CRITICAL ACCLAIM FOR LEIGH RUSSELL'S
DEAD END

'All the ingredients combine to make a tense, clever police whodunnit'
- Marcel Berlins, The Times

'I could not put this book down.'
- Ann Marie Muldoon, Newbooks magazine

'A brilliant talent in the thriller field.'
- Jeffery Deaver

'An encounter that will take them into the darkest recesses of the human psyche'
- Barry Forshaw, Crime Time

'Well written and chock full of surprises, this hard-hitting, edge-of-the seat instalment is yet another treat... Geraldine Steel looks set to become a household name. Highly recommended.'
- Amanda C M Gillies, Euro Crime

'Good, old-fashioned, heart-hammering police thriller...a no-frills delivery of pure excitement.'
- SAGA Magazine

'the critical acclaim heaped on Russell thus far in her literary career is well deserved'
- Mike Stafford, bookgeeks.co.uk

'a macabre read, full of enthralling characters and gruesome details which kept me glued from first page to last'
- GS, www.crimesquad.com

'cleverly thought out, gripping and convincing... I couldn't put this book down... can't wait for the next Geraldine Steel story to come out'
- Helen M Hunt, bookersatz.blogspot.com

'a series that can rival other major crime writers out there... Can't wait for the next one!'
- Best Books to Read

'a classic British cop...Geraldine proves great fun and a character who grows on the reader with every successive title in the series'
- Maxim Jakubowski, lovereading.co.uk

CRITICAL ACCLAIM for *Cut Short*

'*Cut Short* is a stylish, top-of-the-line crime tale, a seamless blending of psychological sophistication and gritty police procedure. And you're just plain going to love DI Geraldine Steel.'

- Jeffery Deaver

'Russell paints a careful and intriguing portrait of a small British community while developing a compassionate and complex heroine who's sure to win fans.'

- Publisher's Weekly

'an excellent debut'

- Mark Campbell, Crime Time

'It's an easy read with the strength of the story at its core.......If you want to be swept along with the story above all else, *Cut Short* is certainly a novel for you.'

- crimeficreader, itsacrime.typepad.com

'Simply awesome! This debut novel by Leigh Russell will take your breath away'

- Amanda C M Gillies, eurocrime.co.uk

'an excellent book...Truly a great start for new mystery author Leigh Russell.'

- Michael Lipkin, New York Journal of Books

'*Cut Short* is a book I had to read in one sitting... excellent new series'
- Beth, Murder by Type

'a surefire hit - a taut, slick, easy to read thriller'
- Melanie Dakin, Watford Observer

'a pretty fine police procedural, with a convincing if disconcerting feel of contemporary Britain.'

- PPO Kane, The Compulsive Reader

'*Cut Short* featured in one of Eurocrime's reviewers' Top Reads for 2009'

- Amanda Gillies, Eurocrime

'*Cut Short* is not a comfortable read, but it is a compelling and important one. Highly recommended.'

- Radmila May, Mystery Women

'well written debut psychological thriller'

- stopyourekillingme.com

'gritty and totally addictive debut novel'

- Sam Millar, New York Journal of Books

'If you're a real fan of police procedurals, you'll probably enjoy this read'

- Claudette C. Smith, Sacramento Book Review

'I found *Cut Short* to be a fantastic read, taking me only days to finish. I thought it to be well-written and well-paced, with a fresh batch of intriguing characters to go along with a fresh tight plot.'

- James Garcia Jr., Dance on Fire

'Leigh Russell may look like your everyday school teacher, but unlike most other English tutors she is also a bestselling crime writer'

- Tori Giglio , Bushey News

'an excellent story, skilfully built and well told'

- Sue Magee, www.thebookbag.co.uk

'intelligently written, gripping crime fiction'

- Helen M. Hunt, Bookersatz Blogspot

'I look forward to the second book in the series'

- Nayu's Reading Corner

'a very excellent book!'

- The Book Buff Blog

'a wonderful series'

- Clarissa Draper, clarissadraper.blogspot.com

'difficult to put down'

- Calum, The Secret Writer

DEATH BED

LEIGH RUSSELL

NO EXIT PRESS

First published in 2012 by No Exit Press,

an imprint of Oldcastle Books Ltd,

PO Box 394,

Harpenden, Herts, AL5 1XJ

www.noexit.co.uk

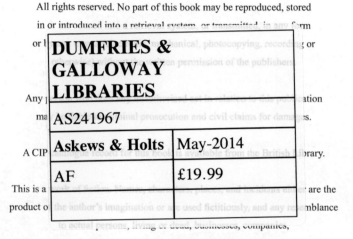

ISBN

978-1-84243-839-8 (open market ed)

978-1-84243-885-5 (hb numbered/limited ed)

978-1-84243-594-6 Print

978-1-84243-596-0 Epub

978-1-84243-595-3 Kindle

978-1-84243-597-7 Pdf

2 4 6 8 10 9 7 5 3 1

Typeset in Times New Roman 11pt, by SunTec, India

Printed and bound in Great Britain by CPI Group (UK) Ltd, Croydon, CR0 4YY

Dedicated to
Michael, Jo and Phill

Acknowledgements

I would like to thank Dr Leonard Russell for his medical advice, all my contacts on the Metropolitan Police Force who have been so generous with their time, Heather Bonney at the Human Remains Unit at the Natural History Museum for her expert knowledge, my editor Keshini Naidoo for her guidance, and the wonderful team at No Exit Press for their support and assistance.

'"He knows death to the bone -
Man has created death."

W B Yeats

PART 1

1.

TAKE ME HOME

Music thumped out a regular beat, any melody obscured by the fluctuating din of voices. Struggling towards the bar with the rest of the clamouring throng, Donna felt sick. She had drunk too much on an empty stomach and the coke wasn't helping either. Telling herself she was old enough to know better, she manoeuvred her way over to the toilets and swore when she saw the long queue. A wave of nausea washed over her and she felt as though she would suffocate in that hot, noisy bar. She fought her way back to the table in the corner and tapped Lily on the shoulder.

'I'm going out for some air.'

Lily smiled up at her.

'Orange juice,' she yelled in reply.

'I'm going out,' Donna shouted. 'I can't breathe in here.'

Lily nodded. Donna wasn't sure if she'd heard her or not.

'I'm going outside,' she repeated. 'You coming?'

Lily shook her head and said something that Donna couldn't make out. She turned and made her way through the door and onto Camden High Street. Pausing in the entrance, she leaned unsteadily against the door jamb and took a few deep breaths that only made her feel dizzy. A couple of men were standing on the pavement in front of her, smoking. Donna was aware of their eyes following her as she staggered forwards. One of them held out a spliff. She took it and inhaled gratefully. It didn't make her feel any better.

'Not bad looking,' he commented, loudly enough for her to hear.

'You know what they say about black girls,' the other one replied and whistled.

As she hurried past them her heel caught on an uneven paving stone. She felt her ankle turn over and almost lost her balance. Startled, she registered that something was wrong and, looking down, saw a thin high heel lying uselessly on the pavement beside her left foot. 'Sod it,' she grumbled. Behind her she heard the two men laughing. 'Pricks,' she muttered under her breath. Afraid she was going to throw up in front of them, she hobbled to the corner and turned off the main road into a narrow alley where she stood for a moment, steadying herself with one hand against the wall and leaning forward, waiting to be sick. She wasn't. Reeling, she turned back to the main road. All she wanted was to get home, but a large group of raucous young men had gathered on the corner of the High Street and she would have to limp past them to reach the station. In desperation she decided to return to the pub and find Lily, but her head was spinning and she couldn't remember which way to go. One of the youths on the corner had turned and was watching her curiously as she tottered on one heel.

While she wavered, a car drew up beside her and a man got out. Seeing Donna sway, he ran round the front of the vehicle in time to catch her by the elbow and steady her.

'Are you alright, Miss?'

'Fine, fine. Get away from me.'

She stumbled and almost fell over.

'You really shouldn't be out on the streets alone in your state.'

'I'm going to the station. I'm going home,' she mumbled, close to tears. 'I need to find Lily. I'm with Lily.'

'Is there anyone at home to look after you?' the man asked. 'You're in no state to be left on your own.'

'I'm fine,' she lied.

She was trembling, afraid she was going to pass out, yet at the same time overwhelmingly grateful for his concern.

She had left her jacket in the bar, but it was a warm evening and she felt uncomfortably hot.

'I think I'm going to be sick.'

'I'll tell you what. My car's here. I can take you home. It's alright,' he smiled reassuringly. 'I'm a police officer.'

He pulled an identity card from his wallet and held it in front of her face but her eyes wouldn't focus properly.

'Come on, let's get you home.'

Donna nodded her head in relief and was fumbling in her bag for her front door key when a thought struck her.

'What about Lily?'

'What?'

'Lily. My friend, Lily. My flatmate.'

'Don't worry about her. She hasn't been too bothered about you, has she?'

He sounded impatient and Donna realised he was right. Where was Lily when Donna needed her?

'Come on, let me take you home,' he urged again.

One thing was for sure, there was no way Donna would make it home by herself.

'My shoe's broken,' she explained and began to giggle helplessly as the man put his hand on her shoulder and guided her to his car.

'Here we are,' he said.

Donna clambered in, hoping she wouldn't chuck up, and relaxed. Her shoes were no good to her with one heel anyway. It was a relief to remove them, they were beginning to rub, and wearing them all evening had made her calves ache.

'I live by Highbury Fields,' she told him as she leaned back and closed her eyes.

It wasn't far but they seemed to be driving for ages. When she looked up again they were passing Kentish Town station which didn't seem right. Donna sat up and tried to work out where they were.

They passed Tufnell Park tube and soon after that she recognised shops on Highgate High Street. Everything looked blurred but at least she knew the road they were on, and the policeman must know where they were going. She closed her eyes again. She just wanted to sit without moving.

'If you want to know the way, ask a policeman,' she sang under her breath and sat up, gripped by a sudden anxiety.

'You are taking me home?'

'Don't worry, we're almost there.'

Donna leaned back feeling nauseous again.

The car slowed down and opening her eyes she saw they had turned off Highgate Hill and were driving past a pub on their left. Without warning, she leaned forward, bent almost double in the seat, and threw up all over her jeans.

'I'm sorry, I'm so sorry,' she mumbled.

The whole drive was turning into a nightmare, but the policeman didn't even seem to notice she had been sick, although it stank. He drove on, staring straight ahead.

Looking up, Donna saw a small patch of grass, like a village green. Turning to look out of her passenger window she caught sight of a church on the other side before they turned sharply right into a narrow lane screened from the road by a row of tall trees.

'Where are we?'

She tried to scoop some of the puke off her jeans with a tissue but it stuck to her thighs, sticky and disgusting.

'This is where I live.'

'Take me home. I want to go home.'

'I brought you here so my wife can look after you until you

13

sober up. Then I'll take you home. You passed out in the car back there and you've been sick. If you vomit while you're unconscious, you can choke. That's dangerous and you shouldn't be left alone. It was either bring you here or take you to the hospital, and they're busy enough on a Saturday night as it is. My wife's a police officer as well. She knows what to do.'

'Where is she?'

'She's waiting for us inside. Now don't worry, everything's going to be fine.'

She fumbled with her seat belt while he opened double wooden gates with a remote control.

'I can't get this off,' she grumbled as they drove in.

'Here,' he released her and helped her out of the car into darkness behind the high wooden gates which had slammed shut behind them. Sharp gravel pricked the soles of her bare feet as she followed him across the drive under the shadow of the trees. The front door closed and the man put one hand against the small of her back, propelling her towards the stairs. Donna resisted.

'Don't worry, my wife's expecting you.'

For the first time he sounded irritated.

'Why doesn't she come down here then?'

'Come on, there's a bed all ready for you.'

The man grabbed hold of her wrist and half led, half dragged her up a carpeted staircase. She was dimly aware of passing a landing and a closed door, before lurching after him up a second narrow wooden flight of stairs. With a growing sense of alarm, she wondered how his wife had known about her.

'Did you phone her?' she asked, her voice thin and fretful.

The man didn't even turn round.

At the top of the stairs he opened a door, pulled her inside and kicked the door shut behind her. Donna blinked. The room was very dark and it smelled foul. A skylight was covered with a black blind. Very little light came through narrow slits down the sides. She couldn't make out much in the dimness, but she could see there was no one else there.

'Let me go. I want to go home. Where's your wife?'

She could barely speak, she was so frightened. Too late, she felt coldly sober, alert to the danger she was in. With an impulsive strength she jerked her arm free and rushed for the door. It was locked. A naked light bulb clicked on and she looked round and gasped. The wall opposite was covered in shelves displaying nightmarish objects.

Suddenly the man grabbed her by the throat and thrust her so she fell backwards onto a bed in the middle of the room. For a second she lay mute with terror then she began to scream, kicking out, trying to scratch him, horrified, while he twisted her round until she was lying lengthwise on the mattress. Swiftly, the man shackled her wrists and ankles with cold metal manacles attached to the bed, then sat back on his heels, astride her body.

As she stared, his face came into focus. The shadows from the light behind him exaggerated the length of his narrow pointed nose, and his eyes gleamed darkly at her. Slowly his thin lips curved in a smile.

'There's no point calling out for help. The house is pretty isolated so don't think any of the neighbours will hear you if you make a racket. They won't. No one will. Except me, of course.'

He climbed off the bed and left, closing the door firmly behind him.

Alone in the darkness Donna tried to calm down so she could think about what to do, but she couldn't stop sobbing.

2

USUAL TERMS

Douggie's straw-coloured hair flopped over his eyes as he waited, head lowered. At last George set his glass down.

'Got a job for you, sunshine.'

Douggie squinted across the table.

'Oh yeah?'

It was best not to seem too keen.

'Usual terms,' George went on in his husky voice.

'I was thinking - ' Douggie began.

'Don't think,' George interrupted him. 'Just listen.'

Douggie wiped the froth from his mouth with the back of his hand and leaned forward. He glanced around the pub but no one was paying them any attention. Just two blokes sat in the corner over a pint. He turned back to his companion.

George was his contact with a group that suited Douggie down to the ground; he'd always been a sucker for a smart set of wheels. Since meeting George he'd been given the chance to drive some real beauties - BMWs, Jags, SAABs, Porsches, Douggie had driven them all, and he'd seen most of them dismantled too, battered, beaten and all but crushed before being loaded into a container along with other cars for scrapping and melting down; nothing logged in, of course.

Douggie knew which scrap yards were safe when there was a motor that needed to disappear without trace. It was hard watching some of the vehicles go, but he knew it would be too dangerous to hang on to them. He never speculated about why the cars had to be destroyed. All he wanted was to drive them and collect the dosh, no questions asked. It wasn't as though he was taking any risks. He'd never been asked to drive a getaway car, for example. To be honest, he quite fancied the idea of a high-speed chase across London, like in the films, but in reality he knew the streets would be crawling with filth and it was impossible to escape once they were after you. Best to keep a low profile and stick to the steady jobs. Not only was Douggie reliable, but he had a clean driving licence, totally legit. He'd never so much as skipped a red light or been caught on a speed camera. He knew that once his licence was marked he might be less valuable as a driver for whoever was running George so he was always careful, and George knew he could trust Douggie to keep his trap shut. It was a sweet set up, and it suited Douggie just fine.

'There's a job,' George said, lowering his voice so Douggie had to strain to hear.

'Are you free tonight?'

Douggie nodded.

'You can pick the wheels up from the corner of the car park here.'

'Hang on, isn't there a camera - '

'So what if there is? What's the problem? You're only picking up a set of wheels. No one will be looking for it. Not yet. You do what you're paid to do, and by this time tomorrow no one will be able to find the car even if they want to. No evidence.'

He winked at Douggie and took a swig of his pint.

'Keep it out of sight overnight then get rid of it first thing tomorrow morning.'

Douggie narrowed his eyes, considering, and reached a decision. He would drive it straight to the lockups.

'There's not going to be a problem, is there?' George asked, when Douggie didn't reply straight away.

Douggie shook his head.

'No, you're alright. There's no problem. I know what to do, you know that. So, what's the car?'

'It's a black SAAB 9-3 Sport Saloon.'

Douggie grinned and gave a low whistle.

'I can't tell you the number - could be anything by now – but it'll be in the car park like I said, right in the corner by the bins.'

'What if someone else is parked there?'

'They won't be. Relax, it's all taken care of. Just do the job, will you? All you have to do is pick up the car and get rid of it. Don't worry about anything else.'

'I'll sort it then. What time will the car be out there?'

'Just after midnight. That's as much as I know for now. We're alright then?'

George raised his glass and drained it with an air of finality.

'No worries. Cheers.'

'See you around, sunshine.'

George stood up and sloped off without looking back.

Douggie finished his pint and sat for a moment wondering whether to have another one but he was going to be behind the wheel soon and wasn't prepared to take any risks with his licence. You never knew when you might be stopped, for no reason. He was hungry but he had to be back at the pub to pick up the car in just over an hour, so there was no time to go home. Instead he decided to go for a walk to clear his head, grab a pizza and come back for the car. In the morning he'd take it along to the scrap yard where Jack would deal with it as a priority, no questions asked, and Douggie would collect the cash from George the following evening when the job was done. It was that simple.

Half an hour later Douggie left the pub. He waited until he was out on the street before he flipped open his phone and called Mary.

'I won't be in till late, love … I've just bumped into an old mate and we're going to have a few beers together … I don't know what time I'll be back so don't wait up ... I'll see you tomorrow then.'

Mary was used to his erratic hours. She probably thought he was out on a bender, but she knew better than to ask questions. It wasn't a bad life, when all was said and done, and soon he was going to start saving up for his own wheels. In ten months he'd be thirty and he was planning to treat himself. A red MX5 drove by, about 1998 and well maintained, its headlights up, its soft top closed. The engine roared beautifully through the dual exhaust as Douggie watched it slip past. He reckoned he could afford one like that before long. Whistling, he strolled along the pavement towards the pizza place.

3

KEEPING SECRETS

Geraldine put down her knife and fork and took a sip of wine. It was now or never, she thought. Her niece, Chloe, had gone up to bed.

'She says she's tired, but I bet you anything you like in two hours' time she'll still be awake, texting her friends,' Geraldine's sister sighed. 'It's impossible to keep on top of it all.'

Despite his wife's protests, Geraldine's brother-in-law had gone into the living room to watch football.

'It's the final,' he explained.

'It's also rude,' Celia replied.

'Don't worry on my account,' Geraldine smiled. 'You don't have to be formal with me, for goodness' sake.'

'And I've no doubt you girls have plenty of things to gossip about,' her brother-in-law added with a grin as left the room.

A few seconds later they heard the buzz of the football commentary, interrupted by an occasional roar from the crowd. The game was on.

Geraldine poured herself another glass of wine and raised the bottle. Her sister shook her head.

'I'd better get this lot cleared up - '

'As it happens I do have something to tell you - '

'Well?'

Celia settled back in her chair.

'What is it?'

Geraldine hesitated.

'OK, is it a boyfriend or the job?' Celia asked. 'Or – is it about…'

Her voice tailed off.

Geraldine had recently discovered that she had been adopted after the birth of her mother's only natural child, Celia. The surprising discovery explained the marked difference in their physical appearance. While Celia resembled their blonde mother, Geraldine's hair was very dark brown and, unlike her blue-eyed sister, her eyes were almost black. The fact of her adoption itself hadn't shocked Geraldine so much as learning about it in her mid-thirties. That the circumstances of her birth had been kept secret from her all those years had felt like a betrayal and it had taken her a while to forgive Celia, who had known about it for years. But her adoption was not what she wanted to talk about. Her transfer to the Met had been confirmed, and she was relocating to work as a Detective Inspector on the Murder Squad in London.

After months of uncertainty, the move went ahead at breakneck speed once her transfer was confirmed. Thanks to a generous inheritance from her adoptive mother, she had been able to put her flat on the market at a price that attracted a first-time buyer almost immediately, and she had exchanged contracts on her brand new flat in London without having breathed a word to her sister about it. She knew Celia wouldn't want her to move away from Kent, especially since their mother had died less than a year ago, and the longer Geraldine left it, the harder it became to tell Celia. Now time had run out and she had no choice.

Geraldine looked around, hoping for inspiration.

'This is a lovely kitchen,' she said at last. 'You've done a great job on it.'

She felt lightheaded, slightly tipsy.

'Is that what you wanted to tell me?' Celia asked, smiling. She didn't get up from the table.

'Come on, Geraldine. Spit it out.'

'I'm moving.'

'Moving?'

'Yes.'

'What do you mean, moving?' Celia frowned. 'You've hardly been in that flat five minutes, and you love it there. Why do you want to move? You're not moving in with your young sergeant, Ian Peterson?'

Geraldine shook her head with a chuckle.

'No, nothing like that. I've told you before, there's nothing going on. He's getting married soon.' She paused. 'It's just that I'm not going to be working for the Kent constabulary any longer. I've been transferred.'

'Transferred?'

Geraldine leaned forward and poured herself another glass of wine. She stared at the yellow liquid slipping from the bottle, aware of Celia's eyes on her, then looked up. Her sister pushed ash blonde hair off her face with the back of a hand, her eyes fixed accusingly on Geraldine. For a horrible instant, Geraldine thought Celia was about to cry.

'What do you mean, transferred?'

'I mean I'm going somewhere else.'

'Yes, I realise that. I'm not a moron. But where are you going?'

Geraldine relaxed slightly. Celia angry was easier to cope with than Celia going all weepy on her.

'I've been transferred to the Met. I'm going to be working for the Homicide and Serious Crime Command in London.'

She couldn't hide her excitement any longer.

'It's a fantastic opportunity for me. I'll be staying with the

CID – sometimes you have to go back into uniform to get into the Met, but they were recruiting and it was exactly what I wanted, and the DCI put in a good word for me - '

'*It was exactly what you wanted?*' Celia repeated. 'Why? Don't you want to be near us? To Chloe? To me?'

'Don't be silly. Of course I do. It's nothing personal. But this is the Met, Celia. It's a great chance for me - '

'What's so great about London?'

Celia gave an exaggerated shudder and pulled a face.

'It's just so exciting. If you're in the police, London is where everyone wants to be.'

'Huh.'

Celia drank her wine, her face sullen, refusing to look at Geraldine.

'And it's quite a lot more money, with the inner London allowance - '

'You don't need more money, with what mum left us.'

Geraldine shrugged. She had expected a negative reaction from her sister but was disappointed all the same.

'I thought you'd be pleased for me. It really is a good career move for me.'

'Oh, you and your bloody career.'

There was a pause.

'So, we'll be seeing even less of you than we do now?' Celia said at last.

She stood up and began clearing the table.

'It's not like I'm going to the other side of the country, Celia. It's only London. I can be down here in not much more than an hour.'

Celia sat down again with a loud sigh.

'*Can* isn't the same as *will* though, is it? Well, I am pleased for you, of course I am, but you have to promise me you'll come and see Chloe regularly. Now mum's not here, it's even more important - '

She broke off, her face twisted into an uneasy frown.

'I can't take mum's place,' Geraldine said gently.

She reached out and put her hand on Celia's, both palm down.

'I know that. But you are - ' Celia paused. 'You are her aunt after all.'

There was another pause.

'So when are you going?'

'Tomorrow.'

'Tomorrow?'

Celia withdrew her hand abruptly.

'What do you mean, tomorrow? How long have you known?'

'It all happened very suddenly - ' Geraldine said lamely.

'Why didn't you say anything?'

'I'm sorry, I know I should have told you before now. I meant to tell you – I kept meaning to – but I was afraid you wouldn't like it and you were so upset about mum.'

She gave an apologetic shrug.

'I bottled it.'

'Keeping secrets seems to be a speciality in our family,' Celia replied ruefully. 'But you will come and stay with us, often, won't you?'

'Of course I will. And I won't be that far away.'

'Well, I suppose it makes no difference if you're investigating murders in London or Kent,' Celia said. 'You'll still be tied up seven days a week when you're on a case.'

Geraldine suppressed a smile, relieved that she had finally shared her news with Celia.

4

CRY INTO THE SILENCE

Donna opened her eyes. Her head pounded with a sharp pain slicing across the top of her skull and her neck was so stiff that when she tried to move an agonising spasm shot down into her shoulders making her cry out. Her wrists and ankles felt as though they were burning. Cautiously she raised herself as far as she could without shifting her head and was shocked to discover she couldn't move her limbs. She thought she was paralysed but after a few seconds remembered that she had been tied down by her wrists and ankles. Fighting to control her panic, she pulled her right arm up as far as she could and twisted her head until the pain became unbearable. Out of the corner of her eye she could just see her raised hand at the periphery of her field of vision. Squinting into the darkness she struggled to distinguish what was holding her down and made out the metal links of a chain, cold against the sore flesh of her wrist. Startled, she swore out loud and even that movement in her muscles made her face sting.

She had no idea what was going on, apart from the horrifying realisation that she had been chained to a bed. Her lips felt dry and cracked, and her mouth tasted of sick. If she hadn't been suffering such severe pain she might have suspected she was the victim of an appalling prank, but this was no joke. Between her legs she felt damp and sore where she had soiled herself and there was another even fouler stench in her nostrils. If no one came to release her soon she was going to die, shackled in this fetid room.

'Think,' she told herself fiercely, but it was hard to focus. Worse than the chains chafing at her skin, worse than her intense thirst, was her terror of the stranger who had taken her captive. If she could only recall how she had arrived in this place, she might be able to work out what to do. She remembered going to Camden with Lily, and then something about her shoe. The heel had come off in the street, but before that she had been in the pub with Lily and she had gone outside by herself, feeling sick, drunk and high on coke. Some men had laughed at her when she tripped on the pavement. After that she could recall only a giddy jumble of images. She had thrown up in a car. What car? She must have got into a car. Whoever was driving that car had brought her to this place. Tears welled up in her eyes as she reconstructed what must have happened. Even young children who could barely talk knew better than to get into a car with a stranger, but in her befuddled state of mind she had done just that.

And now she was going to die for her stupidity.

'Help!' Donna struggled to cling onto the faint hope that someone would notice, but it hurt to call out and her voice was no more than a hoarse rasping, all but inaudible in the darkness. Her captor had told her the house was empty and however much noise she made no one would hear her. Giving way to despair she wept. Her chest heaved and her nose ran, but she couldn't move to wipe away the dribble of snot stinging salty on her cracked upper lip. She licked it and retched. Her thirst was unbearable.

'Help! Somebody please help me!' she moaned.

The air reeked with the combined odour of sweat and excrement that mingled with a putrid stench like rotting fish. She concentrated on taking shallow breaths through her mouth in an attempt to block out the smell. In the silence something stirred. She stopped breathing and listened, every muscle tensed. A faint scuttling, a rustling.

It was probably a mouse.

'Help!' she yelled, a feeble cry into the silence. She imagined rats gnawing her feet as she lay tethered, maggots crawling over her flesh.

'Help! Help!'

She opened her eyes and saw a figure framed in a halo of light.

'Have you come to rescue me?' she whispered.

The man gave a low laugh that seemed to ripple round the room as he switched on the light and revealed his face.

'You said you were a policeman,' she whispered, remembering.

The man approached the bed and stood above her, studying her face.

'Let me go.'

It was difficult to frame the words because her mouth was so dry it hurt every time her lips moved. She tried to raise her head.

'Let me go. Please let me go.'

'There's no point in struggling. You can't escape.'

His calmness only exacerbated her hysteria.

'Let me go,' she shrieked.

'Don't be frightened. There's no need to be frightened. I'm not going to hurt you.'

Donna blinked up at him in surprise. The man turned away and she called out in sudden panic.

'Don't go. I'm thirsty. Please. I need water. Please. I'm dying of thirst. Please, give me something to drink.'

The man moved away out of her line of vision. Donna twisted her head round as far as she could trying to see where he was, but he had disappeared. She closed her eyes to stop the light burning into them. The pain in her head felt even worse when they were shut. She opened them and saw the man was standing beside her again, holding a chipped white mug.

'I've brought you some water.'

His voice was tender as he leaned towards her and held the cup to her lips.

'Don't drink it too quickly,' he warned as she strained to lift her head upright, gulped and choked.

Donna lay back swilling water round her parched mouth. It slipped down her throat, cold and wonderful. Her headache faded slightly into a dull throbbing and she felt her body's tension relax a little. Perhaps she wasn't going to die after all, chained to this filthy bed in this stinking room.

'What do you want with me? Let me go, please.'

'I'm not going to hurt you,' he repeated gently. 'Don't be afraid.'

'But you *are* hurting me. These chains are hurting me. It's agony.'

She hoped he could understand what she was saying. Her voice sounded strange.

'Don't worry. By the time we're finished here you will understand that nothing will ever hurt you again.'

A spasm of terror ran through her.

'You're going to kill me.'

The man shook his head vehemently.

'No. Just the opposite.'

'What do you mean?'

He didn't answer.

'What do you mean?'

He moved away and a few seconds later the light went out. In the darkness she heard the door close.

5

SENSE OF PURPOSE

Geraldine had been to the office in Hendon, getting her bearings. Usually acute with people, the faces she encountered passed in a haze, she was so excited to be joining the Met and so exhausted from the strain of moving. The buildings looked more like a quadrangle of four-storey flats constructed around a playground than a police headquarters, with four blocks surrounding the central parade ground used in the passing out ceremony for recruits. Geraldine had been kitted out with a desk, a computer and a phone, minimal but sufficient for her needs. Working in cramped conditions didn't bother her. She was used to it and anyway, the less time she spent gazing at a computer screen the better, as far as she was concerned. All the same, sitting at her own desk in the Homicide and Serious Crime Command in London for the first time was a thrill, especially as the inspector who shared the room with her was on leave, so she had the office to herself.

 The equity on her flat in Kent hadn't amounted to much but with her pay rise and the money she had inherited from her mother's estate she had been able to get a mortgage on the flat she wanted, just off Upper Street in Islington. It was a glorious summer's day and she abandoned her unpacking to spend the morning exploring the area on foot. She stumbled across a market full of pricey curios and antiques that looked authentic, rails of retro dresses and accessories on the pavement, and boutiques stuffed with amazing and wonderful garments of gorgeous fabrics: velvet, silk, tulle and net decorated with pearls and costume jewellery, splashes of brilliant colour. She could have spent hours looking around.

Controlling an urge to linger in the market she moved on and discovered Highbury Fields, a series of grassy plots bordered with trees, the pathway thronged with pedestrians, joggers, runners and cyclists. Everyone she saw looked young and healthy, enjoying the sunshine. Peaceful and open, it was a different world to the busy streets beyond Highbury Circle where the roads were jammed with traffic, the pavements packed with people rushing past. She turned and walked back to emerge opposite Highbury and Islington Station where she crossed the busy junction back into Upper Street. On the opposite side of the road was a row of elegant residential houses, half concealed behind railings and trees. She walked on past shops, hair salons, a pub on the corner of Islington Street, a Japanese restaurant. The shops gave way to blocks of flats as she walked on towards Angel, past the large white town hall and Islington Museum where cafes spilled tables, chairs and blackboards onto the pavement, giving the street a Mediterranean air. Tired of walking, she sat outside a café drinking coffee and soaking up the atmosphere.

'This is my home now,' she told herself, but she felt as though she was on holiday in Italy or France.

Leaving the café, she bought a few groceries and walked slowly back to her flat, past white and brick terraced houses with elegant arched windows and narrow balconies with wrought iron railings. The flat in Waterloo Gardens had appealed to Geraldine as soon as she saw it. The ground floor of the building was occupied by two businesses: a flooring company with a cheerful red awning, and an internet firm concealed behind mirrored windows. The first and second floors of the block were private flats accessible only through tall metal gates opened with a remote control or a keypad. Inside the security gates was a car park for residents and the entrance to the flats. Geraldine's flat had two small bedrooms, one of which she would use as an office, an L-shaped kitchen and dining area, a living room and small bathroom. It was perfect for her.

At first she had appreciated having time to settle in and roam around in her new surroundings, but after a couple of days a familiar boredom seized her. Work gave her a sense of purpose, a distraction from the sense of emptiness that dogged her. Sorting out her belongings reminded her of sifting through her adopted mother's possessions after she had died. It was pointless brooding about her adoption, but she had nothing else to occupy her thoughts beyond arranging for the gas and electricity to be connected, and sending off letters and emails registering her new address. She'd heard of twins separated at birth who felt something had been missing all their lives, and wondered if she had a twin somewhere. It was possible. Certainly she might have siblings or at least a half-brother or sister.

She had distanced herself from the area where the truth about her adoption had been kept from her for so long, but she couldn't banish it from her mind. She would have to return to the adoption agency at some point to find out more about her birth mother. All she knew was her name, Milly Blake, and her approximate date of birth. On her last visit to the agency, her social worker had shown Geraldine a letter in which her mother had refused contact with the daughter she had given away at birth. Now Geraldine wanted to take another look at it, because she thought there had been an address on the letter. Trained to recall such details, she was furious with herself for not being able to remember it clearly.

She sat in her London flat staring at a faded photograph, all that her unknown mother had left her.

31

6

A LOW PROFILE

Douggie took the car to Jack's, avoiding the main roads and junctions with traffic lights where he knew there were cameras. It never did any harm to be careful and Douggie had been in the business for a long time. He was a survivor. Whistling, he spun the wheel and pulled the sun visor down. It was a beautiful day but he kept the roof up, just in case. There were a few coppers who just might recognise him if he was unlucky and Douggie wasn't one to take risks. Far better to keep a low profile.

As he drove in Jack gave him a nod to let him know there was a space round the back, away from prying eyes. Douggie got out and Jack walked over, smiling.

'Nice set of wheels,' he said, sizing the car up. If he'd been a cartoon character, dollar signs would have lighted up in his eyes.

'What's it to be, Douggie?'

'A quick demolition, mate, no questions asked.'

'Well there's a surprise.'

They both laughed and Douggie tossed Jack the key.

'Seems a pity, mind,' Jack said, walking round the car.

Douggie didn't answer. They both knew the car was too hot to keep.

'But leave it with me. I'll have her stripped and gone in no time.'

'Cheers.'

'A bloke called up asking for you,' Jack said as they walked back across the yard together.

Douggie was on his guard at once.

'What bloke?'

Jack shrugged.

'He didn't give his name. He wasn't asking about you specifically, mind. He was just after someone to get rid of a car for him. I said he could bring it here but he said he wanted something else. Something more definite, he said. Whatever that means.'

'Who was he?'

'How should I know?'

'Well why did you tell him about me if you don't know who he was?'

'Don't lose any sleep over it. All I told him was to go to the King's Head and ask for Douggie.'

'But you don't know who he was. Shit, he could've been anyone.'

'He wasn't a copper, if that's what's worrying you. He was way too posh for that.'

'Posh? What's some posh bloke want with me?'

Jack shook his head with a grin, rubbing his thumb and forefinger together suggestively.

'Just because a bloke talks posh, it doesn't follow he's going to be loaded,' Douggie pointed out, rattled that Jack had mentioned his name. 'What did you go and give him my name for?'

'I didn't.'

'You just said you told him to ask for me at the pub.'

'Yes, but I only said Douggie. There must be lots of guys called Douggie knocking about. Common as muck you are, mate.'

He laughed and slapped Douggie on the back.

'Don't worry about it. You're alright.'

'I suppose,' Douggie agreed half-heartedly.

He took the bus back and nipped into the pub for a quick pint. He wasn't in the mood for serious drinking, but it was on his way home and he had a pocket stuffed with cash so it was daft not to stop for a bit.

'Someone's been in here asking for you,' the landlord told him. 'Smart looking geezer.'

'Who was he?'

In familiar surroundings, with a pint in his hand, Douggie was interested rather than nervous.

'I've no idea. I never saw him before. He's not here now. He left straight away, didn't even stop for a drink.'

'What did you tell him?'

'I told him he might catch you later.'

'What did he look like then?'

The landlord shrugged.

'I didn't notice his face. He was wearing a hood.'

'I thought you said he was smart?'

'It was the way he spoke. He had an upper class accent.'

'Well, I'll be back this evening then. Perhaps he'll turn up again.'

'Maybe he will, maybe he won't.'

Douggie waited in the pub all evening but the man with the posh voice never showed up.

*   *   *   *   *   *   *

Lily sprawled in front of the telly with an apple and a packet of crisps. She was starving so she went out to Highbury Corner where the shops were open till late. Not having grown up in a city, she wasn't comfortable out on her own on the streets at night and hurried into Budgens, the first food shop she passed.

'I bought us some pastries,' she called out as she opened the front door.

The flat was dark and silent.

'Donna?'

There was no answer.

She settled herself in front of the television again and scoffed both pastries. It served Donna right. She had abandoned Lily to make her own way home from the pub in Camden the previous evening, even though she knew very well that Lily had only lived in London for a few months and was nervous about travelling on the tube by herself at night. Lily supposed her flatmate must have picked up a bloke in the bar on Friday. Now she was stuck in the flat, too nervous to go out by herself. She didn't have any other friends in London. Donna was fun and knew cool places to go, and didn't seem to mind Lily tagging along. On the contrary, she usually paid for Lily's entrance as well. She was generous like that, a good friend, or so Lily had thought.

She watched a film with Hugh Grant, and nibbled her way through the large bar of chocolate she had bought to share with her flatmate. It was unlike Donna to go off without saying anything, but they had only been sharing a flat for a couple of months and Lily didn't really know her very well. Obviously Donna must be well off, because she had bought a flat overlooking Highbury Fields. Donna had said she needed to let out the spare room to help pay her mortgage, but she seemed to have plenty of cash to throw around. Lily suspected the real reason Donna wanted a tenant was for the company. When Lily had admitted she could no longer afford the rent and her share of the bills, Donna had told her not to worry about the bills.

'I like you, Lily. I like having you live here. You can forget about the bills for now and just pay the rent.'

'Oh my God, Donna, are you sure?'

'Yes. Don't worry, it's really not a problem.'

'But - '

'It's only money. And you're such help around the flat.'

Lily looked at her watch. It was half past ten on Saturday night and she was sitting at home wondering what to do while life passed her by. She tried Donna's phone again but there was no answer. She imagined Donna going out and forgetting all about her dull flatmate. It was awkward because she couldn't have a go at Donna as long as she was living in her flat paying a very low rent, but that was no excuse for Donna to take advantage of her, dropping her when she no longer wanted her company. She should have said something. A brief call, 'Sorry, I'm going out with friends tonight,' would have shown some respect.

Lily did her best to ignore the possibility that something terrible might have happened, but although she tried to reassure herself that Donna must have gone home with a man, she couldn't help worrying. What if Donna had been mugged or raped? She lay awake in bed listening to the plumbing creaking and rumbling ominously in the darkness, and wished she had never come to London.

7

COLLECTION FROM LIFE

Suspended in pain, Donna had lost all notion of time.
'Let me die, please let me die,' she whispered but couldn't hear her own voice, aware only of pain pulsing through her brain.

Sudden light dazzled her and she closed her eyes. When she opened them the man was standing above her. He reached down to stuff something into her parched mouth, choking her. 'Slow down. What do you think you're doing? Do I have to teach you how to eat?'

Tears slid from the corners of her eyes as she understood that he was angry, but the dry bread was like sandpaper in her dry mouth and she struggled to swallow.

'Here. Drink this.'

She recognised the chipped white cup in his hand and opened her mouth. Leaning down he put his arm around her shoulders and she groaned as he raised her head off the pillow. He held the cup to her lips and she gulped the chilly water.

'Someone ought to teach you some manners. I gave you something to eat. You were hungry, weren't you?'

He dropped her back down on the bed and she fell with a jolt. Pain shot across her neck and shoulders and she fought against crying out.

'I asked you a question.'

'Yes. I was hungry.'

'So? What do you say?'

'Thank you,' she muttered. 'Thank you for the food. Thank you.'

'That's better.'

He turned away from her. 'No,' she called out. 'Don't go. Stay here, please. I want to know what's going on.'

'Nothing's going on.'

She took a deep breath and gagged at the horrible smell in the room.

'Please. I can't stay here. I'll die if I stay here. Let me go.'

'You're not going to die.'

'You can't keep me here. Let me go.'

'You know I can't do that.'

'Why not? What do you want with me?'

The man didn't answer. She turned her head slightly to follow him with her eyes. He walked over to the far wall where she could make out irregularly shaped objects lining the shelves, all creamy beige in colour. She couldn't tell what they were.

'Let me go,' she begged again. 'Why are you keeping me here? What am I doing here? It's a mistake. It must be a mistake.'

She was talking to herself as much as to him.

'What is all that?'

He turned to look at her.

'I was wondering when you were going to wake up to what's here, in this room, right in front of you. I'm surprised you haven't asked me about it before now.'

'What is it?'

She was curious in spite of her pain and trepidation.

'This,' he waved his arm in a circle, 'is a collection so precious no one could put a value on it. It's a collection from life.'

He selected an object and held it up in front of her: it took her a second to realise that it was the inverted top of a human skull.

'That's horrible,' she blurted out, with sudden recklessness. 'Is that what makes the room stink so badly? You should chuck them all out.'

He strode across the room and glared down at her. For a second she thought he was going to hit her as she lay there, powerless to avoid his blows. She closed her eyes and heard his voice raised in agitation.

'You don't understand. How could you? Some of these items are thousands of years old. When you're dead and gone, while you are rotting, they'll still be here, unchanged.'

He returned to the shelves, picked up a carved object and gazed at it reverently.

'Look at this.'

'You're crazy,' she stammered, too frightened to be cautious.

His lips curled as he approached the bed and held the thing in front of her face so she could see it close up. The handle was about a foot long, made of what appeared to be light coloured wood, pine perhaps, pitted and pock marked, the ends slightly bent. The middle of the shaft was carved in a spiral pattern. Thin strips of leather had been threaded through a hole at one end and plaited into a single strand, which then divided into two strands each again divided into four.

'Do you know what this is?' he demanded, his face suddenly alive with excitement.

She stared at him in horrified fascination.

'It's a whip!' he told her, raising it triumphantly above

his head. Donna whimpered and cowered back against the stinking sheets.

'Don't hurt me,' she whispered.

He seemed amused by her reaction and stroked her arm very gently with the strands of the whip. It tickled, tan leather showing pale against her dark skin.

'You don't imagine I'd use this on you? You're the one who's insane.'

His bark of laughter startled her.

'Do you have any idea how precious this is? This whip comes from America where it belonged to Chief Sitting Bull himself. He had it fashioned from the thigh bone of an enemy.'

He held it up again, admiring it against the light.

'From the thigh bone of an enemy?' she repeated. She wasn't sure if this was really happening.

The man replaced the whip carefully on the shelf and returned to loom above her.

'I wouldn't soil this precious object on a filthy bitch like you. That's a disgusting idea.'

Spit sprayed from his thin lips; she felt a globule of saliva slide across her cheek, but couldn't move her hand to wipe it away.

There was a click and the light went out. Donna rolled her eyes frantically from side to side. She couldn't bear to be left alone again in darkness that was never silent. The chains holding her clanked when she stirred, the bed creaked beneath her and sometimes she heard pattering of raindrops on the skylight, or tiny animals scuttling past. The hideous stench became overpowering and her aching muscles tensed as a fresh sound shuffled softly and steadily across the floor.

'What are you doing?' she croaked.

The man didn't answer. The noise stopped and she heard the door open. With a wrench of her neck she turned to look. Silhouetted against the light from the stairs the man was leaning over, dragging a black bin bag across the threshold.

'What is it? What's in there?'

Still he didn't answer.

'Where are you going? You can't leave me here. Please, don't leave me here.'

The door closed behind his bent figure, leaving Donna in darkness. Even with her eyes tightly shut, she couldn't ignore the shadowy objects on the shelves. They grinned at her, as her mind spiralled out of control with fear and hunger until she thought she would go mad.

8

CONSTERNATION

Dave rolled over, stretched out and yawned. A Sunday morning lie in was just the job. He wished he could do the same every day.

'Must be nice not to have to get up for work in the mornings,' he'd said to his dad when the old man had retired.

'Don't wish your life away, son.'

The trouble with sleeping for so long was that it made him feel groggy when he finally woke up, although that could have been the hangover. He smiled. It had been a good night. Liz was still asleep. With a grin he reached over and drew the tip of one finger very gently across her rounded upper arm, like an insect crawling over her skin.

'Bog off, Dave,' she said without opening her eyes. 'I know it's you.'

'What is?'

'Get lost.'

He threw himself on her and set about tickling her until she screamed for him to stop.

'Best thing for a hangover,' Dave said cheerfully as he tucked into a cooked breakfast while Liz lit a cigarette, inhaled and threw her head back to blow smoke at the ceiling.

'Aren't you eating?' he asked, fork raised. 'It's nearly twelve. You should have something.'

'I feel more like throwing up than eating anything after last night.'

Dave laughed. 'Lightweight.'

'I know my limits.'

'Clearly you don't,' he laughed.

He wiped his plate clean with his last piece of toast.

'That was terrific. Shame you couldn't join me.'

He stood up and put his arms round her.

'What now?'

'You can start with putting the rubbish out. That bin stinks.' She pointed at the kitchen bin, overflowing with a week's garbage topped off with the remains of a takeaway curry.

'And while you're at it, we're nearly out of fags.'

'Alright. I'll run round and get some fags and I'll pick up a paper at the same time.'

He swore as he tugged at the bag of rubbish which slid slowly out of the bin.

'Don't spill it,' Liz fussed.

'Got it.'

It was threatening to rain as he opened the front door, crossed the narrow paved front garden, dropped the bag in the bin and used the lid to cram it down.

'Just going round the corner then,' he called out. He turned off into an alleyway that was a short cut to the newsagents at the station. A foul smell grew stronger as he advanced and he saw that someone had dumped a bulging black bin liner on one side of the path. He swore. People had no respect, leaving their stinking rubbish on a public path. The smell was almost overpowering, making him gag and he stumbled, accidentally kicking the bag which tipped over and fell on its side blocking the path. He reached down and grabbed the bag. It felt slimy. 'What the fuck is in here?' The bag wasn't even tied up properly because as he yanked it to one side it fell open and he drew back in horror at the sight of a bloody, bruised and swollen face staring up at him, unseeing, from inside. He turned away and was violently sick.

Dave blinked and shook his head, stepping forward to take another look. There was no mistaking what he had seen. He stood for a moment unable to think then reached out to close the bag, but couldn't bring himself to touch it again. Dread seized him and he felt himself trembling. He looked up. There was no one else in sight. With a frantic lunge he pulled the two sides of the bag together to conceal its horrific contents before running back the way he had come.

'Liz! Liz!'
   'What is it? Don't tell me you've spilled the damn rubbish - '
   She caught sight of his face and stopped.
   'Not feeling so clever now? You and your big breakfast. You look well sick - '
   'There's a woman in a bin bag out there in the alley.'
   'What?'
   'There's a woman in a bin bag, in the alley.'
   'Tell her to bugger off. What's she doing out there anyway?'
   'No, no, she's dead.'
   'What?'
   Liz leaped from her chair.
   'Who the fuck is she?'
   'How the hell should I know?'
   'You're not pulling my leg?'
   She gazed at him in consternation, registering his pallor and staring eyes.
   'Are you sure? Perhaps you'd better check - '
   He shook his head.
   'I'm not going out there again. It's horrible, Liz, horrible. Her eyes – and the smell, Jesus - '

He put one hand over his mouth then dropped it abruptly.

'I've got to wash my hands.'

He ran over to the kitchen sink and began frenziedly lathering the soap.

Liz followed him.

'We'll have to tell someone,' he said, still furiously scrubbing his hands.

'Tell someone?'

'What else can we do? We can't just leave it there. We'll have to call the police.'

'What about the council?' Liz suggested. 'Can't they do something?'

'The council? What are you talking about? What can the council do? This isn't a dead rat we're talking about.'

'Shouldn't we call a doctor?'

'The police bring their own.'

'We can't have the police snooping round here. What if they want to question us? What if they find the dope?'

'Don't be stupid, Liz. What are you on about? Why would they want to come here? We have to call the police. They have to investigate a murder.'

'You don't know it's murder. She could've taken an overdose. Maybe it's a suicide.'

'Don't be a fucking idiot, Liz. The body's in a bin bag. No one crawls into a bin bag before they commit suicide. Someone killed her and dumped the body there. Oh bloody hell. What are we going to do?'

'Calm down. Here.'

She lit two cigarettes and handed him one.

'We've got to think,' he said, inhaling hard.

His hands were still trembling.

'You're right,' Liz said. 'We've got to phone the police.

I'll move the dope and you make the call.'

'Fuck the dope, there's a dead body in the alley.'

He sounded slightly hysterical.

'Calm down, Dave. The way you're carrying on they're going to think you had something to do with it. Dave - '

She stared at him with sudden apprehension.

'You didn't – I mean – is it someone you know? Do you know who she is?'

'No I bloody don't. And you'd be in a right state if you'd seen it – her. Now fuck off and stash the dope while I call the police.'

9

WORKING TOGETHER

Geraldine had planned to spend Sunday unpacking. She had slept really well, got up early, showered and gone out for breakfast, putting off her chores in spite of her good intentions. Finally she had returned to her flat and settled down to sort out the packing cases. Apart from her furniture all her belongings had been delivered to the living room, as the largest space in the flat. The move had been rushed and she hadn't bothered with labelling anything so it was a bit of a lucky dip delving into the cases. She was carting an armful of utensils into the kitchen when her phone rang. She was on call, and having just moved to London didn't expect to be given much time off, so she wasn't surprised. A familiar exhilaration shook her, followed as always by a sour sense of guilt. She was pleased to be working again, but the call meant someone had died. With a quick glance around her living room filled with boxes, piles of books and heaps of clothes, she set off for Hendon and the start of her first case in London.

'Here we go,' she sang as she drove, in a tuneless chant. 'I'm on my way, I'm off to London.'

The traffic crawled along in places even though it was Sunday and the journey to Hendon took longer than she had expected, so she arrived with no time to look around before she was due at an initial briefing. As Geraldine walked in a young female officer beamed at her and Geraldine returned the smile. She had been told the Met would seem informal compared to the Kent force. The other woman approached and held out her hand. She had a warm, firm grip and an alert, friendly grin.

'Hi, I'm Sam Haley, Detective Sergeant. I think we're going to be working together.'

'Detective Inspector Steel,' Geraldine responded to the relaxed approach from a junior officer with slightly frosty formality.

The sergeant didn't seem to notice Geraldine's reserve.

'I can show you around if you like. I know you're new to the Met. I did a stint up North but most of my time has been spent here in London, which suits me. I'm a Londoner born and bred. Where have you come from?' She spoke very fast, with an air of suppressed energy.

There was something wholesome about her stocky build and glowing complexion that gave the impression she was used to fresh air and exercise. Her blonde hair was cropped in a bob at the front and cut very short at the back, sloping into the nape of her neck. Geraldine returned the sergeant's smile but before she could respond the room fell silent. The briefing was about to begin.

The detective chief inspector was standing beside the incident board where a photograph of a young black woman was displayed, her face bruised, her bottom lip split and one eye swollen and bloodshot. It was difficult to tell what she must have looked like before she had been viciously battered, but she could have been beautiful.

'Good afternoon.'

The detective chief inspector looked slowly and deliberately around the assembled officers. Geraldine had the feeling he was taking in every detail of her face, although his gaze only lingered on her for a second. He was tall and burly with broad shoulders and a square chin, his dark hair flecked with grey, still physically powerful, a man who could pack a punch if he chose to. There was an air of arrogance about him, perhaps suggested by his surprisingly well-educated accent.

'I'm DCI Reg Milton, for those of you who don't already know me,

Senior Investigating Officer on this case.'

He turned to the incident board.

'We're investigating the violent death of a young black woman, aged somewhere around twenty. The body was found early this afternoon in an alleyway near Tufnell Park station.'

He read out the post code and the exact address.

'The body was discovered, wrapped in a black dustbin liner, by a David Crawley, tenant of a ground floor apartment where he lives with his girl friend, Elizabeth James. So far we have no identity for the victim, but there's little doubt we're looking at suspicious circumstances. There's a Gold Team meeting here tomorrow with the borough commander and someone from media and communications, and the Safer Neighbourhood Inspector will also be present.'

He glanced around the room again.

'Hopefully we can sort this out very quickly, certainly before the papers get too busy. So, let's get going and gather as much information as possible before the meeting tomorrow.'

Geraldine discovered she was indeed scheduled to work with Detective Sergeant Sam Haley and their first task was to interview David Crawley, the witness who had discovered the body.

'We can get to Islington in time for tea,' the sergeant chattered cheerfully as they walked over to the car.

Geraldine nodded without answering.

'The canteen at Islington's nothing special,' Sam went on, 'but it's worth going there at tea time. There's homemade banana cake, if we're lucky.'

'Fine. But we'll see David Crawley first.'

'Yes gov, but if the banana cake's all gone you'll be sorry.'

She laughed and Geraldine couldn't help laughing too. She had a feeling she was going to enjoy working with Sam Haley.

10

ONE DEAD STRANGER

It began to drizzle as they drove past Tufnell Park station.

'We've taken the wrong turning,' Sam called out, leaning forward to squint at the road names.

'Do you want to check the sat nav?'

'No. It's easy. We're virtually there. We just need to go back to the tube station and pick up Tufnell Park Road at the junction. It's one of the roads off there. Yes, we've gone too far.'

They turned round and found the street they wanted. As they turned into it they saw a police cordon blocking access further down. Almost all the spaces along the road were taken but they managed to park a few doors away from the alleyway where the body had been found earlier that day.

Geraldine checked her phone before she got out of the car.

'There's still no news of the victim's identity,' she said, screwing up her face at the rain.

Sam put up a large black umbrella. Huddled together underneath it they hurried along the path towards the forensic tent up ahead, spanning the width of the alleyway. They pulled on their white suits and blue overshoes before shuffling sideways between the fence and the edge of the tent, to the entrance. Geraldine's ankles were damp and rain had dripped inside her collar, but she forgot her discomfort at the familiar rush of adrenalin at starting on a case, all her senses alert as her thoughts focused on one dead stranger. Inside the tent there was an air of quiet industry. Scene of crime officers were busy taking photographs, scrutinising the ground and placing small items carefully in evidence bags.

Geraldine looked down at the dead girl lying flat on her back on a black plastic sheet, a bin bag that had been split open, before turning to a scene of crime officer.

'Any idea who she is?'

The scene of crime officer shook his head.

'No, ma'am.'

'She was fully clothed?'

Geraldine nodded towards the body which was half hidden by a pathologist kneeling beside it on a folded blanket. She moved to one side to gain a clearer view. The pathologist had cut the victim's clothes open to expose her flesh. In the bright lights the dead girl's lower abdomen had a faint green tinge, blood stained fluid had leaked from her nose and mouth and her tongue and eyes were protruding slightly. Her feet were bare, narrow and bloody, with bright red weals encircling her ankles. Geraldine could see one of her wrists, similarly scored. The stench was foul.

'If she was fully clothed, wasn't there anything in her pockets to indicate her identity?'

'No ma'am, there was nothing at all in her pockets. No ID, no purse, no phone, nothing.'

'What about her prints?'

'We're sending off everything we can, DNA, prints, whatever we can find.'

'Well, let's hope they come up with something before the meeting tomorrow,' Geraldine said. 'Can you tell how she got here?'

'The bag must have been carried most of the way, but it was dragged along for the last few feet, from that direction.'

He pointed to the Tufnell Park Road end of the alley.

Geraldine stepped over to the pathologist, a grey-haired man absorbed in his work.

'What was the cause of death?'

'I'm nearly done,' he replied without turning round.

He clearly wasn't prepared to talk them through it so they had to wait while he completed his preliminary examination. Controlling her impatience, Geraldine gazed around. Strong weeds sprouted through cracks in the uneven path which was littered with cigarette butts and lager cans.

'Nice place to end up,' Sam said under her breath.

The pathologist stood up at last and leaned forward, rubbing his knees.

'I'm Gerald Mann,' he said, turning to Geraldine.

He had sharp eyes, crinkly with laughter lines which his solemn expression couldn't conceal.

'DI Geraldine Steel. So, what can you tell us?'

'We have a black female in her late teens or early twenties. I won't commit myself to the cause of death right here and now, but the victim was badly beaten about the head before she died, subjected to a sustained and severe beating over a matter of days or possibly weeks. She's been dead for at least two days, probably longer. There's no question we're looking at an unlawful killing. As to whether it was deliberate or not, well, that's for you to determine, but it might be significant that she's recently lost a finger.'

He took a step back from the body and Geraldine saw that the dead woman's right index finger was missing.

'What happened?'

The pathologist shook his head.

'I'm not sure yet. But she was shackled - '

He pointed to deep weals on the dead woman's wrists.

'I can't say the exact cause of death yet, but my gut feeling, in view of the obvious evidence, is that we're looking at the victim of a particularly brutal murder.'

'Aren't they all?' Sam grimaced. 'They always say that,' she added, turning to Geraldine who was surprised to hear the sergeant sounding churlish.

'And you came here hoping to see a murder victim who's been well-treated?' the pathologist retorted.

'Wait, are you saying whoever killed her cut her finger off while she was still alive?' Geraldine asked, keen to defuse the tension between her colleagues and focus their attention on the body.

'You'll have my preliminary findings first thing in the morning.'

'Thank you. We'd appreciate a full post-mortem report by midday tomorrow. There's a briefing after lunch, and the more information we can gather together by then, the better.'

The pathologist was already packing his bag.

'I'll see what I can do.'

The body was carried swiftly along the alley to the waiting mortuary van. Within minutes it had driven off and the scene of crime officers followed, until only one was left, along with a uniformed officer posted outside standing guard in the rain.

'Four o'clock. Time for banana cake?' Sam asked hopefully. Back in the fresh air she seemed to have recovered her good spirits.

Geraldine shook her head.

'Before we go anywhere we need to interview the man who found the body, and then we're going to speak to a few of the neighbours, find out if anyone saw or heard anything suspicious. But I want to stay out here for a few minutes first.'

'What for?'

Geraldine shook her head again.

'I don't know exactly. I just want to get the feel of the scene. Remember everything.'

'We've got lots of photos.'

'It's not the same.'

'I know, but – it's nearly tea time.'

'We're not leaving until we've finished,' Geraldine repeated firmly.

'Do you know how many unsolved murders we have in London? We always sort them in the end. It won't be a problem.'

Geraldine stood, immobile, gazing at the scene.

'It's so hard to picture it. It's night. A car draws up in Tufnell Park Road just at the end of the alley. SOCOs confirmed that the bag was dragged into position from that end.'

'The alley's quite near the main road,' Sam pointed out.

'But did the killer come here deliberately because he knew about the alley?'

'It's possible he drove up Junction Road, cruising along slowly looking for somewhere to dispose of the body, but it's more likely he'd selected his destination in advance.'

'Yes,' Geraldine agreed. 'I'd say he knew where he was going. You can't see the alley from the main road.'

'And he wouldn't have wanted to hang about searching for a suitable spot,' Sam added. 'There's always a chance someone might be out on the street. Even at night you can't be sure there'll be no one around.'

They stood looking around for a few moments.

'So he was driving along,' Geraldine resumed, 'spotted

the alley, or probably knew about it already, parked the car, carried the bag half way along, dropped it, and drove off. It would probably only have taken a few seconds, and he was gone.'

She nodded to herself.

'That makes sense. Now, let's see what Mr Crawley can tell us.'

Sam gave a loud sigh.

'Well, if there's no cake left, I'll know who to blame,' she grumbled.

Geraldine burst out laughing.

11

SHOCK

They turned off Tufnell Park Road and followed Littlefield Close which took them past the other end of the alley. The woman who came to the door was tall and skinny with a mop of curly hair that gave her a slightly comical appearance. She puffed frantically at a cigarette as she threw a cursory glance at Geraldine's warrant card.

'I'm Liz. We've been waiting for you.'

She nodded then turned aside, wracked by a dry cough.

'You'd best come in. He's in the kitchen. Dave!' she yelled, her voice suddenly loud. 'Dave! They're here. Come on then. This way. They're here, love,' she called again as she led Geraldine and Sam along a narrow hall. 'He's had a bit of a shock and -' She broke off as they entered an L-shaped kitchen which had been extended to provide a dining area along the back of the house. Through the window they could see a small, untidy garden.

'The garden's ours,' Liz told them, as though they were potential purchasers come to view the property.

'Shall I put the kettle on?'

'No, thank you. We won't keep you long. I just need to ask Mr Crawley a few questions for now, and my colleague will speak to you in the other room.'

'I didn't see anything,' Liz replied, suddenly wary.

'You might remember something Mr Crawley said when he found the body and it's possible he might have forgotten something especially as, like you said, he's had a shock.'

'Fair enough. Come on, then.'

Liz led Sam out of the kitchen and Geraldine turned to David

Crawley sitting silently at the table. Beneath his light brown moustache Geraldine saw that his lips were trembling.

'Mr Crawley, I'd like to ask you a few questions about what you saw. Are you alright?'

'Yes.'

'When did you find the body?'

He shrugged.

'We had our breakfast, brunch I should say, at about midday. We got up late,' he added with a rueful grin. 'We had a late night.'

'Did you recognise the deceased?'

Crawley shook his head.

'Tell me how you found the body.'

'I went out to get some cigarettes and a paper. The alley's a short cut to the nearest shops, down by the station. The first thing I noticed when I went in the alley was this horrible smell. You couldn't miss it.'

He screwed up his face, like a small child about to cry.

'I noticed it as soon as I was in the alley and it got worse and then ...'

He broke off, no longer seeing Geraldine perched on a stool in his kitchen but a dead body stuffed into a bin liner. She thought back to her first view of a cadaver. Even knowing what to expect she had been shocked and could only imagine how horrific it must have been for David Crawley to stumble on a corpse without any warning, just round the corner from his own front doorstep.

'What happened?' she prompted him gently.

'When I was about half way along the alley I saw a black bin bag lying across the path. I thought it must have fallen over. I bent down to move it to one side but the bag wasn't properly closed and that's when I saw the face staring up at me. It was like she knew I was there.'

He shuddered.

'What time was it when you discovered it?'

'Afternoon, really. I suppose it must have been about one. You can check, because I called you lot almost straight away.'

'Almost? Why the delay?'

He shook his head.

'I don't know. Just the shock, I suppose. At first Liz didn't believe it.'

'Did she go outside and look?'

'Not bloody likely! I wouldn't let her see that. Then I made the call and – have they taken it away yet?'

'Yes, but the road will be closed off for now while we examine the area. Mr Crawley, did you manage to get a good look at the dead woman?'

He looked at her in surprise.

'Not a good look, no. As soon as I saw what it was I ran home as fast as I could.'

'Mr Crawley, think carefully please. Did you see the dead woman's face?'

'Yeah I saw it. That's what I've been telling you. That's why I called you lot.'

'Mr Crawley, the bag was closed when the police arrived. The woman wasn't visible.'

'I know. I closed it. There's young kids living along the street. You don't want them seeing something like that.'

'And you said you'd never seen the dead woman before?'

'Never.'

'You're sure of that?'

'Positive.'

'It was horrible,' Liz said, pulling on a cigarette.

'Tell me exactly what you saw.'

Liz frowned and examined the tip of her cigarette.

'I didn't see it myself. Only Dave came in and he'd gone all white, you know, like people do when they're in shock, and he said 'there's a woman out there in the alley,' something like that. 'What's she doing there then?' I asked him. 'Tell her to bog off.' That's when he told me she was dead, and we called you.'

'What time was it when he found the body?'

'About twelve. No, it must have been later than that because we didn't have breakfast – lunch – until twelve. Then he went out to get some fags and that's when he found it – her. So it must have been about one or one thirty. I don't know exactly.'

'Had either of you been outside at all earlier that morning?'

'No. We'd only just got up. We'd had a late night.'

'Were you together all the time on Saturday night?'

'What? You think he nipped out to knock off some woman in the middle of the night?'

She gave a nervous laugh.

'Just answer the question, please.'

'Yes, we were together.'

'Did you go out on Saturday evening?'

'Yes. We went to the pub on the corner – you can ask them, they know us. On the way home we got a takeaway from the Indian. And then we came home, watched a film on the box and went to bed.'

'What time did you arrive home?'

Liz shrugged.

'It must've been around eleven when we left the pub, so I guess we were home about half past. We watched a film and went to bed.'

'What time was that?'

Liz shook her head.

'I don't know. I was a bit tanked-up. I think it was about two.'

'Think carefully, Liz. Is it possible you heard anything after you'd gone to bed?'

'Apart from Dave snoring?'

Liz laughed and shook her head.

'Did you hear any cars pulling up in the street?'

'There's always cars. I didn't notice anything in particular.'

Dave's story matched his girlfriend's. Beyond having stumbled upon her body he knew nothing about the dead woman.

Geraldine scowled as they drove off.

'She was chucked in a dustbin bag and dumped like so much rubbish.'

'It made no difference to her. She was already dead when she was left there.'

'Even so,' Geraldine remonstrated, 'it makes a difference. To begin with it tells us the killer had no respect for the body - '

'Respect? He killed her. What sort of respect was that? If he could beat the crap out of her while she was alive why would he care how he treated her when she was dead?'

'But to dispose of her like he was putting out rubbish in a dustbin bag, was that an expression of anger towards his victim, something personal, or perhaps a racist attack, or does he value all human life so little?'

Sam shrugged as she turned the wheel.

'Maybe he just wanted to get rid of the body. It seems a practical enough way of doing it.'

Geraldine nodded but she had a feeling this killer was not so straightforward.

'And we don't know we're looking for just one man,' Sam added. 'There could be more than one person involved.'

'It's usually a man though, isn't it? A man working on his own. Murder's not a sociable activity as a rule.'

Geraldine sighed. All they could do was speculate about the killer; they didn't even know the dead girl's name.

12

CAUGHT OFF GUARD

Douggie turned off the main road. As he reached the next corner a black car pulled into the kerb just ahead of him. Out of the corner of his eye he took in the shining bodywork of a well-maintained BMW. He'd barely registered the door opening before the driver sprang out and seized him by the throat. The man spun him round, at the same time grabbing his left wrist and twisting his arm up behind his back until Douggie felt as though his shoulder was being ripped apart. He had a confused impression of polished brown leather shoes and a long dark coat. He would have yelped in pain, but the man was clutching his throat so tightly he could hardly breathe. Caught off guard, he lost his footing and only the man's vice-like grip beneath his chin stopped him pitching forwards and crashing into the side of the car. He gagged, struggling to breathe, and the man loosened his hold slightly.

'Nice car,' Douggie wheezed.

The driver's window was open and he detected a whiff of vomit.

'Douggie Hopkins?'

'Who wants to know?'

He had recovered sufficiently to register the man's posh voice and was curious to see him, but when he tried to swivel round his assailant slammed his head against the roof of the car.

'I've got a job for you.'

'Who are you?'

For answer, the man crushed Douggie's nose against the car until his eyes watered.

'What sort of job? Bloody hell, there's no need to break my nose.'

'I want to get rid of a car. Permanently. Someone said you'd be able to help me.'

'Is that all?'

Douggie attempted a laugh.

'You could've just asked. I'm your man. It'll cost you, mind.' Cost you extra for nearly breaking my fucking nose, he thought.

'I'll give you two thousand pounds, but no more questions.'

'Two thousand? That should do it,' Douggie replied.

His nose ached horribly, squashed against the side of the car, but it was worth getting a bruised face for two thousand quid. He would have done the job for less, although he didn't say so.

'The car has to be completely destroyed, and it must be done tonight.'

'No problem. I'll torch it.'

'Yes, set fire to it and burn it, burn it, burn it until there's nothing left!'

'Yes, alright, I get it,' Douggie gasped. 'Don't worry. Nothing like a fire for getting rid - '

The man tightened his grip on Douggie's throat suddenly, almost suffocating him.

'Shut up,' he hissed. 'Shut up!'

Douggie wondered what the geezer was getting so worked up about. If he hadn't been skint, Douggie would have been tempted to forget the whole thing. But two thousand quid was two thousand quid.

The man relaxed his hold on Douggie.

'Do you know Elthorne Road?'

'Off Holloway Road?'

'Yes. Walk along Elthorne and wait outside the art college, at one o'clock tonight. Got that?'

'Yes.'

'A black BMW will drive past and park at the end of Boothby Road. Don't move until the driver has left the car. The keys will be in the glove compartment, with half the money.'

'No problem. What about the rest of the money? You said half the money would be in the car.'

'You'll get the rest when the job's done. And remember, whatever happens to the car, it's nothing to do with me. My work's too important for me to take any chances, but you - ' He gave Douggie's arm a sudden twist. 'Remember, Douggie, I know where to find you.'

'Don't worry, don't worry,' Douggie babbled, 'you've come to the right man.'

Two thousand quid, he thought, although the job had to be done that night, which meant he'd have to torch it. That was a nuisance because it involved a long walk, but he couldn't risk hanging onto the car until the scrap yard opened in the morning. There was something unnerving about this man. He wasn't the kind of car thief Douggie was used to doing business with. Still, he stank of money. Two thousand for this job and there could be more where that came from.

'Two thousand quid then?'

'Two thousand.'

At five to one Douggie was standing at the corner of Boothby Road as instructed when a black BMW drove up and parked on the other side of the street. He couldn't be certain but he was pretty sure it was the same car his face had been squashed against earlier that evening. He touched his nose at the recollection, fingering the bruise. A dark figure in a long hooded coat jumped out of the driver's seat and vanished into the darkness. Douggie caught a glimpse of the man flitting into view beneath a street lamp before he disappeared altogether.

'Vicious bastard,' Douggie muttered as he drew on his gloves and turned his attention to the car.

He was looking at a 7 series 4 door auto saloon BMW, about four years old but well looked after. He ran his hand reverently along its smooth side, gleaming in the moonlight, before he opened the door. A faint sour smell of vomit ruined the pleasure and he wrinkled his nose in disgust. But cars could be valeted. He sat behind the wheel and stroked it, then leant across and checked the glove compartment. The key was there along with the cash, which he counted quickly beneath the dash board. He couldn't see anyone, but you never knew who might be watching from the shadows. Satisfied, he turned the key in the ignition and the engine purred into life. He drove with the window open along deserted streets and out onto the waste ground of Epping Forest. The car ran like a dream. As always, the temptation to keep it was almost irresistible, but he remembered the man's words.

'Remember, Douggie, I know where to find you.'

Reaching his destination, he glanced around. The place was deserted, as he had expected. A quick check of the car revealed that the boot was empty. Douggie shone his torch round the back seat. There was nothing there, not so much as a sweet wrapper. As his torch moved, his eye was caught by something glistening beside a dried up pool of vomit on the floor by the passenger seat. He leaned forward for a closer look and saw a gold chain with a shiny pendant attached. Douggie hesitated before reaching across to pick it up, but it was clean and didn't smell so he slipped the trinket in his jacket pocket thinking it would make a fine gift for Mary. Then he turned to the business of torching the car.

13

SICK WITH WORRY

Lily made a special trip to the shops for ingredients to make Donna's favourite spaghetti supper. Donna had seemed pleased to discover that Lily enjoyed cooking and didn't mind clearing up.

'I thought you'd be great to have around.'

'I'm not as good as my mum,' Lily had replied. 'She makes the most amazing spag bol.'

But the weekend passed and Donna didn't come home. Lily ate the spaghetti on her own.

There was still no sign of Donna when Lily woke up on Monday. Following her usual routine, she ate breakfast in front of the television before going to work. As she stood up, she heard something that stopped her in her tracks. She turned round to look at the blonde newsreader who had just announced that the body of a young black woman had been discovered on Sunday near Tufnell Park tube station in North London.

'...Police do not yet know the dead woman's identity and are appealing for information.'

A uniformed policeman appeared on the screen.

'We need to establish the identity of the victim. Anyone who thinks they might be able to identify this young woman should contact the police immediately...'

He described the victim as a black female in her late teens or early twenties, slim, wearing jeans and a sleeveless turquoise t-shirt. The blonde newsreader returned to introduce another item of news with a smile that revealed perfectly even teeth.

Lily almost tripped over her feet in her haste to reach the phone. She gave her details and explained the reason for her call.

'It's about the dead woman they found. I think I might know who she is.'

'Just a moment, caller, I'll put you through.'

It seemed to take ages before another voice came on the line. While she waited Lily tried to picture what Donna had been wearing on Friday evening but she couldn't remember. Donna had so many clothes.

'I just saw the news on the telly, about a black woman who's been found dead somewhere in North London. I think it might be my flatmate. At least,' she paused, suddenly uncertain, 'my flatmate's gone missing. We were at a bar and she just disappeared, and she hasn't been home since and she's not answering her phone and I thought maybe she'd gone off with, you know, with a bloke, but now... now I think she might be the one you found.'

The woman on the other end of the line asked for her name and address.

'When did you last see your flatmate?'

Lily hesitated. She had been out with Donna on Friday night and it was only Monday morning now, but if she told the police how recently she'd seen Donna they might not take her call seriously. She thought she remembered reading somewhere that a person wasn't officially considered missing until they had been gone for a week, but there was no point in lying.

'Friday. We were in Camden, and she just disappeared.'

She felt like crying and was glad the woman at the other

end of the phone couldn't see her. The woman asked a few questions then thanked Lily for contacting them with her information, and the call ended.

There was nothing else Lily could do now but wait. She couldn't face going into work so called in sick and then regretted it because at least work would have taken her mind off Donna. But she was genuinely sick with worry, and guilty about being so angry with Donna for not keeping in touch.

Once Lily calmed down she decided she might have been jumping to conclusions. London was a big place, and nothing like her village in Norfolk. There could be lots of reasons why Donna hadn't come home over the weekend. Maybe it was merely a coincidence that Lily had seen the report of a dead black girl just when her flat mate had gone off for a couple of days. If Lily's mother was right, people were killed every day in London. The dead girl could be anyone. She wondered if she should contact hospitals to see if Donna was ill or had been in an accident, but instead made up her mind to carry on as though everything was normal. The chances were that Donna would walk through the door at any moment, and Lily didn't want to look like a nervous fool.

She fetched Donna's clean washing and set up the ironing board in front of the television, carefully changing the setting on the iron when she picked up one of Donna's silk shirts. When the news came on she leant forward, but there was no further mention of the dead girl. Every so often she picked up her phone and punched in Donna's number.

'Hi this is Donna. I'm not here right now but leave me a message and I'll get back to you right away.'

14

WORDLESS RAGE

Sam hesitated at the door to the morgue. Her face had lost its characteristic healthy glow and her expression was strained.

'Are you alright?' Geraldine asked with sudden understanding. 'Not everyone can take it. My last sergeant was really quite squeamish and it's OK - '

'I'm fine, really,' Sam interrupted her. 'I don't mind the place. It's all part of the job. It's just the smell that I can't stand, and when it's in a confined space it gets me right in the stomach.'

She pulled out a pungent nasal decongestant stick and applied it liberally before pulling on her mask and nodding to indicate she was ready.

Geraldine gave her a sympathetic smile before slipping on her own mask. She hadn't forgotten the horrible stench inside the forensic tent in the alley. Although she was prepared for it, when the door opened she was immediately hit by a sickening odour of putrefaction overlaid with antiseptic. Her face mask couldn't completely block it out. She glanced back at the sergeant who was staring straight ahead.

The round shouldered pathologist, Gerald Mann, was bent over the cadaver. He glanced up when they entered, eyes bright beneath wispy white eyebrows as he nodded in recognition. He reminded Geraldine of her childhood Father Christmases.

'What do you think?' she asked as she approached the slab, trying not to breathe in too deeply, while Sam hung back.

'This is not a pretty corpse, Inspector, and the circumstances of her death are frankly barbaric. We are looking at a woman in her early twenties at most, probably younger, who was beaten and left to die in her own excrement.'

'She was chained by both her wrists and her ankles. Look here, the imprints of the links are clearly visible, quite large and made of iron not steel. There's a residue of rust here, and again here. The flesh on her wrists was quite extensively damaged from chafing, so I'm guessing she was shackled for - ' the pathologist broke off, frowning, 'well, at least a couple of days, but probably considerably longer. It looks as though she tried to free her right hand, because the skin on that wrist is more severely damaged than the other and the bruising extends up her hand where she tried to force it through the manacle. She was lying flat on her back on a fairly soft surface, probably a bed. We found some fibres of white cotton in her hair and under her nails that could have come from bed sheets. They've gone off for analysis.'

He was silent for a moment.

'What can you tell us about the missing finger?' Geraldine prompted him.

'It's impossible to determine whether the right index finger was cut off while she was alive, without examining the site where the injury was inflicted. There's no blood on her clothes but she's wearing short sleeves so that's not conclusive, and there's no way of ascertaining the extent of the bleeding, if any.'

Geraldine studied the dead woman's face, misshapen with swellings, one eye closed beneath an inflamed lid, the other seeming to stare straight back at her in wordless rage.

'Can you be more specific about the beating?'

'She suffered a powerful blow to the side of her head with some hard object, resulting in a fatal cerebral bleed. Her nose was broken, her cheek bones smashed. Her arms and shoulders suffered severe bruising probably from the same blunt instrument, or there may have been a series of impacts if she was thrown around, perhaps in the back of a van, or even dragged downstairs, before she died.'

He pointed to the woman's shoulders.

'So it was the blow to the head that killed her?' Geraldine asked after a brief silence.

'Her skull was fractured by a severe blow. Cause of death was cerebral bleeding but the shock might just as easily have killed her anyway in her weakened state. She was severely dehydrated and her stomach was empty. There was nothing in the duodenum or the intestinal tract, in other words she hadn't eaten anything for at least two or three days before she died. She was absolutely filthy, and soiled herself several times before she died.'

He heaved a deep sigh.

'So young.'

'Was she raped?'

'There's no sign of any violent sexual encounter although she had recently been sexually active, and she had an abortion some years ago when she must have been quite young, possibly underage. She wasn't raped, but it looks as though she was chained to a bed before she was battered to death.'

'When did she die?'

'I can't say for certain. She was left outside during the night but had already been dead for at least twenty-four hours before that. The plastic bin bag offered some insulation of course, but we don't know the conditions she was kept in before last night.'

He pointed at the greenish tinge that spread across the dead woman's abdomen up to her chest and down her upper thighs.

'Discoloration has spread but there's no blistering. I'd say she's been dead for two or three days, maybe longer.'

'Can't you be more specific?'

He shook his head.

'I could hazard a guess at three days, but without knowing the circumstances under which the body was stored, and the temperature it was kept at, I can't give you an exact time of death.'

He turned back to the body.

'She wasn't wearing any shoes but the skin underneath her feet isn't scratched or torn so it doesn't appear that she walked anywhere barefoot. It looks as though her killer removed her shoes. And her finger, of course, which was sliced off with a small razor sharp saw.'

Geraldine frowned impatiently.

'This was presumably a personal attack, but until we know who she was that line of enquiry remains closed to us.'

'Why not just kill her at once and be done with it? Why torment the poor girl like that?' Sam asked, unable to hide her frustration. 'It doesn't make sense to tie her up then starve and beat her if he was going to kill her anyway.'

'Unless he wanted her to suffer,' Geraldine replied. 'Or perhaps he never intended for her to die and it all went horribly wrong.'

The pathologist shrugged and touched the dead woman's disfigured hand gently.

'It was certainly horrible.'

Sam shuddered.

'What are the chances she was still alive when her finger was cut off?'

'As I said, I can't form an opinion with any confidence as the body was moved, so there's no way of telling if the wound bled.'

The pathologist paused.

'There's another thing. Two of her molars were recently extracted, almost certainly after she died. There would still be traces of blood on her gums if the teeth had been removed while she was alive. Now, what would anyone want with a finger and two of her back teeth, I wonder?'

'Maybe he started to remove her teeth and fingers hoping to conceal her identity but didn't have time to finish the job,' Sam suggested.

'Or he could have taken them as a trophy,' Geraldine said.

She didn't add that if that were true, they were more than likely looking for a multiple murderer - one who had already killed or would kill again, someone who found a perverse gratification in keeping ghastly mementos of his victims.

'That's crazy,' Sam said, and it occurred to Geraldine that, for all her bravado, the sergeant was still very young.

'Tell me about it,' she replied softly.

15

MEMORY OF THE DEAD

After visiting the morgue on Monday morning, Geraldine went back to her office in Hendon to spend a few hours gathering all her data together, before returning to the police station in Islington. It was annoying having to spend so much time travelling through London traffic, but there was no help for it. At least she was learning to find her way around without Sam Haley to drive her. Islington was a large station very close to where she now lived. She hurried in the back entrance, and was directed to the conference room where the senior police officers were gathering to discuss the case. Detective Chief Inspector Reg Milton was already there, deep in conversation with an elegantly dressed black woman. Geraldine wished she had thought to go home and change. She could easily have done so, her flat was very near. She sniffed softly, trying to detect whether the odour of the morgue was still clinging to her clothes and hair, just as the memory of the dead woman haunted her thoughts.

There was a flurry of activity at the door and half a dozen people came in together and sat down. Everyone introduced themselves around the table before the meeting opened. Geraldine knew the borough commander and head of Islington police station, Chief Superintendant Andrew Rogers, by reputation, and had met him briefly in the past. He nodded at her as she introduced herself. Geraldine knew they had to pay careful attention to the local community. At the same time, she couldn't help thinking they might achieve more if the meeting were less formal, and restricted to police personnel. This felt like a publicity campaign rather than a briefing for a murder investigation. Also present were the Safer Neighbourhood Inspector, who would be familiar with local crime hotspots and villains. Finally, a woman from media and communications was there to draft a press release and keep them apprised of any press interest. So far the woman's death had only been briefly reported in the news but it was just a matter of time before the papers caught hold of it and started ferreting around. There had been a lot of fuss in the media about police victimising black youths. Reporters would be quick to whip up a furore if the police were slow to find the killer of a black woman. The tone of the meeting seemed to suggest that failure in this case would be politically incorrect, as though the victm's colour somehow made a difference. Geraldine wanted to cry out in protest. The victim was a human being. The colour of her skin made no difference.

The meeting dragged on, seeming to focus more on concerns about public perception of the police than the case itself. Geraldine read out her report on the post-mortem findings, but that only led back to a discussion about the press release.

'We're still no closer to knowing who she is then?' the Safer Neighbourhood Inspector asked. 'You know what the media are going to make of that.'

He nodded at the press officer, the woman the detective chief inspector had been talking to when Geraldine arrived.

'Was there nothing on the body to give us any sort of clue as to her identity?' she enquired.

'Her prints and DNA have been sent off, but there was nothing else to tell us anything. She had nothing on her but her clothes – totally nondescript, jeans and a t-shirt, common cheap High Street brands. No shoes. No watch,' Geraldine said. She refrained from adding, 'No right index finger and no name.'

As if on cue, a constable came in with a message for the detective chief inspector.

'We had a call this morning, sir, from a woman who thinks she might know the identity of the Tufnell Park woman. Her flatmate's gone missing and matches the description of the deceased. She's about the same age, and - '

'How long has this woman been missing?' the borough commander interrupted impatiently.

'We're not sure yet, sir. A constable's gone round to question the woman who reported it.'

'What's the missing woman's name?' the borough commander demanded. 'Has the body been positively identified yet?'

'We're following that up, sir. The call's only just come through. The missing woman's name is Donna Henry and we're trying to contact her mother, who only lives at Baker Street so we're hoping we'll get her in soon to view the body.'

The commander nodded and the constable withdrew. Geraldine thought it was going to be difficult for anyone to identify the dead woman, her face was so bruised and swollen, but she kept her concerns to herself.

After the meeting she went straight to the morgue. Mrs Henry arrived soon after, expensively dressed in a clingy grey cashmere suit and real pearls. Well-spoken and surprisingly calm about the coming ordeal, she was convinced the dead girl couldn't possibly be her daughter. Geraldine wondered if her own mother had felt the same confidence about her daughter when she had given Geraldine up for adoption at birth. She remembered every word of the short letter her mother had written to the adoption agency: 'I know she'll have a better life without me.' But the young mother couldn't have *known*.

She led Mrs Henry into the viewing room. The body had been cleaned up, and there was no whiff of putrefaction in the room to taint Mrs Henry's delicate perfume. The dead girl's face had been smoothed down, her nose and cheek roughly reconstructed, her split lip covered so that it was clearly visible only if you looked closely, and with her eyes closed it wasn't immediately noticeable that one eyelid was puffy. Despite her obvious injuries, it was now possible to see that the dead girl must have been quite beautiful when she was alive.

Mrs Henry glanced down at the dead girl's face, winced, and shook her head just once before stepping back.

'That's not Donna.'

She turned away dismissively, seemingly unconcerned about her daughter's disappearance.

'No, that's not my daughter. Donna will turn up. She always does. I never know where she is from one week to the next, but I've brought her up to make sure she has enough money on her to get a taxi if she's out late, so she can always get home safely.'

She spoke as though having money for a taxi was a cast iron guarantee against misfortune. Geraldine hoped for her sake she was right as she showed Mrs Henry out.

Meanwhile they were back to square one with the investigation. If the anonymity of the victim was worrying for those concerned about the public image of the police force, it was also frustrating for the detectives working on the case. Twenty-four hours after the discovery of the body they should have been questioning the victim's family, sifting through possessions, consulting known contacts, and putting together a timeline to plot her movements immediately before she died. They were all impatient to move the investigation forward, but time was passing and they were getting nowhere.

PART 2

16

A LONG SHOT

Geraldine was pleased to be away from her desk as she and Sam drove back to Tufnell Park. She wanted to keep busy. The alley was still being searched but they had no idea where the woman had been killed, and with every passing hour, the trail leading to her killer would be growing colder. If he hadn't left the area already, he would be busy covering his tracks while they rushed around, clueless and increasingly uneasy.

They had attempted to talk to the occupants of properties in Tufnell Park Road on either side of the alleyway that morning, but only one old woman had answered the door to the flat above Dave Crawley's. Grey-haired and bowed, she didn't speak much English.

'Yes?'

Geraldine had held out her warrant card and introduced herself.

'We'd like to ask you a few questions.'

'Yes?' the old woman had repeated.

'We want to ask you a few questions.'

The woman had shrugged.

'He not here.'

She had begun to close the door.

Geraldine had waved her warrant card in front of the old woman again.

'Police.'

The old woman's eyes had narrowed in understanding as she pulled back in alarm.

'What you want, missus? He not here.'

'Were you here last night?'

'Night? Night?'

'Here. Home.'

Geraldine had pointed at the floor.

'Were you here last night?'

The woman had smiled suddenly, revealing strong yellow teeth.

'Ah home. Yes.'

She nodded, pleased to have understood.

'Home. I live in house. Yes. And the man. Is my son.'

'Did you - '

Geraldine sighed.

'Last night. Did you hear anything unusual?'

The old woman had shaken her head and made a tutting sound with her tongue, vexed at not being able to understand.

'He not here. And I no speak good. He not here. He work.'

'Thank you. We'll come back later.'

'Yes, missus. Thank you.'

None of the other neighbours had been at home during the day. It was a different story when they returned in the evening. They started again with the flat above Dave Crawley and this time a young man came to the door.

'You again? Ma said you'd be back.'

He leaned against the door jamb staring at Geraldine through a greasy black fringe.

'This is about the woman found in the alley, isn't it? Have you got him yet?'

He spoke fluently but with an obviously Eastern European accent.

'Have we got him? Who do you mean?'

'The killer. Has he been arrested yet? The man who killed that woman in the alley.'

'What makes you think it was a man?'

He shrugged.

'You just assume, don't you? I mean, it's always a man, isn't it?'

'Did you notice anything unusual last night?'

'No.'

'Did you see any unfamiliar cars in the street?'

'No.'

'Did you hear any cars stop outside some time after midnight?'

'No.'

They rang the bell of the ground floor flat beside the alley and a youth of about eighteen came to the door. He introduced himself as a student and after a fleeting hesitation invited them in.

'It's the police asking about that woman they found,' he announced as he led them into a small living room.

Two other young men looked up from a game of chess and Geraldine and Sam posed the same questions to all of them.

One of the lads thought he might have heard a car draw up outside during the night, but he couldn't tell them what time he'd heard it or anything else about it.

'Can you describe the sound of the engine?'

He shook his head and his eyes flicked back to the chess board.

'It was just a car.'

'Could you tell which direction it approached from?'

'No.'

'Can you remember if it came from Junction Road or the

other direction?'

'I don't know.'

'What time did you hear it?'

'I don't know. It was just a car, you know. I don't even know if I heard it. I was asleep. I might just have imagined it.'

Or made it up to try and sound helpful, Geraldine thought. Time waster. The chess players returned to their game.

'Sorry we couldn't be more help,' their flatmate apologised as he showed them out.

They questioned the neighbours who lived opposite, but no one had seen or heard anything.

'Why is everyone so bloody unhelpful?' Sam grumbled. 'It's like no one cares that someone's been killed. No one saw or heard anything!'

'To be fair, it's unlikely anyone would notice a rubbish bag being dropped in an alley in the middle of the night.'

'Well, it would make our job a whole lot easier if someone had seen, and made a note of the car number,' Sam replied with a grin, her usual good temper restored.

A team was examining CCTV film, listing registration numbers of vehicles that had driven off the main road along Tufnell Park Road and cross referencing them to see if anyone with a history of violent behaviour had been driving in the area on Saturday night, but it was a long shot. The killer probably hadn't been driving a vehicle registered in his own name, and the number plates might not have been legitimate. The chances of identifying the killer that way were slim. And they still didn't know the victim's name.

17

THE AGONY OF MOVING

Donna recollected climbing a lot of stairs and supposed she must be in an attic. The burning in her wrists and ankles had woken her from a dream of Lily's cooking and she could almost taste the food in her mouth, as she lay there nauseous with hunger. No light penetrated the slits around the blind that covered the window so she assumed it must be night. She was dimly aware of a subtle change in the atmosphere. The room felt somehow emptier and the rank musty odour had gone. As if to compensate, the sickening smell of excrement and sweat seemed stronger. Lying in her own filth, she couldn't believe she had ever been clean. Her past life was a dream. As she became fully awake, pain dominated her consciousness so that the foul smell, even her hunger and thirst, faded into insignificance beside it.

A distant door slammed. She felt the vibration of footsteps before hearing them and then sudden light dazzled her. Squinting up at the man, she saw he was holding the chipped cup out towards her and endured the agony of moving her head to gulp at the water.

'Thank you. Thank you,' she mumbled.

Her head began to clear slightly.

'I'm so hungry.'

For a second she thought he was angry again, so she added hurriedly, 'thank you for the water. Thank you.'

He raised his hand, not to strike her but to force food in her mouth. She swallowed and gagged, her tongue too sluggish to search for crumbs stuck to her lips, her eyes watering with disappointment.

'Would you like some more?'

'Yes please. I'm starving. Please.'

A feeling close to joy seized her as he pushed another mouthful of bread between her lips. It slid awkwardly down her throat and this time she didn't choke. She looked up at the man and he smiled at her.

'Thank you,' she repeated.

He leaned forward and fiddled with something by her neck.

'There.'

He stepped back.

'I've loosened the chains so you can sit up now if you want.'

She wriggled her hands but her wrists were shackled as tightly as before, only the chains were longer so she could move her arms further from the bed. She raised one arm, the movement arrested by a terrible pain in her shoulder. Glancing down, she saw her wrist, raw and bloody from the chafing.

'Sit up,' he ordered. 'That way you'll be able to see better.'

'See what?'

'The collection of course.'

He went over to the shelves and after some deliberation selected a small irregular bowl and held it up above his head.

'This Tibetan drum was once a human skull. I don't know exactly how old it is, but it could be several thousand years. The Buddhists used them in tantric rituals when they made sacrificial offerings to their protective gods.'

'I don't understand. Where does it come from?'

'I just told you, it comes from Tibet.'

'No, I mean, what's it doing here?'

'I bought it. They're not hard to come by if you know where to look. In Tibet, and parts of Nepal and China, it was commonplace to use human skulls for drums and begging bowls.'

He took another one from the shelf and held it in front of his face. She could see his eyes gleaming as he gazed at a small bowl decorated with delicate blue mosaic.

'You're looking at a fourteenth century Aztec human skull overlaid with turquoise.'

He replaced it carefully on the shelf and picked up an undecorated upturned skull.

'This one was found less than two hundred miles from here. It had been hidden underground since the last ice age, over ten thousand years ago.'

He held out his hand.

'Look, you can see scratches where the soft tissue was scraped away, and marks where someone banged the jagged rim with a stone to try and smooth it down so it could be used as a drinking cup.'

He grinned suddenly.

'They've got a replica of a skull cup like this on display in one of the London museums.'

He returned the skull cup to its shelf and picked up a small comb.

'It's not just cups and bowls. The pre-Aztec civilisations took human bones from their dead relatives and used them to make combs like this one, and buttons. I've got one somewhere.'

He felt on the shelf.

'Here it is.'

He held up a tiny object, too small for her to see clearly.

'And this one's a needle. They turned bones into household items after their relatives died.'

'How did they – get them out?'

She dropped back on the bed, exhausted from the effort of supporting her head.

'They removed the flesh and muscle. None of that's any use once a person's dead, is it? Decay is inevitable. Only bones are permanent. Femurs, tibias, skulls, they used them all.'

'Why?'

He frowned at her.

'What do you mean, why? Don't you understand anything? People die and rot away, decompose to nothing, but bones remain. The Aztecs understood that. So a bone from a woman who was good at sewing would be made into a needle, to preserve the gift. Or they might make a button out of someone's bone to keep their memory alive.'

He ran his hand along the edge of the shelf and picked up a small bone which he held up to the light. Despite her lethargy she could tell it was precious to him, and curiosity overwhelmed her disgust.

'What is it?'

'This one is a phalanx,' he explained as though he was a teacher.

'A phalanx?'

'A fingerbone.'

He stroked the small bone and smiled.

'Each bone is unique. Like you.'

He turned to Donna.

'You're unique.'

She stared up at him through her pain and exhaustion. 'Thank you,' she whispered, aware that he had said something kind, and afraid of provoking his temper if she didn't respond.

Exhausted, she closed her eyes and succumbed to darkness.

18

TOO CLOSE FOR COMFORT

'So Donna Henry's gone missing, and we've got an unnamed body.'

The detective chief inspector tapped a series of pictures showing Donna Henry's smiling face and the corpse that had been discovered near Tufnell Park station.

'They're both attractive black women in their early twenties. Is there a connection here, or are we wasting resources following up Donna Henry's disappearance, if she *has* disappeared?'

He looked at Geraldine facing him across his desk.

'What do you think?'

'There's no reason to assume anything's happened to Donna Henry,' she said slowly. 'The chances are she'll turn up.'

'That's what her mother said, isn't it?'

Geraldine flicked through her notebook and read aloud. 'Donna will turn up. She always does. I never know where she is from one day to the next.'

'Her mother should know, I suppose.'

'Yes, sir.'

He smiled, but his voice revealed his irritation.

'Call me Reg. It bothers me, though,' he went on, gazing down at the photos with a worried frown.

He turned to his screen, clicked on a map and twisted his monitor around so Geraldine could study it with him.

'We've got a triangle. Tufnell Park where the second victim

was found is less than two miles from the pub in Camden where Donna Henry was last seen, and two miles from her flat in Highbury Fields which is three miles from Camden Town. It's all a bit too close for comfort, isn't it?'

He looked up at Geraldine. It took her a few seconds to realise it wasn't a rhetorical question. She liked Reg Milton's seemingly consultative approach but she didn't know anything about him or his reputation, so resolved to be cautious. The detective chief inspectors she'd worked with in Kent had been quite domineering and she wondered if Reg was equally controlling, just less forthright in his approach. At any rate, he seemed to think there was a connection between the two women and Geraldine agreed with him.

'I don't think it's a coincidence either, sir – Reg – a victim turning up and another woman going missing at the same time.'
    'Because?'
    'I don't believe in coincidences.'
    'What about their colour? Is there any significance in them both being black?'
    'We can't rule that out, although it might be more relevant that they were both young and good looking.'
    She paused, realising she was speaking about both women in the past tense, as though she believed Donna Henry was dead.

Reg nodded and leaned forward in his chair, resting his elbows on the desk, his finger tips touching.
    'I see we're thinking along the same lines, Geraldine. Of course, that's not necessarily a good thing,' he added, with a smile. 'Oh well, let's hope we're both wrong and the missing woman turns up.'

He sighed.

'She's only been missing for three days and I wouldn't have given her a second thought if it wasn't for this dead woman. Let's focus on finding out who she is. Until we know her identity, we won't be able to work out if there's any connection between them, will we?'

After she left the detective chief inspector's office Geraldine went straight to the Major Incident Room where Sam Haley was chatting to one of the women entering data onto the computer system. Geraldine checked the details they had for the dead woman but all they knew about her so far was what they had established from examining her corpse.

She went to consult the Safer Neighbourhood Team but they had nothing on David Crawley or any of his neighbours.

'Littlefield is a quiet close, gov'nor,' the sergeant told her. 'There was a bit of bother going on at one time between two of the neighbours, and we had a domestic along there a few months back, but nothing out of the ordinary, and other than that it's quiet. All the houses have been converted into maisonettes, some owner occupied, some rented, and there's a small block of flats left over from the sixties. It's a bit of a hotch potch in many ways, but there's no trouble to speak of. Sometimes there's a bit of a barney along the main road by the station, of a weekend, but there's never been any real trouble in Littlefield. Until this.'

He shook his head, as though the alley that ran between Tufnell Park Road and Littlefield Close was a child who had unexpectedly misbehaved.

'Neither David Crawley or his girlfriend is on our radar, and no one we're interested in lives in the street. Some of the tenants aren't English of course, but they're no bother.'

Geraldine and Sam drove to the burger bar along Holloway Road where David Crawley worked as a grill chef. It was part of a chain and the first manager they spoke to didn't seem to know who he was. The second was more helpful.

'Dave? Yes, I know Dave. He's alright, is Dave. Has something happened to him?'

'No. We'd just like to ask you a few quick questions, for the purpose of elimination.'

'Elimination? Is he in some sort of trouble then?'

'No, but we'd appreciate your answering a few questions. How long has Mr Crawley been working here?'

'Oh at least a year, maybe two. That's a long time for us. I could look it up, if you like.'

'No, that's fine. Is he reliable, would you say?'

'What, Dave? Oh yes. He turns up on time and puts in a good shift. He's no trouble. Nice guy too. Bit of a laugh.'

His landlord wasn't able to offer them any other useful information.

'Crawley? In Littlefield Close?' he repeated, shuffling through a fat file. 'He's been in the property for seven years and he's never caused any problems. Pays his rent. He went through a phase.'

'A phase?'

'Yes. First it was a hall carpet, then it was a hoover, and then there was ... something else. Oh yes, a chain on the door. But he settled down after a while. They usually do. He pays his rent on time, and frankly that's all I'm interested in, as long as they look after the place.'

Back at Hendon, Geraldine checked how the review of CCTV footage from Tufnell Park station and the wider surrounding area was progressing, although she didn't hold out much hope of finding anything significant. They didn't even know what they were looking for. Finally, she set up a TV appeal hoping to try and jog someone's memory.

'The body of a young black woman was discovered near Tufnell Park tube station in North London last Sunday morning. Police are appealing for information.'

'It's like looking for a needle in a haystack, without actually knowing where the sodding haystack is,' Sam grumbled.

'Let's wait and see.'

Geraldine did her best to sound encouraging.

'You never know what we might find.'

'You're right,' Sam agreed uncertainly. 'Something's bound to turn up.'

19

STILL MISSING

The other women were nattering, heads bent over desks, busy at keyboards. One of them passed around photographs of her new grandson and Lily made suitably admiring noises. When her phone rang, she jumped.

'Hello?'

'Is that Lily Smalls?'

'Who is it?'

Lily knew better than to acknowledge her name before she knew who was asking.

'This is Detective Sergeant Haley.'

Lily felt her heart palpitating and for a second she couldn't breathe, let alone speak.

'Lily? Are you there?'

'Yes.'

'Lily, the woman who was found in Tufnell Park on Sunday morning isn't your missing flatmate, Donna.'

'What? Where is she then?'

'I'm sorry, I'm afraid we don't know that.'

'So who's the woman you found, if she's not Donna?'

'We're working on establishing an identity now.'

'You mean you don't know who she is.'

'Like I said, we're working on that.'

'Well, how do you know she isn't Donna then?'

'Donna's mother has confirmed the body we have isn't her daughter. It's not Donna.'

'What – '

'We thought you'd like to know, but please contact us when Donna turns up so we can take her off our list.'

'But - '

'Thank you.'

The line went dead.

'Are you alright, Lily?' one of her colleagues asked, and immediately several pairs of curious eyes turned to look at her. 'You do look pale.'

There was a general murmur of agreement.

'She does look pale,' another voice chimed in as though Lily wasn't there.

'Are you sure you're alright?'

Lily found her voice. 'I'm fine, thank you.'

That was a lie. She wasn't fine. She still didn't know where Donna was. An official looking letter had arrived at the flat that morning addressed to Donna and Lily was worried. What if the electricity bill hadn't been paid? She wasn't sure what she was supposed to do. She didn't even know what arrangements Donna had made for paying the mortgage. She imagined going home one day to discover bailiffs emptying the rooms, seizing Lily's belongings, such as they were, along with the contents of the flat.

'Are you sure you're alright?' someone asked her.

'I said I'm fine. Stop going on at me, will you!' Lily snapped.

Several colleagues looked round at her in surprise and she realised she had been quite rude. Embarrassed and agitated, she stood up.

'Actually I don't feel well. I'm going home,' she announced.

She scurried from the room, but she didn't go straight home. Instead, she took the train to Angel and found the police station off Upper Street. She wasn't sure what she was going to say when she got there, but Donna was still missing and no one seemed to be doing anything about it. It was time to force the police to take her disappearance seriously.

A few people were sitting on a row of metal seats which were fixed to the floor along the wall on the far right. After a few seconds' hesitation she marched up to the desk, her legs trembling. A woman looked at her, unsmiling, from behind a glass screen.

'Yes?'

'Can I speak to - '

Lily fumbled in her purse for the card the inspector had given her.

'Detective Inspector Geraldine Steel. I have some information for her. It could be important.'

Someone shifted in one of the chairs behind her. Out of the corner of her eye Lily saw a man staring at her and regretted having spoken so loudly. Not everyone liked people who gave information to the police. The woman behind the screen took Lily's name and asked her to wait while she made a call.

'The inspector's not in the building. Would you like to see someone else?'

'No.'

'What's it about?'

Lily hesitated then bottled it.

'It's alright,' she said. 'I'll just go.'

She turned on her heel and fled, wishing she hadn't given her name.

When the doorbell rang that evening, Lily wasn't surprised to see the detective inspector standing outside.

'You'd better come in,' she said. 'It's about Donna isn't it? Is there any news?'

'You came to see me at the police station,' the inspector reminded her. 'What was it you wanted to tell us?'

She spoke kindly, but Lily could tell she was feeling impatient.

Lily hesitated, wondering how she could justify her panic visit to the police station.

'I don't want to waste your time, but – can I get you a cup of tea or something?'

'No, thank you. Now what it is you wanted to say?'

'It's just that I've been thinking, and I wondered if Geoff might have got something to do with it, kidnapped her or something.'

It sounded stupid, but it was the only thing she could come up with on the spur of the moment.

To Lily's surprise, the inspector produced a notebook and leaned forward attentively.

'Who's Geoff?'

'Donna's ex, Geoff. I only met him once. He seemed like a nice guy but Donna told me he was boring and that's why she broke up with him. She said he was pathetic.'

'Pathetic?'

'That's what she said. I don't think she'd been seeing him for very long, but he had a thing about her.'

'What sort of thing?'

'She said he kept pestering her, wanting to see her, but she wasn't interested.'

'How long ago did they split up?'

Lily shrugged.

'I don't know really. Not long before I moved in and I've been here two months.'

'Was she seeing anyone else?'

'No. She said she just wanted to have a good time. She didn't want to be tied down. Not yet anyway, not at her age.

That's what she said anyway.'

'So how did Geoff take it when she ended their relationship?'

Lily shrugged again.

'I don't know really. Like I said, she finished with him before I moved in here.'

'Did she say anything about how he reacted?'

'No. Only that she was glad to see the back of him.'

The inspector sighed and shut her notebook.

'Lily, I understand your concern, but we can't suspect Donna's ex has done something to harm her just because she left him.'

'Well I don't think he would've been very pleased about it. And now she's gone missing and I just think something might have happened to her and someone should be doing something about it.'

'We're doing everything we can, Lily, but your flatmate's only been missing for four days and people do usually turn up. It's rare for anything else to happen.'

'She seems very anxious,' Geraldine told Sam when they met later on. 'She's a lot more worried about Donna's disappearance than Mrs Henry is.'

Geraldine didn't respond when Sam said she thought it strange that Mrs Henry wasn't concerned.

'Don't you think it's odd?' Sam persisted.

'What?'

'About Mrs Henry. How can a mother not care if her own daughter goes missing?'

As she finished writing up her notes, Geraldine couldn't help thinking of her own birth mother, who didn't seem to care about her at all. However hard she tried to put the knowledge of her adoption out of her mind, she seemed to be constantly reminded of it, and decided to confront the social worker again. This time she would insist on being put in contact with her mother. Alone in her office, she closed the door and looked up the number of the adoption agency. She had to wait a few moments before the social worker dealing with her case came on the line.

'Hello, Geraldine, it's Sandra. How can I help you?'

The social worker sounded weary.

'I want to meet my mother.'

There was a pause.

'You've seen your file, Geraldine. I'm afraid your mother has declined to meet you. I thought we established that on your last visit. I'm sorry but there's nothing more I can do about it. If you'd like me to arrange for you to talk to someone - '

'You don't understand,' Geraldine interrupted. 'She made that decision a long time ago. People change. She might feel differently now. At least you could ask her.'

'I'll see what I can do, Geraldine. And remember, if you'd like to talk to someone, we can arrange that.'

'I'd like to talk to my mother,' Geraldine insisted.

She didn't care that she sounded petulant. Until she heard the words from her mother's own lips, she would never accept her rejection as final.

20

A POSITIVE IDENTIFICATION

Geraldine was writing up her decision log where she was expected to record reasons for all her actions, in case her performance was later challenged. While she struggled to concentrate, a call came through. The dead woman had been identified and the detective chief inspector was holding a briefing. There was a quiet buzz of anticipation as the team assembled and Reg Milton came in.

'We've had a positive identification,' he announced in his slightly pompous manner.

Geraldine glanced automatically at the photograph of the dead woman's battered face displayed on the board.

'Her name's Jessica Palmer, also known as Jessica Jones. Nineteen years old. She was working in Archway at a massage parlour.'

He enunciated the last two words very slowly as though putting them in speech marks.

'We had her prints on file from when she was picked up for soliciting three years ago.'

His shoulders drooped slightly as he added, 'No one's reported her missing.'

As soon as the meeting was over Geraldine checked the dead woman's records for herself. Jessica Palmer was born in Newcastle. At sixteen she'd left home. Her mother had reported her missing at the time, but the girl had disappeared without trace until she was picked up soliciting in Soho two years later.

Geraldine went to find Sam.

'Come on.'

'Where are we going?'

'To a massage parlour.'

'Nice!'

They found the incongruously named Paradise Parlour in a side street near Archway station. The windows were covered with grubby pink shutters, the door was closed, only a small sign lit-up in pink fairy lights informing customers the place was 'Open 7 Days a Week Midday Till Late.'

Geraldine led the way into a dingy reception area where a girl with jet black hair sat behind a desk filing her long nails.

'Yes?'

Geraldine held out her ID card and the girl lowered thick false lashes that concealed her eyes.

'Just a minute. I'll fetch Angie.'

She scrambled to her feet and vanished into the interior of the salon to reappear a moment later with an older woman, heavily made-up, full-breasted and attractive in a blowzy sort of way. She must have been good-looking when she was younger. Now her looks were ruined by black circles beneath her eyes, wrinkled smoker's skin and a hard expression.

'What is it now?'

Angie glared at Geraldine, who held up a photograph of Jessica Palmer.

'Do you know this woman?'

'What's it to you?'

'Don't waste my time. Do you know her?'

'She used to work here.'

'Used to?'

'That's what I said.'

'When did she leave?'

Angie shrugged.

'She went off a few weeks ago.'

'Why?'

'How the fuck should I know? One day she was here, the next she didn't show up and that was the last we saw of her. Not so much as a phone call to say she wouldn't be coming back.'

'Didn't you wonder what had happened to her?' Sam asked.

Angie grunted.

'These girls, thcy come and go. We're quite casual here, it goes with the territory. But my records are all above board,' she added, suddenly wary. 'You can check the books. It's all in order.'

'We're not investigating you,' Geraldine assured her.

'Oh really? Here for a massage are you then? Or is this a social visit?'

'We're investigating the murder of Jessica Palmer, also known as Jessica Jones.'

Angie stared at Geraldine for a moment without speaking, her expression unchanged.

'What happened?' she asked at last.

'That's what we're trying to find out.'

'Well, I wish I could help you - '

'We want to speak to everyone who works here.'

'They're busy.'

'Look, Angie, this is a murder investigation, so business may have to be suspended while we question everyone on the premises, and I need addresses of anyone else who works here. We can do this discreetly or I can have you closed down until I'm satisfied we've spoken to everyone.'

'Alright,' Angie growled. 'You can see the girls in the back

LEIGH RUSSELL

office. This way.'
'Send them in one at a time and we'll get through this as quickly as we can.'
'Very nice of you, I'm sure.'
'And we'll start with you.'

Angie's answers were predictably guarded. One of the masseuses claimed not to recognise Jessica, another said she might have seen her at the massage parlour, only one admitted straight away that she and Jessica were friends.
'How long have you known her?'
'A while. She's a mate.'
'Have you seen her recently?'
'She's around.'
'When did you last see her?'
The girl shook her head.
'I don't know. I saw her – I don't know. She's around. We went for a drink the other night. We had a few drinks and Jess got wasted and said she felt sick. Then she went off and never came back. That's the last time I saw her.'
'Didn't you wonder what had happened to her?'
'I thought she'd got lucky, you know, pulled.'
'When was that exactly?' Geraldine asked again but the girl just shrugged.
'Where did you go?'
The girl gazed around the room without answering.
'Can you remember where it was? This is important.'
The girl shook her head.
'I don't know. It was just some pub she knew.'
'And you haven't seen her since?'
'Good friends, were you?' Sam asked.
'She's a mate,' the girl repeated, her voice and face devoid of any expression.

Geraldine had to look away to hide her disgust when the girl
didn't visibly react on hearing Jessica had been murdered.
She was too spaced out to feel anything, and somewhere a
callous drug dealer was profiting from her loss of humanity.
It almost made Geraldine want to join the drug squad.

'Do you have any idea who might have killed her?'

The girl appeared to be considering.

'No.'

'Did she have any regular customers?'

'Only Robbie.'

'Who's Robbie?'

'You asked about regulars. He's Jessica's regular.'

'Were they having a relationship?'

'God, no. Nothing like that. He's old. Jessica didn't even
like him. She said he freaked her out. She didn't want to do
him, but Angie said if Robbie asked for her Jessica had to go
with him, and he always did ask for her. I thought she might
have left to get away from him. He's a creep.'

'Why did she see him if she found him so repulsive?'

'For the money, of course. If we don't see clients, we don't
get paid.'

'Doesn't Angie pay you?'

'Angie?'

The girl laughed hoarsely.

'Angie doesn't pay us. She provides us with – all this.'

She waved her hands around, indicating the premises.

'And she takes her cut in return.'

Geraldine glanced at Sam, who was scowling.

She turned her attention back to the masseuse.

'What can you tell us about Robbie? Think, please. This
is important.'

'Not to her it isn't.'

She gave a nod at Jessica's photo.

'What can you tell us about him?'

'He liked Jess.'

'What's his other name?'

'I don't know. Blokes here don't tend to give their full names, not real ones anyway.'

'Can you describe him?'

'He's always sweaty and he's a big bloke.'

'What do you mean, big? Is he tall?'

The girl gazed around, glassy-eyed.

'Yes, he's tall. He's a big guy, really solid, you know.'

'What else can you tell us about him? Is he white? Black? Asian?' Geraldine prompted her.

'He's white and his hair's dark, combed over like he thinks that fools anyone.'

'Would you be able to identify him?'

The girl shook her head, animated for the first time.

'No, no.' She sounded scared. 'I can't remember him. I don't know. I – I only saw him once.'

Angie gave them an address and mobile phone number for Jessica but resisted passing them a list of Jessica's clients, claiming it was confidential information. Geraldine pointed out she was obstructing the police in a murder investigation, and Angie caved in at once. There was only one Robert on the list of Jessica Jones' regular clients, Robert Stafford. He had booked in for a massage every Tuesday evening for a couple of months but had given no contact details.

'No address?'

'Don't be stupid. We don't ask, they don't tell. As long as they pay what difference does it make to me where the punters live? Probably not his real name either, what else would you expect? But this one hasn't been in for the last two weeks and he's not the only one. I've lost several of my regulars recently since your lot decided to do a raid,' she added sourly.

'If he turns up again call me immediately, without alerting his suspicion.'

'Working for you now, am I?'

'No, you're trying to keep your business going and avoid us closing you down. Can you describe him?'

'Tall and broad, built like a tank, dark hair, clean shaven, pale face, if he's the one I'm thinking of.'

'Could you give a description to an E-fit officer?'

Angie shook her head.

'Not bloody likely. I see so many blokes. After a while you find you don't really look at them very closely. Not that most of them are much to look at anyway.'

'What now?' Sam asked as they left.

'You're going to find every Robert Stafford who might have visited the massage parlour here regularly on Tuesday evenings. Check CCTV in case he came by car.'

'We're assuming Robert Stafford is actually his name,' Sam said.

'It's all we've got.'

'Evidence from a girl so stoned she didn't even notice her best mate had gone missing.'

'Would you want to be clear-headed if you worked there?'

'I'll get onto it.'

Sam nodded, tense. They both knew they were clutching at straws.

21

HELL TO PAY

Douggie had been having a run of bad luck on the dogs and was skint. He was still owed a thousand quid for torching the BMW but doubted he'd ever see that. He'd been an idiot not to insist on full payment in advance, but there was something about the geezer that had stopped him asking. He drained his glass and was about to leave when George sauntered in. Douggie hurried to join him at the bar.

'I'm buying.'

He slapped his money down and followed George to a corner table.

A few minutes went by in silence before Douggie came out with it.

'There's no point hassling me,' George answered sharply. 'I'm only the messenger. I can't hand jobs on if there aren't any, can I? Be reasonable. If you're not needed any more then you're not needed, and there's fuck all I can do about it.'

'Not needed any more? What's that supposed to mean?'

'It's not supposed to mean anything. Jesus. There's just nothing happening right now, that's all. It's a quiet time. Everyone's on holiday. Things are bound to pick up again after the summer.'

'What are you talking about, everyone's on holiday?' Douggie grumbled into his pint. 'I'm not on holiday. You're not on holiday.'

'Chance'd be a fine thing. Fancy a few weeks in the Bahamas, me. Look, I want my cut, same as you. It's not my fault there's no jobs on right now.'

'Who's on holiday then?'

George shook his head.

'You know I can't say.'

Douggie put his empty glass down on the table and wiped his mouth with the back of his hand.

'There's other people can get me jobs,' he muttered.

'Whatever you say.'

'I've got other contacts, is all I'm saying. You're not the only one passes work my way.'

'Well, piss off to your other contacts then and leave me to drink my pint in peace.'

Douggie felt a brief surge of rage but held it down.

'You're alright mate,' was all he said.

It wouldn't do to fall out with George. Like he said, things were bound to pick up again soon.

George grunted and nodded.

'Soon as there's a job on, I'll let you know.'

It was late when Douggie got home. He fumbled with his key, stumbled across the step and kicked the front door shut behind him. He hoped he hadn't woken Mary or there would be hell to pay. He reached for the light, but before he could flick the switch something closed on his left hand and twisted it round behind his back, pushing him up against the wall. At the same time, leather gloved fingers gripped him so tightly round the throat he struggled to breathe.

'Hello again, Douggie.'

He recognised the voice at once. It was the man who had given him the car to torch. The man who owed him another thousand quid. What the hell was he doing in the flat? Douggie groaned as the man loosened his stranglehold slightly and jerked his left arm further up behind his back.

'Let go,' Douggie gasped. 'You're breaking my fucking arm.'

'We had an arrangement,' the man said, giving Douggie's arm another tug.

'I know. I've done it, just like you said.'

The man loosened his grip on Douggie's arm.

'How did you get in? You've no business here. And where's my money? You owe me. If you've touched Mary - '

'The money's on the table.'

'I want it in tens and twenties,' Douggie blustered. 'Fifties aren't so easy to get rid of.'

The man laughed, a puff of moist breath in Douggie's ear.

'Money's always easy to get rid of. So tell me. What happened to the car?'

'Don't worry. I got rid of it like you wanted.'

'How?'

'What difference does it make now?'

The man twisted Douggie's arm so sharply he yelped.

'Tell me. I want to know.'

'Is that you?' Mary called from the bedroom.

The man tightened his grip on Douggie as though to warn him.

'It's only me, love. I – I just knocked my shin.'

'You've been drinking again.'

'Go back to sleep. I'll be in soon. Don't get up.'

He held his breath but she didn't come out into the hall.

'Well?'

'I torched it.'

'Where?'

'I drove it out to a place I know in Epping Forest and

torched it. Nothing left that could be traced, see? No prints, nothing.'

'You're sure no one saw you?'

'You think I want to get banged up? I went straight there on Sunday night and no one saw. Look, I'm telling you, there's nothing to worry about. I don't mess about. I didn't even wait for the scrap yard to open in the morning. The car's gone alright. You can rely on me. That's why you came to me, isn't it? I'm a professional.'

Unexpectedly the man let go and shoved Douggie in the small of his back, pushing him to the floor. Douggie put out his hands to break his fall and hit his head against the wall with a painful thud. He clambered to his feet and clasped his head in his hands.

'How did you get in?'

There was no answer. He stumbled backwards and felt the wall behind him, which was lucky because he was shaking so much he could barely stand. Pressing himself against the wall he peered into the darkness. A figure appeared briefly silhouetted against dim orange light from the corridor outside before the front door slammed shut.

Trembling, Douggie felt his way to the living room and flicked on the light. The money lay on the table, secured beneath an ashtray. He fingered the notes, wondering how the geezer had found his way in. Suddenly decisive, he ran back to the hall and turned on the light. The front door was closed. He examined the lock but it didn't appear to have been tampered with. He checked all the windows but everything was shut. He went into the bedroom. Mary was fast asleep, her mouth wide open, snoring gently. She certainly wouldn't have let a stranger in and then fallen asleep. He must have picked the lock, only instead of breaking in to rob Douggie, he had left him a thousand quid better off. A robbery in reverse. If the stranger hadn't put the frighteners on him it would have seemed funny.

He went to the kitchen, opened the fridge and knocked back his last can of lager. Fishing out a half bottle of whisky he gulped down a generous slug, followed by a second, until the bottle was empty. He felt better for a moment until it sunk in. An intruder had been in his flat, poking around. Pent up rage swelled in his head until he felt it would explode with the pressure, and his chest heaved. Gripping the handle of the fridge, he leaned forward and banged his forehead against the cold metal door, fighting an urge to roar out loud in fury. Instead he smashed the empty whisky bottle violently against the wall. Glass flew everywhere, crunching beneath his feet as he swayed and stumbled. Blood welled up on his hand and he felt a sharp sting where a shard of glass had sliced into his thumb. 'Shit!'

He grabbed some kitchen towel and winced as he pressed a wad of paper against the wound. But worse than the pain was his fear that the stranger might return. He shoved the bloody notes back in his pocket as Mary appeared in the doorway, white faced with shock at the sight of blood spattering the floor.

'Oh Douggie,' she said, 'what have you gone and done now?'

'It's alright,' he told her. 'There's nothing to worry about.'

He hoped that was true.

22

MURDER IS MURDER

'I'm shattered.'

Sam slumped into a chair beside Geraldine in the Major Incident Room, arms flopping over the edge of the seat, legs splayed, head flung back.

'That's me done for the day.'

Even when exhausted, she radiated energy.

Geraldine logged off her computer and they left the building together.

'Fancy a drink?'

'Only if you agree not to talk about the case, gov.'

'That sounds like a good idea. And it's Geraldine.'

'OK Geraldine. What do you fancy? How about a karaoke night to take our minds off work?'

Seeing the expression on Geraldine's face, Sam laughed. 'Salsa?'

'I was thinking more like a quiet drink, or maybe something to eat if you're free?'

'I've got no plans for this evening, and I'm starving,' Sam replied promptly. 'How about a curry? Or there's an all-you-can-eat Chinese not far from here that's not bad.'

'Not bad?' Geraldine echoed. 'Is that the best London can offer?'

They ended up going to a small Indian restaurant close to the office. It was almost empty, but it was cheap and the food was surprisingly good.

'How does the Met compare with Kent then?' Sam asked.

Something in her tone suggested she was confident Geraldine would be favourably impressed with London.

'It's different in some ways.'

Sam waited and Geraldine suppressed a smile at her sergeant's childlike enthusiasm.

'It's less formal, which I like, but at the same time I get the impression a lot of officers don't really know each other. In Kent I knew most of my colleagues, one way or another.'

'It's a much smaller force in Kent. The Met has about a fifth of the entire UK police force.'

'Yes, I know.'

'But don't you find it more exciting?' Sam insisted.

'London is, certainly,' Geraldine agreed. 'But as far as the investigation goes, murder is murder wherever you are.'

'No talking about the case.'

Sam raised a reproachful eyebrow and Geraldine laughed.

'Have you worked with the DCI before?' Geraldine wanted to know.

'No.'

'What do you think of him?'

They agreed that Reg Milton seemed like a decent detective chief inspector, and gossiped briefly about the fellow officers they had both met. Geraldine held back from being frank about her colleagues, and suspected Sam was being similarly cautious. They didn't yet know one another well enough to speak freely, and she approved of the sergeant's discretion.

'That was great,' Geraldine said as they finished. 'I didn't realise how hungry I was.'

'I'm always hungry. We could go for a drink?' Sam suggested, but Geraldine excused herself. She wanted to do some more unpacking before she went to bed.

It was past ten when she reached home and put the kettle on

before settling down to open a few more boxes. She wished she could be like her sergeant, who seemed happy to put the case out of her mind when she left work. It wasn't necessarily helpful that Geraldine couldn't stop thinking about Jessica Palmer's battered face and disfigured right hand. At least now they knew the identity of the dead girl they should begin to make rapid progress. Tomorrow they would look into Jessica Palmer's life before she started working at the Paradise Parlour, and track down the man Angie knew as Robert Stafford. Geraldine hoped that was his real name.

Her priority was to find Jessica Palmer's killer. Until the case was resolved, she wouldn't be free to pursue her investigation into her own past. She had already made up her mind she was going to return to the adoption agency and press them for more information about her birth mother. If they still refused to disclose her whereabouts, Geraldine was prepared to take matters into her own hands. She finished putting away her towels and bed linen and set to work on her books. She had decided to defer sorting them out until after the move, something she regretted now that the time had come. First she spread them out on the carpet so she could see the covers. Once they were out of their boxes she began putting them into alphabetical order before placing them on the bookshelf. It took a while but she kept going, determined to finish the task before going to bed.

Methodically she placed her books on the shelves, distracted by an image of the dead woman's beaten and bruised face. If only it were possible to pigeonhole people as easily as books, rearranging them into a logical pattern that would help her find what she was looking for: a brutal killer concealed somewhere among the millions of people in London. Geraldine hoped Jessica's death had been quick even though it had clearly been violent. She couldn't help speculating about what Jessica Palmer had looked like before she had been beaten to death. The mug shot on the police files wasn't particularly flattering and was several years out-of-date, but she must have been pretty despite her sullen expression.

The most unusual aspect of the case was that the killer had removed one of his victim's fingers and two of her teeth, all probably after she was dead. The sensible explanation was that he had been trying to conceal her identity but, if that was the case, why hadn't he just cut off both her hands? If he had been intending to remove all of her fingers, why had he left the task incomplete? He hadn't even removed her clothes, which might easily yield forensic details. Had he been interrupted? Whichever way Geraldine considered it, the facts made no sense. She looked along her rows of books and sighed. Life was never simple but at least she had a competent and energetic sergeant. She still missed working with her previous sergeant, Ian Peterson. They had become friends, and she hoped Sam and she would develop a similar close relationship.

23

BLOOD

The next morning Geraldine received a call from the pathologist.

'Inspector, it's Dr Mann here, from the morgue. I hear you have an identity for the dead woman brought in on Sunday?'

'Yes. She's called Jessica Palmer, also known as Jessica Jones. She was last seen a few weeks ago, although no one seems sure exactly when she disappeared. We've contacted her mother who's coming in tomorrow to make a formal identification, but we've got a positive match from her prints.'

'Good. It's always best to know who you're dealing with.'

'Exactly. Was there anything else?'

'Yes, there is something you should know.'

He paused.

'I told you we found some fibres in the dead woman's hair and underneath her nails.'

'Yes.'

'We've got the results of the analysis. They were white cotton, most probably from a bed sheet. There were traces of blood on the fibres, but it isn't the same blood group as the dead girl, Jessica Palmer.'

'There was someone else's blood on the fibres you took from her?'

'Yes. It looks as though there was someone else's blood on the sheets or pillows where Jessica was lying before she died.'

'Can you tell how long it had been there?'

'No. It was only a trace. It's being tested for DNA but that will take a few more days.'

'We need those results as soon as possible please.'

'Yes, of course. It's being treated as a priority. All I can tell you for certain is that it wasn't Jessica's blood.'

'You're absolutely sure of that?'

'There's no doubt about it. The blood group confirms it.'

Geraldine went to find Reg Milton and pass on the information she had received from the morgue.

'The blood traces have been sent away for DNA analysis.'

'Let's not go jumping to conclusions, but there's a good chance this will give us the identity of the killer,' Reg Milton said, but he looked grave.

Neither of them voiced the equally likely possibility, that the blood could have come from a previous victim, indicating they might be looking for a serial killer.

Geraldine abandoned writing up her decision log and went to see how Sam was getting on tracking down people named Robert Stafford.

'There are three possibilities living in the area. One near King's Cross, one in Highbury, one at Arsenal.'

'Right, we'll start with those three then. Come on, let's go and pay these Robert Staffords a visit,' Geraldine said.

'Here's hoping we find the one we're looking for.'

The first Robert Stafford they visited lived in an expensive new apartment block near King's Cross station. The man who opened the door was young, slim and in his twenties, with untidy curly brown hair.

'Robert Stafford?'

Geraldine held out her ID card.

'That's me. How can I help you, officer?'

He sounded friendly but his eyes were guarded.

'Is there anyone else living here called Robert Stafford? Your father, perhaps?'

The young man looked amused.

'You think I live here with my father? In a one bed flat? No.' He laughed.

'It's just me, I'm afraid. My parents are in Northampton and my father's name isn't Robert. It's Dennis.'

The second address was a small terraced house in Highbury. A tired looking woman opened the door.

'Yes?'

Geraldine introduced herself and asked if Robert Stafford was in.

'Robert? Yes. He's here. Why? What's he supposed to have done?'

'We'd just like to ask him a few questions.'

'Hang on. Robert! Robert!'

As soon as Robert Stafford appeared in the hallway Geraldine knew they were wasting their time. Short, wiry and black, he couldn't have been less like the description of Jessica Palmer's client.

The third Robert Stafford lived in a side street of terraced Victorian properties near the Emirates Football stadium, a short walk from Arsenal underground station. Geraldine rang the bell to number 2b, labelled Stafford. No one answered. She tried again then knocked loudly.

Finally a woman came to the door and peered out at them.

'Bugger off or I'll call the police.'

'We are the police.'

Geraldine held out her warrant card.

'What do you want?'

'We're looking for Robert Stafford.'

The woman's worried expression relaxed slightly.

'Upstairs. First floor.'

She started to close the door.

'We tried his bell but he's not answering. Do you know if he's in?'

The neighbour shook her head.

'I don't know him, not really. I see him in the hall sometimes, that's all. Why? What's he done?'

'We just want to ask him a few questions, that's all. One more thing. Can you tell me what he looks like?'

The woman put her head on one side, thinking.

'He's a big bloke, you know, tall. And he always looks as if he's sweating.'

Geraldine felt the skin on the back of her neck tingle.

'He's very pale, doesn't look healthy, if you ask me.'

'What about his hair?'

'Dark brown, I think.'

Geraldine handed the woman a card.

'Please call me straight away on this number if you see him come back. And don't tell him we've been here looking for him. That's very important.'

'I knew it. He's been up to something, hasn't he?'

The woman snatched the card and started to close the door.

'One more thing,' Geraldine stopped her. 'Have you ever seen Robert Stafford with a black woman?'

'What?'

'Have you seen a black woman with Robert Stafford?'

'No. I've never seen him with anyone.'

'Thank you. You've been very helpful.'

The door slammed.

'Why would Jessica Palmer have visited him here?' Sam

asked as they walked back to the road.

'I wasn't thinking of Jessica Palmer necessarily. What about the missing girl, Donna Henry?'

'Do you think Jessica Palmer's death and the other woman's disappearance are connected then?'

'It's possible.'

'Why? Because they're both black?'

'Because they're both attractive young women in their twenties, who disappeared within a couple of miles of each other. Don't you think they could be linked?'

'I don't see why. This is London. There are millions of people living here of all different ethnicities, all crammed together, and people are constantly moving on, leaving home, changing jobs, searching for a better life, or running away from something – it doesn't mean anything's happened to them.'

'But two women vanishing so close together and at almost the same time, you don't really think that can be coincidence, do you?'

'I can't see the connection. Donna's a wealthy woman, Jessica's a prostitute.'

'The connection is that one of them is dead and the other one is missing.'

'You're in London now, Geraldine. People go missing all the time. There no reason to suspect Donna Henry's been murdered.'

Geraldine wished she shared her sergeant's optimism.

24

A QUIET GIRL

The busy main thoroughfare of Holloway Road was jammed with traffic in the middle of the day. Geraldine and Sam crawled from one set of red lights to the next while drivers revved and beeped their horns, motorbikes weaved between the cars, a siren screamed out from an invisible emergency vehicle, and pedestrians streamed along the dirty pavements. People scurrying in and out of Holloway Road station swerved to avoid one another like partners in an ungainly dance routine. They turned into a shabby side street and the tumult of traffic switched to a background hum. Not for the first time since her transfer to London, Geraldine was struck by the abrupt shifts of atmosphere in this city of contrasts.

The landlady occupied the ground floor of her grubby white house and let out the upstairs rooms. She opened the door and introduced herself as Mrs Benton.

'This is my property,' she told them firmly as though Geraldine had come to challenge her right to live there.

'I'm afraid one of your tenants is dead.'

'I'm sorry to hear that.'

An expression of irritation crossed the landlady's face; she was obviously thinking of her rent.

'She was murdered,' Geraldine added.

The landlady had the decency to look shocked.

Geraldine held out a photo.

'Yes, that's Jessica,' Mrs Benton said. 'She's a quiet girl. Or she was, I suppose I should say. You'd hardly know she was there. I thought I hadn't seen her lately but I never ask questions. As long as they don't make a racket and the rent's paid on time, it's not my business what they get up to, is it? Sometimes they come home at night, sometimes they don't. To be honest I prefer it when I don't see them.'

'Did Jessica ever have any visitors?'

'No. Never.'

'Does anyone else live here?'

'Yes, I've got one other tenant lives upstairs, Ellie Oliver. Now she's a respectable girl. Works at the post office.'

'How long has she been living here?'

'About a year.'

'And Jessica?'

'Almost six months.'

'Is Ellie in?'

'I think so.'

'My sergeant will speak to you and Ellie Oliver while I take a look at Jessica's room.'

'It's this way. I've got the key. I suppose it's alright to go in?'

'It's quite alright, Mrs Benton. In fact it's a necessary part of our investigation.'

'Yes, yes. Of course.'

The landlady led Geraldine upstairs to a small bedroom which smelt of cheap perfume. The worn carpet was littered with pages torn from glossy fashion magazines showing models in glamorous evening gowns that contrasted starkly with the cheap, creased clothes hanging in a small wardrobe. The bed was a mess and a small chest of drawers was covered with a clutter of make-up, shampoo and bottles of nail polish.

'I'm sorry it's in such a state,' the landlady burst out, flustered. 'If I'd known she left the place looking like a tip I'd have tidied before you came up here.'

'Please don't touch anything,' Geraldine replied sharply. 'Leave everything exactly as it is. Thank you, Mrs Benton.'

The landlady dithered on the threshold as Geraldine pulled on her gloves.

'Thank you,' she repeated firmly.

'Right. I'll be downstairs if you need anything.'

Mrs Benton turned away and Geraldine shut the door.

There was nothing in the room to link Jessica Palmer with anyone else, as though her life had passed in total isolation; no diary, no address book, no computer, not even a phone. In the top drawer of the chest Geraldine found a handful of small photographs of the victim. In one of them Jessica was wearing a pastel green off-the-shoulder evening gown that looked too large for her thin frame, the pale colour stunning against her dark skin. Around her neck she wore a star shaped pendant with one blunt point where a tip had snapped off. The other pictures showed her in different outfits, dresses, jeans and t-shirts. Her hair was short and frizzy or long and sleek, different in each picture. The only common feature was her thin face and the chain with the broken star which she wore around her neck.

Geraldine slipped the photograph with the pale green dress into her pocket and continued searching. The dress itself was hanging in the wardrobe along with a grubby pink gown and a short black frock. The drawers were stuffed with underwear, clean and unwashed seemingly thrown in together. In one drawer Geraldine discovered a small red velvet jewellery case containing a collection of cheap silver rings, a necklace of fake pearls and strings of tiny colourful glass beads, but no chain with a broken star pendant. A small block of cannabis had been stashed at the back of the drawer beneath a pile of knickers, and there was a half empty bottle of cheap vodka under the bed.

The other tenant had not been able to give Sam any useful information.

'We passed each other on the landing,' she'd said, 'but I didn't know her. We didn't really speak to each other. It's best not to get too friendly with neighbours, I think. Once you start, you never get rid of them.'

Geraldine had an uneasy feeling she had overlooked something important as they left but then her phone rang and she forgot about Jessica Palmer's room. The surveillance team watching Robert Stafford's flat was on the line.

'He's here, ma'am.'

'Are you sure it's him?'

'Looks like it. A tall dark-haired bloke just entered the premises using a key. He's inside now.'

'I'm on my way. Don't do anything unless he tries to leave in which case detain him.'

'Yes, ma'am.'

Geraldine and Sam drove straight to Arsenal. On the way Geraldine made a quick call to the station to check with a constable who had been looking into Robert Stafford's background and learned that as a teenager he had been a member of the National Front. She told Sam who agreed that the information might have a bearing on the case.

'He was only a member for six months,' Geraldine said. 'And he did go to Jessica Palmer regularly for massage, but even so … It's certainly interesting.'

When they arrived the surveillance officer confirmed what he had told her on the phone. The suspect was still there.

'Watch the front. Is there a constable at the back?'

'A car, yes ma'am. I called for back-up while you were on your way, just in case.'

'Good.'

Geraldine hurried up the path with Sam at her heels and a moment later Robert Stafford opened the door in response to her knocking. He studied Geraldine's ID card with apparent interest.

'You know, I thought about joining you people once.'

He smiled at her, his face greasy with sweat.

'I could have been drawing a nice pension by now.'

He let out an exaggerated sigh.

'But what can I do for you two lovely ladies?'

Beside her, Geraldine heard Sam sniff disapprovingly.

'You are Robert Stafford?'

'Yes. What's this about, Inspector?'

Geraldine held out the photograph of Jessica Palmer she had taken from the dead woman's room.

'You know this woman?'

'Er, yes, I do,' he replied, evasive now. 'She works at a massage parlour I sometimes visit. But I wouldn't say I know her, exactly.'

'Her name's Jessica.'

He nodded.

'You saw her regularly at the Paradise Parlour near Archway.'

'I did, yes, for a while.'

'And you stopped going there a few weeks ago.'

'That's right.'

'Why did you stop going there?'

'That's not a crime, is it?'

He smiled half-heartedly.

'Just answer the question, Mr Stafford.'

He shrugged.

'No reason. I went there because my back was playing up. It's an old rugby injury that bothers me from time to time. I'm not getting any younger.'

He pulled a face.

'I stopped going because my back was feeling better. No point in paying for treatment when you don't need it any more, is there? Look, inspector, what's this all about? Has she been complaining about me? Because I can tell you right now I never so much as touched the girl. And I paid in full, every time.'

He paused, and looked at Geraldine.

'Has something happened?'

'What makes you say that?'

'Well, let's see. The two of you take the time to come here and show me a picture of this girl. It's not rocket science, is it? What's happened then? What's she been saying about me? Because I assure you, whatever it is, she's lying. I never laid a finger on her.'

'We'd like you to accompany us to the station, Mr Stafford. We'd like to ask you a few questions.'

'I'm not going anywhere.'

Robert Stafford's face had changed. He looked paler than before and was sweating profusely. He went to close the door but Geraldine was too fast for him. As she slammed the door open and leaned the flat of her hand against it, he barged past her and leapt down the front steps. Sam moved to block the path and squared up to Stafford, who hesitated long enough for Geraldine to seize his wrists and cuff him. Geraldine was surprised that, although quite short, Sam held herself with a physical confidence capable of halting a man like Stafford in his tracks. The sergeant didn't appear in the least fazed by the encounter while Stafford groaned and complained loudly about police brutality as Sam grabbed his elbow and propelled him towards the car.

'No need to break my bloody arm,' he grumbled.

On the point of arresting him, Geraldine heard herself say instead, 'We need you to come with us to the station to answer some questions.'

She couldn't have said why, but she wasn't convinced he was the man they wanted after all.

'Even though he so obviously resisted arrest?' Reg Milton asked her, when she voiced her reservations later on.

'We need to search his flat, sir.'

'Looking for what exactly? A journal where he confesses to murdering Jessica Palmer?'

'No, sir. We need to find a star shaped pendant with one piece missing.'

She showed the detective chief inspector a photograph of Jessica Palmer and explained that the victim had been wearing the same chain in every picture found in her flat.

'But it wasn't on the body and it wasn't in her room. So I wonder if her killer kept it.'

'As a trophy you mean?'

'It's possible, sir.'

The detective chief inspector looked sceptical.

'What about her missing teeth? Wasn't it your assertion that the killer had taken them as trophies? Just because something's missing doesn't make it significant. People lose things all the time.'

Nevertheless he agreed to arrange the search Geraldine had requested.

'Thank you, sir.'

'My name's Reg,' he reminded her, smiling.

'Yes, sir – Reg.'

It felt strange addressing her senior officer by his first name, but she didn't want to be regarded as a county mounty.

'I don't think I could've have stood up to Stafford the way you did. He's a big bloke,' Geraldine said to Sam when she saw her later on.

Sam laughed.

'That's nothing. You should see my ninjutsu instructor.'

'Ninjutsu? Like jujitsu?'

'Yes. It's a form of Japanese martial art.'

'I see. So you were about to toss Robert Stafford over your shoulder when I stepped in and cramped your style by cuffing him?' Geraldine grinned and Sam chuckled.

'Something like that, only I didn't want to hurt the poor man! I'm not joking, Geraldine. I've been training for ten years.'

Geraldine wasn't convinced the sergeant would have got the better of a man like Stafford if she hadn't caught him off guard. She hoped Sam wasn't going to court danger by overestimating her own physical prowess. But there was something about the way he had caved in to the sergeant that seemed to confirm Geraldine's suspicion that Stafford wasn't a brutal killer.

25

A POSSIBLE SUSPECT

'Mrs Carson's on her way.'

'Who?'

'The Palmer girl's mother.'

Geraldine went to the morgue to speak with Jessica's mother, a tiny woman who had identified the victim as her daughter.

'I hardly recognised her. Why did this happen?'

She reached out with a claw-like arthritic hand to grasp Geraldine's sleeve and her bloodshot eyes filled with tears.

'Why my Jessica?'

'I'm very sorry, Mrs Carson.'

'Who did this to her?'

'That's what we want to find out. Can you think of anyone who might have had a grudge against your daughter?'

'A grudge?' the little woman repeated as though in a daze.

'Anyone who might have been angry with her?'

'Angry with my Jessica?'

'Can you give us a list of her associates?'

Mrs Carson looked at Geraldine in bewilderment.

'Who were her friends?'

'Her friends at school?'

'Did she still see them?'

'I don't know. She left home when she was just sixteen. Her sixteenth birthday.'

'I know. We're interested in her life here in London. Do you know who she mixed with?'

126

Jessica's mother gave a low sob and pressed one hand against her mouth.

'I don't know,' she whispered, dropping her hand and shaking her head. 'I don't know. She didn't keep in touch. She didn't get on with my husband. They never saw eye to eye. They used to argue all the time and then when she left - '

She broke down sobbing.

Geraldine waited a moment before she continued.

'What did they argue about?'

'She used to stay out till all hours. You know what teenagers are. But Martin didn't like it that she stayed out all night. He knew how I used to worry so he wanted her home early. They used to argue all the time.'

'When did she last see him?'

'When she was sixteen. She left home and we haven't seen her since. She called me to say she was alright and that she had a job as a beautician doing all the make-up for ladies, in a shop, you know. I begged her to come home but she just laughed and said "Not bloody likely." And that was the last time I spoke to her. I reported her missing but they just said she'd left home of her own accord, and if she didn't want to come home there was nothing they could do about it. If they found her and brought her back, they said she'd only run off again. But they didn't know that, did they?'

As she stared at Geraldine, her eyes glittered with growing anger.

'The police didn't care. And it's no different now, for all your fine talk. I see what you're thinking.'

'We are doing our best to find the person who killed Jessica - '

'But she wasn't a *white* girl, was she? Oh yes, I know how it is with you, all of you. Do you know how many times my nephew is stopped in the street, every week, just for being a black boy?'

'Mrs Carson, police officers do their best to treat everyone fairly - '

'Not a day goes by, not one day, when that boy isn't hassled going about his business, and he's a good boy. Is it any wonder some of them go off the rails, when they are treated like scum, whatever they do. And now my Jessica - '

She began to cry again.

Geraldine spoke quietly.

'Mrs Carson, I give you my personal assurance that we are doing everything we can to bring Jessica's killer to justice. Now, can you answer one more question? Did you ever see Jessica wearing a chain with a star pendant?'

'Oh yes. Her father gave her that, before he left us. She was only little, and when the chain got too small for her she put it on a longer one. She wore it all the time. She said it brought her luck, although what luck she ever had in her life I don't know.'

She moaned softly and dropped her head in her hands.

'I'm going to find out more about Stafford,' Geraldine told Sam when she returned from the morgue. 'See what you can dig up on him as well. We might as well focus on him. We've got nothing else to go on.'

Sam looked at her curiously.

'We don't need anything else, do we? Stafford's our man.'

'He's a possible suspect,' Geraldine agreed cautiously.

'It's got to be him. Look at the way he sweated when you spoke to him, and how he resisted arrest. Why would he be so reluctant to answer questions if it wasn't him?'

'There could be any number of reasons. Lots of people don't like being taken to a police station, or locked in a cell for that matter. He might be claustrophobic. Not wanting to come with us doesn't prove he's responsible for Jessica Palmer's murder any more than his sweating does.'

Geraldine took Sam with her to search Robert Stafford's flat. He was a tidy man, his clothes neatly folded or hanging in the wardrobe. The bathroom was spotlessly clean. Everything appeared to be in order. They didn't find Jessica Palmer's chain, or anything else that suggested any possible connection between him and the dead woman. They did discover a handful of letters from a woman called Evelyn, and a few phone calls established that Stafford had left a wife behind in Scarborough when he moved to London. There were no photographs anywhere in the flat, and nothing apart from the letters to suggest he was married.

'She seems to write to him a lot,' Geraldine said, looking at the dates on the letters. 'I wonder if he ever answers. He left Scarborough six months ago and it doesn't look as though he's been back to visit her.'

'She doesn't sound like an abandoned wife. Listen to this. 'Don't stay out in the sun too long without covering your head, and remember to drink plenty of prune juice',' Sam read aloud. 'Prune juice!'

She pulled a face.

'No wonder he left her in Scarborough!'

They took the letters and returned to the station where a band of journalists were blocking the entrance.

'What can you tell us about the man helping you with your enquiries into the Tufnell Park murder?'

'Would the police be taking this murder more seriously if the victim wasn't a prostitute?'

A strident voice called out above the clamour, 'Isn't it true you'd be doing more if the victim wasn't a black woman?'

Geraldine hurried past, ignoring the shouts. She hoped her gut feeling was wrong and Robert Stafford would indeed turn out to be guilty of murdering Jessica Palmer. If not, then they were no closer to establishing the identity of her killer, for all their efforts.

Back at her desk she reread the post-mortem report. The victim had been chained by her wrists and ankles, the imprint of large metal links discernible on her cold bruised flesh. Geraldine stared at the photograph of Jessica Palmer in her green frock until every detail of it was imprinted on her mind, right down to the broken metal of the star around her neck. Her lucky charm.

26

SHARP EDGE

Donna chewed at her bottom lip until she tasted bitter salty blood on her tongue. The manacle on her right wrist had been looser than the left one so she had been working away, trying to force it through the metal ring until she thought she must have gouged all the skin off the back of her hand, twisting and wrenching it against the sharp edge of her shackle. Finally she had pulled it free and now her hand lay beside her on the bed, raw and bloody. It was too agonising to raise it in the air to gauge the damage. She felt sick with pain. She had no idea what to do with her free arm but lay motionless, hardly daring to breathe in case the movement disturbed the burning in her hand. She was worried that her wounds would become infected from contact with the filthy bed, but there was nothing she could do about it. She tried lifting her arm to rest her injured hand on her stomach but any attempt to move it was excruciating and she gave up.

She forced herself to stay awake, determined to conceal her small victory from her captor. Somehow she had to keep one step ahead of him if she was ever going to escape. But what could she do with just one hand whilst the rest of her remained chained to the bed? The burning in her hand helped her stay awake; she was afraid of falling asleep in case she didn't wake up again. It was hard to concentrate while pain dominated her thoughts but she had to plan ahead. Somehow she had to take advantage of her situation and take her captor by surprise before he noticed her hand was no longer shackled, but she couldn't remember if she was battling the man or the pain. Her hand was free and that meant she had a hope – but a hope of what?

She couldn't stay focused. Her head throbbed. She closed her eyes and heard herself moaning as she surrendered to confusion.

… In the darkness a voice was calling her. When she opened her eyes her grandfather was standing in front of her.

'Grandad? What are you doing here? I thought you were dead. We went to your funeral… '

Her grandfather smiled but he didn't answer. Yellow light dazzled her and she saw he was holding out a chipped cup.

'You brought me a drink,' she said without speaking and he grinned.

He knew what she was thinking.

'I'm so thirsty.'

Suddenly her grandfather reached forward and seized her wrist. Someone was screaming in her head, the sound flooding through her ears, deafening.

'Did you think I wouldn't notice?' her grandfather was shouting.

Her wrist felt as though it was on fire. She stared in horror as yellow flames flickered up her arm. Her grandfather laughed and she felt something tighten around her right wrist, scraping the bone. She shut her eyes and pain shot from her wrist in bursts like fireworks exploding.

When she opened her eyes again sunlight was streaming into the room through a gap in the blind. Both her wrists were so tightly secured to the bed she couldn't move at all and she was so thirsty she would have cried if she'd had the energy.

Turning her head she looked around. A skull stared back at her from the shelf opposite, its empty eye sockets fixed on her in a horrid glare. Its teeth grinned at her and she recognised her grandfather.

'You came back,' she whispered.

'Of course,' he replied. 'You knew I would. It's time to leave.'

'Where are we going?'

'We're going on holiday.'

'I haven't packed my things.'

'There's no time. We have to leave right now.'

'But - '

'Come on!'

He seized her by the wrist.

'Stop it. Let go. You're hurting me,' she protested, but he only tightened his grip on her and pulled harder until she screamed out in pain...

'Be quiet.'

The man had brought her water and bread. Donna gulped at the water.

'Slow down,' he said. 'You'll make yourself sick.'

As if in response to his warning she gagged and vomited, turning her head to one side just in time so that water trickled into her ear. The pain in her arm was excruciating. She could no longer bear it.

'Help me, please,' she begged. 'What do you want from me?'

The room spun unsteadily. The grinning skull seemed to vibrate.

'It hurts so much. Please help me.'

There was no answer so she opened her eyes but the room was completely dark. With a start of surprise she realised the pain had gone. Aware that she was dying, she trembled with a fierce joy. Soon it would be over and the man wouldn't be able to hurt her anymore.

The light was blinding.

'Drink,' her grandfather told her but she couldn't open her mouth.

'Drink,' he repeated, urgently.

Donna tried to move her lips but nothing happened. She felt herself slipping into darkness.

'Come on,' her grandfather said. 'I've been waiting for you.'

PART 3

27

A GRAND JOB

Geraldine wanted to find out as much about Robert Stafford as she could before questioning him. In the meantime it wouldn't do him any harm to sweat in a cell overnight. He had no form, not so much as a parking ticket. All she knew about him was that he had briefly been a member of the National Front as a teenager, had a wife in Scarborough, and was employed as a bouncer at a North London pub.

The landlord of the Victory was very positive about him.

'Robbie's reliable and he's a stickler for checking ID. Not that we aren't careful who we serve but it's difficult to tell nowadays.'

Robert Stafford had been working at the pub for four months.

'To be honest, I'd be sorry to lose him. Good bouncers aren't that easy to come by. There's plenty of blokes think they can do the job, but it takes a cool head under pressure. Robbie doesn't let the underage girls talk him round, and he's got the physical build to carry it off if the lads want to play rough. He's got the knack, manages the customers well when they've had a few too many.'

'What about his injury?' Geraldine asked but the landlord shook his head at her.

'He never mentioned any injury and he's certainly fit enough. There are circumstances where a physical presence is a big help, and he's got that alright.'

He grinned.

'Would you fancy your chances getting past him if he was blocking the doorway?'

Geraldine remembered how Sam had stopped Stafford in his tracks when he'd attempted to scarper.

'That depends on who you are.'

Robert Stafford had moved to London six months earlier, leaving his wife behind in Scarborough. It was quite a trek but as it was her day off, Geraldine decided to go and speak to Evelyn Stafford face to face. She took a train to York where she was met by a local officer who drove her the last part of the journey. It was a sunny day with a few fluffy clouds scudding about overhead. Geraldine gazed at fields and distant gentle hills but was too distracted to enjoy the scenery as she planned her questions for Evelyn Stafford.

Number forty-two was situated beside a drab hairdressing salon.

'I don't suppose I've got time to watch a bit of the match, ma'am?' her driver asked. 'It's the cricket festival this week and the cricket ground is only just round the corner.'

'Wait here,' she answered shortly. 'I won't be long.'

She rang the bell and was about to lift a polished lion's head knocker when the door was opened by a stout woman with tightly curled brown hair and a heavily made-up face, on which powder was clearly visible in the bright sunlight.

'Evelyn Stafford?'

'Who's asking?'

She studied Geraldine's warrant card.

'What do you want?'

'You were married to Robert Stafford?'

'Still am, not that it's any of your business.'

Evelyn Stafford folded her arms across her ample chest.

'What's he gone and done then?'

Her expression changed suddenly to one of alarm. 'Something's happened to him, hasn't it? I'll fetch my coat.'

'It's quite alright, Mrs Stafford. Nothing's happened to your husband. I saw him yesterday and he's fine.'

'I want to see him.'

'He's in London.'

'London?'

'Yes. I've come up from London to see you.'

'Is he in trouble? What's he done?'

'Mrs Stafford, may I come in? As far as we know for now, your husband hasn't done anything, but we need you to help us eliminate him from our enquiries so I want to ask you a few questions.'

'I suppose you'd better come in, now you're here.'

She led Geraldine into a small neat living room and they sat down.

'Oh, where are my manners? Would you like a cup of tea?'

'No, thank you. I haven't got much time.'

'Well go on then. What is it you want to know?'

'What sort of a man is your husband?'

'He's a lovely man.'

'Why did he leave here?'

'It was when he lost his job. He wasn't the only one,' Evelyn added quickly. 'He was head porter at one of the big hotels in York but they made him redundant over a year ago, along with a lot of other staff. The hotel was taken over and as soon as it changed hands they laid-off a third of the staff. My husband did a grand job for them, but they don't care, do they? One day he was earning good money, what with the tips and all, the next he was out on his ear. On the scrapheap before he reached forty. So he went down South to find work, because a man's got to do something, hasn't he? So what's he got himself involved in? Whatever it is, Robert didn't do it, I can promise you that. He's not one to get mixed up in any trouble. He respects the law.'

She nodded complacently.

Geraldine stifled a sigh. Her journey to Scarborough was turning out to be a complete waste of time.

'We just need to eliminate him from our enquiries.'

'What enquiries? Has Robert been arrested for something he didn't do? I knew it was a mistake, him going to London. I knew he'd get himself in trouble.'

'What makes you say that?'

Geraldine leaned forward slightly in her chair.

'Has be been in trouble before?'

'No, of course he hasn't. I told you he's not one to go getting on the wrong side of the law. But when he lived here he had me to keep an eye on him, didn't he? A man on his own, in London, there's no knowing what might happen. He never should have gone. I knew it. He's been led into trouble, hasn't he?'

Geraldine glanced at her watch. She had travelled all this way to learn that Robert Stafford's wife was still devoted to him.

'Alright, Mrs Stafford,' she said, making a show of putting away her pad and pen. 'I've made a note of everything you've said.'

'And you can tell him - '

'Yes?'

'Well, he knows where I am. Just tell him - ' She hesitated.

'Yes? What is it you want him to know?'

'Tell him he needs to be careful with his diet. He'll know what I mean.'

'I'll give him the message,' Geraldine lied.

She tried a different tack, leaning forward confidentially.
'Just between us, woman to woman, what's he really like?'
Evelyn looked down and folded her arms.
'I don't know what you mean.'
'Does he ever show any violent tendencies? He's tall, isn't he, and strong? I imagine he can be quite intimidating when he loses his temper. He must raise his voice sometimes. Does he ever lose control? Use his fists?'
Evelyn looked shocked.
'Use his fists? I should think not. What do you take me for? I don't know what you want me to say, but Robert's a real gentleman. We've been married for nearly ten years and in all that time we've never had so much as a cross word. Robert's not one of your rough types.'
She sniffed.
'He knows how to treat a woman with respect.'
'And yet he went to London and left you behind,' Geraldine pointed out, determined to provoke her into some criticism of her husband.
'I told you he had to look for work.'
'And - ?'
'And what?'
'How did he get on?'
Evelyn shrugged but didn't reply.

'Why didn't you go with him?'
'What? To London?' Evelyn sounded appalled. 'I can't think of leaving my mother, not now she's all on her own. Robert understood. That's the sort of man he is. And it was better for him to try it on his own. He was hoping to get into the comedy clubs and they work all hours, don't they?'
'Comedy clubs?'

'Yes. He's brilliant with his impressions. It's a gift. He can do all of the film stars. You ask him to show you his Elvis. There's no one to touch my Robert when it comes to impressions. I told him, he could do that programme on the telly, you know, where they do their impressions of the stars. He did turns at our local, but he wanted to try his luck in London. That's the place for it all, isn't it?'

'Are you telling me that in all the time you lived with Robert Stafford you never once saw him lose his temper? Even when he lost his job?' Geraldine asked, bringing Evelyn back to the question of whether her husband was ever violent.

'He didn't lose his job. He was made redundant.'

'Didn't that make him angry?'

Evelyn shook her head and her brittle curls trembled.

'No, Inspector. That's not his way.'

'I appreciate you're keen to show your loyalty, but is there something you're not telling me? You can talk to me in confidence. Nothing you say will get back to Robert.'

'He's my husband. Why would I want to tell you anything I wouldn't tell him?'

'Even though he left you?'

'He hasn't left me.'

'So you don't feel he's abandoned you?' Geraldine pressed her.

'He'll be back.'

'After six months without a visit?'

'He's my husband.'

'Mrs Stafford, do you sympathise with your husband's political convictions?'

'What's that?'

'You are aware that he joined the National Front when he was younger?'

141

'Did he? That's politics is it? I can't say he ever mentioned it, but I'm not one for politics myself. What difference does any of it make to people like us, you tell me that.'

It was no use trying to wheedle information out of her. Geraldine thanked Evelyn Stafford and gave her a card, urging her to phone the station if she thought of anything else to tell the police.

'That was a complete waste of time,' she grumbled as she climbed back in the car.

Evelyn's devotion to her husband appeared unshakeable but Geraldine wondered if she would have something different to say about him if she was talking to her friends. She might have been too proud to reveal her husband's true nature to a stranger from the South.

'A complete waste of time,' she repeated sourly.

28

A STRAIGHTFORWARD QUESTION

Robert Stafford sat down heavily opposite Geraldine and Sam. Pasty-faced and dishevelled, he looked very different from the ebullient man they had met the previous day. There was an unhealthy sheen on his pale forehead and his cheeks were grey with stubble. His hair was no longer arranged in a miserable attempt to conceal his bald pate but hung unkempt and absurdly uneven on either side of his face.

'You don't look too good, Robert. Rough night was it?' Geraldine made no effort to hide her satisfaction.

'This is disgraceful! I've been here overnight and now you've kept me here all day, without any explanation. I demand to see a solicitor.'

'Is there something on your mind you'd like to share with us?'

He dropped his gaze and sat, shoulders hunched, scowling at the floor.

'Let's start at the beginning. We're in no hurry. We can keep you here for as long as it takes. You told us yesterday you were a regular visitor at the Paradise Parlour.'

Stafford mumbled something.

'Speak up please.'

'I went there for the massage.'

'Speak up.'

'I went there for the massage,' he repeated more loudly. 'It helps with my back problems, and it's good for relieving stress.'

'I bet it is,' Geraldine said cynically.

Stafford glared at her.

'You should try it sometime.'

'You went there to see Jessica Palmer, also known as Jessica Jones.'

Stafford mumbled again, looking down.

'You'll have to speak up.'

'I said yes. That's right. It's not a crime is it? She gives a good massage.'

'She wasn't a trained masseuse,' Sam pointed out.

Stafford glanced across at the sergeant, irritation showing in his face.

'I can't help that, can I? I don't ask to see their qualifications before the treatment.'

'Didn't it bother you that she was black?' Geraldine asked.

'What?'

'Jessica was black. Didn't that bother you? It's a simple enough question, Mr Stafford.'

'What do you mean, bother me? Why would it bother me? Are you calling me a racist?'

'It seems odd that you would visit a black masseuse given that you were a member of the National Front.'

'Oh my God, that was more than twenty years ago. So what? Didn't you do stupid stuff when you were a teenager?'

'Are you saying you think joining the National Front is stupid?'

Stafford considered.

'I'm saying I think politics is stupid.'

Geraldine returned to the victim.

'Tell us about your relationship with the black masseuse, Jessica.'

'There was no relationship.'

'You saw her regularly.'

'Her - or one of the other girls. It made no difference to me. She was just one of the girls there. There was nothing special about Jessica. Nothing going on.'

'That's not what we heard.'

'What's that supposed to mean?'

'We were told you used to ask for Jessica. She was a good looking girl.'

Stafford didn't answer.

Geraldine put a photograph of Jessica on the table in front of him.

'That's Jessica, isn't it?'

'It looks like her.'

'She doesn't look like that any more.'

'What do you mean?'

He scowled up at Geraldine without raising his head.

'Jessica's dead, Robert.'

'What happened to her?'

'You tell me. Her face is a real mess now. Black eyes, broken nose - '

'What? You don't think I did that to her?'

He stared at Geraldine, his eyes wide in astonishment. She thought it was genuine.

'I never touched her. I swear to God I never touched her. This is crazy.'

'When did you last go to the Paradise Parlour?'

Stafford shook his head and wiped the sweat from his forehead with his sleeve.

'I want a lawyer.'

'It's a straightforward question.'

Geraldine raised her voice.

'When did you last visit the Paradise Parlour?'

He shook his head.

'I want a lawyer. I'm entitled. And I want to make a phone call. And - '

'Take him away and call the duty brief,' Geraldine said. 'Interview suspended.' She smiled at Sam. It was past the end of both their shifts, but neither of them wanted to go home yet.

'When did you last visit the Paradise Parlour?' Geraldine resumed when the solicitor arrived.

'I don't know. A few weeks ago. I can't remember exactly. I don't keep a diary.'

'You saw Jessica Palmer there?'

'Yes.'

'Speak up please.'

'Yes. I saw her.'

'And then you suddenly stopped going to the Paradise Parlour, just when Jessica Palmer disappeared.'

'Now there's a coincidence,' Sam commented.

She turned to Geraldine.

'Only we don't set much store by coincidences, do we?'

'Why did you stop going there?' Geraldine insisted.

Stafford looked at his lawyer before answering.

'I told you, I went there when my back was playing up.'

'You went there regularly, every week, and then you just stopped going because your back suddenly stopped playing up?'

'Yes, I've told you. I went there for a while and then I stopped. I didn't need the massage any more.'

'Come on, Robert, you'll have to do better than that. Why did you stop going to the Paradise Parlour? There must have been a reason.'

'My client has already answered your question,' the solicitor put in, his voice dry and indifferent.

'You stopped going because you knew Jessica wouldn't be there any more.'

'That's not true.'

Stafford glanced frantically at the solicitor who was gazing at the table.

'I went there for a massage when my back was hurting, and that's all.'

'Your back hurt every Tuesday in June and July?' Sam asked.

'I already told you, it's an old rugby injury. Weekly massage relaxes the muscles and relieves the tension. It just happened to be Tuesdays that I went. It could have been any day but Tuesdays fitted my work rota. And when my back wasn't aching any more I stopped going. I would have gone if I'd needed to but there's no point paying for a massage when you don't need one is there? I'm not made of money.'

'What had Jessica done to annoy you? Or was it something she refused to do for you?'

'My client has already answered that question,' the lawyer replied.

'Does your wife know about your visits to the Paradise Parlour?' Geraldine asked.

'What?'

'Your wife. I met her yesterday.'

'Evelyn?'

'Yes.'

'Is she here?'

Stafford looked over his shoulder as though he half expected to see his wife march into the room, brandishing a bottle of prune juice.

'Does she know about your relationship with Jessica?'

'There *is* no relationship,' he replied, his voice rising in frustration. 'She's just a girl who works in the massage parlour.'

He gazed at the photograph that Geraldine had put on the table.

'Or she was,' he added quietly. 'The last time I saw her she gave me my usual treatment. I paid up and I left and I haven't seen her since. I can't say she's so much as crossed my mind. I'm sorry to hear she's dead but it's nothing to do with me.'

Stafford looked at the solicitor who sat stony-faced at his side.

'Why am I here?'

He waved his arm around the room and turned back to Geraldine.

'Why the hell do you want to pin this on me? Are you telling me I'm her only client? Like I said, I'm sorry to hear the girl's dead but I had nothing to do with it. Why would I? She's nothing to me. Nothing. Now, I'd like to go home.'

He shut his mouth and folded his arms as though to signal that he wasn't going to say another word.

'Charge my client or release him,' the solicitor said, brisk for the first time.

'Yes, you can go - for now,' Geraldine replied, too tired to push any longer for a confession. 'But don't leave the area.'

'We'll be speaking to you again very soon,' Sam added.

Stafford muttered angrily under his breath.

29

THE DEVIL'S FACE

Peter made his way slowly down to the towpath. The rain had given over and he liked to spend time on a bench beside the canal, watching the occasional boat glide past. It was a pleasant spot to sit and contemplate, as long as the rain held off. He wasn't hungry yet but would probably go along to the homeless shelter later on for something to eat. As he had expected, it was deserted down by the canal. The footpath came to an abrupt end by the entrance to the tunnel where the waterway went underground. Few people ventured this far along the path so the last bench was usually free. Peter's blistered feet stung like hell as he limped up to it, sat down and scoured the path for cigarette butts. Spotting one he leaned forward, picked it up delicately between his forefinger and thumb and brushed it against his trouser leg. He lit up and leaned back puffing contentedly. After a while he pulled an almost empty can of lager from the pocket of his raincoat and flung his head back to down the last dregs. Then he stood up and, with a furtive glance towards a narrow boat moored on the opposite side of the canal, tossed the can into the bushes behind the bench.

There was no one about as Peter shuffled to the end of the path to take a piss in the undergrowth at the foot of the tunnel wall. As he relieved himself he glanced up the slope and spotted a pile of clothes someone had chucked from the top of the spiral stairs down onto the weedy slope that ran alongside the brick wall. It was rare for boats to go in or out of the tunnel, and he was invisible from every angle, hidden below the wall and the overhanging trees. In any case, it wasn't a crime to investigate a pile of rubbish someone had chucked away. He scrambled over the low lip, one brick high, at the bottom of the staircase and clung to the cold metal railing as his foot caught in a tangle of ivy on the ground. Avoiding thick nettles he reached out for the clothes and froze, one arm extended. The devil's face was staring up at him from the weeds, black with white staring eyes.

Letting out a yell, Peter leapt down onto the path and charged back past the bench, the blisters on his feet forgotten. He was racing along so fast he almost barged straight into a man jogging towards him. A young woman was running at his side and Peter nearly shoved her into the canal.

'Oi, watch out!' the man shouted angrily as he swerved to one side.

'The devil's here, I saw the devil,' Peter babbled, seizing the man by the shoulders.

'There, by the tunnel, it's the devil.'

He turned and pointed towards the stairs with an arm that trembled.

'Leave it out, mate,' the man said taking a step backwards.

'Come on, Giles. He's drunk.' The woman pursed her lips.

'A face,' Peter repeated. 'The devil's face.'

'He stinks,' she added, wrinkling her nose.

The two joggers moved quickly on. As they reached the stairs, the man looked over at the slope.

'Bugger me,' he said in surprise. 'There is something there. Oh Jesus, what is that?'

The woman was climbing the stairs. She looked over her shoulder and began to scream, over and over, while the man fumbled in his jacket, pulled out a mobile phone and dialled 999.

'Police. There's a dead body down by Islington Tunnel.'

He paused, listening, then gave his name and waited to be connected to the police.

'Yes, there's a body, by the entrance to Islington Tunnel,' he repeated.

He turned to his companion who was still screaming.

'Shut up will you, Elaine. I can't hear a word.'

She clapped a hand over her mouth and sat down with a bump on the step behind her, where she dropped her face into her hands.

'Yes, it's a dead body. I'm sure. Thank you.'

He rang off and turned to the woman.

'The police are on their way. They said to wait here and not touch anything.'

She shuddered.

'Come on, let's go and sit on that bench until the police get here. It's alright, Elaine, we'll be able to leave soon.'

He led her back down the steps, away from the stench, and along the path to the bench.

'That tramp seems to have disappeared.'

'He said it was the devil.'

'Come on. Oh thank God,' he added as they heard a siren approaching.

'The police are here.'

A minute later two uniformed officers came bounding down the stairs. Giles stood up and ran to meet them.

'Was it you who called in to report a body, sir?'

'Yes.'

'Giles Brown?'

'Yes. It's right here.'

Giles led the policeman to the foot of the stairs and pointed to where a dark face was clearly visible, lying on a rough pillow of weeds and bracken.

'I see sir. And you found it?'

'Yes. Well, there was a tramp.'

He described how he and his companion had been jogging along the canal path when a filthy tramp had barged into them, gabbling about seeing the devil's face.

'The devil's face, yes sir.'

The constable was scribbling in his notebook.

'He'd seen the body, you see.'

The other police officer had been examining the body.

'It looks like she jumped.'

He peered up at the wall.

'Only she missed the water and landed at the side of the path instead.'

He studied her face, swollen and bruised from the impact.

A few people had gathered on the canal path.

'Poor cow.'

'Drugs probably.'

Attracted by the police car parked by the gates at the top of the stairs, a group of young teenagers were watching from above. Their voices floated down in snatches.

'Has she snuffed it?'

'Course she has, dickhead.'

'Did she jump?'

'Pushed, innit.'

The police officer who had been checking the body turned to his companion.

'It looks like a suicide but we should call out the Homicide Assessment Team. She's been pretty badly bashed about. Come on, let's clear the area,' he went on loudly while his colleague summoned the rapid response team.

30

AROUND MIDNIGHT

'Another body has been found this morning.'

The assembled team were staring at the incident board in shocked silence.

'One for us, it seems,' the detective chief inspector continued, clearly doing his best to sound vigorous. 'A young black woman was found on the canal path by Islington Tunnel, off Muriel Street.'

'My God,' a constable burst out.

'Is it Donna Henry?' someone else asked.

'We've no identification yet. There was no purse or phone with the body, but it's possible we've found Donna Henry. The assessment team has been out checking the scene and now we're taking it over because it looks like Jessica Palmer's killer's been at it again. The victim was starved, beaten and chained by her wrists and ankles.'

He paused.

'And as you can see, her left leg has been amputated below the knee.'

The detective chief inspector turned to the incident board where a photograph of the second victim was displayed, her face beaten, eyes swollen. Apart from the second victim's missing lower limb, there wasn't a great deal to distinguish her image from that of Jessica Palmer.

'So it's looking like a hate crime,' Sam said.

'Not necessarily, but the possibility increases our need to be cautious with the media. As if the case isn't tricky enough anyway.'

Reg Milton sighed.

'I'll speak to the press office straight away, before anything gets out, if it hasn't already. We need to handle this very carefully. No one speaks to anyone outside this room about the investigation or the victims. Is everyone clear about that?'

There was a murmur of consent.

'The victim was fully dressed above the waist. We're hoping more clothing and shoes might turn up as the area's searched. Well, let's get going.'

Geraldine turned to Sam.

'Let's see what the post-mortem can tell us and then we'll check out where the body was found.'

Geraldine studied post-mortem reports closely, but she also liked to hear pathologists' comments in person shortly after bodies had been examined. The reports were invariably considered and accurate, but there was always a possibility a thought might crop up in conversation that could suggest a line of enquiry she might not otherwise have considered. Following procedure sometimes wasn't enough.

'No stone unturned, eh?' Sam responded when Geraldine explained her reason for going straight to the morgue after the briefing.

'That's what I say,' Geraldine replied and was surprised when the sergeant laughed.

'I know. You say it all the time actually.'

Geraldine was pleased that Sam felt comfortable enough to tease her, and they drove to the morgue in companionable silence.

'At least this one doesn't smell so bad,' Sam said with forced cheerfulness when she opened the door. Geraldine had the impression the sergeant was bracing herself to view the mutilated corpse.

The pathologist looked up and nodded as they entered.

'Another one for you,' he said. 'We don't know who she is. Her prints and DNA have been sent off.'

'When did she die?' Geraldine asked.

She tried to focus on the dead woman's face, comparing her injuries to those sustained by Jessica Palmer, but her eyes were drawn to the crudely amputated leg.

'Within the last twenty-four hours.'

'Can't you be more specific about the time of death? Stop hedging and make an educated guess.'

Geraldine took a deep breath and forced herself to control her impatience. It wasn't the pathologist's fault if he couldn't be more accurate, he was just doing his job.

'It was probably some time last night, around midnight, give or take an hour either side.'

They stood in silence for a few seconds staring at the dismembered body. The face was grotesque, eyes bloodshot, nose and cheeks swollen. They had a photograph of Donna Henry that her flatmate had given Geraldine, but the dead woman's face was so misshapen it was impossible to be certain it was her. The skin on her arms and legs was scratched, her right hand and wrist were a mess of bloody torn skin.

'The victim was in her mid to late twenties,' the pathologist resumed. 'She had looked after herself, her hair had been well-cut, although you might not think it to look at her now, and her clothes look expensive, but she has recently been chained and starved, exactly like the last girl, and she was severely dehydrated.'

He pointed to her face and arms as he went on.

'Many of these injuries to her head, arms and upper body were caused while she was still alive, but her left leg was clumsily amputated at the knee after her death.'

Sam looked troubled.

'Are you sure she was dead? Only you said you couldn't tell if Jessica Palmer was alive or dead when her finger was cut off, and if this was done while she was still alive - '

The pathologist was quick to reassure her.

'The two are quite different and in this case, yes, I'm sure it was done post-mortem. There's no evidence of bleeding, no sign of the blood vessels contracting and no sign of blood depletion in the body, all of which would be present if the amputation had been carried out while she was alive. The signs are not so clear cut – if you'll pardon the pun - with the removal of the finger, where the blood vessels are much finer. This amputation wasn't done with the rather delicate saw that was used to remove Jessica Palmer's finger. A much larger heavy duty blade was used to sever the leg. There are other post-mortem injuries probably resulting from her fall, some skin damage and broken bones. The victim was already dead when she was dropped from a considerable height.'

'What's the cause of death?' Geraldine asked.

'Similar to the last one, only in this case the injuries to her head certainly occurred after she died, probably in the fall, the nose broken and one cheek bone smashed. She was severely dehydrated and malnourished, and she was chained before she died.'

He pointed to the dead woman's wrists and ankles and glanced up at Geraldine.

'Is this beginning to sound familiar?'

'Was it the same chain as the one used on Jessica Palmer?'

'Either that or one exactly like it.'

Dr Mann touched the dead woman's lips delicately with the tip of a finger.

'But the other conclusive piece of evidence so far that we're looking at the same killer is that this victim had two molars removed after she was dead, just like Jessica Palmer. The same two teeth. It's possible the facial injuries were sustained during the extraction.'

'That's weird,' Sam said.

'Yes, it's certainly an odd pattern,' the pathologist agreed cheerfully. 'It's almost like a calling card, as though the killer wants us to know these women were killed by the same hand.'

'Taunting us, you mean?' Sam was indignant.

'I don't suppose he gave us a second's thought when he was pulling out his victims' teeth and sawing off body parts,' Geraldine said. 'There's something else going on here, some other reason he wants them.'

'As a souvenir, you mean?' Sam said. 'Then why doesn't he just take their teeth? It all sounds damned odd, if you ask me.'

Geraldine frowned.

'The man who did this is damned odd.'

'You said the teeth he extracted are the most conclusive evidence so far? Might there be more?' Geraldine asked.

The pathologist nodded.

'I found traces of white fibres under the victim's finger nails. I've sent them away for analysis but I'm guessing they match those we found on Jessica Palmer. It's the same man alright.'

'So he's killed twice,' Sam said.

'Possibly more than twice,' Geraldine answered quietly. 'We don't know whose blood was on the fibres found under Jessica Palmer's nails. Someone else's blood had stained those sheets before she was there. This girl here could be the killer's third victim, or for all we know there could have been more before that - and others to come if we don't find this man and stop him.'

'That's certainly a concern,' the pathologist agreed.

'This woman was killed around midnight,' Sam said.

Geraldine nodded. The same thought had occurred to her.

'It was around half past ten when Stafford left us,' Sam continued.

'He'd have had to work quickly.'

'But it's possible,' Sam insisted. 'And he'd certainly be strong enough to do - that.'

She nodded at the victim's left leg before turning to the pathologist.

'You said she was killed around midnight, give or take an hour or two either side?'

He nodded.

'Well that gives us until one, and he left the station at ten-thirty. That would give him nearly three hours, Geraldine, easily enough time to kill her and drive the body here. You don't think we could have panicked him into doing it? Or perhaps there are two of them and his partner killed her and he disposed of the body once he got back, and our questions had nothing to do with it.'

'No, I think this man works alone. They usually do. But finding him is the extent of our responsibility. Whatever he chooses to do, it's not down to us,' Geraldine said firmly. 'Even if he felt provoked by our questioning, we're not to blame for his actions.'

'Or hers,' the pathologist added.

Sam looked surprised.

'Surely you don't think this could have been done by a woman?'

'Why not?' Geraldine asked.

'A woman could be strong enough to overpower these girls,' the pathologist agreed.

'And would be more likely to take them unawares,' Geraldine added.

'I suppose so.'

Sam didn't sound convinced.

'Still, the likelihood is we're looking for a man, and Robert Stafford's not out of the frame yet,' Geraldine said. 'But whoever it is, we have to find this killer before he – or she - kills again.'

Geraldine glanced at the dead woman and shivered with a sense of Déjà vu.

31

CONCEALED FROM EVERY ANGLE

The entrance to Islington Tunnel wasn't far from the morgue and Sam and Geraldine drove straight there. Neither of them spoke in the car, each lost in her own vision of a woman lying dead on a cold steel table.

'We don't even know it's definitely Donna Henry yet,' Sam muttered as they drew up in Muriel Street and parked by the gate that led down to the canal.

On the opposite side of the road was a residential estate, a care home for the elderly beside it on the corner. In front of them, to the left of the gate, they saw a patio with bushes in wooden planters and a sign 'Please do not steal from this community garden.' Geraldine glanced around the quiet road with fleeting anxiety. It wasn't far from her own flat. They walked through the gate, between high black railings, onto a tarmac walkway which forked immediately. They followed the left hand path down shallow steps concealed beneath the branches of a tree to a spiral staircase with metal railings, which led to a circular wooden platform constructed around a tree trunk. Under other circumstances it would have been an attractive, leafy garden. To the left of the staircase rose the high brick wall of Islington Tunnel where the canal passed under the road, and a steep weedy slope running down to the water below, now mostly concealed beneath a forensic tent squashed into the narrow space between the stairs and the wall.

'That's where she was found,' a constable told them. 'Lying on the grass. She must have been chucked over the railing from the stairs. It would only have taken a moment to park a car outside the gate, carry the body down to the top of the spiral staircase and throw her over. He wouldn't even have needed to take her down to the platform.'

'And there'd be no one here at night,' Sam added.

Geraldine looked around. To her left the high wall towered over them, ahead and to her right thick foliage obstructed her view of the canal, and the path behind was similarly hidden. The stairs were concealed from every angle.

'None of this is overlooked,' she added, speaking to herself as much as to Sam. 'This place was carefully selected by someone who knows the area well. He must live around here somewhere.'

Just saying it gave her a sense of reassurance that they were closing in on this faceless killer. Only she knew that wasn't true.

She turned and looked down at the spot where the body had been found. Stout nettles, dock leaves, ivy and other undergrowth covered the ground. A rotting log lay nearby and a few grey rocks were scattered around.

'There was a smear of blood on one of the rocks,' a scene of crime officer told them.

'And when the medical officer examined the body – well, have you seen it?'

'Yes, we've just come from the morgue.'

'Were there any fingerprints on the railing? Have you checked along the top where he would have been

161

standing?' Sam asked.

The officer shook his head.

'We found a thread from the dead girl's jumper caught in the wire at the top of the stair rail, which confirms where she was thrown over. We've taken casts of all the shoe prints and fingerprints we could find up there, but there are too many really, all overlaid and indistinguishable. I can't imagine we'll get anything useful out of that lot.'

Geraldine looked round.

'Have the people in the boat on the opposite bank been questioned? And the flats across the canal?'

'Yes. The first officers on the scene set that going,' the constable told her. 'The boat people all said they'd slept through the night and didn't see or hear anything. There were a load of muddy footprints on the path, and trampling around in the mud. And it gets worse.'

The scene of crime officer nodded at the constable.

'We had to chase some youngsters off the slope here,' the constable said. 'They were looking for souvenirs, sliding all over the mud. They were only kids.'

It was hopeless. Everyone in the flats across the canal would be questioned but the staircase was hidden by trees. Geraldine stared up at the cracked brick wall, ivy growing across it, and sniffed in the damp musty smell of the canal, its water flowing black and silent below them.

They went up on the bridge to see if anything useful had been discovered there but once again the scene of crime officers had drawn a blank. A police block had been set up on Muriel Road but the street hadn't been closed earlier that morning and traffic had been passing before the police arrived. None of the CCTV cameras around the estate recorded activity on the opposite side of the road where the body had been carried through the gates. The killer hadn't used the path that ran alongside the canal. He had simply hurried through the gate, taken a few steps through the branches of an overhanging tree to the top of the stairs, dropped the dead body and slipped back to his car. No doubt his face had been concealed inside a hood for the few seconds he was there.

'He had this all planned out,' Geraldine said. 'He's checked for CCTV. The last deposition site wasn't on camera either. We'll check all the CCTV and try to track cars approaching and leaving the areas where the two bodies were found but he may have used a different vehicle each time.'

'You think he's got rid of the car?' Sam asked.

'I suspect this killer is too clever to hang on to any car he uses for long.'

'Could this one be Donna?'

Geraldine didn't answer.

The man and woman who had reported the body had been interviewed but they had nothing significant to add. The woman had been too shocked to say much, and it was clear they weren't aware of the extent of the dead woman's horrific injuries. All the man could tell them was that a tramp had stumbled on the body first and then vanished.

'The tramp sounds like Peter,' the constable said. 'He often hangs around here and he matches the description the jogger gave us.'

'What do we know about Peter?'

'He's harmless enough, not much between the ears, but he's light fingered and would have nicked the dead woman's belt if he'd been anywhere near her. Don't worry, we'll pick him up and check his story.'

'Let me know if there's anything about it that doesn't stack up.'

'Yes ma'am.'

But Geraldine knew this had been too carefully planned to be the work of a passing vagrant.

32

WILD ACCUSATION

Mrs Henry seemed vexed at being asked to return to the morgue for a second time to identify a body the police suspected might be Donna.

'Any dead black woman, they're all the same to you are they, Inspector?'

'Mrs Henry, your daughter's flatmate reported her missing - '

Mrs Henry sniffed.

'That feeble minded little thing would dial 999 if a car backfired.'

'But your daughter is missing, and we have a body that matches her description - '

'You mean she's black.'

'She's black, in her twenties and well dressed, and we'd like to eliminate Donna from the investigation. I'm sorry to put you through this a second time. It must be very painful for you.'

'It's not exactly my idea of a pleasant evening. Come on then, let's get this over with. But it's the last time I'm doing this. I'd know if anything had happened to my own daughter.'

That Mrs Henry's confidence in her maternal instincts was misplaced became apparent as soon as she saw the body. The dead woman had been cleaned up as far as possible and her face looked peaceful. With her eyes closed the swelling wasn't so obvious, the bruising was barely discernible against her dark colouring, and her disfigured limb was concealed beneath the covering. Mrs Henry recognised her at once. She stumbled and clasped onto Geraldine's arm, her face contorted as she fought to maintain her composure. Geraldine waited.

'That's her,' Mrs Henry said at last, her voice slurred. 'That's Donna. You got it right this time. That's my Donna.'

'I'm so sorry.'

Mrs Henry turned to Geraldine, her eyes blazing.

'You're sorry? Are you going to get the bastard who did this to her?'

'We're doing our best.'

'Two black girls dead and you're doing your best? Why didn't you find him after the first one? How many more girls are going to die before you do something?'

Her eyes glared in wild accusation.

'If this was a white girl - '

'Our investigation would be just as rigorous. I promise you, Mrs Henry, we're doing everything we can. My team is working round the clock to find your daughter's killer.'

'Do you even have a suspect yet?'

'I'm afraid I can't discuss the investigation.'

'You can't discuss it?' the angry mother repeated, her glossy lips curled in a snarl.

'He's a white man, is he? And this is just another black girl to you, isn't it? My Donna - '

She broke off, suddenly overcome with emotion, and turned back to the body.

'Why?' she howled. 'Tell me why, Donna? Didn't you know to keep yourself safe? Didn't I tell you?'

She wrapped her arms around her own body and bent forward, wailing without restraint.

'Mrs Henry, we can discuss this later if you need some

time, but we would like to know if there's anyone you can think of who might have wanted to harm your daughter?'

'Harm Donna?'

She turned to Geraldine, wiping her eyes angrily on her sleeve and sniffing back her tears.

'Was there anyone who might have had a grudge against her?'

Mrs Henry shook her head.

'She was a wonderful girl, a wonderful girl.'

She turned her head away and began to cry again.

Emotionally drained from her encounter with the distraught mother, Geraldine wanted to be alone so she went out for some lunch. She ordered a pasta dish but only picked at her food, feeling slightly nauseous. She hoped she wasn't going to be ill. More than anything else she would have liked to go home and rest, but her day's work was far from over. With a sigh she gulped the bitter dregs of her coffee, picked up her bill, and set off.

Donna's flatmate was aghast to hear that she was dead.

'Can I see her?' Lily asked, eyes glistening.

'Mrs Henry has already formally identified her daughter's body so I'm afraid that won't be necessary or possible.'

'This is all my fault. I should have reported her missing sooner.'

Geraldine reassured Lily there was nothing more she could have done.

'By the time you noticed she had gone it would already have been too late to do anything to help her. Now, it would help us if we could go over your statement again. When did you last see Donna?'

Lily repeated her account of the evening at the pub in Camden.

'Is there anything else you can tell us about Donna? You mentioned an ex-boyfriend, Geoff.'

Lily seemed surprised that Geraldine had remembered.

'I thought you said he wasn't important.'

'Things have changed now, Lily. This is a murder investigation and we have to follow up any potential lead, however slight. Now, can you tell me his full name?'

'He's just Geoff. That's all I know.'

'Can you describe him?'

Lily frowned then jumped up.

'I can do better than that. I've got a photo we took, if I can find it.'

She led Geraldine into a small bedroom and turned on her laptop. Geraldine waited while she searched through a folder and printed out a photograph.

'Here.'

She held out a small picture of Donna standing beside a dark-haired man who had his arm around her. His face was half turned away, a straight fringe skimming the top of his eyes as he looked down at Donna who was smiling into the camera.

'We took that on the South Bank,' Lily explained. 'Geoff took us on the London Eye.'

'Thank you.'

Geraldine slipped the picture in her wallet.

'Do you know where Geoff lives?'

Lily shook her head.

'I don't know. Donna never said. We only met up together with him once. She wasn't going out with him any more when I moved in here. She said they were just friends, but I know he wanted to get back with her.'

'How could you tell that?'

'He was all over her. He couldn't take his eyes off her and he kept wanting to take pictures of her. It was a bit creepy really. I'm sure he was just waiting for her to go back to him, and when he realised she wasn't going to he killed her so no one else could have her!'

Her eyes grew wide with fear and Geraldine let her talk, listening for anything factual in Lily's wild accusation.

'Do you suppose he'll be after me next?'

'What's prompted you to think that, Lily? Have you ever heard him making any threats?'

'No, but now I've told you about him, he might work it out and come after me.'

'I think that's highly unlikely.'

'You said it was unlikely he had anything to do with her murder and now he's your prime suspect.'

'No, Lily, he's not a suspect, any more than you are. He's someone who knew Donna, so we need to question him in case he has any information that can lead us to her killer.'

'But it could be him,' Lily insisted.

'It's not impossible, but you shouldn't jump to conclusions. We certainly won't. Now, do you know where he works?'

'I think he works in the library round the corner in Essex Road. He's a librarian anyway. They're the sort of people no one ever suspects, aren't they? That's how they get away with it.'

Geraldine nodded. She had heard enough to track down Donna's ex, and more than enough of Lily's fanciful theories. What she needed was facts.

33

DRUNK AND DISORDERLY

It was four days since Douggie had cut his thumb and it still hurt like hell. Mary had taken him to the hospital where they had waited hours before a doctor had cleaned the wound and sent him home, telling him to keep taking pain killers if the hand continued to bother him. Troubled by his injury, not to mention the fact that his flat had been broken into, he went out to the pub. The doctor had warned him to avoid drinking too much alcohol while taking pain killers but he needed to settle his nerves. To make matters worse Mary knew something was up and had been going on at him, driving him nuts, until he had to get out of the flat.

He'd been drinking steadily for half an hour when he noticed a stranger watching him from the other side of the bar. Douggie turned away and knocked back another short then peered round. The man was still staring at him. Douggie had no clear idea what the man who'd broken into his flat looked like; with a shock he realised he could be looking straight at him. He put away another Scotch and glanced around. Still the man was looking at him. In a rage Douggie leapt to his feet and strode across the bar. The room swayed as he walked but he stayed focused on the other man's face.

'What the hell are you looking at?' Douggie bellowed.

'Are you talking to me?'

'What if I am?'

'I don't know what your problem is, mate - '

'You are!'

Douggie almost lost his footing as he lunged at the seated man, fists clenched, face twisted in fury.

'You keep away from me, you hear?'

He swung again and knocked the other man off his chair. Suddenly lots of voices began shouting.

'You ever go in my flat again and I'll fucking kill you!'

'That's enough of that,' someone said loudly.

Hands seized Douggie by the shoulders and pulled him backwards, arms flailing.

'Get off me!'

Everything was confused after that until a policeman appeared, snapped handcuffs on Douggie and shoved him into a car.

'Mind your head.'

Douggie complained loudly that the handcuffs were hurting his injured hand.

'You've got no right. You're picking on the wrong man. He's the one broke into my flat. Did you see the way he was looking at me? He's the one you should be taking in, not me.'

No one paid him any attention so he leaned back and closed his eyes, just for a moment.

'Come along.'

Douggie woke with a start.

'Drunk and disorderly,' a voice barked. 'Come on, let's empty your pockets. You can sleep it off in a cell.'

'Fuck off. Leave me alone.'

Douggie tried to push the police officer out of his way and almost fell over.

'Calm down.'

The policeman grabbed him by the arm.

'Come on, let's do this quietly and then you can go home in the morning. Lucky for you the other bloke isn't going to press charges. Now, what's your name?'

'Douggie.'

'Douggie what?'

'It's Douggie and you can mind your own business. I'm not the one who should be here. It's not me - '

'Alright, Douggie. Are you going to be sensible now?'

Douggie's anger fizzled out; all he wanted to do was lie down and go to sleep. He gave his name and address and the policeman removed the handcuffs.

'Empty your pockets. Come on, I haven't got all night.'

Reluctantly Douggie slapped his keys and wallet on the counter.

'Let's be having your trainers, unless you want to bother removing the laces? Thought not. Anything else in your pockets? You'll get it all back in the morning.'

'Give me my shoes.'

'You can have them back tomorrow. That's a nice little trinket you've got there,' the desk sergeant added, picking up a thin silver chain.

A small star shaped pendant swung from it, one point broken off.

'Get your hands off it, that's mine.'

'Where did you pick this up then?'

'It's mine, I'm telling you.'

'Come on now.'

Douggie yawned and stumbled as a policeman led him away, still grumbling.

The desk sergeant continued dully listing Douggie's possessions.

'Hang about,' he said, suddenly alert because he thought the chain looked just like one they had been told to look out for. He shook his head, dropped the chain gently into a bag with Douggie's keys and wallet, paused, then drew it out again and stared at it for a moment before going to check. It turned out he was right. An inspector from Hendon had sent round a photo of a black girl wearing a chain exactly like the one on the desk in front of him.

'Just call me eagle eyes,' he called out to a sergeant who was passing.

'Don't you mean bird brain?' his colleague replied with a laugh.

Early next morning Geraldine was writing up her log when her phone rang.

'Holloway Road have a necklace matching the description of the one you're after, ma'am.'

'I'll go and take a look.'

At least it would get her away from her desk she told herself while she drove there, trying vainly to suppress her excitement.

'I've come about the chain,' she told the desk sergeant.

'Chain?'

'Yes. You called about a star pendant - '

'Oh yes, of course. Hang about.'

The desk sergeant went away and returned a moment later with a bag containing a delicate silver chain. He picked it out of the bag and put it on the counter.

'There you go. The night duty sergeant took it off a drunk and disorderly who came in last night.'

Looking at the chain, Geraldine felt a sudden elation when she saw that one point of the star had snapped off.

'Where's the owner?'

'He's still sleeping it off in the cells, ma'am. We'll be waking him up and sending him on his way soon. He was involved in a brawl last night, but no one's pressing charges.

From the sound of things he got off lightly.'

Geraldine nodded. She wasn't really listening.

'Give it to me,' she said, brusque in her impatience.

'Ma'am?'

'The chain.'

She held out her hand and the sergeant dropped it gently onto her outstretched palm.

'I don't think it's real silver,' he said. 'Probably not of any value, ma'am. I don't suppose it's the one you're looking for. You'll have to sign for it of course,' he added quickly as Geraldine slipped the chain into her pocket.

'Who did you say it belonged to?'

'A bloke by the name of Douggie Hopkins,' the sergeant read the name and address from his records.

'Good. Whatever happens, make sure Douggie Hopkins doesn't leave here before I've spoken to him.'

'Yes, ma'am. Are you going to sign for that - '

But she was already hurrying back to her car.

'You've got Jessica Palmer's chain?' the detective chief inspector repeated.

He paused for a second before questioning her briskly, staring closely at her all the while.

'Are you sure?'

Geraldine nodded.

'Where was it found?'

'It was found in the possession of some small-time crook who got picked up in a pub brawl along the Holloway Road last night. His name's Douggie Hopkins. I've examined the pendant under a magnifying glass and so has Sam. I've sent it off for closer inspection, but there's a piece missing which makes it an exact match to the one Jessica Palmer's wearing in her photos.'

Geraldine could barely control her elation.

'It matches exactly. It's the same one, I'm sure of it. Can we arrange a search warrant for his flat while he's still being held?'

'Where is he now?'

'He's in Holloway Road cells, sir. I'm going along there to interview him soon, but we can't hold him just on this. He's going to say he found it, isn't he?'

'What do we know about him?'

'The safer neighbourhood team at Holloway Road tell me he does jobs for a bunch of car thieves.'

'He's a car thief?'

'Not exactly. He disposes of stolen vehicles for a set-up operating down in Fulham. They move around a bit, but Fulham Motor Vehicle Crime Unit have been after this gang for months. They seem to work in several areas, mainly stealing high value cars to order, that sort of thing. It's a slick operation. The plates are changed and the vehicles shifted often before the owners even notice they've gone. Fulham have got their hands on a few of the vehicles, but haven't been able to pin these guys down yet. They're slippery. They've got all the kit to make up plates. But they also get rid of hot cars, which is where Douggie Hopkins comes in. He knows all the dodgy scrap yards, and they say he can make any car disappear in a matter of hours, usually crunched and melted down or sometimes torched.'

'Either way, there wouldn't be much left.'

'Douggie Hopkins could be our man,' Geraldine went on. 'If not, Jessica Palmer's killer might have wanted to shift the car she was in and gone to Hopkins who found the chain in the car. In that case, we just need him to tell us who gave him the

175

car and we've nailed it.'

The detective chief inspector nodded thoughtfully.

'Of course there might be no connection, Geraldine. He might have just found the chain in the street. We need to find out exactly what this Hopkins knows. I wonder how helpful we can get him to be? What else do we know about him?'

'The local team pick him up once in a while for brawling. He's a drinker - or rather, he's a drinker who can't hold his drink. Other than that he has no form, and he doesn't know we're aware of his involvement in car crime. Fulham would prefer to keep it that way. Sooner or later they're hoping Hopkins is going to lead them to whoever's running the operation.'

'And if we let on that we know about his links with the gang they're after, Fulham aren't going to be happy.'

Reg ran his hands through his dark hair.

'We have to question Hopkins about it, sir,' Geraldine insisted. 'He could lead us to whoever killed Jessica Palmer and Donna Henry. This is a multiple murder investigation.'

The detective chief inspector looked up.

'Thanks for reminding me, Geraldine. But remember, we don't know for certain the two women's deaths are linked, even if it's looking pretty bloody likely.'

'They must be. Their injuries are almost identical. I'd say that was conclusive.'

Aware that she had raised her voice, she lowered her head and waited for the detective chief inspector to speak.

'It wasn't the same tool, and a different body part was removed from each woman,' he said at last.

'But it's rare to find one female corpse with a body part sliced off, let alone two so close together, and the same teeth were removed from each of the victims.'

'Are we sure the teeth were removed after they died?'

'That was the opinion of the pathologist, and he ought to know.'

It was difficult to hide her irritation with Reg's ponderous deliberations. Her frustration was exacerbated by her suspicion that he would have taken her views more seriously if she was a man.

'Donna Henry's dental records confirm she had all her teeth,' she went on, 'at least as far as her dentist was aware. Unfortunately the Palmer girl wasn't registered with a dentist, and there are no dental records we can find.'

'Are you sure the two molars couldn't have been lost due to bad dental care?' the detective chief inspector persisted. 'It's easy to be misled by unrelated details that appear to correspond. There isn't always a pattern.'

'It seems highly unlikely they're not connected. According to the pathologist's report two of Jessica Palmer's teeth were removed after she died. And then there's the amputations, and similarity in other injuries, and the evidence they were shackled with the same or at least identical chains. In any case, it's at least a reasonable assumption they were killed by the same person.'

'Yes, it's an assumption, and a reasonable one, Geraldine. It may well prove to be correct, but we don't know for sure yet.'

Geraldine was frustrated by Reg Milton's response, just when they seemed to be making progress. She wondered if he was reluctant to admit they were dealing with a serial killer.

'I want to lean on Douggie Hopkins, sir, find out where he got hold of Jessica Palmer's chain.'

'If you're quite sure it's hers then yes, go ahead. I'll deal with the inevitable fall-out from Fulham.'

'I'll interview him as soon as he's sober enough to talk.'

'Go on then. And in the meantime, I'll get onto the beak to issue a warrant so we can search his flat.'

He paused.

'Do you think Douggie Hopkins could be our man?'

Geraldine met his eye, but couldn't answer. At this stage anything was possible.

34

AS GOOD AS DEAD

'What the hell's going on? You said I'd be going home this morning. Where's my things?'

Douggie sat down, sullen and belligerent.

'Do you know a man called Robert Stafford?'

Geraldine held up a photo of Stafford. Douggie leaned forward slightly to squint at it for a few seconds.

'No.'

Geraldine put the bag containing the broken pendant on the table in front of him.

'Where did you get this?'

Douggie glanced at the chain which was clearly visible through the plastic.

'Never seen it before in my life.'

'It was in your pocket when you were picked up last night.'

'So? What if it was? It's not a crime for a man to get his girl a present, is it?'

'Where did you get it?'

'It's mine.'

His eyes were guarded. He looked worried.

'What's the big deal? Give me my things. I never agreed to this. This is harassment. You've no right to keep me here. I want to go home. Now.'

He stood up.

'You might as well sit down because until you've answered my question you're not going anywhere, however long it takes. Where did you get this?'

'You can't keep me here.'

'Where did you get it, Douggie?'

'It's mine. I didn't steal it.'

'No one said you did. Did I say he stole it?'

Geraldine looked at Sam.

'No.'

Geraldine turned back to Douggie.

'Where did you get it?'

'I bought it.'

'Where?'

'I can't remember. It was off some geezer in the pub. He was skint and needed some cash, so seeing as I'm a generous type, I - '

'This belonged to a woman called Jessica Palmer.'

'Well this geezer must have stolen it from her then, because I didn't. Tell you what, you can give it back to the woman if it's such a big deal. I don't want it anymore. Take it, have it, give it back to her, it's broken anyway. And before you say anything, it was like that when I found it – when I bought it - '

'Jessica Palmer's dead, Douggie. She was murdered.'

'Oh fuck.'

His jaw dropped as he realised the implication of what Geraldine had just told him.

'Look, I never had anything to do with anyone called Jessica, I just found the chain - '

Geraldine leaned forward and spoke very slowly.

'The piece of jewellery that was in your pocket last night belonged to a woman who's just been murdered. That in itself places you as an accessory, at the very least. So unless you start talking, and tell us everything you know, you're going to find yourself facing a possible murder charge.'

She leaned back slightly.

'As it happens, I believe you when you say you didn't kill her, but convincing a jury is another matter entirely. The chain was in your pocket, and you just admitted to us that it was your property.'

She paused.

'You can see how it's going to look, can't you?'

Douggie slumped in his chair.

'Alright, alright. I didn't buy it off a bloke in the pub. I didn't buy it from anyone. I found it. I was going to give it to my missus, but then I saw it was broken so I thought I might get it fixed for her. That's why it was in my pocket and that's the truth.'

'Where did you find it?'

'On the street. Your dead woman must have dropped it.'

'What street?'

'I can't remember.'

'You have to do a lot better than that, Douggie.'

'Look, I drink, alright? I don't always remember what happens very clearly. I was walking along, I saw it on the pavement and I picked it up. That's all I remember.'

When it was apparent Douggie wasn't going to budge from his story, Geraldine ended the interview.

'Shall we chuck him out, ma'am?' the custody sergeant asked.

'No, certainly not. Keep him in for now.'

'Right you are, ma'am.'

He grinned suddenly.

'He's not going to like it, mind.'

'Good. Don't make him too comfortable.'

The sergeant laughed.

'I'm afraid we only offer the best accommodation to our guests here, ma'am.'

While Geraldine was interviewing Douggie his flat had been searched. The only interesting find was a blood stained wad of kitchen towel in the bin outside, but Mrs Hopkins' story that Douggie had cut himself on a bottle he'd accidentally broken checked out when hospital records confirmed her account.

'You don't think he could have cut himself deliberately to hide other blood stains?' Sam asked.

'I'm not sure he's that clever – or quite so stupid come to that,' Geraldine replied. 'But get scene of crime officers in to check and send samples off for analysis. Come on, let's have another chat with Douggie Hopkins, see if some more time in the cells has loosened his tongue.'

To her relief, Douggie seemed inclined to talk.

'If I agree to tell you what happened, can I go?' he asked as soon as he sat down.

Geraldine inclined her head.

'But I won't talk with anyone else here as a witness. This is off the record and I'll only talk to one person. That way it's your word against mine if I don't want to testify to anything in court.'

'That's not how it's done, Douggie.'

He returned her gaze levelly.

'Then you might as well call it a day because I found the chain in the street, right? I can't remember where. And that's all I'm saying.'

He sat back in his chair and waited while Sam stood up and left the room closing the door behind her.

Geraldine turned to Douggie.

'Go on then, I'm listening.'

'This is off the record, right?'

'Just talk, Douggie. Or are you determined to go down for

a murder you didn't commit.'

'Alright, I found it in a car I'd been given to – dispose of.'

He was leaning forward and speaking very rapidly, in a low voice, as though he was afraid someone might be listening.

'That's the honest truth. And if you tell anyone what I just told you, you'll have another murder on your hands because I'm as good as dead if this gets out.'

He bit his lip, visibly agitated, and then put his head in his hands.

'No one is going to tell. This is between us,' Geraldine assured him.

She wondered if her lies were any better because she was telling them in a good cause.

'Now, about this car. Who asked you to get rid of it?'

Douggie shrugged without taking his hands from his face. Geraldine repeated the question. When Douggie dropped his hands from his face she could see he was genuinely scared. This was it, the lead they had been waiting for. All she needed was for him to say the name of the man who'd given him the vehicle in which Jessica had dropped the chain.

'Who was it, Douggie? It's that or a murder charge.'

He nodded, licking his lips.

'This man approached me when I was walking home from the pub on - '

He paused, thinking.

'It was Sunday night. He said he'd give me - five hundred quid to get rid of a car for him, but it had to be done that night. No time to wait for the scrap – for the morning.'

He scowled.

'I said I'd do it. It was only a car. It's not a crime to destroy a car with the owner's permission, is it?'

'Maybe not. Go on.'

'So I drove the car to – well, to this place I know. I didn't want to do it, but this bloke, he'd scared the shit out of me and I couldn't say no.'

'Did he threaten you?'

'He said he wasn't taking any chances and he knew where I lived. The bastard had followed me home. He had it all worked out.'

He scowled.

'And he damn near killed me, put his arm round my throat and almost choked me to death.'

'Can you describe the car?'

He smiled.

'Down to the last tiny detail of the trim, but it'll be no use to you now. I torched it.'

He laughed nervously.

'It was a black 7 series BMW… Lovely motor. Broke my heart to see it go like that. I've never done anything like that before - '

His eyes flicked away from her face and back again, calculating how much she really knew. Geraldine sat, impassive, waiting for him to contradict himself with his frantic lies.

'Anyway, he paid up alright. Two fifty in the glove compartment, just like he said, and – and that was it. Two hundred and fifty quid.'

'You said five hundred just now.'

'Did I? I meant two-fifty. I suppose you're going to take that off me now.'

'You're even cheaper than you look Douggie. And the man? Who was he?'

'Never seen him before in my life and that's the truth. And I didn't ask questions. I just did the job. He seemed like he wasn't short of the readies.'

'Can you describe him?'

'Well no, because the thing is, I only saw him twice, in the dark, and he was behind me all the time. I saw his shoes and they looked expensive and he had this posh voice. When I picked up the car I saw a figure in a hood disappearing up the road, but I never got a good look at him. He was too careful for that. But – no, that's it. I never saw him again.'

Geraldine questioned him further, but either he genuinely had no idea who had paid him to destroy the car, or he was too scared to disclose the name.

'How did he find you?'

'I've no idea. He must have asked around.'

'Who might he have asked?'

Douggie shrugged.

'How the hell would I know that? He just appeared out of nowhere. It happens that way sometimes.'

'I thought you said you'd never done anything like this before,' Geraldine reminded him, but he didn't bother to reply. Geraldine suspected he might be telling the truth when he claimed not to know the man, but he did know where he'd torched the car, and any lead was better than nothing.

35

WILD SPECULATION

They took the M25 to Epping Forest with Douggie Hopkins in the back of the car, and SOCOs following in a van.

'What's this for?' he had protested when Geraldine handcuffed him.

'I'm hardly likely to do a runner, am I? I'm helping you. You should be rewarding me for my valuable information, not treating me like a fucking criminal.'

'Just tell the driver where to go.'

'I'll tell you where to go as well if you don't get these things off me. This is police brutality. I'm an injured man.'

'Oh shut up.'

Douggie subsided, grumbling and cursing, and they drove the rest of the way without talking.

It was raining when they reached the outskirts of the forest. Geraldine hoped they weren't being taken on a wild goose chase, but Douggie seemed to know which way to direct them as he led them deeper into the forest along narrow lanes. At last, they drove off the road into a clearing.

'There it is.'

Douggie raised his cuffed hands to indicate the blackened shell of a car and they stared at the twisted metal in silence for a few seconds.

'It was a real beauty.'

'Not any more,' Geraldine replied.

Douggie sighed.

They climbed out of the car and approached the wreckage. A metallic smell mixed unpleasantly with the stench of damp singed fabric and burnt rubber.

'Don't touch anything,' Geraldine spoke sharply.

'What's to touch?' Douggie replied. 'And with what?' he added angrily, shaking his handcuffs.

'Take these fucking things off!'

Geraldine turned to see what had happened to the scene of crime officers who had followed them there, and saw them at the side of the clearing putting on their kit. There was no need to point out the ruined car to them. Leaving the scene of crime officers to their work, Geraldine returned to London, dropping Douggie Hopkins off on the Holloway Road.

'Is that it then?' he asked, nursing his injured hand and scowling.

'For now.'

'What about my things?'

'You can go and pick them up from the station anytime.'

'Thanks for nothing.'

He turned and slouched off without a backward glance.

The owner of the car was soon traced from the chassis number, a William Kingsley.

'It's only about half an hour's drive if we're lucky,' Sam said. 'More likely forty-five minutes. Geraldine, do you think this could be it? Have we got him? He doesn't have form. I've checked. But it could be a crime of passion. He's married. What if Donna Henry was his mistress and he wanted to silence her before his wife found out - '

While Sam could barely contain her excitement that they finally seemed to be getting somewhere, Geraldine struggled to keep her face impassive.

'Facts, sergeant, facts, not wild speculation. Let's see what he has to say for himself before we go jumping to any conclusions.'

'Yes, ma'am.'

Sam gave a mock salute, smiling.

William Kingsley lived in a small house in Northwood, North West of London. The neat, plump woman who opened the door looked about thirty-five but could have been younger.

'Hello.'

She smiled at them readily.

'Are you collecting the clothes for the old folk? I've got a bag put by, hang on a sec.'

'Mrs Kingsley? We're not collecting clothes.'

Geraldine showed her warrant card.

'It is Mrs Kingsley?'

'Yes. You'll be wanting Bill?'

A man appeared in the hallway, tall and lean, with light gingery hair and moustache.

'Who is it, Denise?'

'It's the police,' his wife said.

William Kingsley frowned.

'What is it? Only I've had a long day and I'm knackered.'

'Mr Kingsley, you own a black BMW - '

'Used to. I sold it a couple of weeks ago.'

'It's registered in your name.'

He looked startled.

'Oh shit, did I forget to send the slip off to the DVLA?'

'Oh Bill,' his wife said. 'You promised you'd do it.'

He shrugged.

'How could you forget? Now we're in trouble.'

'Don't look at me like that. And stop being stupid. The police haven't come here chasing my DVLA form.'

'You said you sold the BMW?' Geraldine checked.

'Yes, that's right.'

'Who did you sell it to?'

William Kingsley pulled thoughtfully at his chin.

'I don't really know who he was. Just some bloke.'

'Some bloke. I see. Where did you meet him?'

'I didn't. That is, he came round. He'd seen the ad I put in Exchange and Mart and called up and came over to take a look. Actually, he hardly looked at the car at all, just listened to me start the engine and said straight away he'd take it. I mean, the car was only five years old and it was in great shape. I looked after it.'

'What was his name?'

'I never asked. He paid in cash and that was it really. Is it important then?'

'Yes. We need to speak to the man who bought your BMW.'

Kingsley cleared his throat nervously.

'He looked well-off.'

'It would help if you could tell us everything you can remember about him, and then we'd like you to go along to the local police station and see if you can pick him out in an identity parade.'

He shook his head.

'I'm sorry, but it was a few weeks ago now, and I only saw the guy for a few minutes.'

He frowned in an effort to recollect and then shook his head. 'No, I can't remember him at all, I'm afraid. I'm really not good with faces. My wife thinks I've got that condition, what do you call it Denise?'

'It's got some funny name. It's basically face blindness,' Mrs Kingsley explained. 'Prosonosa or something.'

'Prosopagnosia.'

'Yes. That's the one. Anyway, he's terrible with faces.'

Geraldine turned back to the electrician.

189

'Please try to remember, Mr Kingsley. Was he white or black? Fair or dark haired?'

'Well, he was white with dark hair, I think, and - '

He paused, struggling to summon up an image of the man.

'You said he gave the impression of being well-off. What made you think that?'

'Well, I suppose he had a posh voice and was well-dressed. He might've been wearing an expensive coat. I can't remember what he was wearing, to be honest, that's just the impression he gave, so I felt I could trust him. I mean, it didn't occur to me to suspect his money was dodgy. If it had, I wouldn't have touched it.'

'Was he tall or short? Anything you can remember might be helpful.'

'I think he was tall, about my height, though I couldn't swear to it exactly.'

Geraldine frowned, thinking about Robert Stafford, tall and dark-haired but speaking with a distinct Northern accent.

'Think carefully, please, Mr Kingsley. Can you remember anything else about this man, anything distinctive? His hairstyle, perhaps?'

The electrician shook his head helplessly.

'Where's the money now?'

William Kingsley frowned.

'Well, some of it went on the bike. I had to get it fixed. And the rest - '

He glanced at his wife.

'Don't look at me,' she protested. 'We've got to eat, haven't we?'

'Did he say anything else at all?'

William Kingsley shook his head.

'If you remember anything else about this man, anything at

all, please let me know, and in the meantime we'd appreciate your help in seeing if you can pick this man out at an identity parade. You never know, you might recognise him.'

He shook his head again.

'I won't.'

'Well we'd like you to try anyway, and apart from work, please don't leave home for the time being, and if you have to go away, make sure you let me know. We'll expect you at the local police station tomorrow then.'

Despite his professed poor memory for faces, there had to be a chance he might recognise Stafford as the man who had bought his car. He might remember his voice.

'I'm sorry to take up your time like this,' she went on, seeing William Kingsley's expression, 'but I'm sure you want to help us in our enquiry into a serious crime - '

'What? Is it a murder or something?'

'Yes, what's this all about?' his wife asked.

'I'm afraid we can't tell you.'

'So you want me to go to the police station and look at a line-up, is that it? How long will it take then? What about my work?'

'I'm afraid it will take as long as it takes, Mr Kingsley. I'm sure you want to co-operate with us.'

'Oh William,' his wife interrupted.

She turned to Geraldine.

'Of course he'll be there, Inspector. He'll go down straight after work, won't you?'

'We should have the identity parade ready mid-morning, so we'll expect you about ten-thirty. We want to get this done as soon as possible. One more thing, Mr Kingsley. Where were you on the night of Saturday the twenty-first of August?'

'We always go out on a Saturday night,' he replied.

191

'The girl from next door babysits and we meet my sister and our friends in the pub,' his wife chimed in. 'It's karaoke night.'

'And after the pub closes?'

Mrs Kingsley looked puzzled.

'We all go home.'

'Does your husband ever get called out to work at night?'

'Never.'

'What do you think? Did Robert Stafford buy the BMW from him? Or is Kingsley himself the man we're looking for?' Sam asked, when they were back in the car.

'I honestly don't know.'

'He says he sold his car but there's no record of any kind.'

'I don't think Kingsley's lying,' Geraldine replied. 'There's nothing to connect him with Jessica Palmer and his wife seemed quite clear he was with her.'

Circumstances might point to William Kingsley but much as she wanted to believe they had found the killer, she didn't think the electrician was their man.

'So it's back to Stafford,' Sam said firmly. 'Kingsley sold the car to a tall, dark-haired man.'

'Who was expensively dressed and spoke with an educated accent.'

'He could have remembered wrongly. Like he said, he sees a lot of people over the course of a week.'

'Just our luck to have an eye-witness who can't remember meeting the killer,' Geraldine muttered.

'Whatever. Lots of people are useless at remembering faces. But the rest of it could fit with what Kingsley and Hopkins told us.'

'I don't see Stafford in expensive clothes.'

'Anyone can buy something that looks expensive. That's

neither here nor there. And as for the accent, didn't Evelyn Stafford say her husband did impressions? He could have put on a false voice to hide his Northern accent.'

Geraldine had to admit the idea wasn't utterly implausible, but it still didn't feel right.

36

CROSSING THE LINE

'So it's looking like Stafford's our man after all,' Sam said brightly as she drove back to the station.

'I still don't think he's the one we want.'

'But he could have bought William Kingsley's car. You admitted as much yourself.'

Geraldine sighed, wishing Sam wasn't pursuing Stafford quite so eagerly. He was their only suspect, but that didn't mean he was guilty. She flicked through her notebook.

'A tall dark-haired man wearing a long coat and expensive shoes, and speaking with an educated accent, who gives the impression he has plenty of money. Douggie Hopkins and William Kingsley are describing the same man, aren't they? As far as we know, he bought a car for cash, leaving no paper trail, a car in which Jessica Palmer dropped the pendant she always wore, a car this man paid Douggie Hopkins to dispose of in a hurry.'

She broke off, frustrated. They had been given an elusive glimpse of the man who had killed Jessica Palmer, but he didn't sound like the Northerner who had visited the massage parlour.

'I just don't think Robert Stafford's our man,' she concluded bleakly.

'Because - ?'

'Well, for a start this is a meticulously planned operation. It's not the work of someone who booked into a massage parlour under his own name before bumping off his regular masseuse. I think the man we're looking for is more devious than that. He paid Douggie Hopkins to torch his car without revealing his identity, if we believe Hopkins, which I do. I don't think Hopkins knows who this man is any more than we do. What are we missing, Sam?'

'I don't know. But I do know that Hopkins is scum. I daresay he knows more than he's letting on. If you ask me, we ought to pull him in, not let him off in exchange for giving us information.'

'You know as well as I do that we depend on scum like Douggie Hopkins to give us information. Sometimes that's all we have.'

'That doesn't justify it. We shouldn't turn a blind eye because he knows something we don't.'

'So what would you do then? Lock up all the petty criminals, the snouts and the messenger boys, ones we can mop up easily – and give up trying to catch the bigger fish?'

'Without foot soldiers carrying out their instructions the ones behind it all would have nothing. They'd be nothing. Lock up all the petty criminals and the game's over for whoever's running them.'

'We're talking about men who stay out of sight pocketing the profits. They're loaded, some of them. They'll always find people to do their dirty work for them.'

'Yes, I know. Of course you're right, in practice. But if something's wrong, it's wrong,' Sam protested. 'We shouldn't have to make allowances for scum like Hopkins, that's all I'm saying.'

Geraldine shrugged.

'Well, you're right too, in theory. But we have to be practical. If a small-time crook can help us put a murderer behind bars, it's got to be a good thing. It all depends on

195

where you draw the line about what you're prepared to tolerate and why.'

'There should only be one line,' Sam insisted. 'And that line is the law. It has to be upheld, regardless. It's not our job to decide when the rules can be bent.'

'Sometimes the means have to justify the ends or we'd never be able to protect the majority of people, and that's our job too. Keeping the public safe.'

'So according to you, if a murderer gives us information that leads to the arrest of a serial killer, the murderer should be rewarded? And how about if the serial killer then helps us find a sociopath?'

Geraldine shook her head, smiling.

'Now that *would* be crossing the line.'

'Oh come on. People pay – what is it now? – sixty quid for parking in the wrong place, or driving a few miles over the speed limit, and here we are, condoning someone torching a car that could have led us to Jessica Palmer's killer. We let him off scot free for telling us about it when he was the one who destroyed the evidence in the first place.'

'Letting Hopkins off for destroying evidence isn't the point. The evidence has gone - '

'Thanks to Hopkins,' Sam interjected.

'All we can do now is salvage what we can from the situation. And if that means striking a bargain with Hopkins for information, so we can try and discover who used that car to abduct Jessica Palmer and kill her, so be it. However you look at it, you can't put torching a car in the same category as murder.'

'Yes, but - '

'It's all well and good arguing, and maybe you can make an ethical case, but here in the real world we have to work with what we've got even if that means ignoring moral absolutes. Now come on, this isn't a philosophy class. What do we know?'

'We know enough to suspect Stafford's the man we're after,' Sam replied, crotchety. 'What makes you so sure he's not guilty?'

'What makes you so sure he is?'

'Think about it, Geraldine. He knew her. He stopped going to the massage parlour just after she was killed, and he was a member of the National Front.'

'For six months, when he was a teenager.'

'Alright, he's a National Front sympathiser then.'

'Possibly. But we don't know that. If he's a racist, why would he ask for Jessica Palmer to do his massage? It doesn't make sense. Surely he wouldn't want her touching him.'

'Maybe he liked humiliating her, seeing her in a subservient role. Perhaps he wanted to control his victims - chaining Jessica up could be an extension of her services in the massage parlour where he saw himself as some sort of high and mighty white boss, with black women as his captives, like his slaves. Maybe that's what he enjoyed.'

'And killing his victims would be the ultimate power trip,' Geraldine added. 'Well, I can see how what we know about Stafford could fit what little we actually think we know about Jessica Palmer's killer but what's his connection to Donna Henry? No, something's not right.'

'You can say that again. The whole thing stinks. A massage wasn't all he was after for a start.'

'We don't know that, Sam. And even if there were other services on offer - '

'*If* there were!'

'That still doesn't mean he killed Jessica, or that he's done anything illegal, unsavoury though the whole thing might be.'

'It means he's a disgusting liar.'

'You might well be right, but even if he was cheating on his wife, that's not a crime. And we don't know there was anything like that going on. He might just be the type to go to a massage parlour like that when he was really only after a massage. His story about a rugby injury sounds convincing enough.'

'But it all fits,' Sam replied doggedly. 'The same night we let him go, Donna Henry was killed. It had to be him. Why make things more complicated than they really are?'

'I just want to be confident we're going after the right man.'

Sam shook her head.

'I can't see the problem.'

'Doesn't it bother you that he booked into the massage parlour under his own name when he could easily have used a false one?'

'Presumably he wasn't planning on killing her when he started going there.'

'We'll bear it in mind as a possibility, but we can't go jumping to conclusions.'

Geraldine couldn't give a satisfactory explanation as to why she didn't believe Stafford was a killer, but her instincts told her the man they wanted was altogether more cunning than the Northerner who had patronised the massage parlour.

Tired and dispirited, all she wanted to do was go home and sleep, but her day wasn't over. After work it was time for her to set off on the drive to Kent where her sister, Celia, was expecting her for supper. Although she welcomed the break, she couldn't put the investigation out of her mind. Despite what she had said to Sam, she wasn't ready to disregard Robert Stafford completely. Sam might be right to suspect Robert Stafford had bought William Kingsley's car for cash, putting on a false voice. Geraldine had come across less likely scenarios in previous cases. In any event, they needed to find out more about Stafford and his associates. They knew he had been a member of the National Front as a teenager. He claimed he no longer associated with them and accepting a massage from a black woman certainly seemed to confirm that he had moved away from the views he'd held in his youth. But such prejudices ran deep. Maybe Stafford was cleverer than she thought.

As she left London behind, the investigation slowly began to drift away from her. It seemed strange driving back along familiar roads. It was only a few weeks since she had left the area but it felt as though she was stepping back in time. When she reached Celia's house, time concertinaed as though she had never left at all.

'You've grown up!' she said, smiling at Chloe who grinned at her.

'Are we going shopping, Aunty Geraldine?'

'You know perfectly well it's too late for shopping, young lady,' Celia replied. 'It's supper and then bed for you. School in the morning.'

'Oh mum.'

'I'll take you shopping next time I come,' Geraldine said.

'Do you promise?'

'Promise.'

'You'll have to come round earlier next time then,' Chloe told her. 'Come on Saturday and we can spend all day shopping.'

'Don't be bossy, Chloe,' Celia remonstrated. 'You know Aunty Geraldine's busy. Eight going on eighteen,' she added, turning to Geraldine.

Behind her mother's back, Chloe stuck her tongue out.

'Isn't this nice?' Celia said when she had finished serving the food. 'Three girls together. We should do this more often when daddy's out.'

Chloe chattered about school and insisted on telling Geraldine all about her best friend, Emma. Preoccupied and tired, Geraldine did her best to appear interested. As soon as they finished eating Chloe stood up.

'Where are you going?'

'I need to call Emma.'

'She can wait. Aunty Geraldine's here.'

'But I've got to speak to her about our project.'

'Chloe, don't tell me you've got homework for tomorrow?'

'It's not for tomorrow but I need to ask Emma about it. Aunty Geraldine doesn't mind, do you?'

'Well, I'd like to see more of you, but if you need to speak to Emma, then that's OK with me, as long as I have a hug first.'

Chloe grinned and ran up and flung her arms around Geraldine.

The rest of the evening passed in stilted conversation with Celia. Geraldine considered telling her sister she had contacted social services about tracing her birth mother, but decided against it. If the reunion with her mother went well, she would be open with Celia, happy to deal with her curiosity. But the topic might remain too painful to discuss freely, and once she knew about it, Celia was bound to keep asking her about it.

Arriving home, Geraldine kicked off her shoes and went into the bedroom where she sat down, opened her bedside drawer and took out the one photograph she had of her mother. Sadness overwhelmed her. She put the photograph carefully down on the top of her bedside cabinet and stared at it, thinking about Celia and Chloe. Girls were naturally close to their mothers but Geraldine had never felt accepted by the woman who had brought her up, even before she had known about her adoption. Although she had always been kind and patient towards her, Geraldine had never felt her adoptive mother sympathised with her or understood her on a deep level.

'That's hardly a suitable career for a girl,' was all her mother had said when Geraldine had announced that she was joining the police force.

Geraldine knew it was deluded to imagine she was closer to a stranger in a photograph than to the woman who had raised her. Perhaps it was merely wishful thinking that she felt a tacit bond with the woman whose face she shared. Remembering Mrs Henry's grief at the mortuary, she wondered whether her own mother had grieved at the loss of her baby, and if she still yearned to see her again.

37

NOT ALWAYS SAFE

Jill ran out, slamming the front door behind her, literally shaking with anger. Adam had gone too far this time. It was one thing making snide comments about her admittedly spiteful sister, but when he started on her parents as well that was intolerable. They had only been thinking of Jill when they'd suggested delaying the wedding until Adam found another job.

'There's a bloody recession on,' Adam had fumed. 'Or haven't they noticed yet? What the hell are they thinking? That I just waited until the invitations were sent out and then deliberately jacked in my job? Do they think I want to spend the rest of my life living off my wife?'

'Don't be so stupid. You know that's not it. They're just concerned, that's all. Wouldn't you be?'

'If a daughter of mine was going to marry someone like me, you mean? I've never been good enough for your bloody parents, have I? But of course, they're paying for the wedding so I don't get a say in it, do I?'

A light rain was beginning to fall as Jill hurried along the street listening to the soft thud of her footsteps on the pavement and the distant hum of traffic. A fine spray shimmered in the light of a streetlamp and she shivered, but having stormed out in such a fury she could hardly sneak back for her umbrella. She was confident Adam would come after her before long, although if he didn't show up soon she wasn't sure what she would do. She'd come out without her bag. No phone. No money.

There was no sign of Adam when she reached the end of the road, damp and disgruntled. It wasn't his first outburst but she understood he was under a lot of pressure. Being made redundant just when they were planning the wedding had been terrible timing, especially as he had only been at the firm for eight months so wasn't even entitled to any sort of decent redundancy package. He'd been so pleased with his new job and now it had all gone down the pan. Of course he'd find another position, he would have to, but while Jill was resigned to the likelihood that it was going to take a while, Adam was still struggling to come to terms with his situation. None of that excused his behaviour though. It wasn't her parents' fault that he was temporarily unemployed.

Jill waited on the corner, hoping Adam would turn up soon. He must have heard the front door slam, must have noticed she'd gone. She heard a car draw into the kerb. Turning round, she was disappointed to see it wasn't Adam, but a stranger in a black car.

The driver wound his window down and peered up at her. He looked worried.

'Are you alright, Miss?'

Jill drew back and glanced along the road but there was no sign of Adam.

'I'm fine,' she stammered, turning away.

'Can I offer you a lift home?'

Jill was startled to hear the stranger's voice right next to her ear. He must have got out of his car and approached her noiselessly. She swung round and took a step back, uneasy at such close proximity.

'I said I'm fine, thank you. I'm just waiting for my boyfriend. He's meeting me here.'

'He shouldn't keep you hanging around on a street corner at this time of night, and in the rain too,' the stranger said, pulling his hood further over his brow. He spoke pleasantly, making no effort to move close to her again, and Jill felt reassured.

'I expect he's been held up in the traffic,' she lied. 'I think I'll just walk home. It's not far.'

'I can give you a lift if you like. It's alright, I'm a police officer. Only you're getting wet and - ' he paused. 'It's not always safe to be waiting around on the street after dark. It's not very sensible, really, is it? You never know who might be watching you.'

Jill shivered. He made it sound so sinister.

'It's fine, I'm fine, really,' she assured him.

The man pulled out an identity card.

'Here's my ID. You should have asked to see it before now,' he reproached her. 'You don't know me. I could be anyone.'

Jill nodded. He was right. She looked back along the street and to her relief she saw Adam running towards her.

'Here's my boyfriend now. My fiancé.'

She turned to the policeman but he was already back inside his car, closing the door. He must have left the engine running, because before she could step over to thank him the dark car roared off down the street.

'Who the hell was that?' Adam shouted as he ran up. 'That man? What was that all about?'

'It's alright, he was a policeman. He just stopped to see if I needed a lift.'

'Is that what he told you?'

'He was alright, Adam. He just offered to drop me home.'

'And you don't think that's dicey? Some stranger asks you to get in his car with him at night and you think that's alright?'

'Don't be so paranoid. I told you, he was a policeman. I think it's nice to know there are police around keeping an eye on things. At least he was worried about me. You just left me hanging around on the street on my own at night in the rain - '

'I didn't leave you anywhere. You rushed out and nearly got yourself picked up by a stranger. What the hell was he doing, offering you a lift like that? I should've punched his lights out.'

'I told you, he was a policeman.'

'Yeah right. That's what he said. You've no idea who he was.'

'Of course I know who he was. You don't think I'd talk to any stranger who comes up to me on the street? God, do you really think I'm that naïve?'

'A policeman in a hoody?'

'It's raining, Adam, or hadn't you noticed? I'm telling you, he was a policeman. The first thing I did was ask to see proof of his identity. I'm not an idiot.'

Adam grunted.

'As soon as we get in, you'd better phone the police and check if he really is who he said he was. For all you know, he could be a pervert.'

'If you say so, although I've no idea who he is. And did you see his car number?'

'Me? You were the one talking to him. Now, come on let's go home. You're soaked.'

Adam seized Jill's hand and together they hurried back along the glistening pavement.

38

A DIFFERENT ANGLE

Having traced the car in which Jessica Palmer had travelled - or been transported - Geraldine hoped they were finally on the track of her killer. When she arrived at the station the next morning, the atmosphere in the Major Incident Room was buoyant. Several officers she barely knew congratulated her on the successful turn the investigation had taken.

'It's far from over yet,' she replied. 'It was simply luck we came across the star pendant so quickly.'

Cautiously, she shared their optimism and was privately pleased with herself for having noticed it was missing, and sent round a message to look out for it.

The detective chief inspector was less effusive. He summoned her to his office where his praise for her efficient detective work was brisk.

'Now we have something to go on it's imperative we sort this out quickly,' he told her. 'The papers have started going to town saying we have a twenty-first century Jack the Ripper on our hands and all that bollocks. We can't afford to let this go on much longer without a result. I'm not having a high profile failure on my patch.'

He glared at her as though she was personally responsible for the killer remaining at large.

'Is that why you want to find the killer?' she asked, put out by his belligerent manner. 'To stop the papers criticising us?'

'Of course not,' he snapped. 'But we need to get a result

soon. Here in the Met we're expected to work at a faster pace than you've been used to. I expect you're already discovering it's not like the home counties here.'

Geraldine didn't answer but she thought she understood where the blame would rest if they didn't find the killer. It seemed the detective chief inspector wasn't the only one fighting to protect his reputation.

'What do you expect?' she imagined Reg defending himself to the borough commander. 'I'm sent some inexperienced county DI, wet behind the ears, who thinks she's still operating in a Kent backwater. I do what I can, sir, but a murder investigation is a team effort and a team is only as strong as its weakest member. I didn't have the right team behind me.'

Geraldine frowned. For all the excitement in the Incident Room, the lead had taken them from a villain who worked for a car theft gang, past a burnt-out heap of twisted metal to an electrician who had forgotten to post his paperwork to the DVLA after selling his car.

There was a timid knock on Geraldine's door soon after she had settled back to work.

'Yes?'

She smiled encouragement at the young female constable peering anxiously round the door.

'I don't know if this is important, ma'am. I wasn't sure whether to come and tell you straight away or not bother you - '

'What is it?'

The constable took a deep breath.

'Kentish Town have transferred a call here from a woman who phoned to report that a man offered her a lift yesterday evening and I thought you might want to speak to her as he was a stranger, or shall I - '

'Put her through, constable.'

'Yes ma'am.'

Ten minutes later Geraldine knocked on Reg Milton's door to tell him a young woman had been approached by an unknown man on Sunday evening in Kentish Town.

'A woman called Jill Duncan was out on her own, waiting on the corner of a street for her boyfriend. They'd had a row and she'd flounced out of the house without her keys or phone. While she was waiting for the boyfriend to come after her, a driver stopped to offer her a lift.'

'And?'

'Don't you think we should follow it up? A strange man attempting to pick a woman up on the street, in the area where the killer's operating - '

'Kentish Town?'

'It's not far away. It could be him.'

Reg Milton looked pensive.

'We can't go around pointing the finger of suspicion at every man who chances his luck with a woman. Think about it, Geraldine. The woman who phoned in was approached while she was hanging around on a street corner. What was she wearing?'

'I don't see what that's got to do with it,' Geraldine snapped, although she knew very well what he meant. 'And even supposing he took her for a prostitute, that doesn't mean the man who approached her isn't the one we're after.'

Reg seemed inclined to agree until he discovered the woman was white and sober at the time of the approach. Geraldine argued that wasn't necessarily significant.

'She was a young woman out on her own in the area we know our killer's operating in. It fits his pattern. He wasn't to know she wasn't drunk.'

The detective chief inspector gave an abrupt nod.

'Let's assume for a moment you're right. Was this witness able to give us any information? Did she get the car registration number?'

'No.'

'Or identify the make of car?'

'No. Only that it was dark, possibly black.'

'And was she able to describe the man?'

'Not really. She said he was tallish, but he was wearing a hood and she didn't really get a look at his face. And he told her he was a police officer but there's no record anywhere of the incident. I checked.'

A dark flush spread across Reg Milton's face.

'Are you telling me you think the killer is one of us?'

'No, of course not.'

'What exactly are you saying then?'

Geraldine hesitated, sensing the detective chief inspector's suppressed fury.

'If the killer's impersonating an officer, if he's using fake ID – well, it could be a lead - '

'A lead?'

He glared contemptuously.

'Has it really not occurred to you that anyone can mug up fake ID, enough to fool women who are drunk or high on drugs, at night, in the dark?' he demanded. 'Even supposing this woman had a lucky escape from the man who killed Palmer and Henry, how does that move us forward when she can't tell us anything about him?'

He passed his hand across his face in a weary gesture.

'Well, go ahead if you want to, have her in, question her

if you think it's worth your time, see if she knows anything useful. But don't bring this report to me again unless the woman has something specific to tell us. We need to find the killer, not write a bloody book about where he might or might not be carrying on. Speculation, Geraldine. It's all speculation when we should be looking for hard facts. And you're to keep any suggestion of the killer calling himself a police officer strictly between us.'

'But - '

'You know how people talk. If this gets out, the rumour might spread that we suspect the killer's one of our colleagues, and anything like that is only going to undermine morale. The case is tough enough, with the black community accusing us of institutional racism, without adding to our problems. So, not a word to anyone else. Is that understood?'

He paused.

'That's a direct order, Geraldine.'

Geraldine understood that the detective chief inspector couldn't allow suspicion to threaten the team spirit of the investigation. Nevertheless she felt uneasy at his readiness to conceal a report that might help alert the public to the killer's methods.

The detective chief inspector's suppression of information played on her mind as she sat in her office with Sam, going through everything Douggie Hopkins and William Kingsley had told them.

'Do you think William Kingsley's information is reliable? He was a bit vague, wasn't he?'

'He was trying to be helpful,' Sam said.

'Someone trying to be helpful is no use to us at all. If anything it tends to make witness accounts less reliable. What we want is clear dispassionate facts. What else do we know about the killer?'

'He has a driving licence.'

'How many times have you been told not to go jumping to conclusions?'

Geraldine paused, distracted by her earlier conversation with the detective chief inspector. She couldn't discuss her disquiet after her senior officer had specifically forbidden her to tell anyone the killer might be impersonating a police officer. Her earlier mood of optimism had faded, and the intermittent ringing of phones and buzz of voices passing along the corridor outside her room wasn't helping her concentration. But she felt guilty about venting her irritation on Sam.

'Let's go for a coffee,' she suggested and was relieved when Sam returned her smile.

Seated in the canteen Geraldine continued thinking aloud. As she talked, Sam leaned forward as though eager to hear every word, and Geraldine warmed to her young colleague. Years of experience weren't the only consideration. Sam Haley was a decent human being, acute with people, and not afraid to voice an opinion or admit when she was wrong. She didn't want to crack the case just to further her personal reputation and advance her own career. Like Geraldine, she was committed to the principle of justice, in this case seeking justice for two dead women. It was too late to do anything to help them, but their murderer must not be allowed to go unpunished – or to claim any more victims. Until he was caught, nothing else mattered.

'There are too many unknowns about Robert Stafford's movements,' Geraldine went on. 'Let's approach it from a different angle and think about the victims. We have two bodies, both now identified. They appear to be totally unconnected. Even if they lived within a few miles of each other, that's a long way in London. They came from completely different backgrounds and their lifestyles were poles apart. Jessica lived from week to week, barely surviving on what she earned from the massage parlour.'

'The place ought to be shut down. It makes my blood boil when I hear about young women being exploited like that. And for what? Because no woman in her right mind would willingly go near some stinking filthy bastard of a man like Robert Stafford who - '

'Yes, it's shocking,' Geraldine interrupted Sam's invective, 'but we're not working for the vice squad and they were all consenting adults.'

Sam scowled at Geraldine.

'Now please, let's focus on the investigation. Donna was from a wealthy family. She'd bought an expensive flat in one of the most sought after areas in London. As far as we can tell, the two women's paths never crossed. Donna never visited the massage parlour. Neither of the victims was associated with any religious group or organisation where they might have come across one another and we can't find anything to suggest they ever met. Let's assume we don't know the killer's identity. It might've been Stafford, but then again it might not have been, so let's keep our minds open to any possibility. Did the killer know both of his victims independently and target those specific women, or were they picked at random off the street, in the wrong place at the wrong time?'

She stopped to drink her coffee. Sam waited.

'We know they were both last seen getting smashed in different areas of North London. They both staggered outside and weren't seen again. It looks like they were just easy prey to someone roaming streets, in which case it could be chance they were both black and in their twenties. But why would they get in his car with him? Jessica might well have been perfectly willing to be picked up on the street, but would Donna have got into a car with a stranger?'

'I agree Jessica would have been easy to pick up even if the killer wasn't Robert Stafford – although we don't yet know it wasn't him. But as for Donna, well I suppose she might have got in a car with a stranger if she was drunk enough, and it probably wasn't just alcohol.'

Geraldine nodded.

'You're right, it wasn't just alcohol. I was going to tell you, we had the tox report about an hour ago. I take it you haven't seen it yet? There were traces of coke in Donna's blood, and cannabis, so she could have been completely off her trolley when she left the bar, with no idea where she was.'

'So it's quite likely a well-dressed, well-spoken man might have enticed her into his car, perhaps with some cock and bull story that he knew her, or was a good Samaritan going to take her home.'

'He definitely sounds the sort to appeal to Donna, with a high class accent and BMW,' Geraldine agreed.

She nearly told Sam that the killer was posing as a police officer, but Reg had been adamant that she mustn't share that information with anyone. Reluctantly she decided to keep that to herself for now.

'Whoever he was, he must have spun some credible story to lure them into his car,' she said lamely.

'Whether he was the genuine article, or just Robert Stafford playing the part, he must have seemed like he was reeking of money, the sick bastard.'

'So where did he take them?'

'Yes, where?' Sam echoed.

'And what's he doing now? Should we be warning young women not to get picked up by men they don't know?'

'Come on, Geraldine, kids of five know that much. There's no point warning girls about what's already been drummed into them, if they then go out and get so off their faces that they don't know what they're doing. No amount of warning's going to make any difference to them then.'

Geraldine stared at her empty coffee cup.

'It looks as though he's taken two women in two weeks.'

She looked up at Sam.

'There's every chance he'll strike again, and all we can do is sit around hoping we find him first.'

'He'll make a mistake sooner or later.'

Geraldine shook her head.

'The trouble is, I'm not sure he will. He's got this all worked out. He knows we're looking for him – it's all over the papers – but he's more than one step ahead of us. He knows the area and he knows who to target. He's cunning, Sam, and clever. We don't know how long he's been getting away with this. Does that sound like Robert Stafford to you?'

'Whoever it is, we'll get him,' Sam said between clenched teeth.

Geraldine wondered if her sergeant was really convinced of that.

39

ADDITIONAL PRESSURE

Since a second body had been found, the case had taken on a more urgent momentum and Reg Milton had called on the services of a profiler. He introduced them to a smiling young woman dressed in a flowing floor-length skirt and a multi-coloured pashmina. With her mass of long curly hair and heavily made-up eyes, Geraldine thought she looked like an art teacher.

'I've worked with Jayne before.'

The detective chief inspector beamed as the profiler looked around, careful to make eye contact with everyone.

'The question we need to ask is why is this man acting in this way?' Jayne asked.

'Killing people, you mean?' someone called out.

'And amputating limbs,' another voice muttered.

Geraldine found herself struggling to focus on what the profiler was saying. Her voice was gentle and reassuring, but she didn't impress Geraldine as having much intellectual rigour. The fact that both victims were black shouldn't have made any difference to the investigation, although of course it put them all under additional pressure from the media. Alienated sections of the population were quick to exploit the case to rack up hostility towards the police, which didn't help in their efforts to gather information. But the murder investigation team had to continue with their work regardless.

'The victims were both chained by the wrists and ankles.

This is a killer who wants to control his victims,' Jayne went on. Geraldine did her best to master her impatience as the profiler stated the obvious, speaking very slowly and in such a low voice that Geraldine found herself straining to catch the words.

'Do you think he's likely to kill again?' the detective chief inspector asked.

The profiler considered for a moment, her curly head lowered, before concluding that seemed likely.

'It's possible the killer may be compulsive.'

'You mean we're dealing with a serial killer?' the press officer asked. No one spoke for a few seconds.

At last the profiler replied.

'It's difficult to say.'

'Anyway, we know he's killed at least twice,' Reg said. 'No one outside the investigating team knew that the two victims' injuries were virtually identical until the details came out in the papers after the second murder, so this wasn't a copycat killing.'

Geraldine frowned, realising that the detective chief inspector had agreed with her analysis all along. She understood why he would argue against her theory, making sure her case was watertight, but it irked her that he didn't acknowledge her work. A forceful character, effective in managing resources, he was hardly a team player. That accusation that had been levelled against her in the past, but at least she had never presented someone else's ideas as her own.

'The press have got hold of it now, but what happened to Jessica wasn't public knowledge before Donna Henry was killed,' he explained before turning back to Jayne.

'Both bodies were found close to each other, so he's likely to be operating in an area where he feels comfortable. And is it a coincidence the victims are both black?' the profiler asked.

'Would that question be raised if they were both white?' a black constable demanded.

'I was only wondering if we are dealing with a hate crime,' Jayne replied.

'Against blacks or against women?' the constable snapped.

'Anything's possible,' the detective chief inspector stepped in. 'We don't know anything about the killer so we can't form any firm conclusions about his motive yet.'

Geraldine strained to control her irritation at this nebulous discussion which wasn't helping the investigation.

'Can you tell us anything about the killer that we don't already know?' she challenged the profiler.

'I suspect he's taken the teeth as trophies because he's pleased with the success of his attacks and that may be why he wants to keep souvenirs of his victims. It may also be significant that he's removed the same teeth each time. The dismemberment seems to be escalating, from a finger to half a limb, which suggests he's likely to kill again.'

'Yes, we'd figured that out,' Geraldine muttered. 'This is merely speculating,' she added more loudly.

'That's all we can do until you come up with something more concrete,' Jayne replied evenly.

'Well, I still think Stafford's our man,' Sam interrupted.

'If Jayne thinks he's likely to kill again then we're looking for a pattern. We know Stafford was a member of the National Front and both the victims were black.'

'Their colour might not be significant,' Geraldine argued. 'Maybe the pattern is that both women were in the wrong place at the wrong time, too drunk to sense they were in danger until it was too late.'

A heated discussion followed a male officer's suggestion that the two women had placed themselves in danger. Sam made no attempt to restrain her fury.

'So you're saying women shouldn't go out after dark? A female curfew, would that do it? Is this just for women who've been drinking, or are you suggesting women shouldn't be allowed out on the streets at all? Perhaps you'd like to chain us all up?'

'That's enough, Sergeant,' the detective chief inspector interrupted her sharply. 'This kind of infighting isn't helping. We're all frustrated at making such slow progress, no one more so than me, but we're agreed we need to gather more information. So let's all work together as a team and see what else we can find out. Thank you for your insights, Jayne.'

Geraldine was worried about the report from Kentish Town but didn't dare take it further without the detective chief inspector's authorization. She approached Reg after the meeting.

'At the very least we should run a check on CCTV, see what cars were in the area at the time of the encounter, and conduct house to house enquiries along the street. There's no need to even mention the idea the killer might be using fake ID.'

She hoped it was false, for all their sakes. The thought that the killer might really be a police officer was too terrible to contemplate.

Reg brushed her concerns aside.

'Useful informants are difficult to spot among the host of attention-seeking cranks and time wasters, with so many people claiming to have seen the killer.'

Geraldine pointed out that Jill Duncan hadn't even mentioned the killer. When the detective chief inspector insisted they didn't have sufficient manpower to pursue the matter she couldn't control her frustration any longer.

'How can we not have the resources? This is a murder enquiry - '

'And I'm in charge. Or had you forgotten that?'

He turned on his heel and strode away.

'What was all that about with you and the DCI?' Sam asked Geraldine when they were back in the relative privacy of her office.

'It's nothing.'

'Well he looked damned stroppy to me. Do you think he's crumbling under the pressure?'

'No, I'm sure he'll be fine. His sort always are.'

Sam looked at her inquisitively but didn't comment, asking instead what Geraldine thought of the profiler.

'I'll take your psychological insights over hers any day,' Geraldine answered, and was surprised to see the sergeant's face light up in genuine pleasure.

40

A MINOR TRAFFIC INCIDENT

It was late morning when Geraldine received a call from South Harrow police station.

'William Kingsley's here, ma'am. You wanted to know what happened at the identity parade?'

Geraldine felt a glimmer of hope until she heard the sergeant sigh down the phone.

'We haven't got anything out of him I'm afraid, ma'am. I think he's done his best. He arrived on the dot of nine but he hasn't recognised anyone. We've got him looking again but he says it's impossible. They all look and sound the same to him, and he doesn't seem able to remember the man he sold his car to anyway. I don't think he's being deliberately obstructive, he genuinely can't help. First off, Kingsley picked out one of the officers making up the numbers in the line up. He kept on about how he's no good with faces. We could try an E-fit, but I think it'll be a waste of time. Kingsley's keen to get away and I suspect he'll soon be ready to agree with anything, just to get finished. He's more interested in the insurance claim. He's making a hell of a stink about it, seems to think we should sort it out for him.'

'Insurance claim?'

'Yes. He said he didn't want to mention it in front of his wife but he received a letter from an insurance company.'

'What letter?'

'The BMW was involved in a minor traffic incident after he claims he sold it.'

Geraldine was suddenly alert.

'Has he got the letter with him?'

'Yes, but there's nothing we can do about it. It's between him and the insurance company. And if the car's still registered in his name - '

'Don't let him go. I'm on my way.'

'But he wants to - '

'Don't let him leave before I get there.'

Geraldine hung up without waiting for a reply and drove straight to South Harrow police station. She found William Kingsley looking agitated.

'You can't keep me here,' he complained as soon as she entered the interview room. 'I've been stuck here for hours and I really need to go. I've got a job waiting.'

Geraldine sat down.

'Mr Kingsley, my colleague mentioned an insurance claim? Please.'

She gestured at the chair opposite her and he sat down, mollified.

'At last someone's listening to me. Only it could affect my premium, couldn't it? It's not just the money. If my wife finds out – she's already mad at me for forgetting to send those papers off to the DVLA.'

He pulled a letter out of his pocket. Geraldine took the crumpled paper from him and unfolded it.

'I'd already sold the car so I can't be liable, can I? If the bloke who bought it from me had an accident, that was his fault, wasn't it? I mean, I know they'll say it was still technically my car, but I'd sold it, the money had changed hands, so legally it's nothing to do with me. You can tell them that, can't you? They'll listen to you.'

Geraldine scanned the letter. The BMW had been involved in a minor accident with another car a week after William Kingsley claimed to have sold it. No one had been injured but the other vehicle had sustained some slight damage. According to Arthur Jones, the driver who had made the claim, the driver of the BMW was at fault.

'It can't affect my insurance, can it?' William Kingsley persisted.

'I need a copy of this,' Geraldine said.

William Kingsley claimed to have sold the BMW before it was involved in a minor traffic accident. If that was true, the likelihood was that whoever had caused the accident was the killer of Jessica Palmer and Donna Henry.

Back at Hendon she told the detective chief inspector about this latest development.

'So the car William Kingsley claims to have sold - ' Reg Milton began.

'To the killer,' Geraldine added.

'Let's make that assumption for a moment,' he agreed cautiously. 'The car was parked in Bruton Place in central London on Saturday the twenty-first, a week after it was allegedly purchased from Kingsley. Let's hope the other party can give us a better description of the driver than Kingsley's been able to come up with.'

'Sometimes people remember these incidents very clearly,' Geraldine replied.

Their eyes met. She was voicing an optimism she didn't really feel but the detective chief inspector's face was glowing, his confidence restored.

Arthur Jones was a stout man in his late sixties, white-haired and ruddy faced. He spoke in a loud forceful tone, like a retired military man.

'I was driving along Bruton Place and some idiot in a black BMW pulled out right in front of me. He just didn't look. I swerved but couldn't avoid a prang. Of course I jumped out straight away but the bugger simply drove off. Yes, shocking, isn't it?' he added, misunderstanding Geraldine's dismayed expression as she realised he might not have had a clear view of the BMW's driver.

'Did you see who was driving the other car?'

'The driver? No. But I got his number alright.'

'Think carefully, Mr Jones. This is very important. Can you tell me anything at all about the driver of the BMW?'

'I can tell you the damn fool shouldn't be allowed behind the wheel of a car.'

'Is there anything else at all you can tell me about him?'

'No. I told you, he drove off.'

'What about the car?'

'Bloody inconvenient. The nearside headlight's smashed and it's going to need a new bumper.'

'And the other car? Did you get a clear view of it?'

Arthur Jones looked puzzled.

'Surely you can trace it from the registration number? I definitely got that. Wrote it down at once. He drove off but I wasn't going to let him get away with it.'

He gave a satisfied nod.

'Which direction did he drive off in?'

'He turned left at the first corner. By the time I got back in my car, he'd gone.'

'And you say he pulled out from the kerb?'

'Yes. Pulled out right in front of me as though the traffic was going to stop for him. Well, I did my best but I couldn't avoid him altogether. It wasn't possible.'

'Can you tell me exactly where he was parked?'

Arthur Jones was explicit about what he had witnessed. It was only a pity he hadn't seen the driver. Scene of crime officers were despatched to check the parking space and the area around it, but ten days had passed since the BMW had been there and with the passing traffic, pedestrians and rain, they couldn't realistically expect to find anything that could be linked to the driver or the car. All Geraldine could do was send a team of uniformed officers to ask people working in Bruton Place if anyone had seen the car, or knew of someone who had recently acquired a black BMW, with the registration number Arthur Jones had taken down. The constables all came back with nothing.

Uniformed officers questioned assistants in the shops off Bond Street, all around the area where Arthur Jones had seen the BMW parked. They showed photographs of Jessica Palmer and Donna Henry wherever they went, but no one recognised either of the victims. Geraldine knew the search would be called off by the end of the day. Although it would probably turn out to be a waste of time, she decided to spend the latter part of the afternoon looking around the area herself.

She took the tube to Bond Street and set off, traversing narrow side streets. The elegant buildings were tall but didn't seem overpowering because of their variety: red brick, stone carvings, gothic towers, green roofs – the area had no consistent style, which gave it a vibrant style of its own. She passed expensive dress shops and jewellery stores, the pavements heaving with women in high heels and men in smart business suits, all hurrying along, eyes disengaged from their environment. The air smelt dry and dirty, flags flapped from buildings, the roads were packed with vehicles, cranes hung aloft and at every intersection she had to pause for traffic lights. Her spirits sank at the enormity of the task, searching for an evil killer in this teeming metropolis.

41

UNSEEING FACES

Geraldine passed boutiques of women's clothes, with striking and often outlandish outfits displayed in the windows, but resisted the temptation to go in. The majority of staff working in them were women. Looking for a tall male suspect, she began with expensive shoe shops and menswear outlets.

A well-spoken man with dark brown hair approached her in the first men's shoe shop she entered. A faint smell of leather permeated the store.

'Can I help you, madam?'

Geraldine enquired whether he or any of his colleagues had recently bought a black BMW. He shook his head, his face a mask of good manners.

Virtually every shop she tried employed at least one tall, dark-haired man with an educated accent and the question received a similar response wherever she went. No one admitted to having recently bought a black BMW and no one in any of the shops had seen a colleague driving a car matching that description. In the last shop she tried, a tall dark-haired man tried to sell her a shirt.

'We have these in just this week direct from Paris.'

'I'm not looking for a shirt, I'm a police officer.'

Geraldine asked him if he had driven a black BMW recently and he responded with a cautious shake of the head.

'I'm afraid not, madam.'

Another customer entered the shop and he excused himself.

Geraldine sighed. She had no idea what she was looking for and decided she might as well abandon her plan of looking for the killer in the vicinity of Bond Street. She could have passed him several times on the pavement, even spoken to him, and she wouldn't be any the wiser. There was no point wasting any more of her afternoon on futile questions. The streets were packed with tiny art galleries. While she was there she decided to look for ideas for an inexpensive print for her living room.

The first gallery she entered displayed sheets of black and white images of faces, among them several iconic celebrities and politicians. A few square white pillars created an illusion of alcoves, the floor was mottled grey marble, the walls and ceiling white. There was a shelf of art books behind a counter on which a signing-in book lay open with a fountain pen attached to a chain. Gazing at repetitive images of unseeing faces staring back at her from the walls reminded Geraldine of photographs on the wall of the Incident Room, and the reason why she had come to Bond Street.

A girl with short white blonde hair was gazing at a magazine. She glanced up as Geraldine approached.

'Feel free to look around,' she said and Geraldine nodded. 'Would you like to sign the visitors' book?'

Geraldine declined.

The second place she looked in had the same white walls and ceiling, but the floor was pitted polished wood. The space displayed large, garish canvases slashed across with bright stabs of colour, bold, vibrant and ugly. A young man looked up from behind the reception desk as Geraldine entered. Gangly, with bony fingers, he seemed very young and eager. He explained the set-up at the gallery, which had opened in 2005 and exhibited both acquisitions and loans. Names of artists Geraldine had never heard of tripped off his tongue. She enquired about a painting of a skeleton depicted in neon colours and wearing a peculiar contraption of feathers on its skull, and the young man told her it was a composition by an up-and-coming young French artist. She went around the entire place without seeing a single canvas she liked.

In the next gallery spotlights focused on elegant classical Greek and Roman artefacts displayed in glass cases on top of white plinths. It was like a museum. Sprucely dressed in a navy blazer, the owner gave an impression of quiet confidence.

'My most valuable possessions are kept on the lower floor,' he told her.

'These are yours?'

He inclined his head and led her down a staircase into a basement where a collection of Greek vases were housed.

'They're lovely.'

She meant it.

The gallery owner pointed to a verse hanging on the wall. 'That's the one I'm looking for.'

Geraldine read aloud: ' "She cannot fade, though thou hast not thy bliss, for ever wilt thou love, and she be fair!" That's Keats' Ode to a Grecian Urn. I studied Keats at school.'

He smiled in acknowledgement and indicated a mottled green bronze urn about seventeen inches high. The price tag read £75,000.

'This one's from the fourth century BC, nearly two and a half thousand years old.'

He touched it reverently with the tips of his fingers as he spoke.

'Unlike us, art is eternal.'

After half a dozen more visits to galleries Geraldine went into a coffee shop, weary and discouraged. She certainly wasn't going to find a print she could possibly afford anywhere around Bond Street. Walking between the galleries she hadn't been able to stop herself making a mental note of people who matched the description of the man they were looking for, but it hadn't helped. Tall, dark-haired, smartly dressed and well-spoken described almost every man she had encountered that afternoon.

The café was busy and noisy, and it was a relief to return to an atmosphere of normality. After queuing for a coffee she sat on a bench and sipped her hot drink, scanning the hurried notes she had scribbled after each visit to a shop or hushed gallery. She decided not to bother entering all the details of her outings on the central computer as none of it seemed relevant.

'How did you get on?' Sam asked her when they passed each other later in the Major Incident Room.

Geraldine shook her head.

'Waste of time. I ended up looking round some of the galleries.'

'Did you see anything interesting?'

Geraldine shook her head again.

'Modern art doesn't do it for me.'

42

A MADDENING CONUNDRUM

Reg Milton was reviewing the case so far.

'I can't help feeling we're missing something,' Geraldine mumbled, not for the first time.

'What about Donna Henry's ex, Geoffrey Hamilton?' the profiler suggested. 'He's tall and dark-haired, with an educated voice, isn't he?'

'Well? How about it?' the detective chief inspector demanded. 'Who questioned him?'

'I did, sir,' a detective sergeant replied and proceeded to read out his notes.

'He was alone all night when Donna was abducted, but he seemed pretty harmless,' he concluded.

'He certainly doesn't sound like the killer,' Geraldine agreed.

'What's that supposed to mean?' Reg Milton asked.

'From what Lily told us, he seems to have really cared about Donna - '

'He doesn't have an alibi.'

'That's true, but - '

The profiler smiled at Geraldine and spoke slowly, as though explaining a lesson to a child.

'You summarily rejected Robert Stafford as a suspect - '

'I've given the matter a great deal of thought and I don't think he's the killer.'

'And now you want to reject Geoffrey Hamilton because he cared for Donna. But that's no reason to discount him.

You have to understand that there's a very fine line between love and fixation. Donna's ex-boyfriend could have been dangerously obsessed with her to a point of jealous rage. It's important to consider whether someone could be guilty before dismissing them out of hand.'

'There's nothing to connect Geoffrey Hamilton with Jessica Palmer,' Geraldine objected, aware she was showing her irritation with Jayne's simplistic psychology.

'I'm not sure that's altogether true. He might have killed Jessica Palmer because she reminded him of Donna Henry, as a rehearsal for killing Donna herself. It's a recognised pattern of behaviour and if he is responsible for the deaths of these two victims, he could continue obsessively attacking women who resemble the object of his desire.'

The detective chief inspector beamed at the profiler as though she had presented him with the answer to a maddening conundrum. 'Go on then,' he said, turning to Geraldine. 'It sounds as though Jayne's pointed us in a useful direction.'

'The DCI treats that bloody woman as though she's some sort of oracle,' Sam burst out as soon as she and Geraldine left the Incident Room.

'Or is he lining-up another scapegoat?'

'What?'

'Oh never mind.'

It wasn't just that Geraldine found the profiler infuriating. That wouldn't normally have bothered her, but she had received a phone call from Sandra at the adoption agency. The social worker had refused to discuss the situation concerning Geraldine's birth mother over the phone and that wasn't good news.

Sam didn't think Geoff Hamilton was a likely suspect either, but at least he was quite tall and dark-haired, and he had a relatively educated voice. In his tiny sitting room lined with books he discharged a series of questions at them.

'What's happened? Have you got any news? Have you arrested anyone yet? Was she - '

He broke off, blinking rapidly, clutching his chin in one hand to conceal the trembling in his bottom lip.

'Tell us about your relationship with Donna.'

'I loved her. I mean, really loved her. She was something special, you know.'

He paused, struggling to control his voice.

'I'd have done anything for her.'

'How did you feel when she dumped you?' Sam asked abruptly.

Geoff shrugged.

'I'm just a librarian and Donna - Donna was amazing. You never knew her. She was beautiful. What did I have to offer? I mean, look at me. I work in a library. It's not even a secure job these days.'

He spread his hands in a helpless gesture.

'She could have had anyone. But we had the same sense of humour and we got on so well. We just clicked, you know how it is. I knew straight away we were meant to be together and I think deep down she knew it too. Sometimes you just know - when something feels so right. There'll never be anyone else for me.'

He heaved a deep sigh.

'I like to think she'd have come back to me in the end.'

He dropped his head in his hands.

'So if this relationship was so right, how come she left you?' Sam made no attempt to conceal her disdain. Geoff raised his head, his eyes watery. Geraldine watched a drip dangling from the end of his nose and wondered what had attracted wealthy, beautiful and fun-loving Donna to this sad, gentle young man.

'She wanted to have some fun before we settled down,' he replied seriously.

'Settled down?' Geraldine asked, interested in spite of her feeling that they were wasting time. 'Were you and Donna planning to get married?'

'Oh yes.'

He sounded so earnest it was hard not to believe him. Geraldine wanted to be clear.

'Donna Henry agreed to marry you?'

'No, not exactly.'

'Had you actually proposed to her?'

Sam sounded incredulous.

'I was about to, but then she said she wanted a break so the time didn't seem quite right.'

For a second Geraldine was afraid the sergeant was going to laugh.

'How long did your relationship last? Before she broke it off?'

'It was about two months, but - '

'Two months?' Sam burst out.

'How did you meet?' Geraldine asked.

'At a club in Shoreditch.'

'Do you often go out in Shoreditch?'

'No. It's not really my scene.'

He gave a nervous laugh.

'I went there with a colleague from work. It was his birthday, you see, and he said it would be fun. He thinks I ought to get out more, but it wasn't my kind of thing, not really. The music was so loud. I can't say I enjoyed the experience, yet that's where we met, that one time I went to a club. Do you believe in fate, Inspector?'

He leaned forward, staring intensely at Geraldine.

'My beliefs aren't relevant. Now, just a couple of other questions before we're done, Mr Hamilton. Do you ever go to a massage parlour?'

He sat upright, raising his eyebrows as though she had made an indecent suggestion.

'A massage parlour? No. I've never done anything like that.'

'And can you confirm where you were last Thursday night?'

'Thursday night?'

'Yes. Where were you?'

'I already told your colleague, I was here. This is where I am at night. What time are we talking about anyway?'

'After midnight.'

'Oh, I'd definitely have been here then. I have to be up early for work. I'm usually in bed by ten-thirty.'

'Can anyone confirm that?'

'What?'

'That you were here at midnight on Thursday? Was anyone else with you?'

'Gracious, no. I was here on my own, like I said before.'

'Did you speak to anyone on the phone at all that evening?'

'No, I don't think so, Inspector.'

'Can you think of anyone who might have wanted to harm Donna? Did she ever mention anyone?'

'No. We didn't talk much about other people she knew. We didn't talk much about anything.'

Unexpectedly, he blushed.

'Did you have sexual relations with Donna Henry?'

'Yes. Yes I did. She was so full of life, so exciting to be with. It was impossible not to fall in love with her.'

'One night of passion, was it?' Sam blurted out.

Geraldine glared at her and the sergeant rolled her eyes and looked away.

'Do you mind if we take a quick look around, Mr Hamilton?'

He turned red, suddenly flustered.

'I'd rather you didn't.'

'Is there any particular reason?'

'I'm not hiding anything, if that's what you're thinking,' he answered hurriedly.

'You won't mind if we take a look then.'

Geraldine was convinced they were wasting time, but as soon as they entered the librarian's bedroom they understood his reticence to show them his apartment. One wall was plastered in photos of Donna Henry, a few deliberately posed, many apparently taken when she was unaware the camera was on her.

The lift was out of order in the dismal block of flats.

'What a depressing place to live,' Geraldine said as they reached the bottom of the stone staircase.

'Lots of people live in blocks like this,' Sam replied brusquely.

Geraldine thought about her own well-serviced flat and changed the subject quickly.

'What do you think of our lovesick librarian? Could he be a spurned boyfriend, determined no one else would have her if he couldn't?'

'No way is he our killer. Can you imagine that wet bloke overpowering a woman like Donna Henry? She would have flattened him with one hand.'

Geraldine laughed.

'He was certainly smitten.'

'I'm guessing she was the first woman he'd ever screwed. He was like a teenager with a hopeless crush. Talk about deluded.'

'Yes. She was never going back to him.'

'The question is, why did she ever have anything to do with him in the first place?'

'I don't think we can completely write him off yet. Something doesn't seem quite right. He was certainly obsessed with her, and what did you make of all those photos?'

'Yes, that was a bit creepy, but he's just a harmless crank with a crush.'

Sam dismissed Geoffrey Hamilton with a wave of her hand.

'If we were only investigating Donna Henry's death, he might have been worth a second look,' she added. 'But as for cutting off body parts, no way would he have done that. He's probably a vegetarian. And he's hardly the sort of man to go around dragging girls off the street.'

'I don't know that Jessica Palmer would have taken much persuasion,' Geraldine replied, but she was inclined to agree. 'He's quite tall though. Going bald, but what hair he's got is dark, and he's quite well-spoken. He'd probably seem posh to Douggie.'

'At least there's a motive,' Geraldine persisted as they reached the car. 'Donna Henry ditched him. In a rage he killed a woman who looked a bit like her, acting out a fantasy, or perhaps confusing Jessica with Donna herself in his blind fury? Then he realised his mistake and went after Donna herself. Maybe he even discovered he enjoyed killing women and cutting them up. What do you think?'

'I think you're beginning to sound like our profiler.'

'Oh dear. That desperate?'

They looked at one another for a moment before getting in the car. They wanted to find a connection between the victims, because if the attacks were random then the killer might be almost impossible to track down. And it didn't take a psychological profiler to persuade them that someone who had committed two gruesome murders in quick succession might strike again very soon. Geraldine pictured the two mutilated bodies lying in the morgue and shuddered.

43

SEARCHING

He stared down at the empty bed with an impatient frown. Donna hadn't lasted long. It was a pity he had brought her home before getting rid of Jessica but he couldn't always control his guests' visits as he would have liked. He hadn't been looking for anyone when he had happened to pass Donna on the street, stumbling around in a drunken haze, and it had been all too easy to bring her home with him. He would have been a fool not to take advantage of the opportunity. Now she had gone it was maddening that he hadn't been able to find another visitor straight away. He had been out all weekend driving around searching, without any luck.

He had nearly picked up a decent girl on Sunday night only her boyfriend had come charging along at the last minute and ruined everything. That was infuriating as she had looked healthy and what was even more annoying was that one of them might have noticed his car. It was just as well he'd had the sense to take it to a scrap yard out of town the next morning, because a uniformed policewoman had been round later that day asking about a black BMW. He was confident he hadn't given anything away, but the narrow escape had shocked him deeply. It didn't cost much to secure the foreman's silence at the scrap yard, but the woman throwing up in his previous car had meant burning it was the only sure way to destroy all trace of her. He would have set light to it himself, but fire terrified him.

It was simple enough to get hold of another vehicle. It wasn't so easy finding visitors to view his collection and they never stayed long, but he hated keeping it all to himself. It was far too important for that. One day he would throw it open to the whole world. Everyone would be able to come and see what was much more than a mere collection of fascinating objects. It was a valuable statement, perhaps the most significant statement ever made by man. And so far, no one still living had seen it but him. It was a pity to leave the rest of the world in ignorance but he wasn't ready for a public display, not yet. The collection had to be completed first. In the meantime he was working hard, adding to his exhibits. It wasn't his fault that some of his specimens were still alive when they arrived. It pained him when they died, overcome by the weakness of all flesh.

He regretted having to chain his visitors to prevent them from leaving but he couldn't risk news of the collection leaking out before he was ready. Most people were ignorant, small-minded fools who believed death was inevitable. In a way they were right, but death didn't have to be the end; genuine artists understood that wasn't the whole truth. He walked over to the bed and stroked the sheet with the tips of his fingers. It felt hard where blood had dried on it. With a sigh he turned away and looked at the shelves that covered one wall. They were filling up nicely, and not everything was even out on view yet. There was more. He picked up a tin decorated with pictures of Big Ben and the words: 'New York – Paris – London – Rome' printed over and over again around the lid. He looked inside it before he replaced it on the shelf. Reaching up, he took down the thigh bone whip and swished it through the air. With a quick flick of his wrist he made it crack loudly and grinned.

'Death be not proud,' he intoned softly, 'though some have called thee mighty and dreadful, for thou art not so!'

His voice rose to a shout on the last two words.

'For those whom thou think'st thou dost overthrow die not, poor death, nor yet canst thou kill me!'

He was stalking round the room now, beating time with the

handle of the whip.

'One short sleep past, we wake eternally, and death shall be no more; death, thou shalt die.'

That was what those girls were too stupid to grasp. He had offered them a chance of immortality and all they could do was whine and bleat about going home. How long could they hope to stay there? Fifty years? Sixty years? And what then? Did they think any part of them could survive without his intervention? He alone could offer them the chance of real immortality, not some mumbo jumbo spiritual fairy tale about a kingdom in the sky, but real physical permanence, right here on earth. Only they were too ignorant to understand.

He picked up the Big Ben tin and sat down on the bed, forgetting about the blood stains, and beat time on the tin like a drum as he recited more verses.

'Full fathom five thy father lies; of his bones are coral made; those are pearls that were his eyes: nothing of him that doth fade but doth suffer a sea-change into something rich and strange.'

Tired out, he returned the tin and the whip carefully to their places. Then he walked along the shelves touching the items in his collection, each one posing its own challenge to the transience of life. He glanced down at the tin. It was time to bring another visitor home with him to admire his collection. He was disappointed the last woman hadn't lasted long enough to appreciate what he was doing for her, but it didn't matter. He would find another guest to come home with him soon, if he had to search all through the night, someone educated, capable of appreciating the collection.

Leaving the attic he paused on the threshold and looked round, smiling. A small child's skull grinned back at him. The child itself had vanished hundreds of years before; its smile would never fade.

PART 4

44

VULNERABLE WOMEN

They had questioned people working around Bond Street, checked CCTV footage from near the bar where Lily had last seen Donna Henry alive, searched the roads approaching the canal tunnel where her body had been found, and the vicinity of Tufnell Park where Jessica Palmer's body had been discovered, cross-referencing registration numbers and descriptions of vehicles that had been in those areas at the times the killer must have been there. Geraldine had spent the entire day reviewing reports, trying to find a connection between the two victims. The whole exercise was time-consuming and tedious, and ultimately pointless because they hadn't come across any new leads.

Late that afternoon Geraldine went back to the bar in Camden where Lily had last seen Donna alive, eleven days earlier. Geraldine hadn't questioned people there in the evening yet. When she arrived the bar was fairly empty but by six o'clock it was packed with people stopping for a drink after work, the atmosphere quietly cheerful. She made her way around the room with a photograph of Donna Henry, asking everyone if they recognised her. One after another the customers said they didn't. Some were apologetic, others just shook their heads and a few turned away without even bothering to answer. Geraldine persevered, watching the door and going over to anyone who came in.

Finally a young man sitting on a bench said he recalled her.

'Do you know her?' Geraldine asked.

'No, but I remember seeing her here. It was just the once and I only remember it because she was so wasted. We had a laugh about it, me and my mate.'

'When was this?'

'Oh, I don't know. It was on a Friday, maybe two or three weeks ago.'

He turned and called out to a man standing at the bar.

'Hey Will, when were we last here?'

'Why?' his friend asked.

'Just tell us, will you? It's important.'

'Alright, it was about a fortnight ago. Who wants to know?'

'It doesn't matter.'

The seated man turned back to Geraldine.

'Yes, it was a couple of weeks ago. We were out the front having a smoke, and the woman in your photo came out. I only remember because she nearly fell over right in front of us. She was so wasted she could barely walk.'

'Was she drunk?'

'I guess. Or something.'

He grinned.

'Where did she go after she left the pub?'

The man glanced around as though that would help him picture the scene in his mind, then shrugged.

'She just went off down the road, I don't know where.'

His friend came over with a couple of pints.

'Yes, we were here on a Friday, must've been the week before last,' he said as he sat down. 'Why? Who wants to know?'

Briefly Geraldine explained who she was and what she was doing there. The second man nodded.

'Yes, I remember. She was well out of it, nearly fell arse

over tit.'

'Did you see which direction she went when she left?'

He pointed.

'She went off that way.'

'And that's all we saw,' the first man chimed in. 'But I can't say I was watching her for long. She just walked by and then she was gone.'

'Did you see anyone with her?'

'No, I don't think so. Not that I can remember. What's all the questions for anyway? Who is she?'

When Geraldine explained that Donna Henry had been murdered, the first man she had spoken to looked shocked.

'I had no idea,' he said. 'I feel shit now, laughing about her like that.'

'You weren't to know.'

'If there's anything we can do - '

'What you just told me is really useful. Is there anything else you can remember about what you saw that evening, anything at all?'

'She was limping,' the second man said.

'Limping? How?'

'Just limping, you know, like she'd hurt her foot. She left the pub, tripped and nearly fell over, probably twisted her ankle as she was wearing really high heels, and then she limped away down the road and disappeared. And that's the last we saw of her.'

'Thank you very much. You've been a great help already. If you think of anything else, please give me a call.'

Geraldine handed each of them her card.

If nothing else, this had confirmed their suspicion that the killer was out on the streets looking for vulnerable women. From what the witnesses had told her, it sounded as though

Donna Henry had stumbled and hurt her ankle. Befuddled with alcohol and cocaine, she would have been an obvious target for the expensively dressed, well-spoken prowler.

'There was no mention of any injury to her ankle in the post-mortem report,' Sam pointed out when Geraldine repeated what the witnesses had told her.

'I suppose it's always possible to miss something like that if you aren't looking for it, and a slight swelling could easily have been covered up in the injuries caused by the chain. In any case, it might not have been serious enough to show up, you know, when you twist your ankle and it's agony for a moment and then it passes off with no lasting damage. It could have been enough to make her limp for a while as she was walking away, pissed and high, staggering along the street.'

Reg Milton agreed that the scenario made sense when she told him about it.

'Good work, Geraldine.'

She tried to conceal her irritation at his condescending tone. 'Now we've pinpointed the direction Donna was walking when she left the bar we know where to focus the search of CCTV footage,' she said.

It wasn't much, but it was something.

'We're going to stop checking CCTV footage,' the detective chief inspector replied quietly.

'What?'

'It's taking up a lot of man hours, and it's not going to come up with anything after all this time.'

'But now we know where to look - '

'Yes, you did well there Geraldine, but you have to appreciate, this is London. There's always heavy traffic on the streets, even at night, and the chances of picking out one car among so many, when we don't even know what we're looking for - '

His eyes slid back to his computer screen.

'That's my decision.'

'Yes, sir.'

He looked up with a smile on his lips, his eyes cold.

'It's Reg.'

Geraldine forced herself to return his smile.

As she left his office she wished her colleagues would stop talking to her as though she had arrived in London from another planet.

'I've seen traffic before,' she muttered under her breath. 'We do have sodding cars in Kent.'

She knew the only way to stop his sniping was to solve the case, but she was beginning to think that was impossible.

45

A DEAD END

Geraldine stayed up most of the night studying CCTV footage from the pub where Jessica had last been seen by her fellow masseuse, assuming the other girl from the Paradise Parlour was telling the truth. The film taken inside the pub was blurred, but Jessica was visible, drinking with her workmate. Geraldine fast-forwarded. Jessica could be seen leaving the pub, but then the film became grainy and it was difficult to distinguish what was happening outside in the street. It looked as though she was walking unsteadily as she moved out of the frame. A dark car drove past a few moments later with a figure in the passenger seat who could have been Jessica, but it was impossible to be certain because it was so indistinct. The IT technicians who had worked on enhancing the film had been unable to make out any identifying features of the vehicle which had only been visible briefly, from the side. Just as it pulled away from the kerb another car had driven up behind it obscuring the registration number.

Eventually Geraldine went home, too tired to focus on the fuzzy grey film any longer. She didn't think she would be able to get to sleep but dropped off as soon as her head touched the pillow and struggled to wake up when the alarm rang.

'Have you been here all night?' Sam asked, only half joking, when she found Geraldine glued to her screen first thing in the morning, fast-forwarding through tapes of Jessica and

Donna on the nights they had disappeared.

'No, I went home last night and came back early.'

Geraldine was aware she sounded irritable.

'Leaving no stone unturned is one thing,' Sam told her, 'but don't you think you're overdoing it? I mean, watching all these films again is a waste of time. If you don't collapse from exhaustion you'll end up comatose with boredom.'

Geraldine leaned back wearily in her chair.

'Until we come up with some new evidence there's nothing to do but review what we already have. What else can we do?'

'Have some breakfast?'

Geraldine shook her head.

'Not now. I want to finish going through these tapes.'

'You don't really think you're going to catch a clear shot of a registration number and Jessica Palmer climbing into the car. You know the film's already been watched right through?'

'As long as there's a chance - '

'You know what they're saying?'

'Who?'

Sam nodded towards the door.

'Everyone on the team, even the DCI, I expect.'

'Don't tell me,' Geraldine muttered. 'They're saying that we're never going to find whoever killed Jessica Palmer and Donna Henry, so we might as well pack up and go to the pub.'

'No. I mean - ' she hesitated. 'Do you know what they're saying about you?'

'About me? Let me guess. I'm a county mounty who doesn't know she's in London.'

She turned back to her screen.

'Now it's time to get back to work, Sam. You've got plenty to do and so have I.'

Sam spoke in a rush.

'They're saying you don't trust anyone else to do the job properly.'

Geraldine looked up at her in surprise.

'What's that supposed to mean?'

'A team of uniformed constables went round Bond Street and before they'd even finished - '

'You mean they were recalled - '

'Whatever. The point is, you went round after them because you thought you could find something they'd missed. Now the CCTV's been watched all the way through and that's not good enough for you, you have to sit up all night viewing it. They're saying you want to do everything yourself because you don't trust your colleagues on the team, and you might as well run the investigation single-handedly since you seem to think everyone else is incompetent. And they're saying that for all your thoroughness, you're no further ahead than anyone else.'

She paused.

'It's not what I think, but it's what other people are saying.'

Geraldine shrugged.

'I don't care what they're saying about me. All I'm concerned about is finding the killer and I wish everyone else would focus on that as well, instead of wasting time and energy on idle chatter.' Her voice rose in vexation and she broke off, afraid of sounding as though her colleagues' opinion of her was justified. 'That's all for now, Sam. I want to get on and I'm sure you do too.'

She turned back to her screen.

'Close the door on your way out.'

'I was only trying to be helpful,' Sam said without moving. 'I thought you'd want to know. The point is you don't need to overwork so much. We're all in this as a team, and we'll sort it out together.'

Geraldine didn't turn round.

'I said, that'll be all, thank you.'

A second later she heard the door close.

As she sat watching the tapes she tried not to be distracted by what the sergeant had told her. After all her excitement at moving to the Met it seemed she had already got off on the wrong foot with her colleagues. And worse than her personal disappointment was the frustration of knowing she was searching for one man in seven million.

'We seem to have reached a dead end,' she told the detective chief inspector that afternoon.

'Yes, the lead on the accident to the car near Bond Street was a disappointment, wasn't it? Despite all your efforts,' he added.

Geraldine remembered what Sam had told her and felt her face go hot.

'So, what do you suggest we do next?' he asked.

'It might help if we broadcast a reconstruction of when Jessica was last seen. We can put together quite a lot of information. We know what she looked like and what she was wearing that night. She was there with a colleague and the CCTV footage gives us the time Jessica left the pub. We know she was drunk and the CCTV seems to indicate she was picked up more or less outside the pub. It's possible someone noticed her getting into a car, and they might come forward if we can only jog their memory.'

'Go ahead, Geraldine. The sooner we get a reconstruction broadcast, the more chance I suppose there is of finding a witness who remembers seeing her,' Reg replied, suddenly eager. 'And it's important we're seen to be doing something,' he added. 'Good thinking.'

Geraldine didn't answer. She hadn't suggested the television reconstruction as a means of making the team look effective, but as an avenue to explore which might help them find the killer. Driven by her desire for justice she suspected Reg Milton was motivated by personal ambition. Geraldine trusted his judgement but she was less sure about trusting him.

46

TOO CRUEL

As far as they knew Donna hadn't been planning to meet anyone the night she disappeared but it was possible she had arranged to do so without telling Lily. Her flat in Highbury had been searched without results so Geraldine decided to check her room in her mother's flat near Regent's Park, in case Donna had left a note there. Mrs Henry buzzed her into a wide entrance hall with deep-pile carpets and elegant watercolour prints on the walls. She took the lift to the second floor and entering the apartment found a spacious split-level living area. The flat was immaculate and obviously expensive.

'Do you live here alone?'

'Yes, my ex-husband went to live in Scotland.'

'Does he come back to visit?'

'He lives in Aberdeen with his Russian wife.'

Mrs Henry waved a manicured hand dismissively.

'How long has be been living there?'

'He moved there when we split-up, nearly twenty years ago.'

'Do you know when he last saw Donna?'

'He was down here about six months ago, in the New Year. I think he probably saw her then. That is, I'm sure he would have done.'

She gave a bitter smile.

'I don't speak to him.'

'But he was in touch with Donna.'

'He's still her father,' Mrs Henry retorted, as though it was inevitable a father and daughter would have a close relationship.

Geraldine didn't even know who her real father was.

'When she was at school he took her out three or four times a year and he used to send her extravagant gifts.'

'And after she left school, did they continue in regular contact?'

'They still saw each other occasionally, maybe two or three times a year. I told you, he lives in Scotland.'

Geraldine made a note of Mr Henry's address.

'Did Donna ever go to Scotland?'

'Never, as far as I know. I can't see why that's relevant.'

'It's impossible to say at this stage what might prove to be relevant.'

'You mean, you still have no idea who did this to my daughter.' Mrs Henry's voice rose in agitation, her self control lost for a few seconds.

'I'm sorry, Mrs Henry, I really can't discuss the investigation with you.'

'But you will tell me - '

'Yes, of course. As soon as there are any developments I'll let you know personally, straight away. Now, it would help us if you could answer a few questions. How long have you lived here, Mrs Henry?'

'I've been here since the divorce. My husband wasn't ungenerous. I sold the house in Hampstead and I've been here ever since.'

'And you and Donna lived here alone?'

'I didn't remarry and yes, it was just Donna and me.'

Geraldine looked around the luxuriously furnished room with its pale yellow walls and cream carpet, and tried to picture a child living there.

'I'd like to take a look at the room Donna slept in when she lived here. How long is it since she moved out?'

'Four months. This way.'

She led Geraldine to Donna's room and stopped at the door. 'I don't go in there.' Her voice was taut, controlled again. 'I don't know what you're expecting to find but please don't move anything. I like to keep it exactly as it was.'

'Thank you, Mrs Henry. I'll just have a quick look around.'

Donna's room was beautiful. The floral wallpaper and carpet were pale pink, co-ordinating with a matching bedcover and curtains. A shelf unit displayed tiny dolls and miniature glass animals. Everything was neat and pretty, and clearly designed for a young girl. There was nothing in the pink bedroom that could add to Geraldine's existing image of the adult Donna Henry who had been brutally battered to death. Geraldine looked through the drawers in a white desk that stood beneath the window and found a diary that Donna had written in her early teens. She flicked through the pages but the twelve or thirteen-year-old jottings about a teacher she had a crush on and a classmate who had copied her school work, had no bearing on Donna's adult life. The wardrobe was full of designer label clothes and there was a collection of *Vogue* and *Elle* magazines on a light wooden bookshelf.

Leaving Regents Park Geraldine drove east to Highbury Fields. By following in the wake of Donna's life she vaguely hoped she might stumble across the identity of someone with a grudge against her, although she was already afraid her attacker had been a complete stranger, impossible to glimpse from visiting Donna's apartment.

Lily smiled nervously when she saw Geraldine at the door. 'Have you found out - '

'I haven't got any news,' Geraldine interrupted her. 'I'd like another look at Donna's room though.'

Crossing the pale blue hall, the walls also decorated with tiny flowers, Geraldine thought about the pink child's room in Mrs Henry's flat, every detail carefully selected to harmonise. Suddenly an image of Jessica Palmer's room slipped into her mind: messy and cramped, the walls badly whitewashed and pockmarked from Sellotape or Blu-tack, one cheap narrow wardrobe overflowing with a jumble of dresses.

Geraldine wasn't surprised that there were fitted wardrobes lining the length of one wall of Donna's spacious bedroom. She opened each of the doors in turn. Tall mirrors inside the doors reflected rail after rail of clothes, enough it seemed for Donna to have worn a different outfit almost every day of the year. One of her handbags alone probably cost more than Jessica Palmer could earn in a month. Some of the outfits were gorgeous. Geraldine touched a long burgundy coat and her fingers lingered. Cashmere. However sordid the circumstances of her death, Donna Henry's life had been passed in luxury. She wondered if Donna had faced her end with any less fortitude than Jessica, who must have been accustomed to degradation and pain. Was it easier to die when your expectations of life were at best callous indifference? With a sigh she moved on, hoping to find a diary or mobile phone in a jacket pocket, but there was nothing of interest that hadn't been picked up by the team who had already searched the flat.

'Did you find what you were looking for?' Lily asked when Geraldine emerged from the room.

But Geraldine didn't know what she had been hoping to find; the room had already been thoroughly searched. Sam's words echoed in her head. 'You want to do everything yourself because you don't trust your colleagues on the team. You might as well run the investigation single-handedly ...'

Her colleagues' sneering was justified, but somehow she couldn't control her need to see everything for herself. If that made her unpopular, she could live with that, but only if her drive helped them to find the killer. Right now, there was no reason to suppose it would.

The morning after the television reconstruction was broadcast, a woman called the station to say that she had seen a black girl matching Jessica Palmer's description leaving the pub on the Holloway Road where Jessica had been drinking with her workmate. Geraldine went straight round to see her.

A short grey-haired woman opened the door and stared blankly at Geraldine.

'Maeve Law?'

Geraldine held up her warrant card.

'Yes. Are you from the police then?'

'That's right. Detective Inspector Geraldine Steel. You called the station about the reconstruction on television earlier this evening?'

'You're quick enough to come when you want to,' the woman replied sourly.

Geraldine watched her fiddle about lighting a cigarette, inhale deeply and blow smoke out of the side of her mouth.

'I'm not sure but I think I might've seen her. She was killed, was she? Is that it?'

'I'm afraid so.'

'Bloody hell. I've got daughters, Inspector, and what happened to that poor girl, well, it's a terrible thing and I hope they lock the filthy bastard up. But I can't say I'm surprised she got herself in trouble, the state she was in.'

'What do you mean?'

'She was pissed.'

'Are you sure?'

'I've been around enough to know when someone's had a few too many. She could barely put one foot in front of the other without falling over. She was pissed alright.'

'What time was it when you saw her?'

'It must've been around ten-thirty. I was walking up from the bus stop and she came out of the pub and went round the corner, off the main road, just ahead of me.'

'Did you see her leave the pub?'

'No, not exactly, but she couldn't have come far, the state she was in, so it's a fair bet.'

'Can you describe the woman you saw?'

'She had boots with very high heels. I think they were black. She wore them outside her jeans and - '

Maeve frowned with the effort of trying to remember.

'I think she was wearing a short jacket. It might have been some sort of fake fur, but I couldn't swear to that.'

She tossed her cigarette end past Geraldine onto the path where it lay, giving off a thin trail of smoke.

Geraldine considered. The killer must have removed Jessica Palmer's boots so he could shackle her ankles more efficiently.

'Did you see what happened to her after she left the pub?'

'Yes. That's the thing. She got into a car with some bloke.'

Geraldine felt the breath catch in her throat.

'What did he look like?'

'I don't know.'

'Please try to remember. Anything at all you can tell me about him might be vital.'

Geraldine struggled to suppress her impatience while Maeve hesitated.

'Did it look as though she knew him?'

'She might have done. I don't know. It's impossible to say, really.'

'And you didn't get a look at his face at all?'

'No, I couldn't see his face, and wouldn't have remembered it if I had. Unless he was George Clooney.'

She grinned suddenly.

'Was he a big man, would you say?'

'Big? Well, he was quite tall because when he got out of the car I could see he was easily taller than her, even with those heels she was wearing. Of course she could have been really short, I didn't get a good look at her either. I just walked past on the other side of the road and I remember thinking, "You've had a few more than you ought, my girl," like you do.'

'Can you remember anything else about the man you saw?'

'I think he was wearing a dark coat, but I didn't see him for long and it was a while ago. I can't be sure about any of this. My memory's not what it was.'

'What you've told me so far is really helpful, Maeve. More than you realise. What about the car? Can you describe it?'

'I remember it was dark. It could've been black.'

'Do you know what make it was?'

'I haven't got the foggiest. It was just a car. They're all the same to me. It wasn't a convertible or anything like that. Nothing I'd recognise.'

'Did the woman get into the car willingly?'

'Well, to be honest, something about that didn't look right. I think that's why it stuck in my mind. She was so drunk she could hardly walk. I got the impression the man almost had to carry her to the car. He was holding her by the arm pushing her along the pavement, and then he seemed to shove her inside and I wondered at the time if she'd really wanted to get in that car with him. I don't know why, it was just a feeling I had.'

She shrugged.

'And then, when I saw it on the telly, it gave me the creeps to think I might have seen her, the girl that was killed.'

'Why didn't you go over?'

'Over where?'

'You said there was something that didn't look right. Why didn't you go over and ask if she was OK?'

Maeve stared coldly at Geraldine.

'It was nothing to do with me,' she said. 'I find it's best to mind my own business. And anyway, it was all over so quick. One minute he was hustling her along, the next she was in the car and they were off.'

'Did the man see you watching?'

'Not bloody likely. I'd already gone round the corner. I only happened to glance back and that's how I saw them together, just for a second, before I walked on.'

Geraldine took down the details.

'There's one more thing. Did you happen to notice if the girl had any injury to her right hand?'

Maeve shook her head.

'No. But I didn't get that close a look at her. I was some distance away.'

'Well, thank you very much. That's been very helpful.'

She gave the witness a card.

'You can call me on this number if you remember anything else.'

'I will. Well, I hope you catch the bugger soon, for all our sakes.'

Geraldine gave a nod.

'I hope so too,' she answered under her breath.

47

LOST CONTACT

After typing up her report, Geraldine set off on the drive back to Kent where she had an appointment at the adoption agency. She had asked the social worker on her case to approach her birth mother once again to try and arrange a meeting. When the social worker had declined to discuss the outcome over the phone, Geraldine thought the most likely reason was that her birth mother still didn't want to have any contact with her. There were only two other obvious options. The adoption agency might have lost contact with her mother and been unable to trace her. Milly Blake could have moved, changed her name, even gone abroad to vanish without trace. Geraldine refused to consider the other possibility - that her mother might be dead. To lose her again without even meeting her would be too cruel.

She tried not to speculate too much about her mother as she drove, but the closer she drew to her appointment the more nervous she became. After all the dangerous situations she had faced in her career, she was caught by surprise at her extreme anxiety over the possibility of meeting her mother. Her thoughts were racing uncontrollably and she realised that she was trembling, her palms sweaty, her mouth dry.

'Pull yourself together,' she muttered crossly out loud, but it made no difference. She was distressed before anything had even happened.

Geraldine entered the rundown Victorian building where

her adoption records were stored, gave her name to the receptionist in the dingy hall and paced restlessly around the hallway. She felt she had been waiting for hours, although in reality it was only a few minutes before a solidly-built blonde woman came into view and Geraldine recognised Sandra, the social worker she had met on her previous visit to the agency.

'Hello, Geraldine.'

Sandra smiled warmly at her as though welcoming an old friend.

'It's good to see you again.'

She turned and led the way along a quiet corridor to an interview room where Geraldine recognised the same drooping plant on the table from her previous visit, and the same dusty box of tissues. It was as though time was suspended in that quiet room.

'How have you been keeping, Geraldine?'

Sandra sounded genuinely interested. She leaned forward as she spoke, her hands in her lap, her head tilted to one side.

'I'm fine, thank you. Work's been busy and I've moved to London.'

'London? How exciting!'

Sandra beamed, as though speaking to a small child who had just won a trophy at school. Geraldine felt impatient. The woman was a stranger, her interest in Geraldine obviously no more than a professional ruse to lighten the atmosphere.

'Yes, I've come all the way from London for this meeting,' she said pointedly.

Sandra hesitated before replying with another question.

'You requested a meeting with your birth mother, Milly Blake. That's right isn't it?'

Geraldine felt a sudden rush of excitement at hearing her mother's name on someone else's lips, as though her private day dream had suddenly become a reality.

'Yes. I want to meet my mother.'

'I'm sorry, Geraldine.'

Sandra paused and shook her head, an expression of regret on her rounded face. Under other circumstances Geraldine would have warmed to Sandra who was clearly doing her best in a difficult situation, but as it was she struggled to suppress her anger at the social worker's fake empathy.

'I'm afraid that's not going to happen,' Sandra continued. 'We've done all we can, but your birth mother has made her feelings clear. This is nothing personal about you, but she doesn't want to revisit the past. She's written more than once to say she doesn't want to have any contact with you.'

Sandra paused.

'She feels that would be best for you both.'

'How can she know what's best for me? She doesn't even fucking know me,' Geraldine burst out, and was immediately shocked at her own loss of control.

She swallowed hard, fighting to control her shaking. It didn't help to know that Sandra was simply doing her job. Geraldine had seen bereaved people resort to rage as a desperate shield against grief, driven by a compulsion to blame. Sometimes anger was all that stood between them and feeling their loss. Geraldine had always believed she'd felt genuine sympathy for their grief but she had never been in that situation. Until now. This wasn't as final as death - but in some ways it was even worse because her mother had deliberately rejected her.

Geraldine's training kicked-in and she gave a taut smile, seething behind a mask of composure.

'Well, that's that then, isn't it?'

She looked directly at the social worker, making no attempt

to conceal the bitterness in her voice.

'You could have told me over the phone instead of letting me come all this way for nothing.'

It didn't help to know that Sandra must understand the real reason for the frustration Geraldine was taking out on her. The social worker's sympathetic expression didn't waver.

'I'm sorry, Geraldine. I'm afraid there's nothing more we can do. We can't act against your mother's wishes, but if you'd like to talk with someone about it, we'd be happy to help you. You don't have to cope with this alone.'

But Geraldine *was* alone. Alone in a world of strangers.

'No, thank you. I'm fine. You're quite right, of course. I shall just have to accept this and move on.'

While she drove back to London she ran over the meeting in her mind and tried not to succumb to an uncharacteristic mood of hopelessness as she considered her situation. No one really cared deeply about her. If she were to crash her car and die, who would actually be affected by her death? She thought about Jessica and Donna, and their mothers' grief. No one would cry like that over her. There were people who would be shocked and upset, of course: Celia and Chloe, her old school friend Hannah, colleagues at work; but her loss wouldn't make a significant difference to anyone's life. Her own mother wouldn't know. As for her biological father, he probably wasn't even aware she existed. It made no real difference to anyone else if she lived or died. Admittedly her work was important, and she was good at what she did, but another detective could do her job equally effectively. So what was the point of her life if the only possible outcome was a death disregarded by strangers?

She had said she would respect her mother's wishes and move on, but she wondered now if she would ever be able to accept this emptiness in her life. Her need to discover the people with whom she belonged felt more pressing than ever. They haunted her dreams, unknown siblings, and the mother who stared out of a photograph with her own face. If the social services were unable to put her in contact with her birth mother, she had the resources and the expertise to trace her for herself. If nothing else, at least the search would keep her hope alive. Anything was better than giving in to helpless despair. But for now she would continue to throw all her energy into the case, the one area of her life where she could make a difference.

48

IN A BAD WAY

'So you only stayed with me all this time out of pity?'
Jon struggled to control his voice.

'You let me go on believing we had a meaningful relationship and all the while you were just feeling sorry for me. 'I can't possibly abandon poor Jon now he's lost his job, and aren't I the saint for putting up with him now when he needs me.' You always did like to play the martyr.'

'What the hell are you talking about?'

'Don't pretend you don't know what I mean. You think I can't see what's going on? Do you think I'm an idiot? As soon as you heard I've found a job – which I was feeling pretty damn pleased about a moment ago – you haven't been able to pack your bags fast enough. Why? Tell me why you're leaving.'

Simon shook his head.

'I don't know. And it's not sudden. I've been thinking about this for a long time, only - '

'Only you stayed because you felt sorry for me. Go on, admit it. You only stayed with me out of pity. So what now? Am I expected to be grateful to Saint Simon?'

'Oh, stop being such a drama queen. It's over, that's all. Finished.'

'And that's it. No explanation - '

'How can I explain? I can't change how I feel. These things happen.'

'No, these things don't just happen. There has to be a

reason. At least let's talk about it, try and work it out. We can't just throw away everything we've meant to each other.'

'Look, I'm sorry but it's over, OK? I'm leaving. I'll call you later, when you've calmed down.'

Simon picked up his case and opened the front door. 'Goodbye, Jon.'

'No. Don't leave like this. Please – can't we talk - '

'I'll call you later.'

Simon slammed the front door.

Jon stood in the brightly lit hallway, shaking. One hour ago he had been feeling so happy. After six months' unemployment he had finally been offered the perfect job, starting in two weeks. It had seemed too good to be true. But he hadn't even had a chance to tell his boyfriend about it properly because, as soon as he'd opened his mouth, Simon had started packing. He must have been waiting for a chance to escape. There had to be someone else involved. Jon clenched his fists and took several deep breaths. He was on his own again, but at least he had a job. He could do without Simon now and good riddance.

'Stuff you,' he said aloud. 'I don't need you.'

Jon had spent too much of his life depressed by loneliness to face an evening on his own brooding about where it had all gone wrong with Simon. The silence of the flat was oppressive and the television didn't help. He went out to a pub he knew where he could drown his sorrows in the company of strangers, and maybe meet someone. Simon wasn't irreplaceable.

'Just one more,' he spluttered and the other guys laughed.

He wasn't sure who they were, but the pub was a

friendly place.

'I think you've had enough, mate,' someone said, patting him on the back.

'You can come home with me if you want a place to kip for the night?'

Jon considered. He was reluctant to go home to his empty flat, but he hadn't met the other guy before and he wasn't drunk enough to go off with a stranger. Not yet anyway. He laughed and staggered over to the bar.

'Give us another one.'

'Hadn't you better slow down?'

'Whisky. Make it a double.'

Jon slapped a tenner on the bar.

'I can afford it. I've got a job.'

'Well done, that's grand. Here you go then. And here's your change. But you'd best make that your last one tonight.'

Jon winked and knocked it back, nearly falling over as he did so. Someone held him upright, and a few people laughed.

'This is fun,' Jon thought, looking around. Aloud, he said, 'I never knew I had so many friends.'

All at once he grabbed hold of the man standing next to him with sudden urgency.

'Going to be sick.'

Someone pushed him out onto the street where he doubled over and threw up. When he straightened up he was alone outside, the noise and cheer of the pub dimly audible through the closed door. Jon looked at the pool of vomit on the pavement and walked slowly away. His head was aching and he wanted to go home and lie down.

'You look like you're in a bad way,' a voice said softly in his ear.

Jon spun round and almost lost his balance.

'Take it easy. Tell you what, I've got my car close by. Can I drop you off? You're in no fit state to be out on your own. Where do you live? Or - '

The stranger hesitated, staring curiously at Jon.

'Why don't you come back with me? I can drop you home in the morning, after you've slept it off. Don't worry, I'll take good care of you.'

Jon shook his head, trying to focus. The man had an educated voice and wasn't at all bad looking. So much for sitting at home by himself fretting over what Simon was doing. This was his second offer of a bed for the night. He clutched the man's arm to steady himself.

'I've got a job.'

'Been out celebrating, have you? I don't blame you. It sounds like congratulations are in order.'

Simon hadn't stopped to congratulate him. He hadn't even phoned, although he'd said he would. Jon smiled as his new friend steered him along the street, towards a waiting car.

49

ON THE MOVE

More than a week had passed since they had first questioned Robert Stafford and they still had no conclusive evidence one way or the other. Morale on the team was low.

'A dark-haired man with an educated voice,' Geraldine said to Sam, who raised her eyebrows.

They had been over this so many times.

'Robert Stafford,' Sam insisted. 'He stopped going to the massage parlour just at the time she was killed. How could he have known she wouldn't be there unless he'd killed her himself?'

'He could have just stopped going,' Geraldine said. 'Angie told us they had a raid shortly before Jessica disappeared and that scared off a few of their regulars. He might have been worried his wife would find out.'

'So you think it was just a coincidence he stopped going then?'

'It could be. Honestly, I don't know what to think. Granted he's tall and dark-haired, and he could have put on a different accent.'

'So you agree he's a likely suspect?'

'No.'

Geraldine shook her head.

'I wouldn't say likely. It's possible, but I still don't think he's the one we want. He just doesn't strike me as a killer.'

The detective chief inspector shrugged when Sam voiced

her opinion.

'All this is purely circumstantial. We can't make an arrest on such a flimsy pretext. There's no point.'

A few other officers exchanged glances, as though they had heard this before.

'He's been warned not to leave the area but we can't charge him without any evidence. If we could at least place Stafford in the area of Tufnell Park on the night Jessica Palmer's body was deposited there, that would be something to work on,' Reg Milton went on. 'Catch him out lying about his whereabouts that night and that would be a start.'

Stafford had told them he was at home on the Saturday night when Jessica Palmer's body had been placed in the alley.

'I went home from work about six. I was on early shift.'

'And where did you go after that?'

'After what?'

'That Saturday night. Where did you go after you went home?'

'Nowhere. I never went anywhere. Like I said, I was at home. I didn't go out.'

His face had dripped with anxiety.

Geraldine went along with Sam's misgivings.

'I'm not sure I believe everything he said either, but he told us he was at home and there's no reason to doubt him. If you ask me, he's in a complete funk and said whatever came into his head. But that doesn't mean he was dismembering a body and disposing of it that night.'

'He could have been,' Sam insisted.

Geraldine didn't bother to answer. They were going round in circles.

Later that afternoon Sam burst into Geraldine's office

without knocking.

'We've got him,' she announced.

Geraldine looked up.

'Don't you knock before you enter a room?'

'We've got him,' Sam repeated, her eyes alight with excitement.

'Who?'

'Stafford. We've got him. He's been lying all along. I said he was lying. He told us he was at home on Saturday night but we can prove that's not true because he was at King's Cross - '

'Disposing of a body?' Geraldine interrupted, smiling at the sergeant's enthusiasm.

'No. But he *was* at King's Cross station. We ran a check on his Oyster travelcard and it showed he was on the move that Saturday night, travelling between Arsenal and King's Cross. We confirmed it was him by checking the CCTV film. So he wasn't at home on Saturday night. He's been lying all along.'

'Was he alone?'

'Alone?'

'He wasn't carrying a body by any chance? Or dragging a suitcase? Perhaps he had a large sack slung over one shoulder?'

'Of course not,' Sam answered impatiently. 'But he told us he was at home all night.'

'Yes, he did. Where did he go on to from there? He didn't go to Tufnell Park, I suppose?'

She had begun to share Sam's excitement, and reminded herself that they needed to remain cautious.

'No, he travelled from Arsenal to King's Cross and back again four hours later, but it's only two miles from King's Cross

270

to Tufnell Park. He could have walked there if he didn't want his movements traced. Perhaps he had the body stored somewhere nearby in a lockup or something and wanted to get rid of it. In any case he could have been out and about on both nights the bodies were dumped, and we now know he lied about being at home.'

'So what was he doing around King's Cross when he told us he was at home?'

Geraldine was on her feet.

'Come on, let's go and see what he has to say for himself now.'

Robert Stafford had changed his clothes and shaved since he had been away from the police station, and he looked respectable. His reaction at seeing Geraldine again was very different to when he had first greeted her on his doorstep.

'What is it now? You've got nothing on me. Why can't you people bloody well leave me alone? I've got nothing more to say to you.'

Geraldine spoke quietly but she was firm.

'Mr Stafford, we'd like to go over your statement with you again.'

'I've told you everything I can remember.'

'You told us you were at home all evening and night on Saturday the twenty-first of August.'

Robert Stafford nodded, circumspect.

'That's right.'

He folded his arms and looked from Geraldine to Sam and back again.

'We'd like you to accompany us to the police station - '

'Oh no, not that again. I'm not going this time. You've already tried it on once. This is harassment. Now bugger off and leave me alone.'

'Come on, now, Mr Stafford, we only want to talk to you.'

They led him to the car, huffing and grumbling.

Geraldine opened the questioning when they were all seated in an interview room in the presence of the duty solicitor again.

'You told us you didn't go out on the evening of Saturday the twenty-first of August?'

'That's right.'

He hesitated and glanced at the solicitor.

'As far as I can remember - '

'Mr Stafford, you were picked up on CCTV at King's Cross station just after midnight that Saturday night, having walked to King's Cross from Tufnell Park.'

'What?'

He sounded genuinely baffled.

'What were you doing in Tufnell Park that Saturday night, Robert?'

'Tufnell Park? You said King's Cross.'

'You went to Tufnell Park from King's Cross.'

'Why would I go to Tufnell Park?'

'You tell us.'

'I never went to Tufnell Park that evening.'

'Think carefully, Robert.'

'I may have a bad memory for dates, but I've never been to Tufnell Park in my life.'

'Do you have any evidence my client was ever at Tufnell Park?' the solicitor asked quietly, 'or is this mere conjecture?'

Geraldine knew they couldn't place Stafford anywhere near Tufnell Park but she watched him closely as she continued to question him.

'Yet you were at King's Cross having told us you were at home all night.'

Stafford wiped his sweaty brow on his sleeve but he didn't

look particularly worried.

'So I was at King's Cross. You can't arrest me for that, can you?'

'Why did you tell us you were at home that evening?' Sam persisted.

He shrugged.

'I forgot. I get muddled with days. It's not a crime to have a bad memory, is it? I do different shifts. I don't work Monday to Friday. I often don't know what day of the week it is. I certainly can't remember what was happening nearly two weeks ago. Can you remember where you were two Saturday nights ago?'

He turned to the solicitor who raised his eyebrows but didn't answer.

'If I was at King's Cross I must have been meeting Eddy. Yes!'

He hit his forehead suddenly.

'I remember. Of course. We went out for a drink. It was his birthday.'

'Who's Eddy?'

'Eddy Hart. He's a mate of mine. He'll tell you I was with him. Ask him. Eddy Hart.'

He was grinning with relief.

'We certainly will ask him, Mr Stafford,' Sam scowled.

'So I can go home now?'

'Yes, you can go,' Geraldine said. 'Once we have Mr Hart's details.'

'But we'll be seeing you again,' Sam muttered.

Geraldine glanced at the sergeant who clearly still regarded Stafford as a suspect. Although they had caught him out in a lie, Geraldine was convinced it was an innocent mistake.

50

DARKNESS MORE PROFOUND

From the fading and returning light visible through the skylight Jon guessed he must have been tied up for about twenty-four hours, but he couldn't be sure. His head was throbbing and he was unable to move. At first he thought he was having a nightmare. He closed his eyes and tried to make himself dream something pleasant, yet time passed and nothing changed. The stench from his emptied bowels was real enough and he had to accept it couldn't be a bad dream after all. Under normal circumstances he would have found his condition intolerable, but stinking filth could be washed away. He was facing something far more terrifying than physical degradation.

His wrists and ankles were firmly secured. He could twist his head from side to side and lift it from the pillow but the effort made him nauseous. He waited until a narrow shaft of light along the edge of the blind illuminated the room and then looked around. Turning his head to the left he raised his arm as high as he could, a few inches off the bed, and made out the links of a heavy chain around his wrist. His right arm was fastened in the same way and although he couldn't see his legs he could feel that his ankles were similarly shackled. He had no idea why he was there or who had done this to him and wondered if this was some sick homophobic attack. He closed his eyes and tried to work out what was happening.

He recalled going out to celebrate finding a job. At the

memory of his earlier relief, he was overcome with emotion. His life had finally taken a turn for the better when, without warning, he had been incarcerated by some lunatic. Tired and distressed, tied up alone in the dark, he felt tears slide across his cheeks while he lay helpless, unable even to wipe his eyes.

'Who are you?' he called out. 'Why are you doing this to me?'

No one answered.

'I haven't done you any harm. What do you want with me?'

In spite of his discomfort he must have dozed off, because when he opened his eyes again he was in darkness. His limbs were still chained and the only difference was that the smell seemed to be getting worse. Through his shirt sleeves the sheet beneath him felt hard and scratchy. Suddenly a naked electric bulb blazed above him. After lying in darkness for so long, the light seemed to burn a hole in his head. He tensed, waiting. Footsteps approached and he swivelled his eyes to squint up at an unfamiliar face looming over him.

'Hello, Jon.'

'What the hell's going on?'

Jon raised his arms up as high as he could, rattling the chains. The stranger smiled and Jon recognised the man who had picked him up in the street when he'd been plastered.

'Who are you?'

'My name isn't important. Names don't matter. Who cares about names? Names can be changed. What's a name? Names die with us.'

The man seemed curiously keyed up, babbling excitedly.

'Die?'

Jon seized on the word.

'What are you talking about? What's going on? Let me go!' He bit his lip to stop himself crying with pain and fear.

'You can call me - ' his captor paused. 'Why don't you call me Victor?'

'Victor? As in victory?'

'Yes, that too.'

The stranger laughed lightly, a chilling sound in the circumstances.

'I was thinking of Victor Frankenstein.'

'The monster?'

The man shook his head, vexed.

'That's a mistake that ignorant people make. Don't you know? Victor Frankenstein was the genius who produced the monster, created new life from the dead. But don't worry. If it's art and literature you're interested in, I can teach you all about - '

'Look, I don't give a fuck about art or literature, and I'm not here to learn about them. You brought me here and tied me up, remember? I didn't ask to be here.'

He rattled his chains again.

'I don't know what you think you're playing at but this whole thing is outrageous. Release me now.'

'I can't do that.'

'Yes you can. Do it now.'

There was a pause.

'What do you want with me anyway? If you're planning on killing me just get it over with quickly, please.'

Jon managed to stop his voice from quivering. He closed his eyes and took a deep breath, impressed by his own courageous words.

'Kill you?'

The man calling himself Victor sounded surprised.

'I've no intention of killing you. Why would I want to do that? The others weren't strong enough, but I didn't kill them. It wasn't my fault they died. Why does everyone accuse me of wanting to kill them when that's the last thing on my mind.'

He seemed to be talking to himself.

'What others? I don't know what you mean. Let me go.'

'I told you, I can't. Not now. You might go to the police and then my work would never be completed.'

'What work? What are you talking about? Let's finish this now. Just let me go,' he added with a feeble attempt at a smile. 'I'm not going to go to the police. Why would I? I don't even know who you are or where I am. Please,' he felt his resolution waver. 'If you're planning to kill me, just do it.'

The other man looked around the room and smiled.

'I'm not going to kill you. I've already told you, it's just the opposite.'

'What the hell do you mean?'

'I'm going to help make sure you never die. Not entirely. Something of you will survive forever.'

'This is insane. Let me go!'

Jon rattled the chains furiously.

'Let me go, right now, or I will fucking go to the police.'

'Look - '

The man waved his hand at the far wall.

'Go on, look.'

Jon looked up. The wall was covered with shelves where hundreds of oddly shaped artefacts were displayed. He hadn't been able to see any of them before in the darkness, but now his gaze travelled along the shelves of strange objects and he gasped. His eyes slid away and he saw another, and another.

Staring frantically at the shelves he counted seventeen human skulls, each one polished and shiny.

'What the hell - ' he burst out.

'Now do you understand?' the man who called himself Victor said softly. 'This is my collection.'

'What's this got to do with me?'

The man smiled.

'You're lucky. I don't usually invite people like you back here to see my collection.'

'People like me? You mean gay men?'

'Don't be so stupid. What difference does that make? I don't care about your sexuality, although that could be interesting.'

He smiled and reaching down began to stroke Jon's thigh. Jon writhed but couldn't avoid the man's touch.

'Get off me, you fucking pervert! What are you doing?'

While he caressed Jon's leg, the man continued speaking in an even tone.

'I usually bring women here, they're so much easier to pick up. I thought women were supposed to be physically stronger than men, but so far they've been a huge disappointment. They didn't last long, any of them, and that does rather thwart the purpose. I want my visitors to be resilient, you see. That's very important for the process. But as it turns out, I think men must be tougher than women after all, so it could turn out to be a real stroke of luck, your turning up like this. You know you're the first man to come here. It's easier to persuade women to come back with me, but you didn't exactly resist, did you? I suppose I should be flattered.'

He leered at Jon.

'Yes, you could turn out to be a very interesting experiment.'

Jon felt a shiver of dread as the man leaned closer.

'Relax. I'm not going to hurt you. You're interested in my

collection, aren't you? You understand, I can tell.'

'What the fuck are you talking about?'

But the man had disappeared from his field of vision. He heard footsteps receding and the light clicked off.

'What do you want with me?'

Jon could hear the panic in his own voice, hoarse and shaky. The door opened, there was a brief flash of light from outside, and then the room was engulfed in darkness more profound than before.

51

IN TROUBLE

Eddy Hart was a bus driver who lived above a row of shops in Kilburn. Geraldine followed Sam up cold stone stairs to a set of doors all crammed together in a row, but no one answered when they rang his bell.

A woman came to the door of the next flat.

'Yes?'

She stared suspiciously at them. Geraldine held up her warrant card and the neighbour's eyes narrowed.

'We're looking for Eddy Hart. Have you seen him today?'

The woman shook her head.

'Not today. I haven't seen him for a while in fact. Is he in trouble?'

'No, we just want to ask him a few questions about someone he might know.'

Early the next morning Geraldine and Sam went along to the bus garage in Shepherds Bush to check out Stafford's story.

'Eddy? I've got a feeling he's off this week,' one of the drivers told them.

He turned and called to another driver.

'Oy, Jake. Have you seen Eddy? Eddy Hart?'

The other man shook his head and the first driver turned back to Geraldine.

'Ask up in the office. They'll be able to tell you more.'

'Eddy Hart?' the woman in the office repeated aggressively. 'Who's asking?'

Her attitude altered when she saw Geraldine's warrant card and was reassured that Eddy wasn't in any kind of trouble. 'I'm sorry, Inspector, I thought you'd come to complain about one of the drivers. Not that we get many complaints,' she added, awkwardly.

'Now, who was it you wanted to speak to? Eddy Hart. Hang on. I'll check the rotas. I don't think he's been in for a few days. No, that's right, he's been off this week on planned leave. Have you tried him at home?'

'He wasn't in yesterday evening.'

'Well if he's gone away he must be back some time tomorrow because he's due here Monday morning.'

Geraldine checked what time Eddy was expected on Monday and they left. There was nothing more they could do until the following day.

'Are you busy this evening?' Geraldine asked Sam as they parted at the end of the shift.

Geraldine wasn't surprised to hear that Sam had an arrangement for Saturday evening, but she felt a faint stab of disappointment all the same.

'Tell you what,' Sam went on, 'why don't you come along? If you'd like to, that is.'

'Thanks, Sam.'

Geraldine hesitated.

'I don't know. I mean, I won't know anyone and if you all know each other - '

'I'm only meeting them for a drink. They're probably all going clubbing afterwards, but I think I'll just go along to the pub then call it a day. I'm knackered. Anyway, you can come for a drink and go on out with them later or not, it's up to you.'

Geraldine nodded.

'Thanks.'

It would do her good to get out, have a few drinks and take her mind off the case for a while, and sometimes a break helped her to think.

'I'm starting to feel a bit stale, to be honest,' she said.

'I know what you mean,' Sam agreed. 'I feel as though I'm just going round in circles with it all.'

'Exactly.'

They smiled at one another, and Geraldine thought how lucky she was to have a sergeant whose ideas so often coincided with her own. The prospect of spending an evening with Sam and her friends suddenly seemed very appealing, and Geraldine caught herself wondering if Sam's friends were all in their twenties or whether some of them might be closer to her own age.

Sam was travelling down from Finchley, where she lived, so they arranged to meet at Leicester Square station and go on to the bar together. Geraldine arrived first and stood, mesmerised by the seemingly endless throng of people moving past. The West End on a Saturday night was heaving. Just as she was thinking of calling Sam's mobile in case she was standing by the wrong exit, the sergeant bounded up to her.

'Hi! Hope you haven't been waiting long?'

'No, I just got here,' Geraldine answered not quite truthfully. 'You look great by the way,' she added and Sam beamed.

Wearing a glittery raspberry-coloured top and heavy make-up, she looked very different to the practical officer Geraldine was growing accustomed to working with, younger and far more glamorous.

'Come on then,' Sam said.

The Soho pub was crowded and very noisy.

'What can I get you?' Geraldine yelled to Sam.

It took a while to be served at the packed bar, and when

she turned round to look for Sam, she saw her colleague surrounded by a group of about ten women who all seemed to be talking at once. There didn't appear to be any men with them. Geraldine carried Sam's drink over.

'This is Geraldine,' Sam shouted, barely audible above the general racket of music and voices.

As though at a predetermined signal, the whole gang of women suddenly moved in unison towards the door, jostling and chattering at the tops of their voices. Outside, several of them lit cigarettes. It was smoky but at least it was possible to hear one another.

'Whose birthday is it?' Geraldine asked Sam when she managed to manoeuvre her way over to her.

'Wanda!' Sam shouted and a young woman in tight jeans turned and smiled at them.

'You haven't introduced us properly,' Wanda said, pouting at Sam who laughed.

'I'm Geraldine.'

She held out her hand but Wanda leaned forward and kissed her warmly on both cheeks.

'It's very nice to meet you,' Wanda said.

'Watch out, she's a plain clothes police officer,' someone called out.

Geraldine felt slightly uncomfortable, although it was clearly intended as a joke; they must all have known Sam was a detective sergeant. Another woman approached Wanda and put her arm around her in a possessive gesture. Geraldine glanced at Sam, who didn't seem to have noticed. A couple of the other women were holding hands. She turned to look at Sam, engrossed in conversation, and wondered how she had become attached to this particular group of women. She hung around on the edge of the noisy group, clutching her drink and feeling awkward, while the women chatted with the ease of old friends.

Not until they gathered together to move on did Geraldine appreciate the extent of her misunderstanding.

'Are you coming?' Wanda asked Sam who shook her head.

'I would but I'm really tired. It's been a long day. You have a great evening.'

'Are you on a case?'

Sam nodded. She and Wanda threw their arms around one another.

'They used to be together,' another woman explained to Geraldine. 'But you're alright, it's over now.'

'She's a lesbian?' Geraldine blurted out, staring at the side of Sam's head.

'Who, Wanda? Well, what do you think?'

The woman smiled.

'But I'm telling you, you've got nothing to worry about. Sam's all yours.'

52

A TRICKY CASE

It was her day off, so Geraldine had arranged a visit from her sister and niece. Although she would rather have been at work she was relieved that she wouldn't be seeing Sam that day. She would have preferred to learn about the sergeant's sexual orientation from Sam herself, but she supposed there was no reason why her colleague should have told her. It had nothing to do with work and their relationship was purely professional. They weren't even friends exactly, they had only known each other for a few weeks. But Sam's friend had seemed to think that she and Geraldine were together as a couple and Geraldine felt hot with embarrassment at the idea. Worse, Geraldine wondered whether she might have led Sam on without realising it. New in London, and keen to be friendly, she had been happy to accept Sam's invitation to go out. She sighed, hoping this wasn't going to develop into a complicated situation, but she couldn't sit around fretting about Sam Haley all morning. She had to get ready for Celia and Chloe.

It was the first time Geraldine had received any visitors in her flat and she was excited about showing it off. They were coming round for lunch so she had intended to be up early to tidy and go shopping but she overslept, worn out after her stressful week, and didn't have much time. Instead of sorting out the papers, books and clothes that had accumulated in her living room, she tossed everything in a washing basket which she shoved in her wardrobe, promising herself she would go through it all that evening after Celia and Chloe had gone. She checked that the photograph of her mother, Milly Blake, was hidden in her bedside drawer where no one could find it.

Having made the flat presentable, she went out to the supermarket to buy what she needed for lunch. Wandering along the shelves she regretted not having planned ahead. Celia was easy to please, but Chloe was a fussy eater and Geraldine hadn't bothered to check what her niece currently ate. In a sudden panic she tried to call Celia but there was no answer. They must already be on their way.

If she hurried there was just time to roast a chicken with potatoes and prepare a bowl of fresh salad, with a variety of soft fruit to follow: peaches, cherries, strawberries, grapes and kiwi, because she thought Chloe liked fruit. In case she was wrong, she also put several cartons of Ben and Jerry's in her trolley. She hurried home to prepare the lunch and lay the table and had barely finished when the doorbell rang. The salad was on the table, the chicken in a tray inside the oven surrounded by potatoes which were browning nicely. Geraldine grabbed her keys and ran down to let her visitors in.

'Why do you keep it locked?' Chloe asked as Geraldine slammed the high metal gates shut behind them.
    'We just do,' Geraldine told her. 'It's for security.'
    'Why don't we have a gate like that?' Chloe asked her mother.
    'Because we don't live in London,' Celia answered shortly. 'This way.'
    Geraldine led them across the car park to the door of her block.
    'Why do you keep the door locked when there's a gate?'

Chloe asked.

'Stop asking daft questions,' her mother told her.

'That's alright,' Geraldine said, laughing. 'The gate's locked to keep our cars safe. And the door's locked because it's the front door. Everyone locks their front door.'

She half expected Chloe to comment when she unlocked the door to her own flat, but her niece just followed her in without a word, sat down and looked around the small square living room. 'Nice telly,' she commented. 'Can we watch?'

'No,' Celia answered. 'We're here to see Aunty Geraldine and her new flat. It's lovely, Geraldine. Are we going to get the tour?'

'Come on, then,' Geraldine smiled. 'It won't take long.' Chloe jumped up and Geraldine took them from the living room to the kitchen with its small table, and then the bedrooms and bathroom.

'That's it! What do you think?' she asked when they returned to the living room.

'It's very nice,' Celia replied politely.

'But - ?'

'But nothing.'

Celia hesitated.

'It's immaculate.'

'You say that as though it's a bad thing.'

'No, not at all. But it's like a show home. I mean, it's like no one lives here.'

'Thank you,' Geraldine said, although she knew Celia hadn't intended it as a compliment.

'I've just moved in after all, give me time and I'll manage to clutter it up a bit more.'

They both knew that wasn't true. Celia had said the same about Geraldine's flat in Kent.

'Well I like it,' Chloe said.

Geraldine smiled.

'Thank you, Chloe. So do I.'

'Can I phone Emma?'

'No,' Celia answered. 'It's rude to phone your friends when you're in company. We're here to see Aunty Geraldine. You can speak to Emma when we get home.'

'But - '

'Come on,' Geraldine said brightly. 'Lunch is ready.'

Chloe went to the bathroom after they had finished eating and as soon as she left the room Celia began speaking very quickly. 'Are you alright, Geraldine? I mean, how are you settling in?'

'I'm fine.'

'Are you sure?'

'Yes, I'm sure. I mean, I'm pretty tired what with moving and everything, and the case is very time consuming - '

'Is it this killer who's taking his victims' teeth? It's been on the news. Is that the case you're working on?'

'You know I can't discuss my cases.'

'I know. But - '

Celia glanced anxiously towards the door.

'That's not what I wanted to talk to you about. I wanted to ask you - '

Geraldine felt uneasy, uncertain where this was heading.

'I'll put the kettle on.'

She stood up but Celia reached out and put her hand on Geraldine's arm.

'Wait. I want to ask you something before Chloe comes back.'

'Why don't you call me and we can talk on the phone?'

'You never answer your phone. Just listen will you?'

Geraldine sat down and they both looked at the door. As if on cue, Chloe came back in.

'Mum, when are we leaving?'

'You've only just got here,' Geraldine said.

'Thank you for lunch, Aunty Geraldine. It was really nice.'

Celia sighed and took her mobile out of her bag.

'Chloe, why don't you go in the hall and phone Emma now that we've finished lunch?'

'Yay! Thanks, mum.'

Chloe grinned, grabbed the mobile and ran out into the hall, closing the door firmly behind her. Celia waited and after a moment they heard the faint noise of Chloe's voice. Celia leaned forward and spoke softly.

'I wanted to check you're OK with the news. We haven't really had a chance to talk.'

'What news?'

'About your adoption.'

'Oh that. I haven't thought about it much. Haven't had time,' Geraldine lied.

She had decided against telling her sister she was searching for her birth mother. Celia had been very close to Geraldine's adoptive mother. Her grief was still raw, and she might view it as a betrayal of their mother's memory.

'Are you sure? You're not just saying that?'

'Of course not. Why would I do that? Now, tell me about what's going on with Chloe before she comes back.'

They chatted for a while and then Celia called Chloe.

'You've been on that phone long enough!'

After a while Geraldine put the kettle on and they sat round the table drinking tea and eating chocolate cake until Celia announced it was time to leave.

Geraldine was slightly ashamed at the relief she felt as she closed the door behind them and slumped on the sofa. Her conversations with Celia were always slightly strained, and she was glad to be alone again. When her phone rang she was pleased to hear the familiar voice of Ian Peterson, the detective sergeant she had worked with in Kent.

'Thought I'd catch up with you, find out how it's all going in the big city. I hope they're keeping you busy?'

His cheery tone lifted her mood and she told him as much as she could about the Palmer Henry case.

'Sounds like you're in your element, with a tricky case like that,' he said when she finished.

Geraldine knew he understood her frustration with an investigation that seemed to be going nowhere, but before she started bellyaching she asked about his fiancee. Ian had announced his engagement just before Geraldine left for London.

'How's the wedding plans?'

'That's partly what I'm calling about. We'll be sending out invitations, but I'm ringing round to let people know we've fixed a date.'

'That's great, Ian. I'll put it in my diary straight away.'

He sounded so happy she no longer wanted to bleat about her problems.

'So do you miss us?' he laughed.

'Not in the slightest. London's great,' she lied, and the conversation drifted back to his wedding arrangements.

'To be honest, I'm leaving everything to Bev, it's more her sort of thing. I'd invite you to the stag do, but - '

She laughed and assured him there was no way she would have accepted. She hoped he didn't realise that wasn't true.

After he rang off Geraldine felt a stab of guilt at the realisation that she missed the sergeant more than she missed her sister, but she had worked closely with Ian Peterson and besides, although she and Celia had been raised in the same family they weren't really sisters. Since she had discovered she was adopted her childhood memories had felt like a sham. Her mother, her father and Celia had colluded in constructing a life for her based on a lie. And now, among all the people she had questioned about the deaths of Jessica Palmer and Donna Henry, at least one person was lying. There were so many lies, and they always led to trouble.

Not that the truth was necessarily easy to face; it was hard to accept that the one blood relative Geraldine knew about didn't want to see her. She sat down on her bed and took the photograph of her mother out of the drawer.

'I'll find you anyway,' she whispered before putting it carefully away. The photograph was irreplaceable; her only link with her mother.

For now.

53

A REGULAR CUSTOMER

Geraldine arrived at Hendon early on Monday morning and reviewed the day that lay ahead of her. She had to write her decision log plus she had expenses claims and other paperwork to sort through, but she couldn't face starting her week with tedious tasks that wouldn't move the investigation forward. There was more important work to be done. Kilburn wasn't far away and it was still early enough to drive there before the traffic built up, so she decided to go and question Eddy Hart before he went into work. Once he was out driving they probably wouldn't be able to catch up with him until the end of the day, and she was keen to wrap up that line of enquiry so they could focus their resources on finding another possible lead, instead of wasting man hours checking out Robert Stafford's alibi. Geraldine was convinced he hadn't killed Jessica Palmer, and the sooner they could eliminate him from the enquiry the better.

She drove to the rundown estate in Kilburn where Eddy Hart lived. The door to his block of flats wasn't locked and she entered the dingy hall and went up a narrow flight of stone stairs to the second floor. Hart's flat had no bell so she rapped as loudly as she could, and after a few minutes a young man opened the door.

'Are you Edward Hart?'

'Yeah. That's me.'

His mouth hung slightly slack giving him a vacant expression. 'Who are you then?'

'Detective Inspector Steel.'

She held up her warrant card, slightly surprised to see that he was barely thirty.

'I'd like to ask you a few questions, Mr Hart.'

'Yeah?'

He didn't seem curious.

'I'm just having breakfast.'

He waved a spoon he was holding.

'Can I come in for a moment? It's just a formality, only we're hoping you might be able to help us with an investigation.'

He hesitated.

'Alright, come on in then, if you must,' he said at last, 'but I hope you don't mind talking while I eat.'

Geraldine followed him into a tiny kitchen where he sat down on the only stool and began scooping baked beans out of a tin. 'I've been away,' he said as though that explained his rudimentary eating arrangements. 'Sorry, did you want to sit down? We can go in the other room if you like.'

'That's OK,' Geraldine replied.

He looked at his watch.

'I've got to get off to work soon.'

'I won't keep you long. I'm interested in a friend of yours, Robert Stafford.'

'Yeah, I know Robert, but he's not exactly a friend. He's my cousin.'

'When did you last see him?'

Eddy sucked on his spoon for a moment.

'I don't know. I was away last week.'

He shoved the spoon in his mouth and looked up at Geraldine. 'Is that it then? Only I've got to get off to work soon.'

'Robert said he saw you on his birthday?'

'Oh yeah, that's right. Only it was my birthday, not his.'

Geraldine nodded. Stafford's story checked out so far.

'You'll remember the date then.'

'My birthday was on Friday but I saw Robert on the Saturday. He was working on the Friday or something, and anyway, I was out with some mates on my birthday. So I saw Robert the next evening. I was a bit hung over.'

A grin transformed his slightly gormless look into a mischievous expression.

'Where did you and Robert Stafford go on Saturday night?'

Eddy gave her the name of the pub.

'After that we got a takeaway and went back to his place and I crashed there because it was late. I do that sometimes, stay over, when neither of us has got work the next day. He's got a spare mattress and he does a great fry-up for breakfast.'

He glanced miserably at the empty baked bean can in his hand.

'So you were with Robert Stafford all night?'

'Yeah. That's right. On the mattress. I told you, he's my cousin.'

'Mr Hart, have you ever been a member of the National Front?'

'The who?'

'The National Front.'

'They're the ones who want to send all the immigrants packing?'

'Yes.'

He sucked on his spoon again before replying.

'Well, I can't say I totally disagree with them. Not that I've got anything against anyone, but there are just too many of them. I mean, we let anyone and everyone in and well, what about the rest of us?'

'Have you ever joined the National Front or the BNP? Or attended any of their meetings?'

'Me? No way. What would I want to do that for? I mean, I can't see the point. Life's complicated enough as it is. Poncing about on the telly, telling the rest of us what to do. What about all the money they waste? That's our money, that is.'

He stood up, tossed his empty can in the bin and dropped the spoon in among the dirty crockery in the sink.

'Thank you, Eddy. You've been a great help.'

Geraldine put away her notebook.

'I'll see myself out.'

'No worries. Robbie in some sort of trouble with the law then, is he?'

'Would that surprise you?'

'Yes, as it happens, it would. He makes such a fuss about rules. Not that I don't agree with him but he can go a bit over the top. You try cheating him at cards and you'll soon know what I mean. And don't get him started on benefit scroungers.'

Not only because Sam would be disappointed that it was looking increasingly unlikely that Stafford was the killer, but also to satisfy her own misgivings, Geraldine went to the pub and the Indian restaurant Eddy had mentioned.

The landlord of the pub recognised Stafford but couldn't confirm when he'd been there.

'It could have been a Saturday. It was a few weeks ago anyhow. Sorry I can't be more precise, but we get lots of people coming through here of an evening.'

The manager of the Indian restaurant was more helpful,

because Stafford was a regular customer. It turned out that on the Saturday night in question, a transaction had gone through at half past midnight on Stafford's credit card, confirming Eddy Hart's account of the evening. Sam wouldn't be happy. No one could seriously suggest that Stafford had sneaked out of his flat without his cousin noticing, dumped Jessica Palmer's body in an alleyway near Tufnell Park station, and returned to Arsenal without his absence being noticed. Robert Stafford's alibi had been confirmed for the night Jessica Palmer's body was left in the alleyway in Tufnell Park, and they were back at square one.

54

LAST SEEN ALIVE

'We have to find something on him,' Sam insisted, her face twisted in irritation. 'Until we nail that racist bastard, we have to keep looking. There must be something, otherwise we've got nothing to go on.'

She wasn't happy when Geraldine suggested they forget about Robert Stafford.

'Forget about him? How can we forget about him? Come on, Geraldine, it must've been him. Who else could it have been? No smoke without fire and all that, and we know what he's like. All we have to do is prove it. What if he was working with an accomplice?'

Geraldine felt sympathy for the sergeant's desperation. It would certainly be a relief to find evidence that would put Robert Stafford back in the frame. The media were whipping up a storm of absurd allegations. Stafford was a bouncer from the North. To make matters worse, his former association with the National Front had been unearthed. Several papers had already cited that alone as evidence of his guilt. But apart from the fact that it wouldn't be right, there was simply no point going after the wrong man because without proof there was no case against him. Even the few officers who had never believed Stafford was guilty were dejected at the confirmation of his innocence, the prospect of more dull hard work that lay ahead, and the unspoken worry that they might never find the killer who had taken such macabre trophies from his victims.

'We must redouble our efforts,' Reg Milton said.

Despite his upright carriage and manner of looking people straight in the eye he seemed uncertain.

'Remember, the Met solves nearly all of its murder cases - '

'Ninety seven per cent,' someone said.

'And I'm not going to let this be one of the very few exceptions,' the detective chief inspector went on. His words were positive but his voice had lost its characteristic vehemence.

'So let's put Robert Stafford out of our minds, get back to what we know and work from that.'

Empty words. They didn't need a pep talk, they needed information. Most murderers were identified because the police were able to trace them through their connection to their victims. If this killer was attacking people at random, it would require an interminable amount of cross-referencing at the end of which they would probably come up with nothing. And while they were at a loss over where to look for the killer, he could be out on the streets eyeing up his next victim.

A young constable suggested sending a female officer out to walk the streets at night pretending to be drunk.

'That way we could catch him at it. The WPC's wired and under surveillance, and as soon as he bundles her into his car we follow.'

There was a brief discussion of the proposal before Reg Milton dismissed it.

'We have no way of knowing when the killer is planning to abduct another victim, if ever. And if he does, we don't know if he's still going to be operating round here. And even if he is, it's a vast area. We can't afford to run a surveillance operation around every pub in North London. If we try this on a small scale, the chances are we'll never be in the right place at the right time. It might sound like a good idea, but it would be a waste of resources.'

'We've got to do something,' the constable insisted.

There was a faint murmur of assent.

The detective chief inspector frowned.

'What we have to do is keep looking. We can start by returning to the pubs where Jessica Palmer and Donna Henry were last seen alive and asking more questions. Perhaps we can jog someone's memory.'

'Perhaps we can't,' someone muttered, expressing the general mood of dissatisfaction.

Geraldine went back to her office to check her messages. It wasn't helpful for the boss to say work with what you know when they didn't know anything. She felt as though she was standing on shifting ground. Supposedly skilled at understanding people, for more than three decades of her life she hadn't known she was adopted, hadn't even known her own name, and now despite all her training in listening to people, she had worked closely with Sam Haley for over two weeks without an inkling that the sergeant was a lesbian. At the end of the day she went to the Major Incident Room and found Sam tapping at a keyboard.

'Let's go for a coffee,' Geraldine suggested.

Sam leapt to her feet.

'Anything's better than this.'

She nodded at the computer.

'About Saturday evening,' Geraldine began when they sat down with their drinks.

She hesitated, feeling self-conscious. If she said the wrong thing relations between them could become strained, which would be awkward as they had to work together. Besides, she liked Sam Haley and was worried she might hurt her feelings if she spoke clumsily. To say she had no problem with Sam's sexual orientation sounded patronising. It might have been better to say nothing, but she had started now and had to carry on.

'Sorry I left so early,' Sam smiled, misunderstanding.

'I didn't do a very good job of taking you out. But you could have stayed, gone out with the girls. I was just wiped out.'

'One of your friends said - '

Sam put her head on one side and waited. Geraldine tried again.

'Your friends seemed to think we might be - '

'What?'

'I think they might have got the wrong idea about us. I don't know what gave them that impression.'

'About us? That was probably Liz. She's always concocting some new piece of gossip. No one takes any notice of her.'

'So you don't - ' Geraldine hesitated.

'Don't worry, I don't fancy you,' Sam said, and burst out laughing.

Geraldine smiled.

'Thanks for the compliment.'

'You know what I mean.'

'Anyway, you're not a lesbian. I am. End of. This isn't Bridget Jones. As far as I'm concerned work is work, and with all due respect, what I do in private is my business. My sexual orientation is nothing to do with you. And being a lesbian doesn't mean I automatically want to jump on every woman I meet. For goodness sake, Geraldine - '

She broke off, exasperated.

'I didn't mean - '

'I know. No offence taken. Let's just drop it, shall we?'

'Right then, back to work,' Geraldine said, relieved.

'Let's go over what we know.'

Sam nodded and bit into a slice of cake as she listened.

'He's tall, dark-haired, well-spoken and driving a dark car, probably black.'

'A tall dark-haired stranger,' Sam laughed, brushing crumbs from her lips with the back of her hand. 'Do you think he's handsome? If we believe what Douggie Hopkins told us,' she added, serious again.

'His statement was corroborated by William Kingsley,' Geraldine reminded her.

It was so frustrating, knowing Douggie Hopkins and William Kingsley had both met the killer, yet were unable to give the police any useful clues about his identity.

'How many tall, dark-haired, well-spoken men are there in London, do you suppose?'

Geraldine frowned at her mug of coffee.

'I've reread Douggie Hopkins and William Kingsley's statements so many times I know them off by heart, but I can't see we've missed anything. Come on.'

She stood up, suddenly decisive.

'Where to?' asked Sam.

'Let's speak to those two again. Perhaps one of them will remember something.'

'Anything's better than being stuck here reading all those statements again.'

Sam stuffed the last mouthful of cake in her mouth, washed it down with a gulp of coffee and jumped to her feet.

'And I think we should start putting a bit of pressure on our friend Mr Hopkins,' Geraldine added.

'About bloody time! Let's make the little rat squeal.'

'Do I detect a touch of sadism, Sergeant?'

'A girl's got to have a bit of fun, ma'am.'

Sam winked and Geraldine couldn't help laughing.

55

RITUAL

He pulled on a pair of rubber gloves before reaching inside the top kitchen cupboard where he kept a catering saucepan he had bought especially for the purpose. It had taken him some time to find one that was large enough. Lifting it down, he removed his carefully selected implements: a butcher's cleaver, a set of saws, a sharp knife, a long handled two pronged fork and a pair of tongs. Although well-used, they were all gleaming, the blades recently sharpened. Crossing the room at a deliberately slow pace, he flipped the switch on the kettle. Every stage in the process was familiar as the steps in a sacred ritual. While the kettle came to the boil, he took a large plastic bag out of the freezer and held it up to the light to study its contents.

No longer excited at preparing small bones for the collection, he was ready to work on larger exhibits, instead of buying them in. One day, he might attempt a skull. Meanwhile, this was the largest specimen he had yet tackled. It was going to be tricky, but it would be worth the effort if he could pull it off. The main difficulty was controlling his impatience. Hacking the foot off at the ankle had been easier than he had expected, and it was now time to complete the task. With the lower leg part inside a plastic bag, he measured its length and relaxed on seeing that it would fit inside the pan. He picked up his knife, slit the bag open, and dropped the leg into the water, adjusting the heat until it was simmering gently.

He poured himself a cup of tea and sat down. While he waited, he tapped one polished shoe against the leg of his stool in time to the tune he was humming. The blue and white cup reminded him of his mother's best china tea set and the tea was exactly how he liked it, hot and strong. Contentedly he leaned back against a cupboard, shifting sideways so its door handle didn't dig into his back. It was one of those rare moments when life seemed perfect. He had done the hard work. All he had to do now was wait.

When he judged the flesh was well cooked, he turned out the gas. The gently bubbling water gave off a subtle aroma. It wasn't unpleasant. Still humming, he laid a folded newspaper on the tray. This he covered with layers of clean kitchen roll. Then he drained water from the pan and placed the leg down on the white paper where it lay, glistening. As gently as he could, he wrapped it in kitchen roll, squeezing it gently to allow its moisture to seep into the paper.

Unerringly the sharpened blade slid through flesh to bone. He was careful. The slightest scratch would render the bone useless, but he had judged it well and the meat came away easily. Gently he scraped off every scrap of soft tissue. By the time he had finished, the paper was streaked with fragments of flesh. He tore off a few clean sheets of kitchen roll and patted the bone dry. With a trembling hand he reached out to stroke its smooth surface. He thought how pleased the owner would have been if she could have seen this timeless memento of her life.

Jon would come to appreciate how privileged he was, viewing the collection before anyone else. Earlier visitors had passed on, but he appeared stronger than the women who had gone before him, and it was important he stayed that way. He was part of the plan. In the meantime, there were preparations to complete. Reverently picking up the bone, he wrapped it first in kitchen roll, and then foil, to protect it.

With the worktops scrubbed, and his utensils stored in the cupboard, he sat down to gloat over the slim foil parcel. Later he would take his new exhibit up the attic and decide where to display it, probably on the same shelf as Chief Sitting Bull's whip. Admittedly the whip was made from a thigh bone while this new specimen was a shinbone, but they were both human leg bones. It was important for the collection to be orderly. It had to make sense.

56

HEADY RECKLESSNESS

The office manager had sent an email round first thing Monday morning.

'Don't forget we're all going out after work today!'

Vicky sighed but she knew everyone had to go, sales personnel, office manager, accounts and admin staff.

'It's a bit of a cheek,' she muttered to Melissa who sat opposite her, 'expecting us to put in time outside working hours.'

'Well, it's not like it's work,' Melissa replied. 'They are taking us out, aren't they? I've got no problem with that.'

'No, I'm not saying I've got a problem with it. I'm not complaining, but I could do without it after a day at work, that's all I'm saying.'

The big boss was in the UK on his annual visit from America. Having spent the weekend in London he was at the office for meetings with the area manager and sales team all day, and after work the staff were all going out for dinner.

'If you ask me, it's a great perk,' Melissa grinned, 'being taken out to a restaurant by the boss.'

'Yes, but it's Monday night. Who wants to go out on a Monday night? They could at least have arranged to take us out on Friday.'

Melissa shrugged.

'I can't see what difference it makes. Not everyone's free on Fridays so a Monday makes more sense, and we've still got to eat, even on a Monday. I think it'll be fun. Are you going home first or have you brought something with you?'

She reached down to pull a carrier bag from under her desk. 'I brought my things in with me.'

She glanced at her watch.

'Are you coming to the loo to get changed soon?'

Vicky shook her head.

'I'm going like this. I mean, it's a work outing, isn't it?'

Vicky enjoyed her job, but she liked to keep regular hours. Although she got on with her colleagues well enough she wasn't completely comfortable about socialising with them outside the office. Melissa stood up, swinging her carrier bag, and grinned.

'Free drinks all evening,' she said and Vicky forced a smile. She didn't often drink, not like some of her colleagues who went out after work most evenings. Vicky just liked to get home at the end of the day. She had gone out with them over Christmas and had finished her evening throwing up in the toilets. Thankfully her colleagues had all been too merry to notice how ill she was, and no one had taken much notice when she had left early, pleading a headache.

Melissa disappeared for over half an hour to get changed, leaving Vicky to cover the phones. Finally they walked in a group to a small Italian restaurant in Baker Street where Vicky found herself squeezed in between two salesmen.

'Come on, drink up,' one of them told her while they were waiting for their food. He had a nice smile and she noticed his eyes linger on her with unmistakable interest. She had never really noticed him before but he was quite attractive. Caught up in a sudden heady recklessness, Vicky drank.

'Why not?' she giggled when he offered to refill her glass.

Everyone else seemed to be having a good time and her journey home was easy enough. Perhaps it wouldn't do her any harm to relax for once.

'Why not indeed?' the salesman laughed as he filled her glass to the brim.

Their food arrived and after that the evening passed in a blur. Vicky was surprised how much wine she managed to put away; after the first two glasses she lost count and couldn't remember if her colleague had refilled her glass two or three times, but she felt fine. She supposed it was because of the huge pizza she had ploughed her way through while drinking. It seemed as though hardly any time had elapsed since they had arrived at the restaurant when the accounts manager stood up. He was in his fifties and looked worn out.

'It's been a very enjoyable evening,' he announced, 'but I've got to make tracks.'

He turned to their boss and explained that he had a long journey home.

'I can't afford to miss my train. Early start in the morning,' he added with forced cheeriness.

'Goodness, it's half past ten already,' someone else said and a few other people began to mutter about having to get home.

'It's still early,' the boss protested, signalling to a waiter to bring another bottle of wine.

'You're not leaving are you?' the salesman asked Vicky.

She realised she couldn't remember his name. She giggled helplessly for a moment before scraping her chair back and getting to her feet.

'It's been a lovely evening.'

She held onto the back of her chair as she spoke.

'But I really need to get going.'

Not until she stood up did it hit her that she'd had way too much to drink. She began to giggle again, for no reason.

'What's so funny down there?' the boss called out to their end of the long table.

Vicky started to shake her head but the movement made the room sway.

'I've had a lovely evening,' she repeated quickly, stumbling over her words. 'It's been really lovely, but I have to go.'

She turned and made her way carefully to the door, hoping she wouldn't throw up in full view of all her colleagues. She could see the tube station over the road and it was only a few stops back to Camden, from where it was just a short walk to her flat. As she crossed the road she tried to remember the name of the salesman who had been chatting her up. She hoped she would see him again soon. When she entered the station a blast of warm air made her feel sick and she struggled to take out her Oyster card and make her way through the turnstile, desperate now to get home.

57

SUDDENLY SCARED

Geraldine and Sam found Douggie Hopkins at home. Although it was early evening he looked as though he had just woken up.

'Bloody hell, what now?' he grumbled when he saw them on the doorstep.

He rubbed his eyes.

'Who is it?'

His wife came to the door and stood just behind him, staring at Geraldine.

'We don't want - '

Geraldine held out her warrant card.

'It's the police, Mary. You go on in. I'll talk to them.'

'We'd like to go over your statement again.'

'It wasn't his fault,' Mary piped up. 'The other bloke just set on him. Douggie never started it. It's the other bloke you should be talking to - '

'Go inside, Mary,' Douggie told her.

He gave her a little shove and she disappeared inside the house, complaining.

'It wasn't his fault. The other bloke just set on him for no reason - '

Douggie looked anxious.

'She thinks you're here about the scrap in the pub.'

'You mean she doesn't know about your car disposal activities?'

'Look, I never stole that motor. It's all perfectly legit. As far as I'm concerned, I just got rid of it for the owner. There's nothing in the law says I can't do that.'

'Douggie, we're not here to investigate you and your dubious operations.'

She glanced at Sam.

'At least, not yet.'

'What are you on about, dubious? That's slander, that is. Insulting an honest man's reputation - '

Geraldine ignored his protest.

'What we *are* interested in is the man who paid you to take the car to Epping Forest.'

'Well, I've already told you I don't know who he was. And what's more, I don't want to know. It was just a job. He's nothing to do with me.'

Douggie's whole demeanour was tense, as though he was suddenly scared.

'This man threatened you, didn't he Douggie? He scares you.'

'Ha! You're having a laugh. It takes more than some posh geezer to put the frighteners on me,' he blustered but his hands trembled as he lit a cigarette. 'I'm not that easily scared.'

He was rattled alright.

'We have a few more questions, Douggie. We'd like you to accompany us to the station.'

He glanced over his shoulder.

'I've got nothing to say. I've told you everything I know. Christ, I took you to Epping Forest, didn't I? You can question me till you're blue in the face but I'm telling you I've no idea who the bloke is. I'd never had anything to do with him before and I haven't heard from him since.'

'Come along now, Douggie,' Geraldine said quietly as

Mrs Hopkins reappeared in the hallway behind her husband. 'Let's not have a scene.'

'Are you still here?' Mary Hopkins asked. 'Did you get the bugger who assaulted Douggie? I hope you lock him up and throw away the key.'

Geraldine sighed.

'We're working on it,' she replied, but she wasn't talking about the man who had been brawling with Douggie in the pub. 'Now, your husband is going to come with us and help us with our enquiries, isn't that right?'

'But it wasn't his fault. What's going on, Douggie?'

'It's alright, love.'

He inhaled deeply and grinned, putting on a show of self-possession in front of his wife.

'Come along now, sir.'

'Douggie - ' his wife cried out.

'Just drop it, Mary,' Douggie called over his shoulder as he followed Geraldine to the car.

At the police station Douggie glared at Geraldine across the table.

'We're not convinced you're telling us the whole truth, Douggie, and it's important we know everything about this man.'

'Not to me it isn't.'

'If you can help us find this man you could be looking at a reduced sentence for illegally disposing of a wanted vehicle,' Sam said. 'Perverting the course of justice, you're looking at a custodial sentence - '

'Oh fuck off and leave me alone will you?' Douggie exploded. 'What do you take me for? I told you, I don't know anything about him except that he was in a hurry to get rid of the car. He didn't want me to wait till the morning to take it to be scrapped. I had to get rid of it that night. It was a business transaction, nothing illegal about it.'

'Why?'

'Why what?'

'If someone pays you to torch a car, there must be a reason. Why did he want to get rid of it so quickly?'

'How the fuck should I know? Look, he didn't say and I didn't ask. It was just a job, alright?'

'OK, let's assume for a moment this mystery man exists and he paid you to destroy the car. You weren't just getting rid of it for your own purposes - '

'Leave it out, will you? For fuck's sake - '

'This man. You said just now he's a complete stranger, and what's more you wouldn't want to know him. So why are you so keen to avoid him? What was it he said? That he knows where you live, wasn't that it? Is that why you're worried about him?'

Douggie frowned.

'I'm not worried. I just didn't like the geezer, that's all.'

'So you keep telling us. But why?' Geraldine persisted.

'Posh blokes aren't really my type.'

'Don't you think we should have told him why we're after the man who paid him to torch the car?' Sam asked as they left the interview room.

'He already knows we're investigating a murder, but I get the feeling Douggie's already told us as much as he knows, or at least as much as he's going to say. We might as well let him go for now. But we'll warn him that we'll be back. There's a chance he'll think better of withholding evidence, if he has anything more to tell us, that is. Although I get the impression he's more scared of the man whose car he destroyed than he is of us.'

'Then we need to keep threatening him with the prospect of going down for a long time until he starts taking it seriously.'

'He'll know we're bluffing. And in any case, how can *we* be more frightening than a killer who knows where he lives? And he's got a wife to consider.'

The same evening they went back to see William Kingsley, but although he was eager to help he had nothing new to tell them.

'It's such a long time ago,' he apologised. 'I'm not even sure I'm thinking of the right man.'

It had not been an encouraging day.

'I wonder where he is now?' Sam asked as they drove back to North London.

'He removes his victims' teeth,' Geraldine replied thoughtfully. 'What does that tell us?'

'It tells us he's mental.'

'He takes the teeth as some sort of trophy. I wonder what he does with them?'

'Perhaps he puts them under his pillow for the tooth fairy. I'm starving. Fancy some chips?'

'What made him cut off Jessica Palmer's finger and amputate Donna Henry's leg like that? He's clearly got a selection of saws, which suggests it's all been planned,' Geraldine went on.

'Of course it's all been planned. No one just randomly cuts off someone's leg for no reason.'

'So what *is* the reason?'

'I can't begin to imagine,' said Sam.

'He's keeping something that was part of his victims. If we could work out what's going on in his mind - '

'There's no point trying to understand someone who's completely crazy. The whole thing's too weird.'

'We have to try,' Geraldine insisted. 'In the end it might be the only way to find him.'

Sam shook her head.

'You can't work out what makes him tick,' she said firmly. 'What he's doing is completely insane, which means by definition it makes no sense. You can't understand it. I can't understand it. No one can understand it. Unless you're mad too. Now, I know where there's a decent chippie on the way home. What do you say?'

'About the chips, or about being mad?'

Sam grinned.

'Well, this job's enough to drive anyone crazy, I'll give you that. Now, about those chips?'

Geraldine smiled, pleased that there was no longer any awkwardness between them.

58

THROUGH THE NIGHT

Having spent evening after evening vainly searching back streets, it was typical that he chanced to spot her one night when he wasn't even looking. He had just driven past Camden station, on his way home, when he caught sight of her on the opposite side of the road. She looked young – perhaps very young – and it struck him that a teenager might be more responsive to his vision than the people he had taken home so far. He speculated about her age as he watched her light coloured coat flap against her legs in a gust of night air. There was no reason for him to pull into the kerb and watch her because he wasn't looking for anyone, and in any case they were on a main road which meant there would be cameras everywhere. But her slight figure held his gaze. As she turned into a side street he pulled out into the traffic and followed her. Once he had turned the corner he drew over but the girl had disappeared, which was just as well because he told himself he had no intention of approaching her. Nevertheless he parked and got out to stretch his legs.

The cold night air startled him; he hadn't realised how hot it was in the car. The side street was deserted. About to get back in the car, he heard someone coughing. Stepping forward he peered into a narrow passageway between two buildings. The girl was leaning against a wall, barely visible in the unlit alley, illuminated only by a faint glow that spread out from the street. He could see she had long fair hair and was wearing a knee length mac and low heeled shoes, and was carrying a bag over her arm. Closer up she appeared older than he had initially thought, probably in her late twenties. She hadn't seen him yet. Abruptly she bent double and vomited. When she straightened up unsteadily he knew what to do. This was too good an opportunity to miss.

He stepped smartly into the alley quickly brushing his hood off his head.

'Are you alright?'

The girl looked up, startled.

'Don't worry. I'm a police officer.'

He waved his identity card in front of her.

'Come on, I'll take you home.'

'No. I'm alright, really.'

It was a half-hearted protest.

'That's what they all say,' he told her, smiling kindly, 'but you don't need to worry. I'm not arresting you. You haven't done anything wrong. I'm just looking out for your safety. Come on now, you're in no fit state to be out on your own. Best to be safe.'

He took hold of her arm and steered her back onto the street, jerking his hood up with his free hand before they left the shelter of the dark passage. He muttered something about the threat of rain but she wasn't listening. Deftly he opened the door, shoved her inside, and clicked the seat belt on.

'Won't be long now,' he said cheerfully as he leapt in behind the wheel. 'We'll soon have you home.'

'How do you know where I live?' she asked as the car accelerated.

He didn't answer.

Vicky could hear her teeth chattering, and felt herself trembling as the car sped on through unfamiliar streets.

Although she stared fixedly out of the window she didn't recognise anything they passed. They seemed to be driving for a long time.

'How do you know where I live?' she repeated anxiously.

She had been an idiot to drink so much that evening but had sobered up enough to realise that she was sitting in a car beside a stranger, with no idea where he was taking her.

'Please stop,' she called out, her voice rising in panic. 'Stop the car. Thank you for the lift but I'd like to get out now.'

Still the man made no reply but carried on driving through the night.

There was no longer any doubt in her mind that she was at risk. The fact that the driver was a policeman made her situation more alarming because he would know how to avoid attracting suspicion. There was nothing for it but to jump out of the car at the first opportunity. They seemed to be travelling along a fairly main road. They had only to slow down for a red traffic light or a corner and she would leap out and make a run for it. By the time the driver realised what had happened, she would be gone. She fumbled with her seatbelt and managed to release it silently. The man didn't look round. At last they stopped at a traffic light and she pulled cautiously on the door handle. It was locked. Struggling to control her alarm she leaned back in her seat and waited. There was nothing else to do until he opened the door and when that happened she would need to keep her wits about her. She couldn't afford to give way to the panic rising in her chest which was making it hard for her to think clearly.

Finally the car stopped in front of a large wooden gate which opened, operated by remote control, and they drove in. Leaning against the seat as though asleep, she threw her head back to watch what was happening through half closed eyes. Her car door opened and a rush of cool air blew across her face. Suddenly, with a shriek of terror, she flung herself out of the car, throwing all her weight sideways against her captor in a desperate attempt to barge him out of the way. He stumbled backwards in surprise. She ran blindly but he followed and seized her by the arm. Vicky spun round swinging her bag at his face. He yanked it from her grasp and the frail gold chain snapped and dangled uselessly. Still gripping her arm, he tossed the bag over his shoulder with his free hand which he then pressed against her mouth, pushing her head backwards until she struggled to breathe. Her head was spinning with alcohol and terror and she felt her legs buckle, so that only his grasp of her arm prevented her falling.

'What's wrong with you?' he hissed, leaning forward so that his mouth was touching her ear.

'I want to help you.'

She could hear his breath wheezing in his chest.

'Come along now,' he went on.

She turned her head and saw that he was smiling at her.

'I've got something to show you. I know you're going to like it.'

PART 5

59

A HINT OF AGGRESSION

After a dull morning Geraldine was pleasantly surprised when Sam suggested they go out for a pub lunch.

'Let's just get away from this place for an hour,' Sam said, and Geraldine agreed.

The atmosphere at the station was tense. Colleagues assigned to the Palmer Henry case who had been enthusiastic at the start of the investigation were now fractious. It felt as though they had done no more than go round in a circle. They had no definite leads and were going over old ground casting around hoping to find something new.

Geraldine and Sam went to a quiet local pub where Sam assured her the food was good. Geraldine ordered a prawn salad and Sam asked for a club sandwich with chips.

'Make that a double portion of chips, will you?' she added to the woman serving behind the bar. 'I'm so hungry, I could eat a horse.'

They sat down and began chatting in subdued tones about the case.

'If you ask me, we're worse off now than when we started because we've been on the case for weeks and where are we? Still none the wiser,' Sam grumbled.

'That's not true. We've come a long way.'

'Really? Well, who have we got as a credible suspect right now? After all this time.'

'It's not even three weeks,' Geraldine said. 'Just be patient.

We'll get there.'

Sam looked around.

'Patient? I tell you what, I wish they'd hurry up with that food. I'm famished.'

'I don't know how you can eat so much without putting on weight.'

Sam grinned and patted her stomach.

'I'm hardly skinny. If I didn't exercise regularly - '

The food arrived and Sam offered Geraldine some chips. Geraldine shook her head.

'Go on,' Sam said. 'I've got loads.'

They ate in silence for a few minutes.

'We've been at it for weeks now,' Sam repeated, 'and we still don't know anything. I just think we should be getting somewhere after all this time, that's all.'

She sprinkled salt and emptied two sachets of ketchup on her chips.

'We've learned quite a lot about the killer,' Geraldine pointed out but Sam disagreed.

'Hardly. A few unsubstantiated comments, that's all we've got.'

'We know more than that.'

'What have we discovered, exactly? He's tall. He's got dark hair. Yes, that narrows it down a lot, doesn't it? There aren't many tall dark-haired men knocking around North London, are there? And all that could turn out to be a load of tosh anyway, just like Robert bloody Stafford. So what have we got? Hopkins, the totally reliable witness. Not. Kingsley, who was making it up as he went along because he's got no memory for faces. Great! We can't put much store by anything either of them told us. For all we know the killer could be short, fat and ginger.'

'Hopkins and Kingsley both said very clearly he was tall and dark-haired, and he spoke with an educated accent,' Geraldine said patiently.

'What? So he was educated.' Sam snorted dismissively. 'Ask anyone to describe someone they met once and they'd probably come up with something similar. You can't set too much store by that.'

There was a hint of aggression in Sam's voice that Geraldine had never noticed before. She couldn't help wondering if it was provoked solely by Sam's frustration with the case or if personal feelings were involved. Perhaps Sam had been hoping something might develop between them, despite her denial that she harboured any feelings for Geraldine.

'Sam,' Geraldine began and paused, uncertain how to express her concern.

'What?'

But Geraldine decided against broaching the subject of Sam's feelings towards her. Sam had made it clear she wasn't interested in anything other than a professional friendship, and to suggest she might want more would only embarrass them both. In any case, Sam's bad mood was no doubt due to nothing more than the investigation, which seemed to be going nowhere.

'What were you going to say?' Sam asked.

'What happened with Wanda?' Geraldine blurted out, curiosity overruling her decision not to pry into Sam's feelings.

She waited, expecting to be told to butt out and mind her own business but instead Sam gave a rueful smile.

'We were together for a while, but it got a bit too intense for comfort. She's so wearing. You know how it is when you're on a case. You can't just drop everything because your partner throws a tantrum. She was always complaining I put my work before her – which I suppose I sometimes did – but in the end it pissed me off. I think we just got fed up with each other. Anyway, she's with someone else now and they seem happy.'

'I know what you mean.'

Geraldine told Sam about her ex-boyfriend, Craig.

'He said he didn't want to play second fiddle to a corpse.'

Sam laughed at that, and Geraldine joined in.

'It sounds funny now, but I wasn't amused at the time.'

'Was it a tough break-up? Did you ever think he was The One and all that?'

'No. We weren't together that long, so I was disappointed rather than upset. But there was someone serious before Craig. We lived together for six years - '

'Six years!'

Sam gave a low whistle.

'And then one day he just walked out, without any warning. I should have seen it coming I suppose, but I was so engrossed in work.'

She sighed.

'Why do we do this to ourselves, Sam? Allow work to take priority over everything else? I could have been married to Mark by now, living in suburbia, worrying about our children.'

Their eyes met across the table.

'That's why we have to stick together, and support each other,' Sam said.

She reached out and put her hand on Geraldine's.

Geraldine tensed.

'Sam,' she faltered, 'I like you a lot. But - '

Sam removed her hand with an apologetic grin.

'Don't panic. I'm not going to jump on you when you're not expecting it. I know you're straight. Isn't that why you've just been telling me about Craig and Mark?'

Geraldine shrugged. That hadn't been her intention.

It hadn't occurred to her to question whether she might be attracted to her colleague, but perhaps Sam was right and subconsciously she had been seeking to establish that she had never fancied a woman and never would. Sam grinned and Geraldine was surprised to feel a flicker of regret. They got on so well, and Geraldine had to admit to herself she was lonely. Maybe she had been talking for her own benefit, reminding herself of the men she had loved, because allowing herself to grow too close to Sam could introduce unwelcome complications into her life.

'Come on,' she said abruptly standing up. 'It's time we got back to work.'

60

MORE THAN HIS LIFE WAS WORTH

Douggie was pissed off. It would wreck his nice little set up if anyone found out the police were taking an interest in him. And what did those bloody coppers mean about getting him a reduced sentence if he helped them out? It was more than his life was worth to say more. Douggie might not know who the softly spoken stranger was, but he knew better than to take his threats lightly. On balance, he'd far rather take his chances with the coppers.

As if he didn't already have enough to worry about, now Mary was in one of her moods for no reason.

'Something's happened, Douggie. I can tell. There's something you're not telling me. I can see you're worried but you don't say anything.'

'There's nothing to say,' he replied crossly. 'And you'd do us both a favour if you'd shut up and mind your own business.'

'This *is* my business, Douggie. You're my business. What's wrong?'

'I told you, nothing's wrong. I'm going out.'

'Don't walk out on me like that!' she shouted.

He'd already had a few pints when George stepped through the door. Thinking his luck had finally changed, Douggie hurried up to the bar.

'Have one on me. No need to thank me.'

Douggie gave him a friendly grin but George turned away

without a word.

'Haven't seen you in here for a while,' Douggie said after a moment's silence. 'Got anything for me then?'

George stared at his pint in silence for a moment.

'It's over, Douggie.'

'What are you talking about?'

'There aren't going to be any more jobs, not for you. They've found someone else.'

He squinted at Douggie.

'It's nothing to do with me, honest. But it's best if you don't talk to me again.'

Douggie made a show of not understanding.

'What are you on about, no more jobs? You can tell them, they're not going to find anyone half as good as me. I'm the best at what I do, you know that. And I've got the contacts, see? You tell them.'

George had almost finished his pint.

'Tell them, George. We've worked together for a long time, you can't just drop me for no reason.'

Douggie knew perfectly well why this was happening.

'It's nothing to do with me, mate. I'm just the messenger boy. If it was up to me - '

George shrugged.

'You've been seen, going in and out the copshop. They don't like it. So that's it.'

George stood up.

'Been nice knowing you, sunshine. Thanks for the pint and all.'

Douggie watched him walk away, cursing that posh geezer and his bloody two thousand quid. It had cost him.

As he opened the front door he called out. There was no answer. He went into the kitchen and then the bedroom but

Mary wasn't there. The flat was empty. Terror hit him and for a few seconds he couldn't catch his breath at the thought that the intruder might have returned and taken Mary away. He tried her mobile but it went straight to voicemail.

'Hello, this is Mary. I can't speak now but leave me a message and I'll call you back soon.'

'Mary, where are you?' he asked out loud.

Although it was late, he rang her sister. No one answered. Despite all the driving he did, he was without a car right now. Careless of expense he took a taxi to Mary's sister's house, rang the bell and hammered on the door. Eventually the door opened on the chain and Mary's sister peered out.

'Who is it? Bugger off or I'll call the police – oh, it's you. What do you want? Have you got any idea what time it is?'

'Mary's gone,' he gasped.

'About time too.'

She began to close the door.

'Wait.'

'She doesn't want to see you.'

'But she's here?'

'Of course she's here.'

Douggie was so relieved he staggered and almost fell against the door frame.

'I thought - '

'Get lost, Douggie. She doesn't want to see you.'

The door slammed.

Douggie waited five minutes then rang Mary's mobile.

'Hello, this is Mary. I can't speak now but leave me a message and I'll call you back soon.'

'Mary, please,' he stammered, but he knew it was no use.

'Oh fuck off then, you stupid cow,' he yelled and hung up.

61

AS GOOD AS THEY SAY

'You look worn out,' Jayne said, as Reg motioned her to sit down. 'Do you really have to work such long hours?'

He didn't answer.

'What's wrong? There's something bothering you, isn't there?'

He shook his head, the gesture belied by his gloomy expression.

'It's not like you, Reg. You look really down. You're not sickening for something, are you? You haven't seemed yourself at all for the past few days.'

Reg still made no reply.

'Is there a problem?'

He put down the file he was holding and scowled.

'Yes. You could say that.'

'Well, I'm sure you're doing your best. You know you always get results in the end. It's not like you to let it get to you this way.'

'There's always a first time,' he replied sullenly, 'and it would have to be on a high profile case like this. It's all over the media about these black girls. You've seen what they're saying, that we haven't got a clue, and the worst thing about it is they're right. We're getting absolutely bloody nowhere with it. Nowhere.'

Jayne nodded. She had seen the tabloids, who were calling the killer The Butcher because he dismembered his victims.

'I've been thinking about what they're saying, wondering why he carves them up - '

'He doesn't carve them up, for Christ's sake. Do you have to talk like a tabloid journalist? Yes, I know he inflicts injuries on the bodies, and I'm also aware that the longer it takes us to get him, the more chance there is he's going to find another victim.'

'You've only been on the case for two weeks, Reg. They can't expect you to get results overnight.'

'It's closer to a month,' he corrected her. 'We've already got two bodies. Who knows when we're going to turn up another one?'

'Well, you can only do your best,' Jayne repeated. 'Why don't you go home and make a fresh start in the morning. Making yourself ill isn't going to help.'

Reg smiled weakly at her.

He picked up the file he had been studying, then threw it back down on the desk.

'Let's have a drink,' he said.

They walked to the pub round the corner and sat down at a quiet table inside.

'You're overdoing it, Reg. You look knackered. What time did you go home last night?'

He shrugged, not meeting her eye.

'You can't keep driving yourself like this,' she insisted.

'The work still has to be done, even when we're getting nowhere. We can't let up for a moment. You know that as well as I do. I have to get a result, Jayne. I have to.'

'Well you can't do it all by yourself. If you ask me it's seems all the responsibility is falling on you, and that's not right.'

'I'm the senior investigating officer. That's how it is. I have to take responsibility. I knew that when I took the promotion, but honestly - '

He heaved a sigh.

She waited, watching the droop of his shoulders and his worried expression.

'I'm beginning to wonder if it was a mistake. I mean, I feel like I'm completely out of my depth. Morale on the team is rock bottom. It's my job to psyche them all up, keep things moving, and I just don't think I can do it any more.'

A couple of women sat down at the next table and he leaned forward, lowering his voice.

'It turns out there may have been more victims than we thought. Blood samples from the victims suggest there were others – what if another body turns up? And another one after that - '

'You can't go on winding yourself up like this,' Jayne interrupted. 'You don't know there'll be any more victims.'

'There will be more. I know there will.'

'Well, what about this new inspector you've got on your team? You told me she came highly recommended. Why can't she take some of the load off your shoulders? It can't all be down to you.'

He forced a smile and nodded at her empty glass.

'Another one? Let me.'

'No, no, it's my round. One more and then I really have to go.'

Reg had worked with Detective Chief Inspector Kathryn Gordon of the Kent constabulary in the past and he trusted her judgement. She had not only written a glowing reference for Geraldine Steel, but had followed it up with a phone call singing her praises.

'She's exceptional. You won't regret having her on your team.'

He had fast-tracked Geraldine through the transfer process, and now she was fumbling around with the rest of the team on an investigation that had so far drawn a blank.

'Yes,' he admitted to Jayne as she sat down again. 'Geraldine Steel came highly recommended, by one of the sharpest DCIs I've ever worked with.'

'Well there you are then, if she's as good as they say she is, you can pass some of the responsibility on to her, can't you?'

Reg frowned and took a gulp of his drink.

'It doesn't work like that. And even if it did, I can't say I've been all that impressed by her so far. She's doesn't strike me as anything special, in spite of her reputation. But it's early days, I suppose.'

He leaned back in his chair, stretching his long legs out in front of him.

'Maybe you're expecting too much of her.'

'Yes, perhaps I am. To be honest, I'm not sure she's making the transition all that well. Being in London's very different to working in the home counties. She might have hacked it in Kent, but I'm not so sure she's up to the pressures of working on the Met.'

'Murder is murder wherever you are.'

'That's what she said.'

'So what if the procedures are a bit different - '

'I don't need you to tell me how to do my job,' he snapped, suddenly irritated by her efforts to comfort him.

'No, of course not. You don't have to jump down my throat. I'm only trying to help.'

'I know,' he said. 'I'm sorry. But I'm beginning to think that having a county DI on the team is more trouble than it's worth.'

'If you're worried about this new woman, why don't you just get rid of her?'

'We're in the middle of an investigation. You know very well I can't push her off the team without good reason, and it's not as if she's doing any worse than everybody else. I can't sack the whole bloody lot of them.'

He sighed.

'Then I think you should talk to her, ask her how she's settling in.'

Reg nodded.

'Yes, maybe I will. Perhaps it's time for a review anyway.'

He sat up and swilled the amber liquid slowly round and round the glass, thinking.

Reg watched Geraldine in the Incident Room the following morning. Seemingly wrapped up in her own thoughts, she took no part in the light-hearted banter flying around between the rest of her colleagues. One of the sergeants, recently returned from his honeymoon, was the butt of the jokes.

'Must be a new experience, wearing a shirt that's actually been washed,' one of his colleagues was saying.

'He didn't realise you could wash shirts,' someone else joked.

'And I do believe it's been ironed,' a constable added.

'I didn't recognise you without the creases in your shirts, Jim,' someone else said, clapping the newly-married officer on the back.

'Have you brought a lunchbox with sandwiches?'

Reg turned his attention back to Geraldine. Catching her eye he smiled, but she turned away as though she hadn't seen him. It was one thing to be self-contained but he was finding his new inspector positively unapproachable and now, having made the decision to speak with her, he wasn't sure how to broach the subject of her fitting in. It wasn't as if she had put a foot wrong. On the contrary, she was conscientious and thorough, and ready to take the initiative even though so far her ideas had led nowhere, like everyone else on the team. But she baffled him and that made him uncomfortable.

Not for the first time, he wished he had resisted pressure from his superiors to include more women on his team. Difficult men were so straightforward, compared to difficult women. He hoped he hadn't made a blunder appointing a female inspector. She might have been promoted beyond her capability, thanks to the positive discrimination that had become so prevalent in the force. He had nothing against women as a rule, but he needed his officers to be professional. While he fully supported equality and political correctness, there was no doubt women were more likely to act irrationally than men.

'How are you feeling, Reg?' Jayne asked him later that morning when she came in to talk him through her detailed analysis of the killer's possible motivation.

He shrugged. Jayne had nothing new to say but at least she was eager to help. He had worked with her on several occasions in the past, and there was nothing standoffish about *her*.

'I was just thinking about what we were talking about yesterday, about Geraldine,' he replied.

'Yes, I've been giving her some thought. She does seem a bit hostile.'

'Hostile?'

'Well, defensive.'

'I've seen it before with officers coming into the Met from outside, getting the idea everyone's looking down on them. Some people take to it as though they've been here all their life, but for others there's a period of adjustment. The trouble is, I can't afford to let the transition distract her from the case.' Reg looked worried. 'She doesn't seem to have settled in, does she?'

'Maybe she's just an unhappy person,' Jayne replied.

'Do you really think so?'

He frowned.

'She came with such good references. I can't work out if anything's wrong or not because she's so tight lipped. I don't really know her at all.'

Jayne nodded.

'Would you like me to talk to her? Woman to woman?'

Reg felt uncomfortable with the implication. He was perfectly capable of talking to Geraldine himself. At the same time, he was relieved to think he might not have to tackle the issue in person.

'Yes. Perhaps that would be best. Find out if anything's bothering her. You'll be discreet, won't you?'

'Leave it with me.'

62

SOUND OF CRYING

Jon was woken by a burning sensation in his wrists. His chest heaved with the effort to breathe. The sound of crying reached him in the darkness. With a sudden effort he tried to raise himself upright and was brought back to reality with a jolt by the fact that his arms and legs were firmly shackled. Distracted by excruciating pain, he struggled to focus on what was happening. He had drunk too much before a man had offered him a lift home. They had climbed up a lot of stairs and after that he thought he must have passed out because he had woken up from a nightmare about skulls to find himself chained in darkness.

The sobbing went on and on, coming to him in waves. He drifted into unconsciousness again for a short time, until he was woken by distant noises, banging and shuffling, a door being opened and closed. Muffled voices reached him, but he was too exhausted to call out into the darkness. Then the light came on and he was too frightened to speak, because he had glimpsed a face from his nightmares. The man was leaning over, gazing down, and someone was making a high-pitched whimpering noise. It sounded like a woman. Unintentionally, Jon groaned aloud.

The man straightened up at once and turned to him, as if he had been waiting for a signal.

'Hello. Are you feeling any better?' he asked cheerfully, as though Jon had gone to bed with a touch of flu.

Jon shook his arms and the chains rattled.

'Look at me!' he cried out.

He barely recognised his own voice, it was so hoarse, and his throat felt raw.

'Take these bloody things off!'

He paused to gulp for air and noticed that the whimpering had stopped. The woman must be listening to him – or else she was dead.

'What's happened to her?' he asked as this new dread struck him. 'Have you killed her?'

'I never wanted to kill anyone,' the man said, clearly taken aback. 'Why won't anyone listen to me? Those others who died so quickly, that wasn't my fault. I wish someone would listen.'

He raised his arm and Jon saw he was holding out a chipped white mug. The man leaned forward and pressed the cold rim of the cup against Jon's bottom lip, a dribble of water sliding down his chin and neck. He shivered with anticipation and closed his eyes as he took a sip of water and felt its icy smoothness on his tongue.

'Isn't this nice?' the man said pleasantly. 'All three of us here together.'

Jon scowled at him. The moaning had resumed, a ragged sound, as though the unseen woman was shaking with sobs.

'It's like a party!' Jon's captor giggled. 'A pre launch party for the collection. I should have brought some champagne up with me.'

'This is nothing to laugh about,' Jon protested, shaking his chains again.

'Please don't keep me here!' the woman shrieked suddenly and Jon heard an echoing rattle of chains.

As the man turned to look at her Jon twisted his head, raising it from the bed as far as it would go, but he still couldn't see the woman lying on the floor.

'Let me go!' she repeated, her voice shrill with alarm.

'Yes, let us both go! We've had enough of this,' Jon joined in.

Without warning the man lunged forward and slapped Jon across the face with the back of his hand, a sudden blow that felt like an explosion on the side of his head. Jon yelped in surprise.

'You're not going anywhere until you understand the collection. You want to know about it, don't you?'

'No I bloody don't,' Jon muttered under his breath, scared to speak out loud in case the man hit him again. There was a salty taste on his lips; tears or blood.

'Let me go! Please, let me go - ' The woman broke off abruptly.

For a few seconds there was silence. The man walked over to the shelves of skulls and other macabre objects and began fiddling with them, humming to himself all the while. He picked up a long ivory coloured stick and brandished it above his head. Strands of leather hung down from it, like coarse hair.

'They don't understand yet. But they will.'

He was talking to himself.

'What is that thing?' Jon asked, intrigued in spite of his terror.

'There. I knew you were interested!'

He turned to Jon with an eager smile.

'This is my collection. It's going to be renowned, celebrated throughout the world. One day it will draw the entire human race together, with a power that goes far beyond the misleading drivel of religion. There's never been anything like it, not since the pyramids. It goes further than the ancient Egyptians ever did, a continuation of the work they began - '

'I don't know what you're talking about. What has any of this got to do with the pyramids, for fuck's sake? What work?'

The man shook his head sadly.

'Such ignorance. The ancient Egyptians knew that every living body was inhabited by a spirit which didn't die when mere physical breathing stopped. That's why they built pyramids to preserve the flesh against decay, as a means to deathlessness.'

He waved his hand in the direction of the shelves and turned back to Jon, his eyes shining.

'My collection is going to open the eyes of the world - '

'You're insane!' the woman's voice shouted out hysterically. 'No one wants to see that disgusting - '

The man dashed across the room and kicked out. Jon watched his body jolt at the impact and heard the woman scream.

'Stop that!' Jon yelled, crying with frustration at his own helplessness. 'Stop it at once!'

His captor turned to him, flushed with anger, and lashed out, hitting Jon squarely in the centre of his face. Pain made his eyes stream and blood filled his mouth, choking him. The man's blurred face glared at him for a second, then vanished. The light snapped off, the door slammed, and the two prisoners were left alone once again in darkness.

Jon turned his head to one side to stop the blood from his nose dribbling into his mouth.

'Are you alright?' he asked.

His lips felt thick and his voice gurgled in his throat.

'We're going to die, aren't we?' she replied. 'We're both going to die here and there's nothing we can do about it. No one knows where we are.'

Fighting an urge to vomit, Jon closed his eyes and tried to ignore the pain that had begun relentlessly stabbing his face.

Beside him, the woman began to cry.

63

ON THE BRINK

After an uneventful morning Geraldine spent an equally tedious afternoon trawling through documents. Just when she thought her day couldn't possibly get any drearier she heard a knock and looked up to see the profiler, Jayne, peering round the door.

'Come in.'

Jayne sat down and smiled warmly at Geraldine.

'What can I do for you?' Geraldine asked, trying to hide her impatience.

'Reg asked me to drop by and have a word with you.'

Geraldine fixed her face in what she hoped was an interested expression.

'We're all committed to working together to reach a successful conclusion to this case.'

'Of course.'

Geraldine forced a smile.

'Reg thinks you may be feeling some resistance towards my work.'

Jayne paused.

Geraldine was perturbed to hear that the detective chief inspector had been discussing her with Jayne. She wondered what else he had said about her.

'We need to talk. I'd like to explore how we both see our relationship moving forward. Working in the Met can seem very different to the home counties - '

'Have you worked in the force outside London then?'

'No. But I'm here to talk about you, Geraldine.'

'Well I've worked on murder cases in Kent and in the Met and it may surprise you to learn that it's actually not that different. When people are murdered they die just the same - whichever force you're on. Take it from someone who knows.'

She smiled at Jayne, no longer bothering to conceal her irritation. She had no doubt Jayne was feeling equally antagonistic towards her now.

'Geraldine, I'd like us to - ' Jayne began.

Geraldine spoke at the same time.

'Now if there's nothing else, Jayne, I really must crack on. Perhaps we can discuss the similarities and differences between the Met and the rest of the force when we're not up to our eyes in the middle of a case. I've got work to do, even if you haven't.'

She turned away pointedly and began typing.

'Geraldine, we need to talk.'

'About what for Christ's sake?' Geraldine's voice rose in exasperation.

'You'll get on a lot better if you listen to what other people have to say. I know what I'm talking about. I'm trained to understand - '

'Oh please, spare me any more of your insights. You want to talk about the way I work, is that it? Well, why don't you listen to me, because I'm also trained in my profession and I can tell you that your so-called insights are no better than anyone else's.'

'Geraldine, I'm trained to see things others don't see.'

'What 'things' exactly have you seen then? All you've told us so far is that you think the killer wants to control his victims because he ties them up. A child of ten could work that one out. You think he might be keeping his victims' teeth as trophies, and the dismemberment is escalating because a leg is more substantial than a finger. What other 'deductions' have you made, Jayne? That someone who's already killed at least twice might strike again. Well, I'm sure no one else would have realised that without the benefit of your insight. Might be this, might be that. I'd like to get on with establishing some facts that will actually help us to find this maniac, so can we please cut the time wasting crap about us wanting to work together and be friends?'

'I never said I wanted to be friends with you,' Jayne retorted. She went out, closing the door forcefully behind her. With a sigh, Geraldine returned to her work.

The rest of the day passed slowly. At about eight o'clock, well past the end of her shift, she went home and had supper while watching the news. Thankfully there was nothing about the Palmer Henry investigation. In her bedroom she touched the drawer beside her bed, half opened it then closed it again without taking out the envelope she kept there. Not for the first time she wished she had more than that one small picture of her mother, the size of a passport photo. A week ago she had seen Geoffrey Hamilton's collection of photographs: Donna's face smiling straight at the camera, the picture Lily had shown Geraldine which had been snapped when Geoffrey had taken the two girls out for the day, another with Donna posing against a background of garden flowers, and a stack of other photos showing Donna's face in profile, Donna putting a bag of apples into a basket in a supermarket, the back of Donna's head disappearing into her flat and even a photo of her closed front door. He had so many pictures; she had just one.

She went to bed and tried to sleep but was unable to settle, disturbed by a nagging idea she had overlooked something. She'd had the same sensation before when she had been on the brink of solving a case, but this time there had been no breakthrough and she dismissed the feeling. After a couple of hours she gave up even trying to sleep, rolled out of bed, slipped the photograph in the pocket of her dressing gown and put the kettle on. She sat down in her living room, put the photograph on the table in front of her and stared at it for a long time.

Milly Blake didn't know it, but before long she was going to meet her abandoned daughter for the first time in over thirty years. Geraldine hadn't yet thought through the ramifications of finding her mother. She might have siblings, probably none older than herself but almost certainly there would be a younger brother or sister, perhaps several. She might even meet her natural father - although that seemed unlikely given the circumstances of her birth and her mother's age at the time, barely sixteen. Whilst her adopted mother was alive Geraldine hadn't been told the truth about her birth. Now she felt as though she had been waiting for this moment all her life. It was like being in love, an unbearable longing to see another person, only this was someone she had never met. Her whole life was going to change utterly. She might discover a complete new family.

It wasn't realistic to expect their first meeting would be like the fairytale she had imagined. She was fully prepared for her mother to greet her with suspicion, even hostility, but she knew their relationship would develop given time. Because once Geraldine found her mother, she wouldn't be satisfied with anything less than a proper relationship. She had waited too long to be brushed-off again. It might be irrational, but she needed the intimacy of a close relationship with her mother.

After all, she and her mother couldn't be very different. They looked so alike, the chances were they would be similar in character as well, which meant her mother would be pleased to see her, even if she had fought to avoid a meeting.

She must have been curious during all those years they had been separated. Maybe she regretted having abandoned her baby but was afraid to contact her daughter because she expected to be rejected, and couldn't bear the thought of losing her again. Geraldine knocking on her door might be the best moment of her life, finally laying to rest a guilt so painful she hadn't been able to summon the courage to look her own child in the eye.

Geraldine hadn't told anyone about her decision to find her mother. She trusted Sam implicitly but still hadn't told her what she was planning. It was private. Sam wouldn't understand. How could she, although it was quite possibly the most significant event in Geraldine's life right now? She might have a sister. A kid brother. Sudden excitement hit her and she wondered if she would ever feel the happiness of this wild hope again - because even if the meeting with her mother went well, the reality of the encounter could never match her anticipation. After a lifetime of isolation she would finally belong somewhere, even if it turned out she wasn't welcome there.

64

DANGEROUS PREDICAMENT

Now there were two of them somehow the situation didn't feel quite so hopeless, if only the woman would stop crying. She was doing his head in, going on and on like that.

'What's your name?' Jon called out.

Anything to stop her incessant snivelling.

'What?'

'What's your name?'

'What's it to you?' she stammered.

'I just want to talk.'

'Why?'

Jon could no longer contain his irritation.

'I've been lying here all on my own for - I don't know how long.'

He felt as though he'd been there all his life.

'For as long as I can remember.'

He thought about his flat, his new job and what had happened to him, and an unexpected rage shook him. In a way, this was all Simon's fault. If he hadn't been so callous Jon might never have jumped into a stranger's car so readily. But there was no point wasting his energy feeling angry with Simon. Right now he had to concentrate on finding some way to escape. There were two of them in this dangerous predicament and they had to work together.

'I just want to talk with someone.'

She didn't answer, but at least she was quiet. He

tried again.

'We have to work together.'

'What for? He's going to kill us.'

'You don't know that,' he answered quickly, before she yielded to hysteria again. 'I'm not giving up that easily.'

He felt strangely heartened by his own words; his voice sounded firm and bold. He would never have dared think so positively if he'd been by himself.

'So what's your name?' he asked again.

'Victoria. Vicky.'

'Vicky,' he repeated and broke off, unexpectedly moved by the banality of their exchange.

The only other person he had spoken to for days was his captor, who was hardly a human being.

With an effort, he controlled his emotions.

'My name's Jon.'

'Who is he?' she asked.

'I don't know.'

'How come you're here then?'

He didn't answer straight away.

'Tell me about you,' he said instead. 'How did you get here?'

'You know,' she answered vaguely. 'He seemed nice and I thought - that is, he said he was taking me home. I was wasted. He told me he was a police officer, and I was stupid enough to trust him. By the time I realised he was lying about taking me home, it was too late. I tried to run away when he was getting out of the car, but ... well, I didn't and now I'm here. I don't even know if he is a policeman. I don't know anything about him, except that he's crazy - '

Her voice shook and she fell silent for a minute.

'So what about you?'

Jon told her how he had gone out and got drunk after Simon had left him.

'I don't get it,' she said when he'd finished. 'This guy was your flatmate and he just walked out? How could he do that? I thought you said he was a friend. Some friend! So is the rent in your name or what? You can find someone else to share your house, can't you?'

'He wasn't just my flatmate.'

'Oh, you mean he was, like, your partner? Oh my God, you're gay. Why didn't you say?'

'Yes. I'm gay. So what?'

'No offence. I'm just trying to understand what's going on, that's all. I mean, what does he want with us?'

There was a pause.

'So how did *you* get here?' she asked, adding 'and you can spare me the graphic details!'

Jon realised she was making a feeble attempt to sound light-hearted and promptly resumed his narrative, before she broke down again.

'That's it, so far as I can remember.'

He closed his eyes when he finished. His throat was burning and he felt exhausted with the effort of talking.

'So what's the plan?' Victoria asked.

'What?'

'You said you're not going to stay here. So, how are we going to get away?'

He didn't answer.

'I said, what are we going to do?'

Now she was feisty, he felt drained of energy.

'We can't stay here,' she persisted. 'We can't just lie here and do nothing.'

'Well what do you suggest?'

'I don't know. You're the one who said you weren't going to give up.'

'Alright, let's try and stay calm. I'm thinking, alright?'

'I thought you had a plan - '

'I said, I'm thinking.'

He wondered if she knew it was hopeless.

'What is all that shit anyway?' she asked after a while. 'All that crap he was showing us?'

'It's his collection.'

'What do you mean, his 'collection'?'

'That's what he calls it.'

'But what is it all?'

He wondered if she had seen the grinning skulls, lined up in a row on one of the shelves.

'I don't know.'

'Jon - '

'Yes?'

'I need the loo. I think - '

Her voice faded and she began to cry again. He didn't know what to say.

'It's alright. You can't help it. You just have to – Look, when we get out of here, we'll soon get cleaned up. What I wouldn't give for a hot shower.'

'A long hot bath.'

'I don't think I'd really want to lie in a bath with me inside it right now,' he replied and she laughed.

'It's so cold in here,' she complained.

'I could do with a nice hot cup of tea,' he agreed.

'Hot chocolate!'

'And hot buttered toast!'

'Stop it! I'm starving. Now, what's the plan? You're going

to get us out of here, aren't you?'

'Sure. Me and superman.'

'You said - '

Her voice wobbled and he realised she was being serious, pinning her hopes on his ingenuity.

'Yes, yes. Don't start crying again. We have to keep thinking. There must be something we can do. There's two of us and only one of him.'

'So one of us can keep him occupied - '

'While the other - '

He stopped. It was a fantasy. They were both chained, hand and foot. What could they possibly do?

'How about if I ask him about his bloody collection?' she suggested.

'The only thing I can move is my head.'

'We have to get him to lean over you then, so you can head butt him and knock him out.'

'But - '

'I'll tell him I think you're dead,' she went on, excitedly. 'Then when he comes over to have a look, you can do it.'

'And then we'll still be tied up here, and the only person who knows where we are will be unconscious, or dead. And so will I, probably.'

They fell silent and a few moments later Jon heard her crying again. This time he didn't try to stop her.

65

LET DOWN

Sam tried to quell her nerves as she knocked on the inspector's door. She was a detective sergeant. She had a perfect right to talk to her superior officer, but she felt awkward all the same. There was no doubt Geraldine had started acting strangely, snapping at Sam for no apparent reason, rejecting any approach as though she couldn't even bear to talk with the sergeant any more, although at first she had been so friendly.

'Yes?' Geraldine barked.
  'Another woman's been reported missing.'
  'What?'
  'A woman called Victoria Benning was last seen leaving an office party in Baker Street on Monday evening and since then she seems to have vanished. She hasn't turned up at work and apparently she's a very reliable employee, according to her boss. She called it in, said they've tried to contact the missing woman but she hasn't answered her phone.'
  'Monday. That's only three days. Can't her boss look into it if they're so worried? There's no reason why her not turning up to work should concern us. People take time off work all the time without telling anyone.'
  'I know, but it seems this woman had been drinking when she was last seen, and she lives in Camden where the killer's been operating.'
  'Well, let's hope she turns up at work tomorrow and gets a bollocking for being a bloody nuisance,' Geraldine said

irritably. 'Is that it then? Only I would've thought you'd be busy right now. I know I am.'

Sam hesitated.

'Can I have a word with you?'

'What is it?'

Geraldine sounded dejected. She didn't invite the sergeant into her office, but Sam went in anyway and closed the door.

'Is something wrong?' Sam asked.

'Other than working on a murder investigation with two victims and no suspect?'

'I just wondered if I've done something to offend you,' Sam burst out, forgetting all of her rehearsed preamble.

'No.'

Geraldine didn't even look up from her screen.

'Only if you've got a problem with me – with anything to do with me or my lifestyle - '

'What are you talking about?' Geraldine sounded surprised.

When Sam raised her eyes she could see the DI was angry, but she'd come too far to withdraw.

'It's just that since we had that talk about – personal stuff - you've seemed different.'

'Different? What do you mean, different?'

'I mean, we were getting on so well – at least, that's how it felt to me. But the last few days you've been different, hostile and bad-tempered with me, and I can't help wondering.'

Sam took a deep breath.

'Geraldine, if you've got a problem with me, or with the friends I have, or with my lifestyle choices, then I find that unacceptable and - '

Geraldine glared at her.

'Are you accusing me of discrimination? I'm the one

who's been discriminated against, ever since I arrived here. Oh I know what they're saying about me behind my back. I've overheard the whispers. County Mounty, I don't know anything about life in the city, I should go back where I bloody well came from – you told me about it yourself. And you dare accuse *me* of prejudice.'

Sam was taken aback. Apart from anything else, it was grossly unfair to be told she was being judgmental, when she was the one who had warned Geraldine what other people were saying behind her back.

'You can't deny you've been awkward with me since you met my friends,' she retorted, determined to pursue her point now she had broached the subject.

'I don't feel the slightest bit awkward with you, or your friends. I don't give a toss what you get up to in your spare time. It's no concern of mine. As long as it's legal. Other than that, frankly I couldn't care less. Why on earth would I? You really think I'm some kind of bigot? You've got some nerve, sergeant.'

Geraldine leaned forward suddenly, put her head in her hands briefly and took several deep breaths before continuing in a gentler tone.

'Look, it's not you, Sam. There is something bothering me, but it's me not you, OK?'

'So you do have a problem with me being a lesbian.'

Geraldine's voice rose slightly again.

'Are you completely self-obsessed? Doesn't it occur to you that other people might have problems that have nothing to do with you and your sex life. This is about me. Me! It's got nothing to do with you.'

She stared wretchedly at Sam.

'It's my problem. So perhaps you'd like to get back to work now, which is what you're here to do. All this is none of your business anyway. Now go.'

'But if it's affecting our relationship, then it is my business.'

'Relationship?'

'Our working relationship.'

'It isn't. The one has nothing to do with the other.'

'Well, I'm sorry but it has. You've been aggressive towards me for days, and it's getting worse, and I'd like to know why. Have I done something to upset you?'

'No, it's not you.'

Geraldine shook her head.

'Look, I'm sorry if I've been vile-tempered.'

'So if it's not me, then what is it?' Sam hazarded.

Geraldine didn't answer for a few seconds.

'It's complicated,' she admitted at last.

Sam was baffled when Geraldine began talking about her mother, with obvious difficulty.

'You know I told you I was adopted at birth.'

'Yes.'

'The thing is – I only found out about it recently.'

Once she had started she seemed keen to talk so Sam sat down, gratified that Geraldine was confiding in her.

'I felt so let down by the woman who brought me up. She allowed me to go on believing she was my real mother when all the time I'd been adopted and knew nothing about it.'

'I expect she intended to tell you,' Sam said. 'She was probably just waiting for the right moment, until she thought you were ready for it. I suppose the longer she left it, the more difficult it became, and then perhaps she died unexpectedly before she had a chance to tell you. She can't have been that old.'

'She was only in her sixties and yes, it was unexpected.

She had a heart attack, without any warning.'

'That's no age. She probably meant to tell you. I mean, don't get me wrong, I'm not excusing the way she kept you in the dark. It would have been best if she'd told you right from the start. But she chose not to and you have to accept that. It must feel weird but nothing's really changed has it?'

Geraldine didn't answer.

Sam could only imagine what it must have felt like to learn she was adopted, with no natural connection to any human being she knew. When she was alone, her isolation must feel absolute.

'So, this is what's been playing on your mind recently? You could have told me.'

'Yes, maybe I should have. Anyway, thanks for listening. Now, let's get back to work!'

Having been dismissed there was nothing else Sam could do except leave the room, but she turned round on the threshold.

'If you ever want to talk some more,' she said softly, 'you always know where to find me. I'm a good listener.'

She had a feeling the inspector needed a friend.

'Sam,' Geraldine called out as Sam was closing the door.

'Yes?'

Geraldine sighed.

'Nothing. It's just that I'm sorry if I've been – unreasonable.'

'Don't worry about it.'

'And Sam - '

'Yes?'

Geraldine hesitated as though struggling for words.

'Thank you again.'

66

ONE MEMENTO

As she got ready for bed that night Geraldine brooded over her conversation with Sam. Her colleague had been helpful, pointing out that Geraldine's adopted mother had probably wanted to tell her what had happened. The right moment might well have been difficult to determine once her mother had allowed a certain period of time to elapse and Geraldine could imagine her mother worrying over the tricky task, putting it off time and again, just as she herself had prevaricated over telling Celia about her own move to London. The longer she had stalled the harder it had become to speak out.

Perhaps her mother had been planning to say something before Geraldine's father had left them, at which point her mother had gone to pieces. Maybe after that she couldn't risk the emotional pain of losing another person she loved. She and Geraldine hadn't exactly seen eye to eye, and it wasn't as though it was an easy secret to reveal at the best of times. It must have seemed increasingly difficult as the years passed and then, suddenly, it was too late. She died without ever telling her daughter the truth.

Geraldine told herself she was keeping an open mind, but a visceral excitement nonetheless grabbed her whenever she thought about meeting her birth mother. Sitting on her bed, she clutched the photograph she had been handed by the social worker at the adoption agency and stared at the

face of her sixteen-year-old mother. They could have been
identical twins if they hadn't been separated by a generation.
All at once she felt unexpectedly tearful. The prospect of
becoming stupidly emotional in her thought processes filled
her with dread. It would make her incompetent at her job.

Her work was the one area of her life where she hadn't
totally screwed up. If she failed there she would have to
acknowledge that her whole life was a disaster. Deep down
she knew she was driven to succeed in her job by more than
an abstract sense of justice, she needed her work to protect
her own self-esteem. It wasn't her ego at stake but her sense
of self-worth, because she had failed in every other area of
her life. Her own mother didn't want her, and the man she
had loved most of all had left her after six years, and she still
didn't understand why. She fell asleep thinking about Mark
and woke in the night startled by a dream of lying in bed
beside Sam. All she could remember clearly was that they
were both naked.

In the dream, Geraldine had been shocked at their situation
but Sam just smiled.
    'Don't worry about it,' Sam had reassured her in the dream,
'you always know where to find me. I'll be right here.'
    She patted Geraldine's pillow.
    'But this is my bed,' Geraldine had protested, scandalised.
'I want you to leave right now. We have to get back to work!'
    'Don't worry about it,' the dream Sam had repeated,
smiling. 'You know where to find me.'

Geraldine glanced at her clock. It was almost time to get
up. Her outrage at the dream had quickly faded leaving her
bemused. She liked Sam, and hoped they might become
friends, but she had never been attracted to other women

and was faintly disturbed by the intimacy the dream had suggested. On balance she decided it must be an expression of her longing to meet her mother. She rolled over to open her bedside drawer and found the precious photograph. When the social worker had given it to her the image had already been faint. She had been keeping it carefully in her drawer to protect it from direct sunlight but couldn't resist frequently taking it out to stare into her mother's impenetrable eyes. She was horrified at the thought of one day finding it was no longer possible to distinguish her mother's features. All she had was this one washed-out photograph and the prospect of her mother's features vanishing filled her with a terrible sadness.

She placed the photograph back in her drawer, resolving to have it professionally framed with protective glass. If she had nothing else, she would at least preserve this one memento of her mother; and a properly treated photograph would survive indefinitely. As she closed the drawer on her mother's face it occurred to her that the killer might be hoarding his victims' teeth motivated by a desire to keep something of them that would survive their deaths. It was a bizarre idea which she dismissed at once. It was time for her to set to work objectively and meticulously, a skilled detective committed to getting results. She had to stop being distracted by her own emotional quest to find her mother, which threatened to cloud her professional judgement.

67

TWILIGHT ZONE

Lost in an uneasy twilight zone between consciousness and sleep, Jon was no longer aware of any pain from the chains rubbing against his wrists and ankles, although he could still feel them weighing him down. Behind closed eyelids he knew the light had been switched on and voices drifted past him. He struggled to retreat into oblivion but something was pulling him back. It was the sound of Victoria, yelling.

'No! No! Get off me! Get away!'

'Come on now, open wide,' Jon heard his captor's voice urging her. 'Open wide.'

Jon jolted awake, shocked into attention. He might be dying but he wasn't going to lie there and do nothing whilst this man forced himself on Victoria. Jon and she had a pact. They were in this together.

'Stop it!' Jon's voice sounded hoarse and distant. 'Leave her alone. Fucking get off her!'

He began screaming, a rasping, high-pitched screech, determined to make enough noise to remind the man he wasn't alone with Victoria, anything to distract him from his sordid purpose.

'Stop! If you hurt her, if you touch her - '

'I'm only looking,' the man said.

He sounded very close.

Jon opened his eyes and saw the man staring down at him.

'She's got strong teeth.'

Jon's screams stopped abruptly.

'Teeth?' he whispered in surprise.

'Yes. What did you think I was looking at?'

The man scowled. Victoria was sobbing.

'What did you think I was going to do to her?' the man bellowed in sudden rage. 'You thought I wanted to kill her, didn't you?'

Jon didn't see the man's arm move, but felt a blow on the side of his head before everything went black. Then bright white spots of light were dancing in front of his face and he heard Victoria calling out his name.

'Say something. Jon, Jon! Did he hurt you? Jon?'

Panic stifled him and he struggled to breathe.

'Leave her alone,' he cried out feebly. 'Kill me. Kill me instead.'

Death would be a relief. He had suffered enough.

'Please.'

There was a strange rushing noise in his ears.

'Let her go. Let her go! Kill me instead of her!'

He opened his eyes. Through a red haze he could see his captor, one arm raised above his head. The man's mouth was open. He was yelling.

'Don't talk to me like that! Don't you dare! You're not going to die here, do you understand? No one dies!'

The man's eyes were rolling wildly and Jon saw his arm descend as if in slow motion. He felt no pain this time, just a numbing cold. He tried to open his mouth but couldn't move.

Everything was empty.

68

A RIGHT TO KNOW

Geraldine wasn't deliberately avoiding her colleagues when she kept to her own office throughout the morning. The fact was, she had a mountain of work to get through. As well as updating her decision log she wanted to read through all the notes she had made talking to people in central London. William Kingsley's BMW had been parked near Bond Street so there must be a chance the new owner of the vehicle worked or shopped in the area, a likely setting for a well-spoken, expensively-dressed man. If she cross-referenced all her notes against the statements taken by the team of uniformed officers who had been sent round the streets in central London, she might possibly come across some detail that would give them a new lead. It wasn't as if they had anything else to go on.

It was a major task for one person to tackle alone but she decided to plough ahead regardless. Sometimes it was more efficient to look at everything by herself as that way she was more likely to notice if something didn't fit.

She thought about her conversation with Sam. 'They're saying you don't trust anyone else to do the job properly' Sam had told her. 'You might as well run the investigation single-handed, as you want to do everything yourself. You think everyone else is incompetent but you.'

But that wasn't the point. Right now she had to stay busy. It helped her banish thoughts of the mother who had rejected her at birth, and who was still eluding her more than thirty years later. Scanning report after report left no space in her thoughts for anything else as she immersed herself in documents.

By early afternoon she was still re-reading statements until her head ached and she had to go to the canteen for something to eat. As soon as she sat down she saw Sam enter the room and hoped the sergeant would want to join her, but Sam didn't respond when Geraldine smiled. Geraldine looked away and sipped at her coffee. She picked up her fork but her appetite had gone. Miserably she toyed with her pasta.

'Mind if I join you?' Sam asked. 'If you can bear some company, that is.'

Geraldine looked up and smiled, waving her fork in invitation. 'Please,' she said gratefully.

She wanted to speak to Sam and was relieved that the sergeant had approached her first.

'We're alright then?' she asked quietly when Sam had sat down.

The sergeant nodded uncertainly.

'I've been thinking,' she replied, and hesitated.

'Thinking about the case?' Geraldine prompted her.

'No, about you and your mother. I think if you really want to find her, there's no reason why you shouldn't - '

Geraldine interrupted her.

'There's something else, but I can't talk about it here.'

She glanced around. A couple of uniformed officers were at the counter asking for tea and cake, sharing a joke with the woman who was serving them.

'It's too personal. I'd like to see you in my office when you've finished here,' she said in a louder voice as she stood up.

'Yes, Gov.'

'It's Geraldine.'

Her eyes held Sam's for a second in a tentative smile. Then Geraldine turned and left. She was still smiling when she reached her office.

It was a lengthy task going over all the statements again and Geraldine was keen to crack on. By the time Sam knocked on her door she was already engrossed in reading.

'Who is it?'

'It's me. You asked me to come and see you.'

'Yes, of course.'

Geraldine looked up. She wanted to carry on with her work but couldn't very well send her colleague away without speaking to her. Not after their recent misunderstanding.

'Come on in,' she repeated, reluctantly closing the file.

'Sit down, Sam.'

They sat for a second without speaking. Geraldine was still mentally scanning the features of people she had seen in the shops and galleries in London.

'Look, if this is awkward - '

Sam stood up suddenly.

'No, no. Sit down.'

With an effort Geraldine switched her attention to the sergeant. Finding relevant information was crucial, but getting along with her colleagues was also essential to the success of the investigation and besides, she really liked Sam Haley and hated the idea of any resentment developing between them. Briefly she told her colleague about her efforts to find her birth mother.

'You'll have to find her if you want to meet her. At least then you'd know if she's prepared to have any sort of relationship with you.'

'A relationship apart from being my mother, you mean?'

'But she isn't your mother, is she? Not really. She just gave birth to you. Someone else brought you up and loved you and everything. You don't even know if your birth mother wants to have anything to do with you now.'

'Yes, I don't know, and that's what's driving me crazy because until I find her there's always a chance she might regret having lost me. It's possible she's just too nervous, or embarrassed, to admit wanting to see me.'

'She didn't lose you,' Sam reminded her. 'She gave you away.'

'She was sixteen. People change. Grow up.'

'And if she still doesn't want to have anything to do with you? How would you feel then?'

Geraldine shrugged.

'Like you said, at least I'd know. If I hear it from her, then I'll have to move on. It's like hearing someone's been reported missing in action. In a way it's almost worse than knowing they're dead, because you can't get on with your life.'

'I suppose.'

'It's exactly like that, not knowing if she's dead to me, as a mother. I don't know how she'd react to meeting me, and it's the uncertainty that's so hard to live with. It doesn't get any easier, because I can't shake off the feeling that if I could only meet her, face to face, she'd change her mind about wanting to know me.'

'Even though she's told the social workers she doesn't want any contact with you?'

'Yes. But imagine how frightening it might seem to her now, the thought of my confronting her after all these years. I can't help thinking there's a chance, if I can only speak to her, tell her I've forgiven her, I understand – she's my mother, Sam - '

'You have to find her then. You have to ask her.'

'You think so?'

'Yes. You have a right to know. But don't forget this feeling you have, that she might welcome you into her life after all this time – well, you could be completely wrong.'

'I just feel there must be something there, some emotional tie.'

'Don't confuse what you want to find with the actual evidence you've got. All the indications are that she doesn't want to see you. That's all I'm saying. You don't want to set yourself up for an even bigger disappointment.'

'Yes, I know what you mean and I'll be careful.'

'Look, it's getting late. I don't know about you, but I'm shattered. Do you fancy a drink?' Geraldine asked.

'I would, but not tonight. I'm seeing Wanda.'

As Sam stood up, Geraldine felt a faint hint of envy. It wasn't that she wanted her relationship with Sam to develop along more personal lines, but she liked Sam and enjoyed her company and she didn't feel like being alone. Somehow it seemed more difficult than ever to meet people now she was living in London.

On a whim she phoned her sister, Celia, when she arrived home.

'Are you busy this weekend?'

'Busy? That's an understatement.'

Celia reeled off a list of her plans, which included ferrying Chloe around to the shops, horse riding, and a party.

'They're having a disco,' she explained. 'Her friend's nine years old and she's having a disco!'

Geraldine gave a non-committal grunt.

'How about you?' Celia asked. 'I suppose you're up to your ears now, living in London.'

'Yes,' Geraldine lied.

'Well, you must come and see us again soon,' Celia replied vaguely. 'I've got to dash, I'm late.'

'Bye,' Geraldine said, but Celia had already hung up.

Geraldine resigned herself to an early night. It wouldn't do her any harm. Before climbing into bed she took the photograph of her mother out of the drawer and placed it carefully beside her bag, so she wouldn't forget to take it with her in the morning.

69

VANISHED WITHOUT TRACE

On Saturday morning, Geraldine put the photograph of her mother carefully into an envelope and went into the framer's on her way to work. Having the picture framed seemed the sensible thing to do but her hand trembled as she handed it over. She felt better when the woman behind the counter spoke confidently about framing it with protective glass.

'You'll be careful, won't you?'

'Careful?'

'I mean, if you lose it I can't get a replacement.'

She didn't add that she had no other keepsakes from her mother, not even memories, nothing but that one small faded photograph.

Driving away from the framer's she felt an overwhelming relief that her mother's image would no longer be at risk from exposure to daylight. She would be able to look at it without fear of damaging it, display it openly on top of her bedside table instead of hiding it away in the drawer like a guilty secret, her mother's features preserved for posterity like the characters depicted on the Grecian urn that inspired Keats' poem she had been reminded of only the other day. She smiled, remembering how she had been intrigued by Keats' idea when she was at school.

'When old age shalt this generation waste, Thou shalt remain,' she muttered to herself. And there was something about 'She cannot fade'. Her mother's photograph would last forever, like a work of art.

A scrap of conversation she had heard recently floated into

her mind.

'Unlike us, art is eternal.'

The words troubled her like a vaguely familiar face she couldn't identify until, with a flash of adrenaline, she realised why they were nagging at her. A protest against the transience of life, they might reveal the strategy of a killer who clung onto his victims' teeth and bones because they would outlast the living, just as she herself had become obsessed with preserving an image of her mother. It was only a hunch, but she couldn't shake off the suspicion that she might have stumbled upon the killer's insane logic.

She had to discover who had spoken to her about art being eternal. Strictly speaking, all the statements she had taken should have been transcribed and stored on the central computer in the Major Incident Room, but Geraldine had questioned some of the people in her own time and, since Sam had mentioned her reputation for preferring to do everything herself, she had been reluctant to record everything centrally. Sam's comment had upset her more than she had admitted to herself at the time, and typing up all her notes would reveal how extensive her double-checking had actually been. As a result, she still had copious handwritten jottings in her notebook yet to be entered on the system. If she couldn't access the expression she was looking for electronically she would have to read through all her notes to discover who had talked to her about art outlasting life.

It needed to be done quickly, but now she could do with help she felt she could hardly ask for it. The detective chief inspector might want to know why she had been questioning people in her own time outside the structure of the investigation, and more importantly, why she'd kept quiet about any information she had gathered. Of course Reg would know she hadn't deliberately concealed anything from the team, but she had certainly failed to follow procedures strictly. She knew she hadn't made a very good impression on the DCI and couldn't afford to risk blotting her copybook again. In any event, in the absence of any information – let alone evidence - Reg was likely to dismiss her idea without a second thought. There was nothing else for it. She would have to conduct the search by herself. It was only a gut feeling, but her instincts had served her well in the past, and she could barely contain her excitement.

As soon as she arrived in Hendon she set to work. She remembered the words clearly but couldn't see them anywhere on the system, so she turned to her notebooks. It took her several hours to scan through them but she still didn't find what she was looking for. As the words referred to art she wondered if she had heard them in one of the galleries off Bond Street. It was a reasonable supposition, so she re-read her notes from that afternoon, trying to reconstruct the conversations from her brief factual notes.

She was wondering whether to return to Bond Street and retrace her footsteps in hopes of triggering a memory, when a note caught her attention.

'3rd gallery. Owner fits description. Edward Barrington.'

She recollected the tall, suave owner of a collection of ancient artefacts. They had discussed a poem displayed in his gallery in which the poet set art above life, because art lasts forever.

'Forever wilt thou love and she be fair.'

The poet described an image of a lover pursuing a beautiful woman on a Greek urn, the characters unchanged since antiquity, centuries after the artist had vanished without trace.

While the idea of courteous, cultured Edward Barrington as a vicious killer seemed far-fetched, Geraldine knew from experience how deceptive appearances could be. She needed to find out more about the art gallery proprietor with the soft, educated voice. Her fingers trembled as she keyed in his name and began to search.

Towards lunch time there was a knock at her door and Sam peered in.

'What are you doing?'

'What does it look like?'

Sam entered the room and closed the door.

'I asked first,' she said with a grin. 'Oh alright, if you're going to pull rank,' she went on as Geraldine raised her eyebrows.

'I was on my way to the canteen and wondered if you fancied some lunch. Or we could go out if you prefer?'

Geraldine shook her head and Sam sat down.

'So, what are you up to then?'

Briefly Geraldine explained the conversation that had led her to suspect the art gallery owner.

'I don't get it.'

Sam shook her head, a puzzled frown on her face.

'This Edward Barrington said something to you about art and you think he's our killer? Why? Because he has a thing about art outliving the artist?'

Geraldine nodded.

'Exactly. The killer is keeping parts of his victims – teeth, bones - '

'We suspect he's removed their teeth and body parts. We don't know he's keeping anything,' Sam pointed out.

'He's hanging onto them because he wants something of his victims to last. Everything – everyone – disappears eventually. He wants to save people from oblivion - '

'By killing them?'

'By preserving something of them. Teeth. Bones. The only parts of us that don't decay.'

'That's crazy,' Sam said firmly.

'You don't expect this to be sane, do you?'

'I'm sorry but all this sounds seriously weird. So, what now?'

'I'm going to speak to the DCI. And then I think we should pay Edward Barrington a visit.'

'But even accepting your theory that the killer's mad, which obviously he is, I still don't understand why you suspect this Edward Barrington all of a sudden. His name hasn't come up at briefings. You haven't even mentioned him before. So he made some random comment to you about poetry and life - '

'It was more than just a passing comment about art outlasting us when we're dead. He had Keats' Ode to a Grecian Urn on his wall. This is something he thinks about a lot.'

Sam looked even more baffled.

'It's a poem about how art is superior to life, because art lasts and life doesn't,' Geraldine explained.

'You're telling me you've got a feeling this man might be a killer because he reads poetry? No, I really don't get it. There may be something weird about people who read poetry, but - '

Geraldine interrupted her firmly.

'It's more than just a feeling, Sam. Edward Barrington's interested in the idea of some part of us surviving our death. He told me he's looking for the Grecian Urn that inspired Keats. I don't suppose he meant that literally.'

Before Sam could say anything, Geraldine told her she had been looking into Barrington's background.

'His parents both died in a domestic fire when he was ten.'

Every trace of his family life had vanished in one night; the entire contents of his home, along with his mother and father. Only ten-year-old Edward Barrington had survived.

'The terrible part of it was that he started the fire himself, trying to light a cigarette. So he was responsible for the tragedy that killed his parents. It seems he ran out of the house in a panic and his parents were trapped inside, probably looking for him. That was the conclusion of the Fire Investigation Team's report.'

Geraldine stopped speaking and the two women sat in silence thinking about the child so violently orphaned, struggling to cope with intolerable guilt. Geraldine pictured the small boy suffering unbearable loss, desperate to cling on to whatever he could of his parents, to prevent them vanishing altogether; the child grown into a man with a macabre collection of human remains, steadfastly resisting the reality of death.

'Forever wilt thou love and she be fair.'

'Poor kid,' Sam commented at last. 'So you really think he could be killing people to keep mementos of them after they die?'

'Something like that. Perhaps he doesn't even intend to kill them,' Geraldine said slowly. 'But he lost his mother and father, and now he's looking for a way to hold on to something that won't disappear like they did.'

'No, I don't buy it.'

Sam shook her head.

'I thought I did, but I don't. Not as a motive for murder. It's too weird.'

'Well, we're going to check it out whatever you think, so we might as well get on with it. We're wasting time here.'

Geraldine stood up.

She was surprised that Reg Milton seemed more receptive to her theory than Sam had been.

'It does no harm to follow it up,' he agreed. 'Although it will probably turn out to be another false trail.'

Registering grey circles under his eyes and an unhealthy pallor on his face, Geraldine felt a flicker of sympathy for her senior officer.

70

FOREBODING

Geraldine was aware that her intuition about the gallery owner, Edward Barrington, might be wide of the mark but she couldn't suppress her excitement as Sam drove them along the Holloway Road and up Highgate Hill. It was possible they were about to come face to face with the man responsible for the deaths of Jessica Palmer and Donna Henry. She gazed out of the window at shops flashing past, and thought about the two dead women. Jessica Palmer had probably never walked along the High Street but Donna Henry might have shopped in Highgate or gone there to meet friends for lunch in one of the many cafes.

When they reached the corner of Highgate West Hill they turned off the main road, approached a pub on their left and slowed down alongside a small green, a church spire visible on the far side.

'This should be it,' Sam muttered.

She braked sharply and turned right up the gentle slope of a narrow road screened from the green by trees. They drew in opposite a row of large terraced houses that looked like authentic seventeenth century Queen Anne buildings. The row of properties was fenced off from the roadway by high black metal railings, apart from the final one to their right which stood slightly apart from the rest of the houses, the ground floor completely concealed behind a tall brick wall with heavy wooden double gates wide enough to let a car through.

Looking at Edward Barrington's house Sam seemed to tune into Geraldine's sense of foreboding.

'Shall I call for back-up?'

'We're only going to question him,' Geraldine reminded her. 'Let's check it out first.'

As they approached the dark gates Geraldine's gut feeling of suspicion returned and she felt an almost unbearable sense of urgency. It was possible they were standing outside the murderer's home right now, only a wooden gate and a brick wall separating them from another victim chained to a filthy bed, another life at risk. They might already be too late to save her.

Peering through a gap between the gates, Geraldine could see a parking space in front of a square brick garage. There was a large window on the first floor of the house and immediately above that a skylight. The right side of the house was covered in ivy and tall shrubs screened it from the property next door. Sam tried a narrow wooden door to the left of the gates and it creaked open so they went in, crossed in front of the garage and rang the bell. They waited a moment then tried again. Sam rapped briskly on the door with her knuckles but no one came to open it.

While Sam went to check the garage door Geraldine followed a narrow passageway which led round the back of the house. A window on the corner rattled when she nudged it but she couldn't wrench it open. She went back to see how her sergeant was getting on and as she walked across the front of the house noticed something glinting on the ground beside the path. She crouched down and saw a shiny black evening bag with a broken golden chain hanging from it, half concealed in the bushes.

'What do you make of this?' she called out in a low voice. Sam hurried over pulling on her gloves and bent down to pick up the bag, holding the chain delicately between a finger and thumb. Geraldine watched as she snapped the clasp open and together they examined its contents: a mirror, a silver make-up bag with lip gloss and mascara, a comb, a key ring attached to a Yale door key and a tiny pink fluffy mouse, a wallet containing around thirty pounds in cash, debit and credit cards and an Oyster travelcard in a black plastic holder. Sam drew out the credit card and turned it around.

'It belongs to someone called Victoria Benning,' she read aloud.

Sam looked up and saw her own alarm reflected back at her from Geraldine's eyes.

'Isn't that the name of the woman reported missing a couple of days ago?'

Geraldine nodded, almost breathless with her growing sense of unease.

'Yes. Come on, there's no time to hang about. I saw a window round the back.'

She led the way, Sam's feet pounding along the path behind her. Reaching the window at the corner of the house, Geraldine turned to Sam.

'Let's do this.'

'Are you sure?'

For answer Geraldine bent down and picked up a large stone which she hurled at the window. The glass shattered. She nodded at Sam who knocked out a jagged shard before reaching in to open the window while Geraldine pulled out her phone to call the station.

'Shouldn't we wait until back-up arrives?' Sam asked when Geraldine had finished speaking.

Geraldine shook her head.

'We may already be too late - '

She didn't finish the thought aloud.

Sam hoisted herself nimbly over the window sill, dropped silently inside and reached out with both hands to help Geraldine.

'I can manage,' Geraldine whispered and Sam stepped back to give her room to climb over.

The window was higher than Geraldine had realised. Scrambling clumsily over the sill, she almost fell to the floor inside but Sam caught her by the elbow and she managed to preserve her balance. Splinters of glass crunched beneath her feet. The room they were in was empty apart from a small polished wooden desk and upright leather chair, a kind of study. They stared at one another for a second before Geraldine turned and led her colleague away from the broken window to explore the silent house.

71

PATHETIC LIVES

Fiona watched people flitting past the window. Outside the sun was shining but it was pleasantly cool inside Barringtons, the gallery in Bruton Place where she worked on Saturdays. She glanced at her watch. It was gone half past four, nearly time to pack up and go home. Only a few people had been in to look around but that was typical. The gallery specialised in artefacts from antiquity and had a reputation for acquiring ancient works of art, and the objects on sale were generally too expensive for impulse buying by visitors wandering in off the street. The owner, Edward Barrington, had contacts all around the world and they received enquiries from buyers in far-flung places, some of them larger galleries and museums, others wealthy individuals with private collections.

She was about to fetch her bag and find Edward to ask if she should close up when an old man entered the showroom.

'Is it alright if I look around?'

'Yes, of course.'

She smiled politely, hoping he wasn't going to linger. It was ten to five. People who walked in off the street usually left after a cursory look, but they sometimes hung around for ages in front of the classical Greek and Roman artefacts displayed in glass cases on top of white plinths. As a rule, Fiona didn't mind people looking. It helped to pass the time, especially when they stopped for a chat, but it was nearly five o'clock and she wanted to go home and get ready for her night out. As the man shuffled slowly around the showroom she glanced at the staircase which led down to the basement, willing her boss to appear and tell her she could leave.

At last, Edward came trotting up the stairs. Fiona thought he had probably been quite attractive once although he was nearly forty, and ridiculously old-fashioned; she sometimes caught him glancing her way, as though he might be interested in her, but all he ever talked about was the gallery. He knew everything about antiquity. She had studied art history at university and her interest in ancient Greece and Rome had landed her the job at Barringtons, but she knew very little about it really. Edward was an expert. He could date an old pot just by looking at it and was obsessed with all his ancient artefacts. Some of them were beautiful, and it was amazing to think they had been made thousands of years ago, but she didn't share Edward's enthusiasm for all of the items in the gallery.

'They're incredible,' she fibbed when he took her down to the basement and showed her the oldest remains stored there. Just because they were ancient, Edward treated them like holy relics when some of them were nothing more than ugly shards of chipped pottery.

'I've got another collection at home.'

'A private collection?'

She had been intrigued, but wary at the same time in case he invited her to go home with him and see it.

'It's private for now but one day I'll open it to the public, and it'll all be on display here. That's why I'm keeping this place going.'

'Why don't you bring it here now?'

'My collection's not finished yet.'

He spoke about it as though it was something really special, his face alight with passion. Fiona nodded, although privately she thought he was a bit weird, getting so worked up over his relics of the past.

By five o'clock Edward was engrossed in conversation with the old man who had wandered in.

'Excuse me. Is it alright if I go now?' Fiona asked.

'Oh my goodness, is it really that late?'

The old man glanced at his watch in surprise, and Edward nodded at her to indicate she could go. Fiona smiled as she stepped out into the sunshine, thinking about the Saturday evening that lay ahead.

Alone in the gallery Edward tidied up, set the alarm and locked the door. It was nearly half past five on a warm afternoon and the pavements were crowded with pedestrians as he made his way to the station. The tube was packed and uncomfortably hot. He didn't get a seat but leaned against the glass partition watching the other passengers, their brief existence punctuated by petty desires and schemes dreamed up to distract them from their future oblivion. He struggled to understand why they bothered going on from day to day, hour to hour, for no purpose. The newspapers exasperated him with their announcements that a footballer was injured, a politician had claimed expenses, a drought was forecast – as though these things mattered. Journalists earned their keep churning out headlines that appeared for a day and were gone, feeding the illusion that human existence was dynamic. No one cared what they printed as long as it offered diversion from the terminal reality of life.

Edward had more in common with the ancient Egyptians than these tired, sweaty commuters who would spend Saturday evening hiding from transience in stupor; drinking themselves senseless, or slouching comatose in front of the television. It wasn't just one ancient Egyptian who took the afterlife seriously, the whole society had appreciated its significance. He smiled, thinking about the breakthrough that would follow the opening of his collection to the public. Like Darwin, he would be the catalyst for an inevitable shift in consciousness throughout the Western world and beyond, because the human spirit couldn't struggle on indefinitely ignoring the truth. He understood that death didn't have to be the end and soon everyone would be liberated from the fear of dying. Books would be written about Barrington's contribution to the history of mankind, and the word would spread in an unstoppable wave.

He looked around the train carriage, travellers cocooned in bubbles of self-importance, and was immediately filled with pity for their pathetic lives and a renewed sense of urgency to complete his collection and reveal it to the world. Other people needed his knowledge. But despite his eagerness to share the collection, anxiety about its reception held him back. None of his visitors so far had appreciated what he was offering. What would happen to his life's work if everyone proved equally obtuse? At first he had dismissed the repeated rebuffs as stupidity, but although he told himself that women who allowed themselves to be picked up by strangers lacked sufficient intellect to appreciate his work, their folly infuriated him. And it wasn't only women who obstinately refused to share his vision. For the first time he had brought a man home to view the collection and in spite of his initial interest, he too had turned out to be a disappointment.

What if no one understood? He would be pilloried for the gift of knowledge he brought to the world. Worse, he might be ignored, his collection overlooked, forgotten. He tried to be patient with his visitors but they let him down every time until frustration overcame him and he lashed out. He had beaten both of his guests unconscious before leaving for work that morning. They should be awake by now, and he would try again. He had to make them listen, had to make them understand that he wanted to save them from death, eternal and absolute.

72

OUR DARK SIDE

Not much light penetrated the house with the blinds closed, shielded as it was on all sides by high walls and trees. There was something unnerving about the silence as they walked from room to shadowy room. With velvet curtains and upholstery, antique wallpaper and polished wooden panelling on the walls, the place was well maintained but in spite of the luxurious décor the atmosphere was cold and forbidding.

'It's like a funeral parlour,' Sam whispered and Geraldine shivered.

They went upstairs. None of the bedrooms looked lived in. Everything was pristine but old-fashioned, as though the house had been untouched for decades. Geraldine ran her finger along the top of a radiator. There was no dust. An unpleasant smell permeated the rooms. Sam gazed enviously at a king-sized bed and fitted wooden wardrobes in the main bedroom. A pair of leather slippers were arranged neatly beside the bed. It was like a show house.

'Very nice, but it stinks. He should get his drains seen to.'

'It's not the drains.'

Having checked the upstairs rooms they returned to the landing where a narrow staircase led up to what must be the attic. Geraldine remembered having seen a skylight from the street. She nodded at Sam who went first. Reaching the top step she glanced round at Geraldine before rattling the door handle. The door was locked.

'Hello?' Sam called urgently.

The smell was much stronger now, like rotting eggs.

'Is anyone in there?'

'Let's not wait,' Geraldine said, unable to curb her alarm.

Sam took a step back down the stairs and rushed at the door, which burst open with a deafening crack. An overpowering stench hit them. Geraldine recognised the smell from the morgue, horribly out of place in this elegant house.

Sam found the light switch and flicked it on while Geraldine looked from the doorway in stunned silence. At her side she heard Sam gasp. In the centre of the room a man lay spreadeagled on a blood-stained bed. He didn't stir and when Geraldine approached she saw his wrists and ankles were attached to the bed by chunky metal chains. Quickly she checked for a pulse and reached for her phone, but there was no point summoning urgent medical assistance. The man was dead, his face beaten and bloody.

'Oh my God, there's another one!' Sam burst out, suddenly flinging herself to the ground.

Geraldine ran round to the other side of the bed where Sam was kneeling beside the body of a fair haired woman who lay on the floor staring rigidly up at her. The woman's wrists and ankles were also shackled with heavy chains, her face bruised and smeared with blood. Sam raised a stricken face to Geraldine and shook her head.

'It's no good,' she said. 'We're too late.'

Geraldine stared past Sam's bowed head at the dead woman, her pale face streaked with blood and dirt, her mouth stretched wide in a silent scream. Across the woman's chin a trickle of dried blood led from the corner of her mouth to a dark pool glistening on the bare floorboards. Her limbs appeared intact.

'Are any of her teeth missing?' Geraldine asked.

'I don't know,' Sam muttered. 'We should have got here sooner. If I hadn't held us up arguing – if I'd listened to you - '

Geraldine shook her head.

'It wouldn't have made any difference.'

She turned away and looked around the attic, for the first time seeing the bare plaster walls, wooden rafters and floorboards, the only source of light a naked bulb hanging from the ceiling. The skylight was covered with a dark blind. She half turned and noticed shelves almost covering the entire wall facing the door. Running her eyes along the misshapen objects on display her gaze was arrested by a human skull, then another, smaller, one. A child's skull.

She walked slowly over to the shelves.

'Bone doesn't decay,' she muttered, staring at rows of curiously hewn artefacts: irregularly shaped bowls, a chunky ring, a whip, interspersed with more human skulls. Gaping eyeholes stared balefully at her above grinning jaws. She looked from a skull to a bowl and back again, and realised the bowl was in fact the inverted top of a human cranium. She glanced along the shelf. More skulls. More bowls. An oddly shaped button. A large needle. It was a vile, grisly collection, all seemingly made of bone which she suspected was human. She wondered how fresh some of the bones were and felt her whole body go rigid with horror.

Pulling on her gloves, Geraldine reached out and picked up a large round tin. Inside were a stack of small brown envelopes, each one dated in neat handwriting. Not all of the dates were from long ago. She flicked through them. With a shock she recognised what must have been the date of Donna Henry's death and picked the envelope out of the tin. It wasn't stuck down. She already knew what she would find inside it but lifted the flap and made out two molars with bloody stumps. Donna Henry's missing teeth. Running her finger over the envelopes she guessed there must be at least a dozen. A dozen different dates. A dozen pairs of teeth.

The tin was trembling in her grasp and she took a deep breath to steady herself.

'He's been busy, adding to his collection,' she said.

'What do you mean?' Sam asked.

She was still kneeling beside the dead woman.

'No ID,' she added.

Geraldine held up a hand in warning.

'Shh.'

'What?' Sam whispered.

'I thought I heard something.'

When the door burst open Geraldine barely recognised the urbane gallery owner in the figure framed in the doorway. His eyes glared, bulging from his face, and came to rest on her as she stood clutching the open tin. With a roar of anger, Edward Barrington launched himself at her. He elbowed her out of the way, knocking her sideways and slamming her head against a shelf as he made a desperate grab for the tin.

'Don't touch it!' he yelled.

Gathering her strength to defend herself against Barrington's frenzied attack, Geraldine lost her footing. At once, his arm was around her neck, squeezing her throat until she was suffocating. Thrashing wildly, her eyes fell on the row of skulls grinning at her. As her chest tightened with the effort to breathe, she had a chilling premonition that she was going to be number eighteen, her polished skull displayed on a shelf in this cold attic.

Before she could recover, she was aware of Sam leaping at Edward Barrington from behind. He released his grip on Geraldine and she saw Sam kick him on the back of his knee to unbalance him, following this with a punch in his side with a straight palm, her fingers bent at the first knuckle, aiming up towards his heart. At the same time she seized his left wrist with her free hand and twisted it up behind him towards the middle of his back. He yelled out in shock.

'This is an act of desecration! Put that down at once! The collection isn't ready. You've got no right to be here, no right to touch anything.'

As Geraldine slumped to her knees, the tin slipped from her grasp and crashed to the floor with a startlingly loud clatter. Small brown envelopes spewed out, spraying teeth across the room like a shower of hail stones.

'Those are mine!' Barrington shouted as his legs gave way and he dropped to the floor.

Sam wrenched his arm until he screamed in pain.

'Stop it! You're going to dislocate my shoulder.'

'Are you alright, Geraldine?' Sam called over her shoulder.

Slightly dazed, Geraldine scrambled to her feet and cuffed Barrington.

'Fine. Where the hell did you learn that manoeuvre?'

Sam grinned.

'Shikan ken? It's something I learned at ninjutsu. It comes in handy.'

She climbed off Barrington, who lay groaning on the floor, and pulled out her phone.

Before long, the attic was crowded with scene of crime officers and had become an official crime scene. Photographers were busy recording images of the bodies in situ, the shelves of bones, and a grisly collection of saws stacked neatly in one corner of the room.

'But what made you so sure it was Edward Barrington?' Sam asked. 'I still don't get it.'

'We all have our dark side,' Reg Milton answered for Geraldine.

She smiled uncomfortably. It seemed the detective chief inspector understood her better than she had realised.

Geraldine leaned against the wall and watched a scene of crime officer delicately collecting up teeth, vestiges of vanished lives.

73

UNREMARKABLE PEOPLE

Exhausted by the stress and exertion of the investigation Geraldine hadn't set her alarm, and it was after ten when she woke up the next morning. Although it was late she didn't stir but lay there, knowing she could lounge around all day if she wanted to. Finally she got up and went out for breakfast: freshly squeezed orange juice, coffee, and an almond croissant. The sky was clear and she sat outside a café enjoying the warmth of the morning. Most of the passers by looked normal; just an ordinary day on an ordinary street. A few other customers were seated outside the café sipping coffee. It probably didn't cross their minds to wonder if one of the pedestrians might be a psychopath or a spy, a paedophile or a drug baron, and Geraldine dismissed the thought at once. When she was working on a case, suspicion became a state of mind but as a rule strangers were unremarkable people, discreetly pursuing their quiet affairs.

She spent the afternoon doing housework and catching up on chores. At last she finished and sat down on her settee. Much as she relished the challenge of adjusting to a new job and a new home, right now she was worn out and suddenly lonely. She thought about visiting her sister but was too tired to drive all that way. She considered phoning a few old friends, just to chat, but couldn't face the inevitable inane questions about the case she had been working on. She would have liked to call Ian Peterson, the sergeant who had worked with her in Kent. He would understand how she was feeling, but he was getting married soon and was bound to be busy.

Any confusion about the nature of her friendship with Sam had been cleared up, but Geraldine still hesitated before picking up the phone.

'Hello, this is DS Haley.'

'Hi Sam, it's Geraldine. I wondered if you fancied going for a drink, or perhaps something to eat, this evening?'

'Oh sorry, that would've been great, but I've arranged to meet a friend.'

'No worries,' Geraldine was quick to reassure her. 'It was just a thought.'

'A nice thought.'

'Another time then.'

'Sure. See you soon.'

Geraldine hung up. She was pleased at Sam's friendly response to her invitation. Life was full of possibilities.

There would be no more opportunities for Edward Barrington's victims to make new friends, or even to sit at home feeling lonely; their futures had been senselessly snatched away by a man who had discovered the fragility of life when he was only ten. At times it was hard to make sense of anything, but right now she wanted to put the horrors of the case behind her. She had her work, her friends and her flat, and Celia, who thought of her as a sister, and soon she would start searching for her mother. For now she was content to spend an evening alone with a glass of wine and the distraction of mindless television. It was enough simply to be alive.